EVEN IF IT KILLS HIM

The pirate captain's eyebrows were furrowed together, and he had a pained look in his eye.

"I'm sorry, son—there's dirty work afoot, and it's no place for children—I mean, I would if I could, but—"

"It's not that," I said.

"Oh." Healy looked a little flustered. "Then what?"

"I've made a decision," I told him. "I'm going to destroy Roger Pembroke. Or die trying."

He almost smiled. But not quite.

"Well, in that case . . ." He dug in his pocket for a moment. "Take another five gold. You'll need it."

He dropped the coins into my hand. Then he ruffled the hair on the top of my head and returned to his conversation without another word. He had a job to do.

And so did I.

OTHER BOOKS YOU MAY ENJOY

BLUE SEA BURNING

THE CHRONICLES OF EGG

BLUE SEA BURNING

GEOFF RODKEY

PUFFIN BOOKS
An Imprint of Penguin Group (USA)

PUFFIN BOOKS
Published by the Penguin Group
Penguin Group (USA) LLC
375 Hudson Street
New York, New York 10014

USA * Canada * UK * Ireland * Australia
New Zealand * India * South Africa * China

penguin.com
A Penguin Random House Company

First published in the United States of America by G. P. Putnam's Sons,
an imprint of Penguin Young Readers Group, 2014
Published by Puffin Books, an imprint of Penguin Young Readers Group, 2015

THE LIBRARY OF CONGRESS HAS CATALOGED THE G. P. PUTNAM'S SONS EDITION AS FOLLOWS:
Rodkey, Geoff, 1970 –
Blue sea burning / Geoff Rodkey.
pages cm.—(The chronicles of Egg ; book 3)
Summary: "In this final installment to the Chronicles of Egg trilogy, Egg and his
friends must defeat the ruthless slave trader Roger Pembroke."—Provided by publisher.
ISBN: 978-0-399-25787-2
[1. Adventure and adventures—Fiction. 2. Buried treasure—Fiction. 3. Good and evil—Fiction.]
I. Title.
PZ7.R61585Bl 2014
[Fic]—dc23
2013025515

Puffin Books ISBN 978-0-14-751443-1

Printed in the United States of America

1 3 5 7 9 10 8 6 4 2

For Rahm

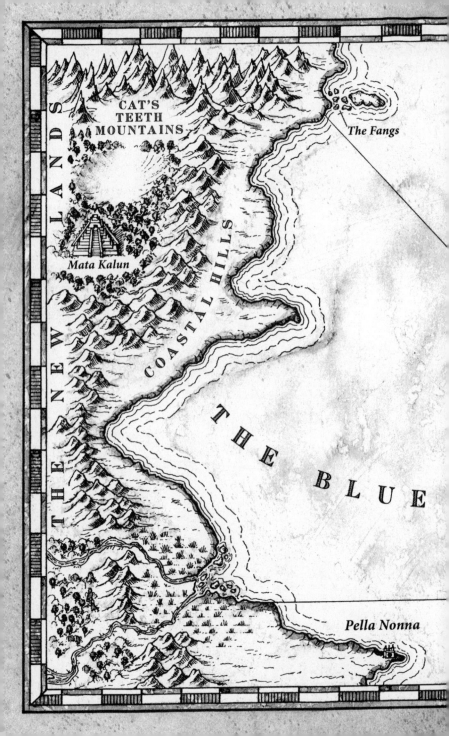

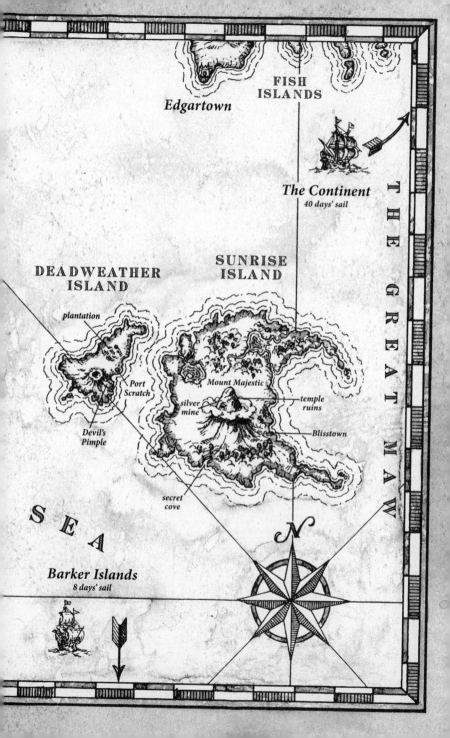

FISH ISLANDS

Edgartown

The Continent
40 days' sail

T H E   G R E A T   M A W

SUNRISE ISLAND

DEADWEATHER
ISLAND

plantation

Mount Majestic

*Port
Scratch*

*silver
mine*

*temple
ruins*

Blisstown

*Devil's
Pimple*

S E A

*secret
cove*

Barker Islands
8 days' sail

THREE PROBLEMS

BURN HEALY'S PIRATE SHIP was sinking. And we were on it.

Cannon fire had torn a hole in the lower hull during the invasion of Pella Nonna. Healy's men had patched it, but there hadn't been time for a full repair before they set sail with me, Guts, Kira, and my brother, Adonis, on board—and as soon as the *Grift* hit top speed, the patch had split open. Now seawater was gushing into the hold as fast as the pirates could pump it out, and we were limping across the Blue Sea, trying to reach Deadweather Island for repairs.

But Deadweather was four days' sail away, and if the half-busted patch got any worse, we weren't going to make it.

So that was a problem.

But there was a bigger one.

A convoy of warships was somewhere over the horizon, determined to blow us out of the water.

The convoy was led by Cartage's colonial viceroy, *Li Homaya,* and his temporary ally, the brutal pirate Ripper Jones. Between them, they had at least three ships, including two massive Cartager men-of-war with more than fifty guns each.

Jones and *Li Homaya* were unlikely partners. The only thing they had in common, other than their tiny Cartager ears, was a blood lust for Burn Healy. They'd been roaming the Blue Sea for weeks now, trying to hunt him down, and if they crossed our path before the crippled *Grift* made port, we were doomed.

So that was another problem.

But there was a third one.

And at the moment, it was even bigger than the other two.

The third problem was this: the crew of the *Grift* wanted us dead.

"DEAD?! WHAT THE PUDDA — *blun* are you talking about?" Guts twitched as he cursed at me in two languages at once. Guts had one hand, a foul temper, and an even fouler mouth. And he was my best friend in the world.

He'd sacked out right after we left Pella and was only just waking up from a much-needed nap. So were Kira and Adonis—the three of them were folding up the hammocks they'd strung under the beams in the aft corner of the *Grift*'s gun deck.

"Just look at them," I said, motioning toward the gun crews behind me. "Do you see the way they're staring at us?"

Guts, Kira, and Adonis peered over my shoulder at the hundred-plus pirates clustered in tight, watchful groups around the two dozen cannon that ran down either side of the deck.

One by one, my friends' eyes widened.

"They are definitely angry," said Kira. She nodded slowly, more thoughtful than scared. Kira didn't scare easily.

Guts twitched again. "One in the striped shirt looks like he wants to — my *glulo* in the *pudda* —."

Kira wrinkled her nose at Guts. "That's disgusting."

"True, tho'," said Guts, scratching his nose with the stump at the end of his left wrist. "Look at 'im. And them ones on the chain pump are *really* givin' us the stink-eye."

Halfway down the deck in front of the mainmast column, four sweat-drenched pirates were heaving their shoulders in time as they worked the big circular crank of the chain pump that drew water up from the flooded hold.

I glanced back at them and caught a look of pure hate that turned my insides to water.

Adonis snorted in disgust. "Stuff it, Egbert! Yer just bein' a girlie wimp!"

Kira's dark eyes flashed as she turned her head to him. "Did you say *girlie*?"

Adonis shrank back in an instant. Like most bullies, my older brother went to pieces when somebody tougher than he was challenged him. Kira was a head shorter and a hundred pounds lighter than Adonis, but she was tougher by a mile.

And I suspected, even though I hadn't seen it happen, that the greenish-black bruise my brother was sporting under his left eye had been Kira's doing.

"No!" Adonis sputtered. "I said-said-said"—he scrunched up his face in the pained look he got whenever he tried to think—" . . . gurgly."

Kira ignored him, turning back to me. "Egg, the ship is sinking, and we might be attacked at any minute. That is reason enough for the crew to be angry. Why do you think this is about us?"

"Because this whole mess is my fault," I said.

And it was true. The only reason the *Grift* had set sail from Pella in such a hurry was because Burn Healy had to rescue me from a public hanging. Which didn't go over well with the man who was trying to hang me.

The man who'd recently crowned himself the new governor of Pella Nonna.

The man who was trying to take over the whole continent of the New Lands and make slaves of everyone who lived there.

The man who'd killed my father.

"It is not your fault, Egg," Kira insisted. "It is Roger Pembroke's."

Her lip curled in a snarl as she spoke his name, and I remembered he'd ordered her own father's death as well, for trying to stop Pembroke from using Kira's tribe, the Okalu, as slaves in the silver mine back on Sunrise Island.

"Bunch of nonsense," Adonis growled again. "Ain't nobody on this ship gonna kill me. My uncle's the captain!"

"He's my uncle, too," I said. "And I'm plenty worried." I was still getting used to the idea that I was Burn Healy's nephew—which I'd only just learned that morning as I stood on a gallows with a noose around my neck.

It had been an awfully strange day. And it wasn't even time for dinner yet.

"Yer just worried 'cause yer a gir—" Adonis stopped himself, with a sideways glance at Kira. "Gurgly wimp."

"Thought you were going to start treating me right," I reminded him. A few hours back, after he'd gone to pieces over our father's death and spilled out all his fears for the future, I'd promised Adonis that I'd stick by him, but only as long as he quit being a bully and a thug.

"I am! Ain't slugged you today, have I?"

"It's more than just not slugging me. Quit calling me names! Especially ones that don't mean anything. I mean, what on earth is a 'gurgly wimp'?"

It was quiet for a moment as Adonis scrunched up his face, trying to work out what he'd meant by that.

Guts broke the silence. "Don't matter who they blame for this mess," he said. "They ain't killin' any of us. Not just 'cause the captain's yer uncle. 'Cause of the Code."

The Code was the set of rules that Burn Healy's pirates had all sworn to live by. And we knew from experience that the Code guaranteed the safety of children.

Or did it?

"Doesn't the Code say children should be treated with mercy?" I asked.

Guts gave a twitchy nod. "Right."

"Well, what if that just means they'll give us a merciful death?"

That stumped him.

Nobody said much of anything for a long time after that. We just huddled in the corner of the gun deck, averting our eyes whenever one of the pirates shot a murderous glance in our direction. Between the gushing leak in the hold and the state of alert over a possible attack, the mood was tense all around, and we didn't want to move around the ship for fear of getting in the crew's way.

I thought about searching out my uncle to ask him if there was any chance his men might kill us. But the last time I'd seen him, he was holding a grave and serious-sounding conference with his officers up on the main deck, of the sort that seemed like a very bad idea to interrupt.

And anyway, if I went looking for him—or went anywhere, for that matter—I'd have to walk past a hundred seething pirates. So I stayed put and tried not to think about the fact that I had to pee.

Instead, I thought about Millicent.

Millicent, who was smart and funny and had long, honey-gold hair that shone in the sun like a treasure.

Millicent, whose deep brown eyes had a fire burning fierce inside them.

Millicent, whose smile was warm and mysterious and made life worth living whenever she turned it on me.

Millicent, whose father was Roger Pembroke. The most evil man in the world.

It wasn't her fault. You can't choose your parents.

And she knew it now, all of it, the full horror of what he'd done, and she was as determined as Kira and I were to stop him before he could expand his slave trade from Sunrise Island to the whole of the New Lands.

I hadn't seen Millicent since that awful morning—less than a week ago, but it felt like a year—in the shadow of Mata Kalun, when my father lay dead on the steps of the temple and our desperate, half-baked plan had fallen apart. Pembroke had split us up, sending Millicent back to her mother on Sunrise Island.

Where was she now? Still on Sunrise, probably. Living at

Cloud Manor, waiting for a ship to take her across the Great Maw to Rovia and some boarding school for rich girls.

How could I get to her? Sunrise was Pembroke's island, full of Rovian soldiers who did his bidding. But maybe I could—

"I want some o' that food."

Adonis's voice cut through my thoughts. I looked up to see that the gun crews were eating dinner. A man from each crew had brought up a bucket of rations from the galley down on the lower deck, and they were all seated around their cannon, digging into biscuits and salted chops.

Watching the pirates eat, my mouth started to water. It had been a long time since breakfast.

Adonis got to his feet. "Gonna get us a bucket."

He started off down the deck with his usual swagger—the kind that made even strangers want to give him a hard kick in the pants. Guts, Kira, and I watched the pirates stare daggers at him as he passed.

"Think he's going to get himself in trouble?" I asked the others.

Kira sighed. "I am sure he will." She stood up. "We should follow him."

Unfortunately, I had to agree.

CHAPTER 2

STICK'S COMPLAINT

WE CAUGHT UP with Adonis on the lower deck. As we headed for the short line of pirates waiting for food outside the galley, we passed the companionway leading down to the hold—and even before we got close enough to peer down the stairs, I could hear the *slap* of water sloshing against the walls below.

Just from the sound, I knew it was bad. But the sight of the water lapping at a step halfway up the stairs nearly took my breath away. I could hear voices somewhere down there, splashing around, and I prayed they were fixing the patch, because if that water level kept rising, the *Grift* wasn't going to be afloat much longer.

As we reached the back of the food line, Adonis took a hard shoulder from a pirate who was walking off with a bucket of rations. Fortunately, my brother had just enough sense to swallow his tongue, and we waited in silence while a grizzled, one-legged cook passed out buckets to the three pirates in front of us.

Then it was our turn. Adonis stepped to the galley door.

The cook didn't even give him a chance to speak.

"Clear off!" he barked, gesturing for us to go back the way we came.

That was good enough for Guts, Kira, and me. But not Adonis. The rest of us were turning to leave when he opened his mouth.

What came out of it reminded me of a bad novel I read once, *Orphan Dora*. It's one of those books where the pitiful-but-plucky main character goes through so many heart-wrenching episodes you'd swear the author's whole purpose was to make whoever reads it cry like a baby.

In the final sequence, little Dora escapes from a chain gang in a coal mine and walks fifty miles through a driving snowstorm to get to the door of a widowed baker whose only daughter had perished in a subplot so boring that I'd skipped six chapters of it. When the baker answers the door, Dora says, in an adorable-even-though-she's-about-to-faint-from-starvation voice, "Please, sir, if I might just have a bite of something old and stale . . ."

And of course the baker's heart breaks for her, and once he's finished bursting into tears, he not only feeds Dora a fresh loaf from the oven, but adopts her and they live happily ever after.

What Adonis said to the cook was very similar, except it wasn't adorable, he didn't say please, and instead of bursting into tears and adopting him, the cook growled, "Eat this," and punched Adonis in the mouth.

It was quite a punch, especially for a one-legged man who you wouldn't think could lay much weight behind his swing. It knocked Adonis off his feet, and he tumbled past us to land in a heap in front of my uncle, who'd just appeared out of nowhere with a handful of his officers.

Burn Healy looked down at my brother with gray-flecked blue eyes that showed a bit of curiosity, but not much more.

Adonis opened his own eyes, saw our uncle the pirate captain staring down at him, and made a noise through his bleeding mouth that sounded like *"shgrf."*

As my brother staggered to his feet, Healy turned his gaze to the cook.

"What happened here, Stick?" he asked in a mild voice.

But its meaning wasn't mild at all. Healy had the unsettling ability to give even the most pleasant-seeming question an undercurrent of mortal threat—so in this case, everyone within earshot understood that what he really meant wasn't just *what happened here?* but *your life depends on how you answer.*

The cook couldn't bear to look Healy in the eye. He stared at the deck as he answered.

"Lost me temper, Cap," he said quietly.

"It happens," said Healy, with a thoughtful nod.

For a moment, the tension crackling in the air began to subside.

"Even so . . ."

Instantly, the tension spiked again. I heard a little gasp as someone sucked in their breath in fright—and then I realized, to my embarrassment, that it was me.

"Two articles of the code come to mind," Healy told the cook. "No fighting among the crew . . . and mercy toward children."

Everyone looked to the cook for his reply. The skin around his eyes was leathery and wrinkled—but when his gaze rose to meet Healy's, his eyes grew so wide that the wrinkles nearly vanished.

I followed his frightened stare to the pistol that had appeared in Healy's hand.

"What do you say to that, Stick?" he asked.

It was silent except for the *slap* of seawater in the hold below our feet.

When the cook finally spoke, his voice was heavy and slow.

"Beggin' pardon, Cap . . . and with all due respect"—he jerked his head toward Adonis—"that one ain't crew . . . and he ain't no child, neither."

Everyone turned to stare at the captain. He was motionless as a stone, his gaze steady on the cook.

Then Healy began to raise the pistol.

I saw the eyes of the pirates behind him narrow as one, their faces darkening.

The pistol stopped moving, its barrel pointed just short of the cook.

Healy extended his thumb over the cocked hammer.

It hovered there for an endless second.

Finally, he eased the hammer back and gently guided it down to rest against the pan. He dropped his arm.

"Top deck. Five minutes. All crew—"

He looked me in the eye.

"—and passengers."

Then he was gone, striding into the gloom of the lower deck.

CHAPTER 3

FREE SPEECH

THE FOUR OF US stood in the warm light of the setting sun, our backs against the wall beside the poop deck ladder. We looked out over the two hundred pirates who were crowded onto the deck's waist, waiting for Healy to appear.

Kira had picked the spot. "It's next to the captain's cabin," she pointed out. "And away from the rail. If they try to throw us overboard, we will see them coming. And there will be time for Healy to hear our screams."

She was clever that way.

And now she was praying, turned away from us as she whispered to the sunset. It was a ritual she performed every morning and night, offering her devotion to the sun god, Ka. I didn't know what the Okalu words meant, but I hoped she was asking for help.

We needed it. The one thing every man on that crew had in common—other than the small flame tattoo on the side of the neck that marked them as Healy men—was a simmering hatred of the four of us.

They were a motley bunch. Better than half were Rovian, but the rest were a mix of Mandars, Ildians, Gualos, a handful of tiny-eared Cartagers, and even some native Fingu. No two men wore the same clothes, just about everybody had at least one prominent scar, and quite a few were missing bits and pieces—rarely anything as major as an arm or a leg, but there were plenty of empty spaces where eyes, ears, and fingers should have been.

Many of their wounds were recent—wrapped in bandages stained copper brown with blood, and reminders of their part in the invasion of Pella Nonna that put Roger Pembroke in the palace where *Li Homaya* had once ruled.

They stood in silence, showing their usual cold-eyed seriousness. Growing up on Deadweather, I'd seen a lot of pirates. And if you stuffed any other group of a couple hundred of them into close quarters like this, there'd be chaos—laughter, yelling, fistfights, the occasional knife getting pulled . . .

Not Healy's men. They were quiet as undertakers. Watching them, motionless even as they continued to shoot us murderous looks, it was clear that the only things keeping us alive were the Code and the captain who enforced it.

Which had Adonis even more terrified than the rest of us. He was sixteen, three years older than me and big enough to be a member of the crew in his own right. If the Code only protected children, and the cook was right that Adonis didn't count as a child, he was in real trouble.

He whispered in my ear, his voice slurry from the punch he'd taken. It seemed to have rearranged some things in his mouth.

"What's gonna happen? Healy gonna tell 'em to lay off?"

"I don't know," I said. "I've never seen this before."

The door to the captain's cabin was to our right. As I answered Adonis, it opened.

Two hundred heads turned to watch Burn Healy step onto the deck, trailed by his hawklike first mate, Spiggs.

He took a few strides into the mass of men, which almost magically ebbed away from him in a perfect half circle.

Then he held up a small hourglass.

"Free speech, brothers," he called out. "Five minutes." He flipped over the hourglass and tucked it into his chest pocket.

A roar of angry voices broke over us as those killer stares turned into words, hurled in our direction with such force that I felt like I was being shoved back against the wall.

Kira was to my left. As the curses washed over us, her hand found mine and squeezed it tightly. I squeezed hers back. Guts was holding her other hand, his head bent down against the storm of words.

It'll be okay. They follow a Code. He won't let them hurt us.

I told myself that. But my body didn't believe it. My heart was thumping so hard I could feel it in my ears.

Then, in an instant, the abuse stopped.

I looked up.

Healy had his hand in the air. "Specific complaints, brothers," he said. "One at a time."

He pointed to one of the pirates closest to him.

"Cost me my money!"

Then another. "Where's our gold?!"

And another. "Left us broke!"

It was even worse than I'd thought. I had no idea we'd cost them money.

"What else besides the money?" Healy asked.

"Pulled our leave! 'Fore it even started!"

"Why's them under the Code? Code's fer captives! This bunch waltzed on like they'd bought a ticket! Get what they ask for, I say!"

"An' *this one*"—a giant bear of a man jabbed at me with his finger—"prances round like 'e's first mate!"

My cheeks burned hot. I'd never pranced in my life, as far as I knew.

Still pointing at me, the bear turned to Healy.

"Due respect, Cap—I been crewin' this ship five years, never once spoke to ye without leave. This one here trots up an' chats with ye like ye's drinkin' buddies in a pub!"

My legs were turning to jelly. And the rumbling fury was building again, so much so that Healy had to raise his hand a second time for quiet.

He pointed at a pirate in the middle of the crowd, a tall Mandar whose head was wrapped in a ragged bloodstained bandage.

"Ather," Healy said. "Speak your piece."

Ather's voice was quieter than the others'. But he was no less angry.

"All I want's what's fair," he said. "Lost an ear and half my scalp takin' Pella. Buried three o' me mates in the sand off that lagoon. We all fought willin'—'cause you an' that Pembroke promised us two weeks' leave and a fat sack of gold when the job was done.

Well, I did my job—an' what I got to show for it? No money. No leave. Out here in a sinkin' ship waitin' to be picked off by Short-Ear scum not fit to wipe me boots."

He nodded in my direction, his voice dripping with disgust. "All 'cause this one needed savin'. What's he to me? Code says I give up my life for this crew. An' I would. But he ain't crew. None of 'em are. Like to slit the whole lot of 'em open. Spill their guts on the deck. Ain't gonna make it square—but I'd sure get a smile out of seein' 'em die."

The words were all the more terrifying for the matter-of-fact way in which he spoke them.

And the truth behind them was devastating.

If I were one of the crew, I'd want to kill me, too.

Healy nodded. "You're an honorable man, Ather. And your point is fair."

I waited for the second part of his reply—the one where he told this Ather why he was wrong, and we deserved to live.

But it didn't come.

"Is that it, brothers?" Healy called out. "Any complaints not yet voiced?"

No one spoke.

"Very well." Healy checked the hourglass, then closed his fist around it. His voice boomed out across the deck.

"Free speech is over. I've heard your complaints. Here is my answer. Firstly—these four passengers, *children or not,* are under my protection. As long as I lead this crew, and my Code is in force, no one touches so much as a hair on their heads."

I felt my muscles begin to unclench. Healy would keep us safe.

"Secondly—I resign as your captain, effective at sunset."

I must have heard that wrong, because it didn't make any sense.

Healy glanced at the red sun, hovering just over the horizon.

"You have twenty minutes to elect a new captain. Choose quickly—and well. The future of this brotherhood is in your hands."

He turned and strode back inside his cabin, shutting the door behind him as a buzz of excitement broke out among the men.

My head was swimming.

If what I thought had just happened . . . had actually happened . . . we had twenty minutes to live.

SHAMED

I HADN'T MISUNDERSTOOD anything. Burn Healy had resigned.

The crew splintered into dozens of urgent conversations about who was going to replace him. Judging by the poisonous look we caught whenever a pirate glanced our way, it was a safe bet that whoever got the job would make killing us their first order of business.

Which was why we were in the middle of our own urgent conversation, about how to get off the *Grift* alive.

"I say we swim for it," said Adonis.

I looked at the horizon. To the west, where the mainland should have been, there was nothing but ocean.

I shook my head. "We're half a day's sail from land. We'd never make it."

"We need a boat," Kira said.

There were six big lifeboats—three on each side of the deck, covered in canvas and tied end to end along the rails.

"Can't just pinch one," said Guts. "Need help puttin' her on the davits."

"Stuff! We'll shove it over the side!" growled Adonis.

Looking at the size of the boats and the way they were secured, it was clear to me that Guts was right. We couldn't get a boat in the water without help, especially since we'd likely get jumped by the crew as soon as we tried.

"It's impossible," I said.

"Unless we can get Healy to give the order," said Kira.

She turned to me. "Go ask him."

Something told me I shouldn't ask Healy for a boat—but my head was so addled I couldn't figure out why, let alone put it into words.

"I don't . . . think . . ."

"Don't *pudda* think!" yelped Guts. "Just go!"

"Why me?"

"Yer the one he likes!"

Adonis looked offended. "Likes me just fine! He's my uncle, too!"

"Don't mean he likes ye," snarled Guts.

"Stuff it, you!"

Kira stepped between the two of them to break up the argument before it could really get going. Then she reached out and pushed me toward the captain's cabin.

"Go ask him, Egg!"

"Can't we all go?" I pleaded.

Kira shook her head. "Better just you. It will be easier to beg if you're alone."

That wasn't comforting.

"Just go! We're wasting time!"

The door to Healy's cabin was only a few steps away. As I walked over to it, my muddled head finally managed to cough up an argument for why I shouldn't ask.

"He's very clever—what if he's got a plan of his own?"

"For what?"

"Not getting us killed. I mean, the whole reason we're in this mess is 'cause he saved my life. After all that, he's not going to let his crew slit our—"

Kira interrupted me. "If he has a plan, asking for a boat won't spoil it. Just *ask*!"

I raised my fist in front of the door. But I couldn't bring myself to knock.

"Get it over with!" barked Guts.

Kira let out an annoyed sigh, marched over to me, and rapped on the door.

"Enter," came the response.

She stepped away, leaving me alone. I took a deep breath and went inside.

Healy's cabin was tidy and spare. He was sitting at his desk, a leather-bound journal open in front of him and a quill pen in his hand. The pen was poised, motionless, over a scrap of parchment.

He spoke without looking up.

"How are you at figures?"

"Sorry?" He was facing away from the door, so I couldn't figure out how he knew it was me. Or maybe he would've asked the same question of anyone who'd walked in just then.

"Figures. Math. Specifically . . ." He lifted the quill, using the feathered end to scratch his head. "Breaking a very large number into a lot of small ones. Are you good at that sort of thing?"

"Not really," I admitted.

"Pity. Shut the door on your way out."

I just stood there like an idiot, trying to get up my nerve to ask about the boat.

He looked over his shoulder and locked eyes with me for the first time.

"What?"

His stare had its usual effect. My brain threatened to shut down completely.

"I'm more than a little busy, son. State your business."

"We . . . ah . . . wondered . . . boat" was all I could manage.

The look in his eye turned to ice, and in an instant I knew I'd made a terrible mistake.

"You want a lifeboat? To flee the ship?"

His voice was as cold and hard as his eyes.

I shook my head, trying to undo the mistake. "N-n-no . . ."

He saw right through the lie. He stood up and walked toward me.

I started to tremble under his stare.

"You really *aren't* good at math. I have six lifeboats and two hundred men, on a ship in danger of sinking."

He was right in front of me now, so close that his broad chest nearly filled my sight.

"If this ship goes down, six boats are just enough to save my crew. If I launch one with the four of you in it . . . and we sink . . . thirty men will die for your selfishness."

I didn't realize I'd been backing away from him until I hit the wall behind me.

I wanted to run and hide, but there was nowhere to go.

He stared down at me from his six-plus feet of height. Those terrible cold eyes drilled right through me.

"I'm going to assume your friends put you up to this, and that the boy I troubled myself to save from hanging is not a coward who thinks only of himself in a crisis."

He took a step to one side and opened his cabin door. Somehow, I managed to stumble out of it onto the deck.

I heard the door click shut behind me as my friends approached.

"What happened?" Kira's eyes were wide with concern. "You look like a ghost."

"I don't feel so good," I said, just before everything went black.

KIRA AND GUTS were floating over me, looking anxious. Adonis was just behind them, his face more confused than worried.

"Are you all right?" asked Kira.

"What happened?" I was lying on the deck of a ship, but for a moment I didn't know what ship, or how I'd gotten there.

"Fainted," said Guts. "Dead away."

Then everything came back to me, and I felt sick with shame. Not for the fainting, although ordinarily that would've been plenty embarrassing, but for what Healy had said about my being a selfish coward.

I'd been in awe of Burn Healy for a long time, and his disgust with me would have been hard enough to take if he'd been just a pirate captain. But now he was my uncle, and somehow that made it much, much worse.

Once I told the others what had happened, Kira tried to comfort me. "It's okay. We made you go in there. And I'm sure what you said before is right—he has a plan."

"Don't worry it," Guts said. "Be fine." But his face was twitching hard, and lately it only did that when he was upset.

I'd let them down. I knew it was a bad idea, and I'd gone and done it anyway.

And now Burn Healy thought I was a selfish coward.

Maybe I was.

"I've got to do something," I said.

"There's nothing to do but wait," said Kira.

I looked out at the sea of pirates, waiting to elect a new leader and put us to death.

"I'm going to give a speech," I said.

"What?" My friends looked at me like I'd lost my mind.

"I'll tell the crew this was all my fault—and they can kill me for it, but they should spare the rest of you, because you're innocent."

"You can't do that!" said Kira, gripping my arm with so much emotion that I felt my eyes start to well up.

"I have to. It's my fault—"

"*You have the map.* If you die, it's all over."

I'd forgotten all about the map in my head.

It showed the way, or so we'd thought, to the lost treasure of the Fire King, and the mystical Fist of Ka that was its centerpiece. The Fist was a sacred object to Kira's Okalu tribe, driven from

23

their homeland and struggling to survive somewhere in the Cat's Teeth mountains.

Kira believed that if she could find the Fist of Ka, it would save her people.

Roger Pembroke had wanted it too, and badly, because he believed it would help him rule the tribes of the New Lands. But once he'd tortured the map out of me and gotten it translated, he'd blown up in a rage—from which I'd gathered the whole legend was a myth, and our desperate efforts to keep the Fist from him were a tragic, stupid waste of time.

But Kira still believed. The look in her eyes told me it was life and death to her.

It didn't matter if she was right or not. She'd stuck with me through a whole lot of trouble, and I owed it to her to make sure the map didn't die with me.

"Listen carefully," I said. "The first hieroglyph is a feather. With a dash and a dot—"

"There's no time, Egg! The election is any minute now!"

She was right. It had taken me hours on end to memorize that map. She wasn't going to get it in her head in five minutes without so much as seeing a copy.

But Healy had a pen and parchment.

Before I knew it, I was knocking on his door again.

This time, he opened it himself. I kept my head down, because I knew if I looked into his eyes, I'd lose my nerve.

"Please—I need a pen and parchment. To write something. Not for me. For others. To help them."

"On my desk."

Then he brushed past, leaving me alone in the cabin.

I ran to the desk. The pen and parchment were still there, along with an inkpot. The parchment was covered with scribbled numbers. I flipped it over. The other side was blank.

I sat down at the desk and copied out the map's ancient hieroglyphs for the second time that week.

Dash dot feather, cup, two dash dot firebird. Spear, sun eye, jagged line stars . . .

My hand was shaking when I started, but by the third line my pen strokes were smooth. It was a relief to finally be able to write out the map for someone who wasn't going to use it for evil—and to finally be rid of the awful responsibility of carrying it around in my head for so long.

It was more than a relief. Once I gave it to Kira—and as long as I could persuade the pirates to spare her life—I'd have done my part to help the Okalu. Even if I hadn't been able to finish the job, I'd at least have tried.

And no one could say I'd been selfish or cowardly about it.

The moment I finished, I ran for the door, shaking out the parchment to dry the ink as I went.

Back outside, the election was about to start. Healy stood alone at the deck rail, studying the horizon while his first mate, Spiggs, moved through the crowd, handing each crew member a gold coin from a large canvas sack.

Kira, Guts, and Adonis were still standing near the poop deck ladder. I walked over to them and handed the map to Kira.

"It's yours," I said. "Keep it close."

She stared at it in disbelief.

"She your — partner now? Cuttin' me out?" Guts was glaring at me from under his shaggy, white-blond bangs, and I suddenly remembered the map wasn't all mine to give.

"Oh, right—Guts has claim to a third of any treasure you find," I told her.

Kira and Guts traded a look that I couldn't begin to figure out. In the week we'd been apart, their relationship seemed to have turned into something more than just friendship.

Or maybe it hadn't. I couldn't tell. And I wasn't about to ask either one of them, because I didn't want to get slugged.

"Now, hang on," Adonis chimed in. "If that map come off our property—"

I was about to tell my brother to stuff it when Spiggs's throaty voice rang out, ending the conversation for me.

"Who's still needin' a coin?" he asked, holding up the sack.

Nobody answered.

"Right, then. Get the vote started."

THE VOTE

HEALY TURNED AWAY from the deck rail and walked back to his spot in front of the crew.

I had a decision to make. Once the election got going, I couldn't interrupt it to plead for my friends' lives. And after it was over, the crew might tear us apart before I could get a sentence out. If I didn't speak up now, I might never get the chance.

I tried to bellow loud enough to be heard in the back of the crowd.

"I have something to—"

"*Shut up, boy.*"

Healy's voice hit me like a mallet. My head swam, my eyes filled with little green and red explosions, and for a moment I thought I might faint again.

After that, I couldn't have found my voice with a spyglass. All I could do was hope I'd get a second shot when the election ended.

Healy gave Spiggs a nod. The first mate called out:

"Who stands for captain of the *Grift* and her crew?"

"I, Roy Okemu."

Roy Okemu was a bald, dark-skinned Mandar nearly a head taller than the pirates around him. Even in a crowd of fierce men, he looked uniquely terrifying. It took a moment for me to figure out why—alone among the bristly, unshaven crew, his face was smooth and hairless, all the way down to his nonexistent eyebrows.

It was like he'd scared off his own hair. And just looking at him, I knew we couldn't expect any mercy if he won.

"I, Jonas Pike."

Pike was an older man, one of Healy's officers. His beard was streaked with gray, and his eyes were keen and narrow. I wondered how close he and Healy were, and whether if he were captain, Healy could persuade him to spare our lives.

"I, Mateo Salese."

Mateo Salese was a Gualo, with thick black hair, olive skin, and an almost musical accent. He was so handsome I immediately thought of Tonio, the gentleman thief in *Throne of the Ancients,* and I wondered if women didn't mind when Salese robbed them, either.

It was hard to imagine a man that handsome slitting our throats. Maybe we'd be okay if he came out on top.

Then it was quiet for a bit, and I was starting to wonder whether our odds of surviving were better with Pike or Salese when another voice startled me.

"I, Burn Healy."

A murmur of surprise rippled through the crowd. Then:

"Jonas Pike withdraws."

"Mateo Salese withdraws."

Roy Okemu just narrowed his eyes. He wasn't withdrawing from anything.

"Any others?" Spiggs called out. No one answered.

"Awright. Okemu and Healy stand for captain. Roy Okemu, state your case."

The men around Okemu stepped back to give him room.

"You all know Roy," he began, in a thick Mandar accent and a voice as deep and rumbling as the volcano back on Deadweather. "On crew eight year. Fight hard. Fair man. Day I join crew, speak not one word Rovian. Today? Speak ten. Maybe twelve."

The crew laughed at the joke. Okemu grinned.

"You want captain knows more words? Don't vote Roy. But I say, for captain words not so important. Action important."

He stopped to let that sink in. There were some nods and grunts of approval.

"We follow Healy long time. Take his mark, obey his Code. We do good, sure. Healy do better. What he take? Quarter share."

More nods. Some grumbling.

"Captain get more, okay. He leader. This fair. But not quarter. Is too much. I be captain, I take one tenth."

A lot of nodding. Even some claps. They liked hearing this.

Okemu held up his hand.

"But hey—gold is gold. Important, yeah. Not most important. Most important is Code. Every man on ship swear Code. We live. We die. All by Code. Yeah? This right?"

Nods and voices of approval all around.

"Article One. First day, they tell me this biggest rule: *'Brethren above all.'* I say, what this mean? 'Brethren'? They tell me brethren is us. Brethren is crew. Brethren is *everything.*"

Cheers. Roy Okemu might not know a lot of words. But he was very good at using the ones he did know.

"Nothing come before brethren! Not treasure. Not woman. Not blood. *Nothing!*"

More cheers. His voice was booming now, and there was anger in it.

"We break this rule, what happen? We die. By *his* hand."

He pointed to Healy. My uncle's face was a mask.

And my heart was starting to race, for him and me both. Because I could see where this was headed.

"I say okay. This fair. Rule is rule. Same for everyone. Until today."

Okemu lowered his voice.

"What happen today in Pella? Everybody know. Nobody want to say. I say it."

He turned to Healy, looking him in the eye.

"You break you Code. You put *him*"—he pointed to me—"front of us. Now we got no money. Now we ship sink. Now maybe we die. Not for brethren. Just for boy."

Okemu's lip curled in a snarl. He slowly shook his head. "This no good. Rule is rule! Even for man who make it. Captain break Code . . . *no more captain.*"

The implication was clear—Roy Okemu wasn't just arguing to be the new captain. He was arguing for the old one's death.

And men were roaring in approval. Not all of them. But enough.

Kira's hand was gripping mine again.

It was all I could do to stay on my feet.

Healy watched his crew cheer the man who'd just urged them to end his life. His face gave away nothing.

Once the cheers had faded into silence, Spiggs spoke up.

"Burn Healy, state your case."

Healy began in a somber voice.

"Our situation is perilous. Our hull is breached, landfall is days away, and two hundred cannon roam this sea intent on our death. Whoever leads you will require your unquestioned devotion."

Healy paused. I could feel the crowd turning on him. The iron loyalty that had held the crew together under him for as long as I'd been on his ship was melting away and re-forming around Okemu.

"Roy Okemu," Healy called out, "is a fair man. And, brothers—what he says is correct. Twenty years ago, I wrote our Code in my own hand. And I have followed it to the letter."

He paused. His eyes darkened.

"Until today. When I broke it. I put blood before brethren. Worse than that, brothers—I'd do it again."

I felt a lump of emotion well up in my throat as Healy nodded to underscore his point. "And if you were to argue that the rightful penalty for my action is death . . . well, boys, you'll get no argument from me."

He was smiling now. For the life of me, I couldn't understand why. And judging by the looks on their faces, neither could the crew.

"More than that," he went on, "in ordering our departure, I cheated every one of you your fair share for the taking of Pella

Nonna. What had you expected? Five hundred gold each? A thousand? Call it the bigger. All in, there's two hundred thousand gold I cost you. Because I put blood before brethren."

He wasn't exactly helping his case. The pirates looked furious. Healy was still smiling.

"But here is my promise to you: I'll put brethren before gold. I take a quarter share, it's true. And over the years, brothers, it adds up. There's a dark and private place near Edgartown, accessible only by me. Inside it is ten million gold."

A little ripple of disbelief went through the crowd at the mention of such a staggering number.

"There's a world of trouble ahead of us. But those who follow me through it—and see that Ripper Jones and *Li Homaya* get what's coming to them—can split that ten million equally. Brothers, if we get this job done together . . . that's *fifty thousand gold* for each of you."

Two hundred mouths fell open in shock.

"Call the vote," Healy said to Spiggs.

Spiggs held up a large canvas sack, open at the neck.

"Inside the sack are two bags. White and black. Coin in the white's a vote for Okemu. Coin in the black's a vote for Healy."

The voting went so fast that a thick sliver of sun was still hanging above the horizon when it finished. Spiggs pulled the white bag out first, and it was so light and thin there was no need for a count.

"Your new captain . . . is Burn Healy," Spiggs bellowed.

A cheer began to form, but Healy cut it off with a wave of his hand.

"Return to your posts," he called out. The men went straight back to business with their usual intensity of purpose. No one looked at us.

The newly reelected captain had just begun a brief conference with his senior officers when Roy Okemu approached him, holding a pistol by the barrel.

Okemu held out the pistol for Healy to take.

"What Code says," Okemu told the captain. "Challenge fail . . . no more challenger."

Healy nodded grimly. "Rules are rules."

Okemu sank to his knees. Healy raised the pistol and pointed it at the Mandar's bald head.

I turned away so I wouldn't have to see it happen. Guts and Kira did the same. Adonis just gawked.

The pistol roared.

"Wot the deuce?!" Adonis muttered. "He missed!"

I looked back at Healy. He was examining the smoking pistol with a curious look on his face.

"Hmm. Not the shot I used to be," he said.

Bewildered, Okemu rose to his feet. Healy handed the pistol back to him.

"All the better. Need every man we can get. Back to your post."

He issued a few terse orders to his officers, then dismissed them and turned to us.

"The four of you. In my cabin. Now."

THERE WAS A SQUARE TABLE in the middle of his quarters. Healy sat us down around it. Dusk had turned the room gloomy, so he fired a lantern and set it in front of us.

"Thank you," I said—meaning *thank you for saving our lives.*

Healy ignored me, and I worried he might think all I meant was *thank you for the light*. I was about to explain myself when he started talking.

"Just so we're clear—they'd still very much like to kill you all." He leaned back against his desk as he spoke, his arms crossed in front of him in a casual sort of way. "If I hadn't called that election and broken their fever, you wouldn't have lived to see the dawn. It's likely I wouldn't have, either.

"Fortunately, I've now solved that problem for myself. But not entirely for you. Technically, the Code only applies while you're on board this ship. If we make Deadweather, and put in with the crew still hard against you, I wouldn't bet on your lasting more than five minutes on dry land."

He shrugged, as if to say that would be a shame, but not much more.

"So: if I were you, how would I avoid such an outcome? By making myself *so incredibly useful* to this crew that by the time we make land, they'd no more want to kill you than throw a perfectly good cannon sponge overboard."

He cocked his head and wrinkled his eyebrows as he fixed his gaze on Adonis.

"You especially. Stick was right—you're no child. Better stop acting like one, or you won't be long for this world. That means treating people with respect. Not just my crew, but your companions here. And the whole rest of humanity, for that matter. Fortune doesn't favor a fathead, son. Get your act together."

Adonis looked like he might throw up. I actually found myself feeling sorry for him. If there was anyone in this world he respected, it was probably Healy, and hearing that must have devastated him.

Then again, he needed to hear it.

Healy straightened up, walking toward the door as he spoke.

"If I might offer a suggestion in the 'making yourselves useful' category—that chain pump is built for four. And the men working it have responsibilities elsewhere."

He held the door open wide.

"Get going."

We all scrambled for the exit. For a moment, I hesitated—because I had an idea that I figured might solve both his problem and mine. But I was still feeling so ashamed from the last time I'd opened my mouth without an invitation that I wasn't about to do it again.

I was walking past him, out the door, when he put out an arm to stop me.

"There's something on your mind."

"No, I . . . don't want to speak out of turn."

He smirked. "Why stop now?"

The others were outside already. He closed the door. "Out with it."

"It's just . . . I mean, that's *so* much money you have to lay out, and it seems unfair Pembroke would get off without ever having to pay your crew for helping him take Pella . . . and we're only half a day out, and if we went back—"

He held up a hand to stop me. Then he gestured to the table. "Sit."

I sat. So did he.

"You want me to go back to Pella Nonna . . . and do what?"

"Destroy Roger Pembroke," I said—and when I spoke his name, the anger came spilling out of me. "You could stop him! I know you could! I saw how you were with his soldiers—they love you! Much more than him. And you've *got* to! If Pembroke takes over the whole New Lands—"

"—*all the better for me.*" Once again, his voice stopped me cold.

"Are you forgetting," he went on, "that it was my men who helped take Pella for him in the first place?"

"But that was . . . before—"

"—he put a noose around your neck. Yes. And in spite of all that, it's not in my interest to destroy Roger Pembroke. To the contrary. I need to help him."

I must have looked as nauseated as I felt. Healy let out a weary sigh.

"The Blue Sea . . . is a complicated place. And not a large one. Sooner or later, everyone's paths cross. Time and again. I've been sailing these waters better than twenty years. And whether you start out as a man's best friend . . . or his worst enemy . . . sooner or later, we all end up with our hands in each other's pockets. Does that make any sense to you?"

"I'm not sure," I said.

"Probably it doesn't. Because you're very young, and I'm going to hazard a guess that you make sense of the world by dividing everything into good and evil. Am I right?"

"No," I said. "I'm not *that* stupid."

"Really?"

"Really," I insisted. "I know there's gray areas."

"Do you? All right, then: Roger Pembroke. Good or evil?"

"Evil," I said instantly.

"No gray there at all?"

I thought back to the last time I'd seen Pembroke—standing in front of the whole city of Pella Nonna, spinning a monstrous lie about how it was me, not him, who deserved to hang for the crime of trading in slaves.

Then a whole series of images flashed in my head.

Pembroke smiling across his breakfast table as he sent me to get thrown off a cliff . . .

Pembroke marching up the road to my house on Deadweather with a company of soldiers, aiming to steal my father's plantation for the treasure he thought was buried there . . .

Pembroke in a dark cell, red-faced with rage, his hands around my throat . . .

And the worst one of all: Pembroke standing at the base of Mata Kalun, giving the order for my father's death.

"No," I said. "Not him. He's all evil."

"What about me?"

"Good," I said.

"Really?" He looked so amused I thought he might break into laughter. "Are you quite aware of how I earn my bread?"

"Gray, then," I said.

He kept smiling. "But not *really* gray. Right? I mean, deep down, I must be quite a fellow. The buccaneer with the heart of gold, eh? Good ol' Uncle Burn?"

I couldn't help smiling myself.

Then his smile vanished.

"You're wrong."

He leaned forward in his chair, his voice low. "I'm a pirate. I rob men for a living. When I have to, I kill them. I've ended more lives than I can count. Most of them not guilty of anything worse than foolishness. And if you think I'm good . . . you're a bigger fool than any of them."

He didn't say it like he was angry. He said it like he was sad.

"For the record, you're absolutely right about Pembroke. That man might just be the devil himself. But the fact of the matter is . . ."

He leaned back again with another deep sigh.

"I'm neck deep in the devil's business. And so is everybody else who might help you. Unfortunately for your fantasies of justice, right now the only man on the Blue Sea with a ghost of a chance of taking down Roger Pembroke is *Li Homaya*. And at the moment, he and I are on opposite sides of the chessboard."

I thought about *Li Homaya*. He'd been the rightful ruler of Pella Nonna—but he'd left the city before the Rovian invasion, taking his two warships with Ripper Jones to hunt down my uncle.

"He doesn't know, does he?" I asked. "He has no idea Roger Pembroke took Pella from him?"

"Not a clue," said Healy.

"But if he did—wouldn't he stop hunting you? And turn right around and go take his city back?"

"I'm sure he would."

I was on the edge of my seat, my voice rising with excitement. "So all you have to do is get a message to him! And then he'll—"

My uncle cut me off with a sharp laugh. "Son, any message I send to *Li Homaya* is going to be written on a cannonball. When next I cross *that* filthy Short-Ear's path . . ."

His jaw tightened, his eyes turned dark as coal—and as I looked in them, I finally saw the pirate who'd ended more men than he could count.

". . . I'm going to kill him dead. Try to find some good in that."

I couldn't.

"Think I'd better go help with the pump" was all I could think to say.

"I think you'd better."

I stood up and walked to the door.

Then I turned around. There was that one other thing I needed to be sure he understood.

"Thank you—"

"There's no need—"

"—for saving my life. Again. And my friends' as well."

The darkness left his eyes. He nodded, just a little.

I turned to leave.

"Wait."

He was standing up, his eyebrows bunched together in a frown.

Twice he started to open his mouth, then stopped.

"Egbert . . ."

"Egg. Please. I hate the name Egbert."

"I would, too." He looked at his feet and sighed again. All those sighs were unnerving. He wasn't the type for it.

"I remember when I met you . . . ," he began. "Pembroke was offering five thousand silver for your life. And I thought it was an awfully steep price for a fruit picker's boy."

He raised his eyes to meet mine.

"But I've just paid ten million gold for you."

For the first time, my brain fully registered the enormity of what he'd done.

The tears came so fast I didn't even have a chance to fight them.

"Oh, Savior's sake! Don't do that!"

"Sorry . . ."

"No, no—there's no tears on this ship—we don't—honestly, stop!" He was dashing around the room in a mad search for something to plug up the waterworks.

"I'm sorry . . ."

"Stop saying—just—don't—*please*!" He finally found a handkerchief, and practically smothered me with it.

I got myself back under control.

"Thank you," I said again, as soon as I could talk.

He grimaced. "Son, as the Savior is my witness, I don't want your thanks. I only brought up the ten million . . ."

He put a hand on my shoulder.

". . . because I want you to be worth it."

CHAPTER 6

TEN MILLION WORTH OF GOOD

"STATIONS!"

The cry rang out from the top of the companionway. Within seconds, the gun deck had filled with a ship-rattling *thrum* as a hundred pirates flooded past us to man the cannon. Half a minute more, and there was a full crew in place around every one, all of them loaded and ready to fire.

The four of us just kept turning the stupid crank of the chain pump, sweat running down our faces like water.

If there's a worse job on earth, I never want to find out what it is. We'd been stuck on that pump twelve hours a day for three full days, in six-hour shifts that left us flat on our backs when they ended, and so sore we could barely raise our arms over our heads when it was time to start up again.

But we'd kept at it without complaint, because it was a matter of life and death. The leak in the hold was only getting worse—a carpenter might have been able to shore it up, but Healy had lost

41

his to a musket ball during the invasion of Pella, and for all their skills, none of his crew had the proper training to fix the ruptured patch.

Our only good fortune was that *Li Homaya* and Ripper Jones hadn't found us yet.

This was the third time the *Grift*'s gun crews had gone on alert. The first two times had been triggered by the sight of sails on the horizon. In each case, the ships turned out to be merchantmen who fled at the sight of Burn Healy's ship—and must have been astonished at their luck when they weren't run down and plundered.

Now it was dawn on our fourth day at sea, my friends and I had just started our morning shift at the pump, and I was praying this would be another false alarm. I'd only just decided how to make myself worthy of the ten million gold Healy had paid for my life, and I didn't want to die in a sea battle before I could get started on it.

It was pretty simple, really: all I had to do was destroy Roger Pembroke.

Simple, but not easy.

And it had taken most of those three days to work out the logic of it. When I first started thinking it over—as much as it was possible to think while turning a heavy crank for six hours straight— I figured Healy's alliance with Pembroke made destroying him a nonstarter in terms of paying my debt to my uncle.

None of my friends suggested it, either. They all had their own ideas.

"You can find the Fist of Ka—" Kira paused to suck in a

lungful of air on the crank's downstroke "—and restore it to my people."

"That's good for the Okalu," I huffed between my own gulps of breath. "But how's it worth ten million to Healy?"

"Rest of the Fire King's treasure . . . might be worth ten *pudda* million," Guts panted. One of the crew had helped him wrap a cloth over the stump of his hand so he'd have some cushion when he pushed down on the pump handle, but it was still much tougher going for him than for the rest of us. "Find the treasure . . . ye can pay him back from your share."

That seemed logical. But something about it didn't quite fit, and it took me until the beginning of the next shift to put my finger on why.

"I don't think he actually wants me to pay him back," I said. "Burn Healy doesn't care about money."

"*Blun* to that! He's a — pirate!"

"But if money's so important to him," I pointed out, "why'd he give up so much of it for me? For that matter . . . why save me in the first place? If his crew left Pella without getting paid, he must have, too. Think how much *that* cost him."

"So what *does* he care about?" Kira asked.

I spent almost a full day thinking about that as I worked the crank or lay splayed out, exhausted, between shifts.

"Honor," I said finally.

"Honor?"

"That's what Healy's Code is all about—honor, and putting the good of your crew ahead of yourself. That one time he got angry with me, before the vote, it was because he thought I was being selfish and cowardly. So I've got to be the opposite of that. Selfless and brave. Helpful to others. Honorable."

Adonis snorted. "Want to be honorable, please ye thanks? *I* can tell ye how, please."

My brother had taken to heart our uncle's advice about not being a fathead. He'd been on his best behavior ever since, and he'd started peppering his speech with strange words (for my brother, anyway) like *please* and *thank you,* because he knew using them was part of being respectful to people.

He hadn't quite gotten the hang of where to put them in a sentence, though. So they kept cropping up in odd places whenever he spoke.

"How's that?" I asked him.

"Go back to Deadweather thanks, help me run the plantation like ye promised please."

Before my father died, I'd promised him I'd get the plantation—which I'd handed over to the field pirates who worked it in exchange for their help against Pembroke—back on its feet again.

But it was likely to be a near-impossible job. And I'd never much cared for the place to begin with. Going back to live there with Adonis and the field pirates was the last thing I wanted to do. Just thinking about it put a knot of dread in my gut.

Even so, I knew I had that feeling of dread because Adonis was right. I'd made a promise. And holding myself to it was the honorable thing.

It took a while for me to figure out a way around that.

"I've got to avenge Dad's death," I told Adonis the next day.

"Thanks how?"

"By destroying Roger Pembroke."

It wasn't just honorable because he'd killed my father. If Pembroke had his way, he'd turn the entire New Lands into a continent-sized version of Sunrise Island—a rich man's paradise, rotten to the core and built by slave labor.

If I could bring him down, it'd mean a better life for thousands of people in the New Lands. Maybe more. Maybe a lot more.

As bad at math as I was, I felt sure that if you added up all the good it would do for all those people, you'd get within spitting distance of ten million gold.

And the more I thought about it, the more it seemed to me— although I couldn't have told you why—that even if he wouldn't do the job himself, my uncle would approve of it.

Kira certainly approved. Not only was Pembroke responsible for her own father's death, but destroying him meant stopping the slave trade that kept her people either under the thumb of Pembroke's Moku allies on the mainland or imprisoned in his silver mine on Sunrise Island.

Guts was fine with taking down Pembroke, too, "long's we find that *pudda* treasure while we're at it."

I had my doubts about the Fire King's treasure. After seeing Pembroke blow up in a rage when he translated the map that supposedly led to it, I no longer believed the treasure and the Fist of Ka existed—at least, not in the way the legend promised.

But Kira still had faith.

"Of course we will find the treasure," she told Guts. "If we can restore the Fist to my people, it will put an end to Pembroke's evil."

I figured there was no point in arguing about the treasure for the moment. And we had to quit talking about the whole thing anyway, because it was making Adonis upset. He couldn't come up with a good reason why I shouldn't avenge our father's death, but the thought that I might not stick around to help with the ugly fruit plantation turned him red-faced and sputtery, and his *pleases* and *thank yous* started to come out sounding like curses.

So we worked the pump in silence after that, except for Kira's whispered prayers to Ka at every sunrise and sunset. I spent the rest of the time trying to puzzle out how I was going to go about destroying Pembroke—and got nowhere, because other than somehow getting a message to *Li Homaya* so he'd quit chasing my uncle and take his warships back to Pella to attack Pembroke, I didn't have the slightest idea where to begin.

NOW, ON THE MORNING of the fourth day at sea, the crews were on alert again—only this time, it wasn't because there was a ship on the horizon.

"OARS OUT!"

The crews amidships turned as one, away from their cannon. Unfastening a dozen giant oars from the ceiling, they began to maneuver them out through the middle gun ports on either side.

As I watched them prepare the ship for rowing, it dawned on me why the air that morning had turned so hot and smothering, with no breeze coming through the ports.

We'd finally reached Deadweather Island. For the moment, we were safe. And I was nearly home.

After the ship docked, four of Healy's men relieved us at the pump. We made our way to the weather deck, stretching our weary muscles and blinking in the morning sun that burned through the island's stifling haze.

The pirate haven of Port Scratch looked pretty much the way

it had when I'd left: a collection of filthy, rotting shacks clustered around a crude port. It was unusually quiet—just one other ship, the *Sea Goblin,* was docked along with the *Grift,* and the streets were mostly empty except for Healy's crew, who were streaming on and off the ship on various errands.

Healy was standing near the companionway, issuing orders. Seeing us eye the pirates on the dock with concern, he smiled.

"Don't worry. They won't kill you unless you give them a fresh reason. Your time at the pump saw to that."

"What is that awful smell?" Kira asked, wrinkling her nose. She was the only one of us who'd never been on Deadweather before.

"Mostly, it's the volcano," I said. "That, and a lack of cleaning up."

Kira's eyes bulged as she raised them skyward and got her first look at the smoke-belching summit that made the whole island reek of rotten eggs.

"Please don't worry, thank ye," Adonis told her. "She don't never blow. Just stinks up the place, thank ye."

"Headed back to the plantation, then?" Healy asked us.

We all looked at each other. We hadn't talked about where we'd go once we reached Deadweather.

"Please, yeh, thanks."

I looked at Guts. He gave me a shrug. "Where else we gonna put up?"

"Looks like the plantation," I told Healy.

"Have you got everything you need? You all right for money?"

I shrugged. "Kind of."

"Well, how much do you have?"

We all looked at each other again.

"None."

Healy sighed and dug in his pocket for a fistful of coins, which he handed to me.

"If you need anything else, we'll likely be in port another day or so. Patching things up, possibly making an ally"—he glanced over at the *Sea Goblin* as he said that—"and then we'll be headed to Edgartown for more of the same. In the meantime, if you come across a decent carpenter, send him my way. I could use the help fixing that breach."

He gave me a friendly pat on the back. Then he did the same to the others.

When he reached Adonis, he grasped my brother by his shoulders and looked him in the eye with a serious but kind expression.

"Keep it up, son. It's hard work being a good man. But you've got it in you." He glanced up at the sky. "Your mother's watching. Make her proud."

I got a little lump in my throat at the mention of our mother.

Adonis did, too. "Thank ye, please," he told Healy in a scratchy voice.

"You're quite welcome, thank you very please," said Healy with a smirk.

Then Spiggs called to him from across the deck, and he left us to make our way off the ship alone.

All of a sudden, I didn't want to leave. The thought of parting ways with Burn Healy, for the first time since I'd learned he was my uncle, didn't sit well.

Not that I had much of a choice. It wasn't like he'd asked me to stay. And sooner or later, he'd be shooting it out with Ripper Jones and *Li Homaya*. I didn't want to be anywhere near that battle if I could help it.

Even so . . .

Before I left him, I had to make sure of something.

The others were already on the gangway.

"Just one second!" I called out to them. Then I ran across the deck to where Healy and Spiggs were talking.

My uncle heard me coming. By the time I reached him, he'd already turned toward me. His eyebrows were furrowed together, and he had a pained look in his eye.

"I'm sorry, son—there's dirty work afoot, and it's no place for children—I mean, I would if I could, but—"

"It's not that," I said.

"Oh." He looked a little flustered. "Then what?"

"I've made a decision," I told him. "I'm going to destroy Roger Pembroke. Or die trying."

He almost smiled. But not quite.

"Well, in that case . . ." He dug in his pocket for a moment. "Take another five gold. You'll need it."

He dropped the coins into my hand. Then he ruffled the hair on the top of my head and returned to his conversation without another word. He had a job to do.

And so did I.

HOUSEKEEPING

THINGS HAD CHANGED at the ugly fruit plantation since we'd been away, and not for the better.

The lower fields were shaggy and overgrown, like nothing had been pruned in ages. Harvesting hooks lay here and there, spotty with rust. And there wasn't a field pirate in sight, although I could hear hoarse voices yelling at each other down near the barracks.

As we approached the house, the first thing I noticed was that the shark's jaws Dad had hung over the front door were gone.

Then I realized the front door was gone, too.

Next to where the door used to be, there were two cannonball-sized holes in the wall. So it probably shouldn't have come as such a surprise when we stepped inside and discovered a cannon in the middle of the living room.

It was surrounded by a thick carpet of shattered bottles, chicken bones, bent playing cards, and some spectacularly broken

50

furniture. Only the couch was more or less in one piece, along with the legless house pirate who was asleep on it with a copy of *Principles of Citrus Cultivation* open across his chest.

"Quint?"

"Back off, ye crapsacks!"

He sprang to his feet—actually, his stumps, which ended where most people's upper thighs are—brandishing a knife that must have been hidden under the book.

Then he realized who we were.

"*Egbert!* And . . . Savior save us, is that Adonis? Thought ye was dead!"

Adonis was furious. "Wot'd ye do to the house, ye stupid—"

"Respect—" I reminded him.

"Foo—ye—*thank ye very much*!" he finished, spitting out the phrase in a way that gave it pretty much the opposite meaning from its usual one.

Quint looked sheepish. "If I'd known ye was comin', I woulda . . ."

". . . not blown holes in the wall?" I suggested.

He shook his head sadly. "Bad night, that was. Lessons learned, I tell ye."

Then his eyes landed on Kira, and his face brightened. He vaulted himself up onto the arm of the couch and stuck out his hand.

"Hello, luv. Don't believe we've met. Quint Bailey, jack-of-all-trades. Don't mind the legs. Clever men get by without 'em."

Kira shook his hand warily. "Kira Zamorazol."

"You are easy on the eyes, darlin'." He turned to wink at me. "Know how to pick 'em, don't ye, Egbert?"

Guts didn't care for that. "Back off, ye *billi glulo porsamora*!"

Quint just grinned at him. "Look who's been hangin' round Short-Ears!" Then he nodded at Guts's stump. "Where'd yer hook get off to?"

"Had it pinched by Natives," Guts muttered.

"Bought it off Ozzy, didn't ye? Got himself a new one down in the Scratch a while back. Prob'ly sell that to ye as well, now he's outta money."

"Wot the deuce!?" Adonis had wandered off into the den, and judging by the fury in his voice, what he'd found there must not have been pleasant.

"I was plannin' to clean that up!" Quint yelled back at him. "Soon's I can find the wheelbarrow," he added under his breath.

"What on earth is going on around here?" I asked Quint.

He looked pained. "Why don't I fix ye a meal? Better we talk on a full stomach."

LIKE MOST OF QUINT'S COOKING, the stew he put in front of us was filling but not exactly tasty, and we had to eat it fast before it hardened. Most of the dining chairs had vanished, so we stood around the butcher's table in the kitchen while he caught us up on what had happened.

Leaving fifty field pirates alone with nobody in charge, several crates of weapons, and enough money to get drunk for weeks had turned out to be, no surprise, a recipe for disaster. In addition to nearly wrecking the house, nobody had done a lick of work in the fields for six weeks, and what should have been a manageable case of planter's blight had now spread over enough of the upper orchard that it was threatening to ruin the entire crop.

The only good news was that the field pirates' money was all gone, so they couldn't buy any more rum unless they went back to work. And somebody—Quint wasn't sure who—had been levelheaded enough to steal all the weapons in the dead of night and dump them over the cliff at Rotting Bluff.

But not before the fifty men had been reduced to thirty-six, mostly due to arguments over card games.

"Fact of the matter is," admitted Quint, "none of us is what ye'd call captain material. We can follow orders all right, 'specially with a hard stick backin' 'em up. But leave us be to make our own rules . . . don't go so well."

"What about Otto?" He was the foreman, and he'd run a pretty tight ship in the past.

"He, ahhh . . . wound up wrong side of the cannon. That rule yer dad had 'bout nobody havin' guns? Smart." Quint nodded appreciatively. "No drinkin' an' gamblin' was another smart one, come to think of it. Reckon it's time to get back to that."

"Gonna get back to all of it," said Adonis firmly. "Me and Egbert are in charge now. Gonna set things right round here, thank ye please."

"Dunno how the lads gonna take that," said Quint. "By now, they's good and used to not havin' no boss on the plantation."

"But there's not going to be a plantation if this keeps up," I said. "It'll fall apart completely."

The whole situation was making me feel angry—and helpless, which was worse. Fortunately, Mung showed up just then, with a smile that filled his whole face, and gave me a big bear hug.

Of all the busted-down pirates who'd worked the fields for my dad, Mung was my favorite. He was missing a good chunk of his skull, which left him unable to talk in more than a gurgle, but even so, we'd always understood each other pretty well.

After he'd said hello to Adonis and Guts, and I'd introduced him to Kira, he asked me a question. The words were incomprehensible, but I got the gist of it. And I was too tired and beaten down to be anything but honest.

"It's a mess, Mung," I said. "I don't even know where to start."

He gave me a kind smile. Then he patted me on the shoulder and told me, in his gurgling way, that it was all going to be fine and I should get some sleep.

I looked at my haggard, heavy-lidded friends. It was only late afternoon, but we were all beyond exhausted from the past few days of hard labor on the *Grift*.

"Let's just get some rest," I said. "Deal with things in the morning."

My bedroom was only a few steps away. I headed for it, glad to be able to lie down in my own bed for the first time in ages.

"I'd be careful openin' that if I was—"

I pushed the door open before Quint could finish his sentence, and I was looking back over my shoulder at him when the monkey jumped on my head and started trying to claw my face off.

The next few seconds were pretty chaotic—not to mention painful—but Mung and Guts managed to peel the little monster off my forehead and heave it back into the bedroom, then slam the door shut before it had a chance to mount a counterattack.

"Yeh, that's Clem," said Quint by way of explanation. "One o' the lads bought him down in the Scratch. But he don't much like people, so, ah, livin' in the barracks didn't go over. Really took to yer room, tho'—happy as a pig in poop in there. Well, monkey in poop. There *is* quite a lot of poop. He don't come out much 'cept to steal food."

"I think I'll sleep upstairs," I said.

IT WAS A LONG WALK up those stairs. I felt like I'd lost before I even got started.

I couldn't leave my brother with a mess like this. But I had no idea how to fix it.

And how on earth was I going to take down Roger Pembroke if I couldn't even take down a two-foot monkey in my own bedroom?

When I reached Dad's room, I didn't dare look inside, let alone sleep there, for fear I'd go to pieces at the memory of him. So I went to my sister Venus's old room.

There was a foot-wide hole burned through the middle of her mattress. Somebody must've poured rum on the fire to put it out, because the whole room stank like a Port Scratch tavern.

I curled up on the edge of the bed and wondered how my sister was doing.

We'd left Venus back in the jungle, raging crazy as she lorded it over the Moku. They were treating her like a queen, and she thought that's what she was. But it was all a mistake. Somehow, the Moku had gotten the idea that Venus was the Dawn Princess—a goddess worshiped by Kira's Okalu tribe, the archenemies of the Moku. So the Moku were keeping my sister fat and happy until the rainy season came, when they planned to sacrifice her to their Thunder God, Ma.

As I thought about her, a nauseating lump of guilt started to grow in my stomach—because I knew that no matter how cruel and stupid Venus had been to me growing up, it was my duty as her brother to save her.

Just like it was my duty to Adonis to stick around and try to help him untangle the mess that was the ugly fruit plantation.

But I was going to leave both my brother and sister in the lurch. Because I had to stop Roger Pembroke. Even though I had no idea how to do it and wasn't even tough enough to stop a monkey from pooping all over my bedroom.

It was too much. If I'd had an ounce of energy left, I would've spent it bursting into tears over how helpless and overwhelmed I felt.

I was kidding myself to think I'd ever be worth ten million gold, to Healy or anybody else.

The thing to do was to run away.

Far away.

With Millicent.

If I was lucky, she'd still be on Sunrise Island. And that was just a few hours' sail from Deadweather.

I could sneak down to Port Scratch . . . hire a boat with the money my uncle gave me . . . slip into Sunrise . . . find Millicent . . . persuade her to run away with me . . .

Just the two of us . . . together . . . leaving all our problems behind . . .

Me and Millicent . . .

Millicent . . .

I WOKE UP around dawn and lay in bed for a while, listening to the birds chirp outside and mulling over what to do next. Twelve hours' sleep had shored up my sense of honor, and I no longer thought I had it in me to run away.

At least, not until I'd helped Adonis clean the house.

I went downstairs, drew some water from the well behind the house, and washed up for the first time in ages. I left two buckets of fresh water in the kitchen for the others, then found an empty bin and a shovel and went to work clearing the mess from the living room.

I'd dumped a full bin of trash behind the stable—it was a relief to see our horses were still alive, and not much more underfed than they'd looked when I left—and was heading back inside to fill another when I ran into Kira.

She was sitting on the steps of the porch, studying the map I'd copied for her on the *Grift*.

"It tells a story," she said.

"I thought you couldn't read it."

"I can't. Just a few symbols. But look—" She pointed to a squiggly *X* with two circles over it. "These crossed slings mean there was a battle. And these two here—" She indicated a pair of symbols, a boat over water next to an eye inside a cloud. "The first is a journey over the sea, and the second is Ma, Thunder God. They journeyed to Ma—the god of our enemies."

"What does that mean?"

"I don't know," she said. "But the whole story is about the Fist. Its symbol shows up over and over again. When we get this translated, we can find it."

The hope in her voice said she still believed the Fist of Ka had all the power the legends claimed for it. And that if she found it, she could save her tribe.

"How on earth are we going to get it translated?" I asked her.

She looked at me like I was an idiot. "The same way we are going to stop Roger Pembroke. By finding the Okalu."

"But how would that help?"

"There are warriors among my people," she said. "Plenty of them. And we have no greater enemy than Pembroke. It's our tribe he uses as slaves in his mine on Sunrise. And the Moku hold our land because of guns he gave them."

Her eyes narrowed. "And he ordered my father's death the same as yours. If we can find my tribe, every Okalu alive will help you against him."

"But what if the Fist isn't—?"

"Fist or no Fist. My people will help."

I nearly leaped up and hugged her. "That's fantastic! I'd never even thought of it."

She laughed. "What—did you think we were going to stop Roger Pembroke by ourselves? Just the three of us?"

I let that go without answering. As Guts joined us, taking a seat on the porch next to Kira, I started to puzzle over how we might get to the Okalu. Our last attempt to reach their base in the Cat's Teeth Mountains had been foiled by both the Moku tribe and Roger Pembroke's Rovian troops.

"How are we going to reach the Okalu?" I asked. "We can't go overland again. It's too dangerous."

Kira had already figured that out, too.

"We'll go to Edgartown. My old tutor from when I lived there, Mr. Dalrymple, is a friend of my people. He will know how to reach the tribe."

"Just gotta get to *pudda* Edgartown," said Guts.

"It's just a few days' sail from here," I said. "How hard can it be?"

PLENTY HARD, IT TURNED OUT.

"Only ships out o' Deadweather that put in at Edgartown," Quint explained to us as he pulled a tray of breakfast biscuits from the oven, "are merchantmen. Most of 'em carryin' ugly fruit fer yer dad . . . may the Savior watch over him." Quint kissed a fingertip and raised it to the heavens. He'd taken the news about Dad's death harder than I'd expected.

"A merchantman's fine," I said. "We've got some money—we can pay our freight." It was the same way Guts and I had gotten to Pella Nonna.

"In that case . . . next one's due in three months."

"We've got to wait *three months* to get a ship?"

As I said it, the door to my bedroom opened, and Adonis entered along with a strong whiff of monkey poop.

"Sounds just right," he said. "Three months be 'nuff time to help me get this plantation runnin', thank ye please."

"What were you doing in there?" Kira asked.

"Feedin' Clem." He showed her a handful of tree nuts. "He ain't so bad after all. Make nice to 'im, he's a right good monkey, please."

The last thing I wanted was to be stuck on Deadweather for three months.

And there was one other option.

I looked at Guts and Kira. "Burn Healy's headed to Edgartown," I reminded them. "What if we hop a ride with him?"

"An' get sunk when he runs into *Li Homaya* and Ripper Jones? *Blun* to that!"

"But the way Healy talked, it sounded like he was going to make for Edgartown *before* he tried to fight them. And he's leaving right away."

Kira shook her head. "His crew would never let us board again. Unless one of us was a carpenter."

Quint looked up from his biscuits.

"I'm a carpenter."

THE LEGLESS CARPENTER

"SORRY I SLUGGED YE, thanks."

I fingered the bruise on my cheekbone. It had swelled up pretty good over the last few hours.

"That's okay. Guess I would have been angry, too."

When it dawned on Adonis at breakfast that we were not only leaving right away, but taking with us the only person in the house who knew how to cook and do laundry, he'd exploded. Like most of his rages over the years, it had been directed at me—only I'd been lulled into a false sense of security by the new, trying-to-be-nice Adonis, so when the old one had suddenly reappeared, I hadn't gotten my arms up in time to block the punch.

After Quint and Guts had pulled him away, he'd spent some time screaming, "SORRY SORRY THANKS!" at me, but it hadn't exactly sounded like he meant it. Then he'd gone into a heavy sulk, and for the next several hours, he'd refused to speak to any of us, or to do anything at all except sit on the front porch and feed tree nuts to Clem the monkey.

I don't know if it was just the tree nuts or what, but my brother and that monkey had really hit it off. Clem screeched and bared his teeth at everybody who came within a few feet of him except Adonis, who was now sitting on the porch steps and scratching Clem's nut-swollen belly as the monkey lay on his back, dozing in the stifling afternoon heat.

Not only was Adonis's latest apology the first thing he'd said to me in hours, but it actually sounded halfway sincere. I figured it was okay to get within swinging distance again, so I sat down on the porch steps beside him.

Adonis bit his lip as we watched Mung hitch the horses to the carriage. By now, my brother didn't look angry, or even sulky. Instead, he looked scared. Once Kira and Guts got back from the western slope of the volcano, where they'd gone so Kira could get a look at the Fire King's tomb, we'd be leaving Adonis alone with the mess that was the plantation.

We'd done what we could to make it easier for him. After I'd cleaned the whole house, I'd gone down to the barracks to find Janks. He was the most dependable man among the field pirates who wasn't already dead, and I slipped him five gold pieces to serve as foreman in Otto's place.

Meanwhile, Quint had washed Adonis's dirty clothes and was inside making a fresh stew so my brother would have cooked meals for at least the next couple of days.

"I'll come back," I told Adonis for the tenth time. "Soon as I take care of things."

He glowered. "S'posed to take care of things here, thank ye. Swore it to Dad 'fore he died."

"I'm going to avenge his death. Seems like he would have wanted that."

Adonis didn't say anything.

"Do you have enough gold?" I'd left him all but three pieces of what Burn Healy had given us, minus what Janks had gotten. "I've still got a bit left if you want it."

He shook his head. "Don't need it please."

Kira came out of the house dressed in her own clothes, still damp from Quint's washing. She'd been wearing an old dress of Venus's when she went up the mountain.

"The house looks much better," she said.

"Thanks." A sarcastic comment about all the help I'd gotten with the cleaning popped into my head, but I figured it was better left unsaid. "Didn't know you were back. Did you find the tomb okay?"

She nodded, looking sorrowful—and I got a little pang of sorrow myself at the thought that if I'd gone along, I could have paid a visit to my mother's grave while we were up there.

But then the house would still need cleaning, and we had to get down the hill to Port Scratch before Burn Healy set sail. For all we knew, he might be gone already.

"Where's yer friend, thank ye?" Adonis asked Kira.

"He went to the barracks. To buy a hook for his hand."

"Is Quint ready?" I asked.

"I think so," she said. She went back inside to look for him.

I stood up. Adonis didn't move, except to keep scratching Clem's belly. It really was odd to see. I didn't know my brother had it in him to be gentle like that.

"Quint thinks Janks will be a good foreman, long as you treat

63

him well," I told him. "Just . . . remember what Healy said about respect, and you'll be fine."

I didn't really believe that. Getting the pirates to pull together and put the plantation back on a decent footing was going to take a lot of clever leadership. And Adonis wasn't clever. Or a leader.

I think he knew that, which was why he was so upset.

"You could come with us, you know," I said.

He shook his head. "This is me place, right here please. Anyway, yer nuts."

"How so?"

"Gettin' on that ship again. Ripper an' that Lilo bloke gonna blow it out of the water."

I'd been trying not to think about that.

"An' that's if Healy's crew let ye on to begin with. Probably won't."

"Well, in that case . . . we'll be back for dinner."

Quint vaulted through the doorway, walking on his hands. Kira was behind him.

"All squared away. Stew in the pot's ready to eat," he told Adonis. "Don't let it sit more'n a day. Give ye a bellyache after that."

Quint had a big grin on his face. Like everyone else on the plantation, he'd been a working pirate before he got too injured to crew a ship, and the prospect of going to sea with Burn Healy had him more excited than I'd ever seen him.

I still wasn't sure how Healy would feel about hiring a legless carpenter, but our plan—to promise Healy that the three of us would be Quint's legs and carry him wherever he needed to go on board—seemed reasonable, assuming the crew went along with it.

Mung signaled to us that the carriage was ready. We'd decided to take it so Quint wouldn't have to walk all the way to Port Scratch on his hands, and Mung was at the reins because our old driver, Stumpy, hadn't survived his last card game.

We had to wait around a few minutes for Guts. In the middle of it, the ground began to shake like a rickety table. Kira looked terrified.

"What's happening?"

"Earthquake," I said. "We get a lot of them."

Quint squinted in the direction of the volcano. "Been comin' more regular lately. Coughed up some ash last month, too."

"Hope she spits lava on ye comin' down," grumbled Adonis. But he must have felt guilty about it, because a moment later, he added, "Sorry thanks."

Guts showed up just then. He had a new hook strapped to his left hand under a leather cowl, and his face was twitching hard.

"Ground's shakin'!"

"Earthquake," I said. "No big deal." Then I nodded at the hook. "Going to name that one, too?" He'd called his last hook Lucy, which had always struck me as silly.

He grimaced. "Nah. Just make me madder if I lose it."

After saying our good-byes to Adonis—Clem woke up and screeched at us, which more or less matched my brother's mood— we piled into the back of the carriage and started off down the wagon-rutted road.

I waved out the window one last time at my brother, and he replied with a hand gesture that would have gotten him shot down in Port Scratch.

"Think he'll manage okay?" I asked Quint.

Quint shrugged. "Probably not."

THE DOCK AROUND THE *GRIFT* was swarming with Healy pirates, all loading gear so fast that it seemed like they might be casting off any minute. I didn't want to interrupt any of them for fear of getting my head taken off, so we stood around awkwardly on the dock until Spiggs strode by and noticed us.

"Looking for the cap?"

I nodded.

"Went to meet the captain of the *Sea Goblin.*" Spiggs pointed up the street. "Check the Blind Goat."

We left Mung with the horses so they wouldn't get stolen for meat and started up the street, which was so filth-ridden that Quint rode piggyback on my shoulders rather than walk on his hands.

"Strange thing, Burn Healy in the Blind Goat," he said, his head so close to my ear I could feel his breath on it.

"Why's that?" I asked.

"It's a Ripper joint," he said.

The Goat was a big, single-story box with walls made of wood so warped that they looked like they might cave in at any second. We were about thirty feet from the place when two burly men popped out the open front door, clutching pistols, and ran around the far corner of the building.

"Stop a bit," said Quint.

I stopped. "Why?"

"In case they's runnin' from somethin', instead o' to it. Wouldn't want to get in the way."

But nobody else followed them out, so after a long moment

standing in the muck of the street, we continued on, stepping through the open doorway into the tavern.

The only light in the place came through either the door or the dozens of cracks in the walls and ceiling, so it took a moment for our eyes to adjust to the gloom. The place was empty except for three grimy pirates who were hunched over the bar, sniggering to each other.

The one standing on the bartender's side looked up to growl at us. "Wot ye want?"

"Looking for Burn Healy," I said.

The men sniggered. "Just missed 'im," said one.

"Do you know where he went?" I asked.

"Down below, I expect," said another, and they all sniggered again.

I didn't get it. "Is there a basement?"

More sniggers. Then:

"He's *dead,* boy."

My stomach fell out at the words.

"Now, hang on, Zig," growled the bartender. "Deal ain't done yet, or we woulda heard it."

The words were barely out of his mouth when a shattering crash erupted from somewhere in the back, like someone had just jumped through a window. It was followed by several gunshots . . . and then a *thud* that I didn't hear so much as feel through the floorboards.

"*Now* it's done!"

"Come beggin' fer help, left with a hole in his head!"

The men at the bar cackled with glee as they slapped hands

in celebration. I looked past them, horrified, at the closed door along the back wall.

The sneering bartender turned back to face us. "Turns out Healy weren't so tough after all. Ripper Jones gonna pay a fine bounty for *that* meat."

He started toward us, pulling a knife from his waistband as he spoke.

"An' as fer your lot . . ."

Quint dropped from my shoulders to the floor. Guts stepped forward, brandishing his new hook. I was getting my fists up, cursing myself for having been stupid enough to walk into a place like this unarmed, when the door in the back opened.

The bartender glanced back over his shoulder, and the color left his face.

Burn Healy was standing in the door frame, a pistol in each hand. In the little room behind him, something heavy and slack slid off a chair, and another low *thud* vibrated through the floorboards.

All three pirates ran past us out the door so fast that they'd vanished almost before the bartender's dropped knife hit the floor.

Healy walked over behind the bar. Through the door he'd just exited, I could see a table, chairs, a lot of broken glass, and several heaps on the floor. Two of the heaps resembled the men who'd run around the back of the building just before we entered.

My uncle set the pistols down on the bar, and then took a bottle of brown liquor and a glass from the top shelf.

"It never gets easier," he said, shaking his head as he wiped the lip of the glass clean with his shirttail. "You spend years building a reputation, so when you need something done, you don't have to shoot anyone to make it happen."

He poured himself a drink. "But the minute there's some chop in the water, everybody thinks they can get over on you."

He drained the glass in one gulp. Then he looked our way. "Why are you here?"

"We've found a carpenter," I said.

Quint vaulted up onto a barstool, then onto the bar itself. He waddled over to Healy on his stumps and stuck out his hand.

"Quint Bailey, Cap. Honor to meet ye. Understand you're in need of a man with my skills."

Healy shook Quint's hand with a wary look on his face.

"Carpenter, are you?"

"Prepped by masters, salted with experience. That's me."

"How much experience?"

"Five years apprenticed in the yard at Safe Harbor. Six on ships: first one press-ganged by His Majesty, next five as chief man fer Warty Creech, rest his soul." Quint kissed his finger and raised it to the heavens.

Healy frowned. "You were carpenter on the *Crow*?"

Quint nodded gravely. "Me last ship."

"Why couldn't you save her?"

"Could've—if the shell wot sank her hadn't taken me legs off." He shook his head at the memory. "I'd been ten feet farther down the deck, she'd be sailin' still. So would I."

"So would Warty."

"Aye . . . That he would."

Quint's eyes crinkled with sorrow, but he didn't shrink from Healy's withering stare.

Finally, the captain spoke. "Come look at my ship."

"THAT'S A BIG BITE, that is."

We were down in the gloomy main hold of the *Grift*, wedged into the aisle between the port hull and the massive pile of water barrels that filled most of the space. Quint was standing on a barrel, examining the ragged mix of hammered planks, grain sacks, oakum, and pitch plugging the two-foot-wide hole that had nearly sunk us on the voyage in.

It had been stabilized, but not truly fixed, and seawater was still bubbling through in spots and trickling down the hull.

Quint whistled appreciatively. "Wot was it? Shell gun?"

Healy nodded. "From a shore battery. How many hours to fix her?"

Quint squinted, thinking for a moment.

"If we can careen her—"

"There's no time. We need to set sail at the tide."

"Can ye wait a day?"

"It's been risk enough staying in port this long. Best guess is Jones and *Homaya* are on a regular sweep between here and the coast. If we're not out by tonight, like as not they'll catch us either docked or in the dead miles."

Quint shook his head. "I can repatch. Shore it up a bit. But if ye want a true fix, I gotta get her out o' the water."

"We can dry-dock her in Edgartown. I just need you to get us there."

Quint snorted in disbelief. "Due respect, Cap—how ye

gonna make port in Edgartown without gettin' strung up fer piracy?"

Edgartown was the colonial capital—the biggest Rovian out-post in the New Lands. I'd never been, but I figured there were plenty of soldiers garrisoned there. And piracy was punishable by death.

"Leave that to me," said Healy. "I just need a patch that'll make the trip."

"At wot speed?"

"Fourteen, if the wind's right."

"Wouldn't risk more'n eight. And no promises if ye see combat. 'Specially against the likes of the *Red Throat*." That was Ripper's ship. "Wot's *Homaya* sailin'?"

"Two Cartager men-of-war. And there's five ships in all—*Frenzy* and *Blood Lust* have joined them."

That last part was news to me. *Frenzy* and *Blood Lust* were pirate raiders that, until now, I hadn't realized were allied with the Ripper. Healy must have learned that since he'd been on Deadweather.

Quint's eyes widened. "All five of 'em? Against just us?"

"That's right."

His mouth fell open. "How in the name o'—"

"No time for the story," said Healy. "How soon to get us repatched?"

"With the right material?" Quint gave the damage another look. "Five hours."

"I need you to do it in two."

Quint was looking a lot less thrilled about going to sea than he had been when we left the plantation.

"And there's the issue of your legs," Healy added.

"Wot legs?" asked Quint.

"That's the issue. How will you get around if we see combat?"

"Reckoned these three'd be my mates," Quint told him, nodding at us. "Haul me where I need to go, plug shot if it comes to that."

Healy turned to look at me with concern. I shrugged.

"If your crew will have us . . . we need to get to Edgartown," I told him.

"There's no guaranteeing we'll make it."

"I understand."

"Not sure you do," he said. "Ever been in a sea battle?"

"I was on the *Earthly Pleasure*."

"That'll be a picnic compared to this."

"I been in battles," Guts offered. "Powder monkey."

"Under whose command?" Healy asked him.

Guts's face twitched hard. "The Ripper," he said, staring at his feet.

Healy didn't comment. Instead, he looked at Kira.

"I have fought on land," she told him. "And I am not afraid to die."

"I'd rather you were," he told her.

Then he looked back at me. "Where's your brother?"

"Up at the plantation."

"To stay?"

"Yes."

Healy stroked his jaw as he stared at all three of us in turn. "Carpenter's mates?"

"Yes, sir."

He grimaced. Then he leaned in toward me and spoke in a quiet voice.

"I'm not your father, boy . . . but if I were, I'd never let you on this ship."

The way he looked at me put a lump in my throat.

"I want to go with you," I said.

His face tightened in another grimace. He stared up at the ceiling planks for a moment, like he was looking to them for permission. Or maybe it was forgiveness.

Finally, he exhaled sharply through his nose.

"Fine." He turned to Quint. "Tell the purser what you need. And hurry."

He was two steps up the companionway when the waver in Quint's voice turned him back around.

"Beggin' pardon, Cap—"

"Yes?"

"We hadn't talked about pay—"

"Get the job done, you'll see a crew share. Fifty thousand gold."

Quint looked confused. "Ye mean, we split fifty—"

"That's the share. You're splitting ten million."

Quint's eyeballs bulged. "I can live with that."

"Let's hope we all do."

MATES

AFTER CHECKING THE *GRIFT*'S STORES against the list of supplies Quint gave him, the purser sent Guts, Kira, and me off with a handful of silver coin to buy extra lumber and nails from Port Scratch's only store. On the way, I stopped to say good-bye to Mung, who'd been waiting with the carriage in case we needed to go back up the hill.

"Please watch out for my brother," I begged him. "Try to keep him out of trouble."

Mung gave me a solemn nod, then gurgled a request of his own. I was pretty sure I understood it.

"I'll do the same for Quint. I promise."

Mung smiled, and I knew I'd guessed right. Then he gave me a hug that nearly squeezed the breath out of me. I had to hurry off after that, not just because I didn't want the crew to think I was slacking, but because I could feel myself starting to get emotional.

The list of things I liked about the ugly fruit plantation was a pretty short one, but Mung was at the top of it.

By the time we got back to the *Grift* with armloads of cut lumber and a bucket of nails, Quint already had a team of pirates hard at work in a makeshift staging area on the lower deck, sawing wood for the new patch. We'd barely had time to set down the wood when a lanky pirate appeared with a tape measure that he spread against each of our upper backs.

"Wot ye doin'?" Guts asked him.

"Harnesses."

He sped away before we could ask him what he meant, but a stocky, square-headed Gualo had popped up in his place, and he answered our question before we even asked it.

"He makes harnesses from sailcloth. For your backs. So you can carry carpenter. I am Ismail. I train you. Come."

Ismail led us down to the hold and gave us a quick tour. It was divided into a cavernous main compartment that held hundreds of water barrels, stacked sideways nearly to the ceiling, and a handful of smaller compartments fore and aft that housed the bread room, sail room, carpenter's room, shot locker, and magazine.

The whole deck reeked of bilgewater and was gloomy even on a sunny afternoon. Just a trickle of sunlight managed to filter down through the ceiling grates in the upper decks, and although a couple of oil lamps hung on hooks, neither of them were lit.

"Lantern only at night," Ismail told us. "And *never* near magazine," he added, pointing to the little room that contained the gunpowder kegs. "Unless you want to go *boom*. Kiss the sky."

In the main compartment, two feet of empty space stood between the stacked water barrels and the hull on either side; fore and aft, there were narrow walkways of the same width separating the compartment walls from the hull.

As Ismail explained our duties, the reason for that empty space around the hull became clear.

"First job of carpenter and mates," he began, "is plug any hole below waterline. With load we got now, waterline about here"— he reached up on tiptoe, extending his arm to mark a space just below the ceiling—"so no worry about holes on other two decks. Only down here.

"When cannonball come through hull, you plug hole. Take you twenty seconds, no problem. Take you forty seconds, you got problem. Take you one minute, whole ship got problem."

He held up a canvas sack and pulled out a squat wooden cylinder about ten inches across, wrapped in canvas. "Each of you get sack with plugs. This smallest plug. For eighteen-pound cannonball. Ripper ship mostly fire this. Short-Ear man-of-war . . ." He held up a slightly larger plug. "Fire twenty-four pound. And if we got bad luck . . ." He showed us a plug the size of my head. "Maybe thirty-six. Too many of these, make big problem.

"Every time you go to hole, take sack with you. Find right size plug, pound in hole with this." He pulled a wooden mallet from the sack.

"Sound easy, yeah? Not so easy. Water come fast. Now— second job of carpenter. Fix masts and yards when they break. Deadeyes, too. This complicated. Take time to teach you. Battle come soon, someone else do job. Just know this—someone on deck yell for carpenter, whoever got him on your back get to deck fast. Anybody got question?"

Nobody did.

"Okay. Now we train."

Within seconds, Ismail had us sprinting every which way at top speed, carrying mallets and bags of shot plugs as we reacted to the shot sizes and locations he called out.

"Starboard magazine, low, twenty-four!"

"Bread room, top by ceiling, eighteen!"

"Three holes port side, amidships! Thirty-six all!"

It was tough work. But it was easy compared to what came next.

"Everybody think they good? Know they job? Yeah?"

We nodded, wiping sweat from our faces.

Ismail smiled and pulled three bandannas from his pocket.

"Okay. Now we work blindfolded."

It made sense, given how little light reached the hold. But it was disastrous. I banged my limbs every few feet, had a forehead-to-forehead collision with Kira that sent us both sprawling, and I'd never heard Guts curse so much. Which was saying a lot.

Once the new patch had been sealed over the breach and the *Grift* got under way, Quint joined us. The sailmaker had finished the harnesses, and Ismail had us take turns sprinting up and down the companionways with Quint on our backs. Whoever didn't carry Quint was given a sack of cannonballs that weighed as much as he did.

Then Ismail made Quint practice jumping in and out of our

harnesses so many times that when we finally stopped for our dinner ration, Quint looked as tired as we were.

We ate under the moonlight on the weather deck, grateful for the breeze that dried the sweat from our shirts. The *Grift* had taken the long way around Sunrise Island, and even in the dark I could see the craggy outline of Mount Majestic rising to the east, along with a cluster of twinkling lights just above the horizon that must have been Blisstown.

I wondered if Millicent was somewhere out there.

And then, for the first time in days, that Cyril fellow popped into my head.

The older boy. The one who'd grown up with Millicent on Sunrise.

The one she'd told me was tall, handsome, and rich, and had just gotten himself kicked out of some fancy boarding school in the Fish Islands for doing something terribly impressive.

The one Millicent had claimed she was going to marry.

Is she with him right now? Under one of those twinkling lights?

A little shard of fury went shooting through my brain, and for a moment I considered jumping overboard and swimming to shore.

But I was too tired to chew, let alone swim miles of ocean in the dark.

After dinner, Ismail had us string our hammocks on the lower deck, and at first we were thrilled to get into them. But it turned out he wasn't sending us to sleep. He just wanted to see how fast we could jump out, unstring the hammocks, and stow them.

We must not have been fast enough for him, because when we were finished, he had us do it all over again.

Twenty times.

Then we did it blindfolded, twenty more times.

By the time Ismail finally let us bed down, I'd grown to hate him. I slept that night like a dead man.

The next morning brought more of the same, along with lessons in repairing deadeyes and climbing ratlines to fix broken spars in the rigging. Whenever he let us pause to rest, Ismail quizzed us on the various commands that governed the ship in combat, and there were so many of them that pretty soon my head hurt as much as my arms and legs did.

But as brutal as the training was, every time I looked around whatever deck we happened to be on, I saw men working every bit as hard as we were. The sailors who handled the rigging were a blur of constant movement, and the gun crews drilled nonstop. If there was a single pirate on the ship who wasn't pulling his weight, I never saw him.

I gradually realized that this was why Healy's men had always seemed so much more capable than other crews—because they worked at it, night and day, until every movement their job required had been practiced so many times that the memory of it was burned deep into their muscles.

That was where the iron discipline came from, too. A man who worked such long hours didn't have time for grumbling. Or mutiny. Or fear.

If I'd had the time to stop and think about it, I would have been grateful for that. My head and my hands were so preoccupied with practicing what I'd do in a battle that I didn't have time to worry about whether there was going to be one. There were five ships out there, bristling with cannon, scouring the Blue Sea for us, and if I'd had nothing to do but sit around and wonder when their masts might poke up over the horizon, I would've paralyzed myself with fear.

But I was too busy to be scared. And when I did have a moment to myself, I was too tired to spend it on anything but sleep.

There was something else about working that hard, and for such long hours, with other people—it bound you to them. Ismail taught Guts, Kira, and me to work with Quint as a team—to plug holes, relay supplies, and cover the narrow carpenter's walks in pairs; to share the load of carrying Quint from place to place; and to keep a map in our heads of where the others were, so we could rush to help them, or call on them for the same, at any time.

It's hard to explain the feeling I got from that. Guts and I had been tight for a while, and Kira as well—we'd seen hard times together, and watched each other's backs. And I'd known Quint as long as I could remember. Next to Mung, he'd treated me better than anybody on the plantation.

But those days on the *Grift* bound us even more tightly, to one another and to the rest of the crew. For the first time in my life, I felt like I was part of something: a small but necessary piece of a whole that was much bigger, and more important, than just myself alone. And it felt good. Not happy good, or exciting good, or even warm-piece-of-jelly-bread good . . . but a deep, strong, lasting good.

Not that I understood a bit of that while it was happening. It was only much later, after things had settled down and I'd had a chance to puzzle it all out. All I remember feeling at the time was a strange sense of stability, of having my feet planted firmly somewhere even though I was in the belly of a boat crashing through the sea.

And I do recall wondering, on the night of the third day, why I'd stopped hating Ismail for working us so hard. But I chalked that up to the fact that he'd given us the rest of the evening off after dinner.

Quint arm-vaulted off to sleep, but Guts, Kira, and I spent a few minutes stretched out on the deck, peering through the rigging at the stars overhead.

"Been thinkin'," Guts said. "Gonna get crew shares out o' this?"

"Why would we?" I asked.

"Quint's gettin' one."

"Quint patched the hull," I said. "And anyway, I think crew shares are only for whoever makes it through the battle."

"And we won't?"

"We're less than a day out of Edgartown. I think we'll be off the ship *before* there's a battle."

"Don't say that!" snapped Kira.

"Why not?"

"You taunt Ka when you make a prophecy. He will prove you a fool."

"Sorry," I said. I didn't understand Kira's religion, let alone believe in it. But just the same, I didn't want to get on the wrong side of her god. "Can I take it back? Say a prayer or something?"

"It is too late for that," she said. She stood up, stretching out her neck. "I am going to sleep so I don't have to smell your burnt flesh when Ka strikes you down."

We followed her down two flights to the wide-open mid-section of the lower deck, strung our hammocks in the dark, and crawled into them to sleep.

As I lay there, gently swaying with the roll of the ship alongside a hundred cocooned pirates, I thought about Kira's superstition.

It seemed a little silly. Healy's best guess had been that Ripper Jones and *Li Homaya* were patrolling the coastal lane between Deadweather and the mainland. If that was true, they were days away from us now.

And by tomorrow night, we'd be in Edgartown. The thought of seeing it for the first time was exciting. Not only that, but there were regular ships, as many as one a day, between Edgartown and Blisstown.

Depending on how things worked out with Kira's old tutor, I might have time to double back to Sunrise and find Millicent.

Maybe she'd come with us to track down the Okalu.

And we'd be together again.

Me and Millicent . . .

Millicent . . .

I drifted off with a smile on my lips.

It was the last calm breath I'd draw for two days.

CHAPTER 10

INCOMING

"STATIONS!!"

The voice cut through my sleep like an ax. My heart was pounding before I even opened my eyes.

There was no light. I was swinging in the air.

And the ship was breaking to pieces.

No. The shudder and rumble was feet—hundreds of them, all hitting the decks at once, above and around me.

Get out of the hammock.

It was swaying so crazily I couldn't settle it. I lifted my legs free and rolled out.

Only one leg wasn't quite free. My foot snagged, but the rest of me kept going. I landed ugly on the deck, breaking the fall with my right hand. When I put weight on it to push myself up, a burst of pain shot from my hand all the way to my shoulder.

Something's hurt.

I stood up. The rumbling of feet had stopped, replaced by the eerie *frip-frip* of a hundred hammocks being whisked into storage all around me.

I couldn't see my hand in front of my face. I was groping for the front tie of my hammock, the pain in my arm creating green starbursts in my eyes, when a pirate thundered past in the dark and nearly bowled me over.

The rumble of feet rose again as the crew streamed past me, headed for the companionway and the gun deck upstairs.

Faster. Stow the hammock.

My shaking fingers found the tie, and as I started working at the knot, the pain settled around my wrist, stabbing daggers through it.

The pounding of feet was drowned out by the heavy rumble of cannon carriages moving into place over my head.

I couldn't get the knot undone.

Calm down. You practiced this.

I gulped air, trying to slow my thudding heart.

It's just a drill. Don't get—

I never heard the first round hit. The next thing I knew, I was on my back, skittering across the deck with things and people raining down on me. Then there was light coming from somewhere and voices were crying out and my nose was full of something smoky and bitter as thunder erupted in the distance.

That's not thunder.

A second round struck the ship like the hand of an angry god.

I was thrown again, battered against the hull. As I lifted my head, I heard the thunder again, and the first thing I saw was Quint's face, dazed and blinking in the blue moonlight filtering through an open portal behind him.

Only nobody had opened a portal.

That hole in the hull wasn't supposed to be there.

Quint's dazed look turned wild and urgent as he whipped his head around to me. "GET US BELOW!"

But I haven't untied my hammock.

He vaulted toward me, and I got on one knee like I'd been trained to do. I was wearing the harness—Ismail had made us sleep in them—and Quint swung into it like I was a saddled horse.

I lurched to my feet and started for the companionway down to the hold. Men dodged past me in both directions. I tripped over someone—alive or dead, I wasn't sure—and nearly fell.

I saw Kira a few feet ahead in the smoky gloom, moving in the same direction as me.

"Guts?!" I called out.

"Behind ye!"

Another round of cannon fire slammed into the ship, sending us all sprawling. Quint landed on my head, tangling us both up in the harness.

The force of the impact had blown us forward, almost to the companionway leading down to the hold. As Quint struggled to untangle the harness, a new sound reached my ears.

Rushing water.

Quint heard it, too. "MAN THE PUMP!" he screamed at the ceiling.

The *Grift*'s cannon fired overhead, with a deafening roar that rattled the ship from end to end.

Quint kept yelling, "MAN THE PUMP!" but my ears were ringing so loud it sounded like he was underwater.

He tapped me twice on the shoulder. Ready. As I got up to take the final few steps to the companionway, an answering cry came down from the gun deck:

"PUMP'S ENGAGED!"

Kira was crouched beside the companionway, trying to light an oil lantern. It was pitch black down in the hold. Even through the ringing in my ears, I could still hear the water.

It sounded like a river down there.

"GO!" yelled Quint, but I was already on the steps.

The water in the hold was ankle deep and roiling. I was blind in the darkness, but the canvas sacks of plugs and mallets were right near where they were supposed to be, floating to the left of the stairs. I picked up a sack, handed it back to Quint, and listened for the direction the water was coming from.

Everywhere. It was coming from everywhere.

I moved forward, hands groping in front of me, until I reached the hull. I could feel a current moving past my ankles, and I walked against it, stutter-stepping through the water, until I found the closest breach.

It was at waist level, the seawater rushing in so fast that it slapped away my hand when I first crossed it. My injured wrist shrieked in protest.

"Wot's the size?" yelled Quint.

I tried to probe it with my hands. In the dark, it was like a living, angry thing. "I don't—"

"Kneel on it!"

I knelt down in the water, pressing my body against the hull so Quint could get his hand out to feel the gushing stream.

"Thirty-six!"

The size of the largest Cartager cannon. Ismail's words came back to me.

Too many of these make big problem.

I straightened up. Quint held the sack open, and I plunged my hand into it, searching for the right plug.

No . . . no . . .

I could feel the water rising up my legs.

Got it.

I lifted a large plug from the sack, tucked it under my right arm—the wrist was throbbing now—and reached back in to grab the mallet.

"Mallet on the left!"

Quint took the mallet from me with his free hand. I gripped the plug with both hands, then stepped forward and knelt down in the water as I shoved the plug into the roaring stream.

It pushed back with such force that the plug smacked me in the face, almost knocking me over.

I tried again, putting my weight behind it. The water batted me away a second time.

The pain in my wrist was excruciating. My body was trembling, my clothes soaked and heavy with seawater. Roaring water filled the darkness all around me.

This was nothing like the training.

Get it done or we sink.

I held up the plug in front of my face and shoved it forward with all my strength. My arms shook as the water struggled to find a way around the plug.

I got it.

Almost. A knifelike stream of water was drilling into my face. I moved my head down and away from it.

Then the spray must have hit Quint, because I heard him curse.

The water kept fighting me. My wrist shrieked in agony. Gritting my teeth against the pain, I kept the plug over the hole as I leaned to my left so Quint could drive it home with the mallet.

"On the mark!"

I felt Quint's thick arm swing around my right shoulder—slowly the first time, measuring his target, then so hard my hands tingled when the mallet struck the center of the plug.

My wrist was screaming.

Two more mallet strikes. I could feel the plug burrowing deep into the tight hole. The razor spray of water died.

Three more strikes, and the plug was flush with the hull.

"NEXT!"

As I straightened up, light began to bleed into the hold, and for the first time I could see the hull in front of me. Kira had finally gotten the lantern lit—it was swinging from a hook by the companionway, casting jittery shadows on the walls—and now she was wading through the water to help Guts, who was trying to stanch a gushing hole along the forward carpenter's walk.

I turned to search for another hole. I didn't have to look far. There was one just a few feet behind us, at the same level as my head.

I splashed through knee-deep water to get to it. This one was eighteen—*the size of the Ripper's cannon*—and I had to stand on a crate to plug it.

That took precious time. When we finished and moved on to the next hole, the water was up to the middle of my thighs.

By the time Quint and I had plugged our third hole, I was nearly waist deep in seawater—and I had to press my ear to the hull and listen for the steady *shhhhh* that gave me a fix on the next one.

It was down low, a foot beneath the water level. I had to unhitch Quint, dive underwater, and fix the plug in place with my bare hands. It took forever to pound it in using my hands and feet.

Sputtering and soaked, with the water up over my waist, I put my ear to the hull again.

This time, there was nothing. Just the distant roar of cannon that promised more would come.

DOWN IN THE HOLD

"BUCKETS DOWN!" Ismail called out from the top of the steps. "Rations coming."

We'd been running a bucket line—passing pails of water up the stairs and dumping them out an open portal—for so long that we were getting a second meal. For all its terrors, there was no fear of going hungry in combat. If you could keep food down, it was yours for the taking.

Early on, we'd had to stop twice to plug fresh cannonball holes, and even with the pump running full speed above us, the water level hardly seemed to budge. But a little after dawn, which had arrived so gray and bleak that we still had to burn a lantern in the hold, my uncle had appeared to survey the situation.

He took one glance at the water level and pulled two full gun crews off their weapons to join the line. Our pace picked up dramatically after that, and by now, the water was low enough that my bucket had started scraping the deck when I filled it.

I sank down on the companionway steps next to Guts and took two biscuits from a pail as it went by. It was quiet enough that I could hear the men above us chewing their food. The *Grift*'s guns hadn't fired in hours, and it had been almost that long since we'd heard enemy fire.

Which wasn't actually comforting, because I'd learned that the cannonballs traveled faster than the sound of their firing. It could be dead silent, and there still might be one speeding right at you. By the time you heard the *boom*, it was too late.

The battle wasn't over. According to Quint, it had barely even started. Down in the hold, we couldn't see anything, and no one had bothered to tell us what was happening. But once the cannon fire had stopped, Quint had explained to us what he thought was the situation, in breathless grunts between the buckets he was slinging.

"Cap's runnin' 'em out. . . . Short-Ear men-o'-war ain't . . . so fast as the others . . . If he makes 'em chase us awhile . . . slow ones'll fall behind . . . we can fight 'em two-three at a time . . . 'stead of all at once.

"Just hope the cap remembers," Quint had wheezed, glowering at the patch he'd built on the port side of the hold, " . . . she don't run like she used to."

"She's holding up fine so far," I said.

"'Cause there's water in her belly . . . slowin' her down . . . Once this lot's bailed . . . top speed gonna be a sight faster . . . put a lot o' stress on that patch . . . 'specially turnin' to port."

At the moment, though, the patch looked solid.

"How's yer wrist?" Guts asked me.

"It's okay." There was a splint on it now, which didn't make it hurt any less but at least gave me some use of the hand. The surgeon had tied it on me a few hours back, after he'd taken care of the most serious injuries and come around to check on us. By then, my wrist was so stiff and swollen I could barely bend it, and it was a relief to get a splint on it so I didn't have to worry about it giving way in a tight spot.

I was still chewing my last biscuit when the order came.

"STATIONS!"

The gunners who'd been on the bucket line were gone in seconds, back to their cannon. I was wondering whether the four of us should keep bailing when Ismail yelled down an order.

"READY IN THE HOLD!"

Kira was closest to Quint, so he climbed into her harness as Guts and I rushed down into the hold. We collected our sacks of plugs and waited for the barrage to come.

Minutes passed. Nothing happened. The ankle-deep water sloshed gently against the hold near our feet. The shadowy lamplight cast moving lines across the faces of the others.

Kira looked as frightened as I felt. Guts's face was twitching up a storm.

The minutes stretched out. The steady pitch of the ship as it cut through the waves might have made me drowsy if my heart hadn't been beating so fast.

Not knowing was the worst part. How far away was the enemy? Were we still running from them? I wanted to clamber upstairs and poke my head out on the deck so I could figure out what was going on.

But it wasn't my job to know. My job was to stand there and wait.

The first hint we got that the ship was turning came when the water began to run over our feet toward the starboard hull. Within a few seconds, the deck had tilted to starboard at such a steep angle that I had to reach a hand out to steady myself against the stack of water barrels.

If we'd been running from our enemies, we were turning back toward them now.

The ship slowly began to roll back to level. Then a sharp lurch jerked us to port.

"Mind the speed . . . ," breathed Quint.

I looked over at the hammered planks of his patch. They seemed stable enough.

Then the *Grift*'s guns roared over our heads, rattling the whole ship and sending my heart leaping into my mouth.

We braced ourselves for the answering shot. But there was only a distant rumble. The enemy volley had missed us.

Over the next ten minutes, the *Grift* made several hairpin turns, its cannon thundering after each one. The turns came so close together that the water at our feet slapped against itself in confused, unruly waves.

I was starting to feel seasick. It might not have been a good idea to eat so much.

The enemy cannon were rumbling constantly, the sound rising with every volley. But at first, nothing hit us.

Then there was a crash and shudder far above us, and as the cannon thunder faded, a voice called out:

"CARPENTER ON THE WEATHER DECK!"

Kira ran to the companionway and disappeared up the steps with Quint on her back. Guts and I were left alone to man the hold.

The cannon kept roaring and the ship kept making its jerky, unpredictable turns, the enemy fire growing louder every second. By the time the next round struck the decks above us, the space between the impact and the thunder had disappeared. Our enemies were close now.

Another round slammed into the upper decks, this one followed by a series of urgent orders, not so much bellowed as screamed from somewhere above.

My stomach was queasy. I tried not to be sick.

Then my eye fell on one of the dozen plugs we'd hammered into the hold.

It wasn't flush anymore.

I looked around. None of them were.

The plugs are coming loose.

"GUTS! THE PLUGS!"

I ran for the closest one, mallet in hand, and pounded it flat.

I turned toward the next closest plug. Guts was already there, banging it back into place.

I moved on to the next one.

And the next.

And the next.

The deck tilted up to meet me as the ship carved out another steep turn to port, rolling onto its side.

Gravity flattened me against the port hull. There was one last plug, far away at the aft end of the ship. I could see it coming loose under the pressure created by the ship's leaning hard into the turn.

Guts saw it at the same moment I did. He was much closer.

"ON IT!"

I was starting toward him, praying the ship would come out of its turn and stop stressing the hull, when a spray of water erupted in front of me, right at the spot of Quint's two-foot-wide patch.

At first, I thought a cannonball had hit us. But the spray was too thin and wide, and nothing had struck the water barrels opposite the breach.

Then I realized what it was.

Quint's patch is failing. If it broke open, we'd sink in a matter of minutes.

I lurched over and began to hammer at it.

The hammering didn't do any good. The spray kept coming. It was getting worse.

The patch was giving way.

"GUTS!"

I fell against the patch, throwing the whole weight of my body at it.

The seawater kept spraying out on either side of me. Through the curtain of water, I could see Guts at the far end of the hull. He'd just reached the last plug, his mallet raised to hammer it flush, and he was glancing back over his shoulder at me with a look of surprise.

Then there was an explosive *pop* as the plug rocketed out of its hole and struck Guts in the head, knocking him off his feet.

A fat column of water roared through the hole.

I started to move off the patch—and felt it bulge against my back, threatening to burst open.

"GUTS?!"

I blinked through the spray, waiting to see him get up.

But he didn't.

"GUUUTS!"

He was on his back, the water pouring down on top of him.

He wasn't moving.

I started to take my weight off the patch again. The spray of water accelerated in all directions. The whole thing was coming apart. I fell back against it and flailed away with the mallet.

As I opened my mouth to scream, the *Grift*'s cannon began to roar again, drowning out my voice and making the whole side of the hull shudder.

"FOUR IN THE HOLD! FOUR IN THE HOLD!" It was the emergency order. If anyone heard it, they'd come running.

I kept screaming it at the top of my lungs.

The cannon were still roaring. I could barely hear my own screams over the noise.

"FOUR IN THE HOLD!"

Guts was motionless on his back, the water cascading down on him, rising up over his ears.

"FOUR IN THE HOLD!" I pounded away at the patch as I screamed, but it was pushing back harder now. The water wanted in. It was stronger than I was.

And Guts was going to drown.

"FOUR IN THE HOLD!"

The cannon roared. I kept screaming for help.

I couldn't let the water in. I had to keep pushing back.

Guts was drowning. Just a few feet from me. And I couldn't move to help him.

"FOUR IN THE HOLD!"

There were pirates on the stairs. Running for me. The first one slammed into the patch with the full weight of his body. The second one squeezed past him and lowered a shoulder against the other side.

"Get on the breach!" the first one yelled at me.

I slipped past the second man and started for Guts. Two other pirates were headed for him at the same time, coming around from the other side of the barrels. The first one got there ahead of me and scooped up Guts, throwing him over his shoulder. I got a glimpse of my friend's face—eyes shut, skin ghostly white, red and pink smears of blood mixed with seawater running down his face from a fat gash over his eyebrow—and the pirate was turning to run him upstairs and I was about to follow them off when the other pirate yelled, *"On the breach!"* and I realized the hole was still gushing water and it was my job to plug it.

The mallet was in my hand. The plug that had struck Guts in the head was near my feet, bobbing in the water. I handed the mallet to the pirate, picked up the plug, and attacked the flood of water that had hurt my friend.

I got it over the breach, and the pirate hammered it home. Then we hammered in a second plug behind the first one, just to be safe.

By now, there were four pirates holding the weakened patch in place, and a new bucket line was forming to bail the hold. Quint and Kira had arrived, and Quint was shouting orders at the pirates on the patch. When he saw me, he pointed to the ceiling and yelled, *"Find the cap! Tell 'im the patch is bust! Take her down to six and no turns to port!"*

As I turned to run for the companionway, my eyes met Kira's for an instant, and I saw the worry in them. I knew it was for Guts, and I wanted to tell her he was okay.

But I didn't know if it was true.

And there was no time. I had to find the captain.

THE FANGS

I TOOK THE COMPANIONWAY STEPS two at a time. When I reached the gun deck, the floor was gritty with sand, and there was so much smoke in the air I could barely see through the haze. I was halfway up the next flight when the *Grift*'s guns erupted again.

The recoil nearly knocked me off the steps.

As I stumbled out into the open air of the weather deck, a cloud of smoke from the guns was rising like a curtain on the port side. Before the smoke choked off my view, I glimpsed a familiar-looking frigate half a mile off port. Its foremast was leaning at a crooked angle, one huge sail cut loose from its spar and billowing uselessly across the ship's deck.

It was Ripper Jones's ship, the *Red Throat*. As it disappeared behind the veil of smoke, half a dozen muzzle flashes blinked from its gun ports.

I hit the deck as cannonballs ripped through the sails over my head. A moment later, a hundred pounds of rigging crashed to the deck behind me.

Right away, I realized I'd been wrong. As bad as it was down in the hold, not knowing what was happening above, this was worse.

I got up and ran for the quarterdeck. Burn Healy was standing at the wheel next to his pilot, Pike. When I got a look at my uncle, I gasped. A bloodstained bandage covered the upper half of his head, including one full eye, and streaks of crusted blood ran down his face and neck to his shirt, which was stained a copper red down to the chest.

In spite of the wound, he was grinning from ear to ear—until he saw me, and then the grin vanished.

"The patch in the hull is bust!" I yelled. "Carpenter says, 'Take her down to six and no turns to port!'"

Healy's good eye widened at the news. He turned to Pike.

"Reef the tops. When the next round's off, bring her to starboard."

Then he ran past me, headed for the companionway. Not knowing what else to do, I followed.

Healy moved fast. By the time I caught up, he was on the steps of the hold, yelling past the bucket line at Quint. Three burly pirates had their full weight pressed against the failing patch, which was still squirting water around its edges. Two more crewmen were pulling lumber from the carpenter's room on the far side of the water barrels.

"Not even reinforced?" Healy was yelling.

"Not at speed!" Quint yelled back.

"Then how fast?"

Quint's face twisted in a pained grimace. "Eight . . . ?"

"Oh, —!"

I'd never heard my uncle curse before. He turned and pushed past me, back up the steps, bellowing as he went.

"THIRD MATE!"

Ismail came running. As he approached, Healy barked orders at him. "Pull a crew from the port side to back up the carpenter!"

"Roger that," replied Ismail as he leaped up the steps for the gun deck.

Healy turned to me. "You're off carpenter duty and running messages for me. Find the gunner, tell him I need cannon at the aft gun ports. Aft! Understand?"

"Cannon at the aft gun ports," I repeated.

"Then find me in my cabin. Go!"

THE SHIP'S CANNON UNLEASHED another round just as I was repeating Healy's message to the soot-blackened gunner. The noise was so deafening that as I ran back up to Healy's cabin, my ears rang like someone was hammering sheet metal inside my head.

Healy was standing over the table with Pike and Spiggs. Pike was gesturing at a chart that was unscrolled in front of them.

"Anything more than two hours from high tide, we'll run aground at the far end," Pike was telling my uncle.

Healy looked at Spiggs. The first mate shook his head. "It's too big a risk. Unless we know what the tide's—"

"We're doing it," said Healy, cutting him off. "Chart the course and brief the sailors."

Pike and Spiggs both winced. Whatever was about to happen, they didn't like it.

Healy opened the door to his cabin and nodded in my

direction. "Tell the gunner all hands starboard and aft. We're running the Fangs."

WHEN I RETURNED from delivering Healy's message, he was back at the ship's wheel, and the *Grift* was in a turn so tight I had to grip a rail with both hands to stay on my feet next to him.

Looking ahead, I realized for the first time that we were close to shore. I could see the coast of the New Lands off our port side, and straight ahead to starboard was an offshore island, stretching east as far as I could see. A channel no more than a couple of miles wide separated the coast from the island.

The *Red Throat* was still half a mile from us, off starboard now and so far aft that I had to crane my neck around the poop deck to find her. A mile or two farther back in the haze were the massive bulks of the two Cartager men-of-war. The only signs of either *Frenzy* or *Blood Lust* were two smears of black smoke on the horizon.

We came out of the turn and the *Grift* leveled off, our bow pointing straight at the channel between the coast and the long island. The *Red Throat*'s muzzles flashed again. I hit the deck, but the volley sailed wide of us. When I got back up, my uncle was watching me with an amused smirk.

"Son, when your number's up, ducking won't cheat the reaper. What happened to your wrist?"

"I, um . . ." I didn't want to tell him the truth, but my brain got stuck, and I couldn't come up with anything else. "Fell out of my hammock."

Healy's smirk widened, and I felt my cheeks turn hot. "What happened to your head?" I asked, just to change the subject.

"Same thing." He winked at me with his one good eye, and I couldn't help smiling.

The cannon roared under our feet. Healy whipped his head around in time to see the *Red Throat*'s crooked foremast fall still farther off its line before the smoke from our guns blocked the view.

"Not bad," Healy murmured. "Pity we can't finish her here."

"Because of the patch failing?" I asked.

He nodded. "Do you understand what's happening?"

"Not really," I admitted.

"Our enemies are down to three ships. And if I hadn't lost the ability to maneuver at speed, we might have settled things right here. But that's no longer an option. So we're plotting a course through the Fangs."

He pointed at the channel in front of us.

"When we get closer, you'll see why they call it that—it's quite shallow, with a lot of exposed rock sticking up like teeth. Very tricky to navigate, and for all his bluster, the Ripper's a rather timid sailor. Couple that with him losing a mast, and it's likely he'll break off. Take the long way around Finger Island and try to catch us on the other side." Healy glanced back at the *Red Throat,* which was coming into view again now that the smoke was clearing.

Its muzzles flashed a third time. Healy didn't even blink, and I had to fight the urge to flop onto my belly.

"But I suspect *Li Homaya*'s got just the right mix of stupidity and arrogance"—he didn't bother to pause even as the boom of the *Red Throat*'s cannon reached us, and its latest round sizzled into the sea not more than ten yards from the ship—"to follow us into the Fangs. If he does, he'll either sink on the rocks or run aground at the far end, and we can finish him off as we please.

And if he's got brains enough not to follow us, he'll have to take the long way around with the Ripper. That'll give us time to position ourselves upwind on the far side before we reengage—which should help compensate for the fact that I can no longer turn to port without punching a hole in my ship. Any questions?"

I thought back to the ominous looks on Spiggs's and Pike's faces. "Just, um . . . the tide?"

Healy's mouth turned down at one corner. "That's the one fly in the ointment. If the tide's too low, there's a chance *we'll* run aground. In which case . . . the forward cannon on those men-of-war will make rather quick work of us."

The voice of a lookout called down from the crow's nest.

"*Red Throat's* breaking off!"

Healy looked back at the Ripper's ship. Her bow was nosing around, turning away from us.

Healy smiled. "And so he goes."

Over the next ten minutes, there were a few final rounds of cannon fire—which kept me sweaty with fear even though they didn't faze my uncle a bit—but soon enough, the *Red Throat* was showing us her stern, the cockeyed foremast poking out to starboard like a broken tree branch.

Healy yawned as he watched her limp off toward the men-of-war, still moving in our direction. "Think I'll snatch a nap while we find out if the Short-Ears are game. You're welcome to string a hammock in my cabin if you don't think it'll end badly for you," he said with a glance at my wrist.

"That's very kind," I said. "But if there's time . . . my friend was injured, and I don't know if—"

"Go."

I HEADED FOR the surgeon's room on the lower deck, where the pirates who had pulled Guts from the hold would've taken him.

A few strides from the doorway, I stopped in my tracks, my stomach dropping to somewhere around my knees.

There was a large canvas bag in front of the surgeon's door, the size and shape of a small man. In another location, at another time, it could have been any number of things. But right there, just then, there was no question what it was.

There was a body in there.

I was staring at it, my eyes filling up, when the door opened and a pirate stepped out, his bloodstained shirt open and his chest wrapped in a fresh bandage. As he strode past me, buttoning his shirt, the surgeon appeared.

I pointed to the body in the bag. "Is that . . . ?"

"Fells. He ran messages for the captain."

I was so grateful to hear it wasn't Guts that I barely registered the news that the last man to hold my new job as messenger was dead.

"Was a boy brought up to you with—"

"Your mate? With the head wound? Yes, a while ago."

"Is he all right?"

The surgeon frowned. "Hard to say. He's conscious now. But I think there may be brain damage. He's got a bad twitch, and he won't stop cursing."

"No, he's just like that."

"Oh . . . Well, in that case, he might just need some time to let the cobwebs clear." The surgeon jerked his thumb toward a door a short way down the hall. "He's in the purser's cabin."

I thanked the surgeon and went to the cabin. Guts was lying on a short, narrow bed. The room was so small I could barely stand inside it.

His eyes fluttered open when I came in, and he looked up at me with unfocused eyes. There was a bandage over his forehead. Underneath it, his face was pale and drawn.

"Battle over?" he croaked.

"Not yet," I said. He looked so awful that for a moment, I worried the doctor had been right about the brain damage.

Then he snarled, "Get back on the line, ye — *porsamora!*" and I figured he was going to be okay after all.

I filled him in on what had happened, and on Healy's plan to go through the Fangs. He nodded.

"Be up in a minute," he said. "Help out."

"It's okay," I said. "Just rest. It's going to be fine."

"Nuts to that. Gotta pull my weight. Earn a crew share."

He scowled and twitched, but then he closed his eyes. I slipped out, then went down to the hold.

There was a flurry of activity around the leaking patch. Kira and Quint were in the thick of it, but I managed to catch Kira's eye and give her a thumbs-up. She nodded and smiled, and I knew she'd understood.

When I got back to my uncle's cabin, he was snoring on the bed. Not sure what to do with myself, I took a seat at the table and waited for him to wake up.

Every few minutes, the enemy cannon thundered, making my heart jump into my throat.

Healy snored through it all.

Finally, after what seemed like an hour, Spiggs poked his head in the door.

"*Sssst,*" he whispered.

My uncle sat up in an instant.

"Five minutes," said Spiggs. Then he left. My uncle yawned and let his head settle back into the pillow.

"Fetch a handful of coffee beans from the galley," he told me. "I'm going to grab another five."

BY THE TIME my uncle came out of his cabin, the *Grift* was well into the Fangs. There were so many sharp rocks poking up out of the sea you could practically jump from one to the next, and steering the ship through them took constant, jaw-droppingly complex adjustments to the sails. Those were made by a few dozen pirates manning ropes on the deck and monkey-climbing in the rigging, all under orders from Pike. He had one hand on the wheel and the other on a sheet of parchment with a detailed list of movements scribbled across it. Every few seconds, he either turned the wheel a few degrees or yelled a fresh order to the men.

Healy appeared at his side, watched in silence for a moment, then turned and strode to the poop deck ladder. I climbed it after him, and when I reached the top, he was at the stern rail, surveying the Cartager men-of-war with a spyglass.

Li Homaya's two massive ships were still in the open water, a mile or two behind us on the starboard side. They were moving toward the coast at a right angle to the *Grift*, their triple decks of cannon unloading a fearsome barrage every few minutes. But the ammunition was wasted—they were out of range, and their cannonballs plunked harmlessly into our wake.

Which was why it was such a surprise when the ship suddenly shuddered like it had been hit.

At first, I thought we'd struck a rock. But when Healy turned and ran to the front of the poop, it wasn't Pike he stared down at for an explanation—it was Spiggs, who was amidships at the starboard deck rail. Next to Spiggs, a pirate was lowering a rope over the side of the ship.

Healy, Spiggs, and Pike all stared at the pirate with the rope like he was the most important person on the ship. I spent a few seconds staring stupidly at him before I realized he was using the rope to check the depth of the water.

He was pulling up the rope when the lookout called down from the crow's nest.

"She's following!"

I followed Healy's gaze back behind us. The first of the Cartager men-of-war was turning her bow in our direction. *Li Homaya* had taken the bait and was headed into the Fangs after us.

Healy didn't spend more than half a second taking it in before he turned back to Spiggs and the pirate with the rope. It was lying limp across the pirate's hands, and Spiggs was staring at it like it was a corpse.

He looked up at Healy.

"Thirteen," he called out.

My uncle sucked in his breath, making a hissing sound through his teeth.

"Thirteen's bad?" I asked.

"No," he said. "It's quite a bit worse than bad."

CHAPTER 13

LOW TIDE

MY UNCLE WAS SHOUTING orders even before he'd reached the bottom of the quarterdeck ladder.

"Four crews to the deck! Run a kedge! Nonessentials overboard! EGBERT!"

"Right here."

He turned and grabbed me by both shoulders. "Find the third mate. Tell him to ax the barrels. Then—"

"'Ask the barrels?'"

"Ax!" He made a chopping motion with the flat of his hand. "Ax the barrels! Then tell the carpenter I need a hole in the gun deck, starboard at the fore, wide enough to pass a cannon! GO!"

I ran to find Ismail, repeating the orders to myself as I went and trying not to worry over what they meant.

I found him on the companionway, helping two pirates haul a replacement sail up from the hold.

"Captain says to ax the barrels!"

Ismail's eyes widened with concern. He left the sail to the others and ran back down into the hold. I followed him.

Quint was still on Kira's back, supervising a group of pirates who were hammering planks into the hull to shore up the still-leaking patch. When I relayed Healy's order about the hole in the gun deck, Quint's eyes grew even wider than Ismail's.

As he opened his mouth, I heard a loud *shhhunk!* behind me. I turned to see Ismail and a second pirate swinging axes at a pair of water barrels atop the stack. One barrel was already busted open, and a second broke apart as I watched, sending a flood of water to the deck.

I must have looked stunned, because I heard Quint behind me.

"Fastest way to dump the weight," he explained. "Bust the barrels, draw the water out with the pump and the buckets. Now quit gapin' and fetch two saws to the gun deck."

As Kira ran Quint upstairs, I grabbed the saws from the carpenter's room. By the time I left the hole, half its barrels had been split open, and the water level was a foot higher.

Five minutes later, two pirates had sawed halfway through a four-foot-wide hole in the forward gun deck, Kira was ferrying Quint back down to the hold, and I was on my way up to Healy for more instructions.

When I reached the deck, a lifeboat was being lowered over the side, with five men and a massive six-foot anchor inside it. My uncle was leaning over the deck rail, calling orders to the men turning the crank of the davit that lowered the boat.

"Hold . . . hold . . . wider . . . away!"

The lifeboat touched the water, and the men in it unhooked themselves from the davit ropes and began to row furiously, moving parallel to the *Grift* and dodging the sharp outcroppings of the Fangs as they went.

There was a fat rope running from the giant anchor back into the *Grift*'s bow. I couldn't understand the point of rowing away with our anchor, but there was no time to stop someone and ask.

Healy headed back toward Pike, who was still at the wheel. As I followed him, I passed a line of pirates staggering up the companionway steps, loaded down with heavy chests and kegs to throw over the deck rails and into the sea.

Nonessentials overboard . . . They were tossing out everything that wasn't tied down.

"Short-Ears' struck! Taking on water!" bellowed a lookout from the crow's nest.

Healy sprang up the ladder to the poop deck.

The two men-of-war were a mile behind us, weaving in single file through the Fangs. The gray sky was beginning to mist, shrouding them both in a haze. But even without the spyglass my uncle held to his good eye, I could tell the second ship was listing badly.

It wasn't going to be above water for much longer. The jagged rocks of the Fangs had done their job on at least one of our enemies.

But the nearer one was still upright and coming at us. I saw muzzle flashes blink from two of her forward ports, and I hit the deck before I could remind myself not to do that.

A moment later, I heard the *boom,* followed by my uncle's voice.

"No need—they're a hundred yards out of range. Is the hole cut in the gun deck?"

"Should be," I said.

"Tell the gunner to ready his oars. And have the third mate move six cannon forward and stand by."

I ran off again and delivered both messages to the gun deck. Instantly, half the men on the deck began to pull the long, un-wieldy oars from their ceiling racks and maneuver them out the gun ports, while the other half started hauling five-thousand-pound cannon on ropes from the middle of the ship to the freshly cut hole in the forward hull.

Either job alone would have been complicated enough. Trying to do both at once was near madness. As I watched, one pirate caught an oar in the face, shattering his jaw, and two more got knocked head over heels when the back of an oar swung around and hit them from behind. When they fell, they lost their grip on the ropes, and their cannon careened out of control, skidding across the deck and crushing a man's leg.

The only men on the whole deck who weren't tripping over each other were the four sweat-drenched pirates at the chain pump, furiously cranking water up and out of the hold.

But by the time my uncle descended the steps, his men had somehow managed to get both jobs done. The oars were in posi-tion, six on each side sticking out the middle gun ports, with four men manning each oar. And half a dozen cannon were lined up at the forward hole.

"Ready!" the gunner called out.

"When the time comes," my uncle told him, "dig in and punt."

Just then, the ship gave a terrible lurch, hurling everyone for-ward. I lost my footing and fell to the deck.

The moment of ominous silence that followed told me exactly what had happened.

We'd run aground.

"SEND THE CANNON OVER!" Healy yelled to Ismail's crews, and the six men closest to the hole rolled their giant weapon over the edge and into the open air, where it vanished in an instant.

"PREP ANOTHER SIX!" Healy yelled as the second cannon rolled forward.

"PUNT THE OARS!" the gunner was yelling at his men, who were raising their oar handles at such a sharp angle that several of them struck the ceiling.

"FIRE THE AFT CANNON!" Healy yelled. A moment later, a pair of cannon thundered from the rear of the ship.

There was an answering *boom* as the Cartager cannon returned fire.

I felt the deck rumble as a third cannon rolled through the forward hole, plummeting out of sight.

The rowers had gotten their oars dug into the sea bottom and were straining against them, trying to prod the ship forward.

The chain pump was cranking so fast it was a blur, the faces of the men on it bright red and glistening.

A fourth cannon went out the side.

The pirates on the oars were putting all their weight against them, grunting from the effort. There was a loud *crack* as one oar snapped, sending its rowers sprawling.

"ALL SPARES ON DECK!" my uncle yelled. Then he grabbed my arm. "Go below and spread the word: *all spares on deck for the kedge!*"

He ran up. I ran down.

I had no idea what a kedge was, but as I spread the word through the lower decks, every man who wasn't trying to keep seawater out of the hold ran for the weather deck.

A gray drizzle was falling when I reached it myself, and it didn't take more than a few seconds for me to understand what *kedge* meant.

The lifeboat that had launched a while back was a few hundred yards ahead of us, at a point where the Fangs gave way to the open water of a bay. The ship's anchor she was carrying had been sunk to the seafloor, the anchor cable rising from the water on a taut line that threaded a hawsehole into the *Grift*'s bow.

Amidships on the weather deck was the upper end of the capstan—the giant, five-foot-high spool that winched the anchor cable in and out. A dozen long, thick poles had been inserted into her slots, and every spare man on the ship was pushing against them, trying to reel in the anchor line and physically drag the *Grift* over the shallows that had beached us.

That was a kedge: a hundred men trying to heave a ship forward through brute force.

My uncle was in the middle of the group, a fat vein on his neck throbbing as he threw his whole weight against the pole in front of him. The men were inching forward, barely making any progress.

I was on my way to join them when the first cannonball struck the poop, throwing up a shower of splinters as it crashed through the ceiling of my uncle's cabin.

The man-of-war was in range. If she'd been sideways to us and able to fire a broadside, we'd have already been dead.

I took my place between two pirates on one of the capstan poles and pushed with everything I had. My wrist, which had settled into a dull throb when I was running messages, woke up and started screaming again.

There was a loud crash from somewhere below, and at first I thought we'd been hit again. Then I realized it was the sound of a cannon falling into the sea. A moment later, six more men vaulted up the companionway steps and joined the kedge.

The capstan was turning, but only by inches. Every few seconds, I took a stutter-step forward.

The next round hit. Two cannonballs shot through the sails overhead, and a third crashed into the quarterdeck next to the wheel.

We kept pushing, inching our way forward. The rain was getting worse, turning the deck slick under our feet. Someone scattered a bucket of sand to sop it up.

There were grunts and groans and roars of fury from the men around me, straining against the capstan poles.

Another cannon crashed into the sea. Six more men came up from below to join the line.

We were at a slow walk now. The rain came down harder. My feet kept slipping. The pain in my wrist was awful.

But not as awful as dying would be.

Another round hammered the ship, blasting away a section of deck rail so close that splinters hit my face. One of the mainsails broke loose from its spars and billowed to the deck. It was on fire.

There was a second fire burning on the side of the deck near the capstan.

The Cartagers were firing incendiaries, the rounds flaming as they came in.

The fires flickered in the rain, then fizzled out.

Thank the Savior for the rain.

Another cannon went overboard. Six more men joined us.

We were at a fast walk now.

A round hit the forecastle. Something was on fire, but I was turning away with the capstan and couldn't see what.

I prayed the rain would put it out like the others.

Then something broke loose, and the capstan lurched forward so suddenly I almost fell. A cheer went up from the pirates, and we were moving at a trot . . . and then faster still, all one hundred of us running in mad frantic circles around the capstan.

The next round of Cartager incendiaries fizzled into the sea behind us.

The ship was free.

TWENTY MINUTES LATER, I was standing in the rain on the poop deck next to Healy, watching the Fangs recede in our wake. The Cartager man-of-war had run aground itself, stuck helpless a mile and a half behind us, its massive bulk nearly out of sight in the downpour.

The smile was back on my uncle's face.

"You know the difference between us and them?" he asked me.

"What's that?"

"*Li Homaya*'s too fat to kedge."

NO MERCY

HEALY'S PLAN WAS to intercept Ripper Jones at the mouth of the bay and finish him off, then turn around and come back to sink the beached man-of-war.

But it didn't work out that way. When we came around the far side of Finger Island, there was no sign of the *Red Throat*. We sailed south, through rain that had slowed to an occasional drizzle, until the lookout cried out just before sunset:

"Red Throat *to the southwest! Turning tail!*"

She must have been pretty far off, because even through his spyglass, my uncle couldn't see her.

"*You sure it's her?*" he called back.

"*Got a cockeyed foremast!*"

Healy handed me his spyglass. "I'm going to check this out."

To my surprise, my uncle went to the mainmast and clambered up the rigging to the crow's nest.

A minute later, he called down an order.

"Full around!"

By the time he returned to the deck, the *Grift* had reversed course and was heading back into the bay.

Spiggs and Pike were shaking their heads as my uncle approached them.

"Wouldn'ta figgered that."

"Thought he had more fight in him."

"Reckon he's headed to Turtle Bay?" Healy asked them.

The others nodded.

"Or someplace like it. Put up and lick his wounds."

"Try an' fix that foremast."

"We'll deal with him soon enough," said Healy. "First, let's finish off the Short-Ears."

But as we sailed back into the bay, not only did the sun go down, but a fog rolled in so thick it choked off the moonlight.

Healy quickly realized that not only was it impossible to aim his remaining cannon in such a heavy fog, but if we kept sailing, there was a good chance we'd wander back into the Fangs and break up on the rocks. So he anchored the *Grift* to wait for sunrise and a break in the weather.

"Six hours' rest for everyone," he told Spiggs. "Savior knows they've earned it." Then he turned to me. The bloody bandage over his head and eye was soiled and drooping.

"Find the surgeon. Tell him I wouldn't mind a look at my eye if he's not too busy. Then get yourself a meal and some sleep. Did your friend come through all right?"

"I think so," I said.

"Glad to hear it."

I'd been walking with him toward his cabin, and just then he opened the door.

The table in the middle of the room was in splinters, a victim of the cannonball that had punched a hole in his ceiling and was now embedded in a crater on the floor.

Healy sighed. "I liked that table. I really did."

I found the surgeon and delivered Healy's message. Then I went to the purser's cabin, where I'd last seen Guts. I opened the door to find Kira with him.

And not just with him, but kissing him.

And not just a peck on the cheek, but a full, passionate—

"*Egg!*"

"— knock, ye *porsamora*!"

They both glared at me, their faces bright red from embarrassment.

"Sorry!" I sputtered. "Sorry! Just . . . I'll be . . . dinner . . . Bye!"

I shut the door in a hurry, feeling my own face flush as well.

I'd suspected for a while that their relationship was changing into something more than just friends. And I was glad for them both.

But seeing them in a clinch like that made me ache, too—because it reminded me of Millicent.

I tracked down Quint in the hold. The patch was stable now that we were at anchor, and he was happy to join me for dinner. We got rations from Stick, then took them up to the weather deck. There was a good-sized crowd up there, eating in the dim light of a few hooded lanterns. By the time we found a spot with enough room to sit, Guts and Kira had caught up with us.

It was too dark to tell if they were still blushing. But I could make out enough of the men around us to see that the crew was as battered as their ship. There was a lot of dried blood and bandages, including some that covered newly missing limbs.

The four of us ate in silence, letting the tension seep away as we filled our bellies. My head was nodding as I chewed. I couldn't wait to finish so I could curl up and fall asleep.

"Do you hear that?" murmured Kira.

"Wot?" asked Guts.

"Voices," she said.

We listened. Over the sound of water lapping at the hull and the low mutter of the pirates' conversations around us, I heard distant voices.

They were yelling, in urgent tones. The few words I could make out weren't Rovian.

"It's the Cartagers," Kira said. "They are trying to free their ship."

"Healy says *Li Homaya*'s too fat to kedge," I said.

"True enough," grunted Quint. "Nothin' gonna free a ship that big. Even at high tide."

"If I know *Li Homaya*, he will not stop trying," said Kira. "And he will never abandon ship. He has too much pride." She sighed. "He is foolish. They are close to land. He could save his men, if only their lives were more important than his honor."

An idea tumbled into my head, knocking me wide-awake.

"What about his city?"

"What?"

"What's more important to him—dying with honor, or getting Pella Nonna back?"

120

"He doesn't know he's lost it," Kira said. "They sailed before the invasion."

"What if we told him?"

"Can't get there nohow. Ship's stuck," said Guts.

"He could go overland," I said. "There must be three hundred men on that ship. And the second one sank slowly enough that most of its crew probably got off. That's six hundred men—with those numbers, they could take Pella Nonna back from Pembroke."

I was up and moving before I'd even finished the sentence. I had to talk to my uncle.

He was in his cabin, a cup of wine in his hand and a fresh bandage covering his upper head down to the left eye. Spiggs, Pike, and Mackie the gunner were all drinking with him. Mackie was still black with soot from head to toe.

"Put in, fix up, and give the boys their due," Healy was saying as I entered.

"Take at least four days," said Spiggs. "More if they get to spendin' it."

"Jones will be longer than that fixing a busted fore with no shipyard to call on," replied Healy. "And full strength, we can take him regardless." Then he turned to me. "Shouldn't you be asleep?"

"I'm not tired," I said. Which was true. A minute ago, I'd been ready to drop, but now I was buzzing.

"And you're here because . . . ?"

He smiled when he said it, but I got the idea I wasn't all that welcome at the moment. I would've turned and left right then if what I needed to ask him hadn't been so urgent.

But I didn't have the courage to just blurt it out. So I wound up stuttering like a fool.

"I j-just . . . um . . . ah . . ."

"Question? Observation? Request? Unsolicited advice?"

"Ah . . . request?"

Healy glanced at Spiggs, who immediately started for the door. "Think I'd better check on the . . . thing."

Pike and Mackie were right on his heels.

"Yes! The thing. Me too."

"Back in five, Cap."

The door closed, and I was alone with my uncle. He sank into his desk chair and gave me a weary look with his one good eye.

"What is it this time?"

I couldn't tell if he was annoyed or amused. I sat across from him on one of the unbroken table chairs.

"I was just thinking . . . if you could . . . somehow . . . get a message to *Li Homaya* that Pembroke took Pella—"

"Why on earth would I do that?"

"He could take his men overland. To win it back. You can still destroy his ship—"

He gave a dry laugh. "Sorry, boy. Not going to happen."

"But without a ship, he's not a threat to you anymore. And just think of all those people whose lives would be better if Pembroke wasn't ruling the New Lands! That's got to be worth—"

"Do you really believe"—he interrupted me, with just enough of an edge in his voice to set my stomach fluttering—"I mean, sincerely believe, that Pella Nonna's better off under the Cartagers? That *Li Homaya*'s a more just ruler than Roger Pembroke?"

122

"I *know* he is," I said. "I've lived in Pella. I've seen what it's like under the Cartagers—"

"Have you, now?" He stood up, towering over me. "Think you can vouch for the Short-Ears as rulers?"

He began to unbutton his shirt.

"Because I've lived under them myself," he said. "And I've formed my own opinion."

He pulled his shirt off and turned around. Just inside the left shoulder blade of his broad, thickly muscled back was a four-inch welt in the shape of a *C*, made of the kind of unnaturally smooth, pink skin left by a severe burn.

"The Cartager who bought me burned that into my flesh. So the world would know I was his property."

My uncle turned to face me again. "I was ten years old. Your mother was eleven. They gave her one, too. It took us five years to escape. And if you knew what those five years were like, you wouldn't bother asking me to show mercy to a Short-Ear."

He put his shirt back on and sat down again.

It was quiet for a while. My head was swimming.

My mother . . .

I knew next to nothing about her. I definitely hadn't known this.

"You . . . and my mother . . . were . . ."

"Slaves. Of the Short-Ears. You might do well to remember that next time you go splitting the world into good and evil."

He went to pour himself another drink. I stared at the floor and tried to understand.

"How did . . . ?"

"There was a raid on the island in the Barkers where we grew up. Cartager brigands. The women and children were sent to hide in the woods. After they killed all the men, the Short-Ears found us hiding there and gathered us up. Sold us on the mainland to a planter with a big spread down on the Southern Plains.

"He hanged any slave who tried to escape. That's why it took us so long. We knew we had to get it right the first time."

I tried to imagine it. I couldn't. My brain just couldn't conjure up Burn Healy as a boy, let alone a slave. And I didn't even know what my mother looked like.

What's more, it didn't make sense. Not the story itself—there was no denying that awful *C* burned into my uncle's back. And it definitely answered the question of why he hated Cartagers so much.

But the connection to what was happening now, to Pembroke and *Li Homaya* . . . It didn't fit. It was all sideways. The Cartagers in Pella Nonna had been the friendliest, most easygoing people I'd ever met. They wouldn't keep slaves any more than I would.

And *Li Homaya,* from what I knew of him, was a swaggering bully with a big head and a heavy hand. But he was no slaver.

The only slaver I knew was Roger Pembroke.

What my uncle was saying—not the words, but the thinking behind them—was all wrong. I knew it in my bones. I just had to figure out how to make him see it.

He was sitting down again. "Have you gotten enough to eat?" he asked in a gentler voice. "I think the cook's got some chocolate squirreled away."

"You were in the south?" I asked. "You and my mother?"

He nodded. "Idolu Masa. On the Southern Plains."

"How far is that from Pella Nonna?"

"Quite a ways. Fifteen hundred miles."

"And this was . . . twenty years ago?"

"Closer to thirty."

"And the men who made you slaves—they were brigands? Not soldiers? And *Li Homaya* wasn't one of them? Or anyone else who—"

"They were Cartagers, son."

"I know. But . . . I mean, we're Rovians. And so's Roger Pembroke. Just because we live under the same king, or have the same kind of ears—"

He cut me off. "It doesn't matter."

I could feel his anger rising. I didn't want to make him angry. But he was wrong.

I took a deep, shaky breath.

"Pembroke is a slaver. *Li Homaya* isn't—"

"Enough." The tone of his voice made me squeeze my eyes shut in fear.

I heard him take a deep breath of his own. I opened my eyes. His good eye was narrowed and dark.

"The simple fact is this, boy: when the fog clears and the sun rises, *Li Homaya* and his men are going to die by my hand. If you want to send him a message, you'll have to swim it out to him."

He drained his glass of wine and stood up. "Now, why don't you get some rest, and eat some chocolate, and be glad you're alive? Because if *Li Homaya* had gotten his wish today, you'd be a corpse right now."

I stood up, nodding.

"You're right," I said. "I'm sorry. And thank you. And . . . congratulations on winning the battle."

"Thanks to you, too," he said. "You did good work today. Your mother'd be proud. Although none too happy with me for dragging you into it." He walked me to the door and gave me a pat on the back. "And don't fret over Roger Pembroke. Life is long—someday, he'll get his."

I nodded. "I know. You're right. I won't fret."

"Good. Get some sleep. And thank your friends for me."

"I will. Good night."

"Pleasant dreams." He winked as he shut the door behind me.

IT TOOK A FAIR AMOUNT of stumbling around before my eyes readjusted to the dark and I found my friends. Guts was lying on the foredeck, snoozing with Kira's head on his chest. Quint was curled up next to them.

I knelt down and nudged Quint awake.

"Sorry to bother you," I whispered. "But I need a favor."

"Wot is it?"

"Can you build me a raft?"

CHAPTER 15

THE MESSAGE

FIRST, QUINT TRIED to talk me out of it. Then he refused to help. But our arguing eventually woke up Kira and Guts, and once I told them what I wanted to do, they came down on my side.

"If you just tell me the Cartager words for what I need to say to him, I can—"

Kira cut me off. "No. I am coming with you."

"Are you sure?"

"Of course. I was *Li Homaya*'s translator for two years. He trusts me. When I speak, he will listen."

"Ain't goin' without me," said Guts.

"Yer all mad!" Quint yelped. "If the Short-Ears don't kill ye, Healy will!"

"For what?"

"Crossin' him!"

"I'm not crossing him," I said.

"Wot else ye call it? Runnin' a message out to his enemy?"

"It's . . ." I didn't know what else to call it, either.

Better to just do it and not think too much.

"Please, Quint—it doesn't have to be anything complicated," I said. "Just something that floats. Big enough for the three of us."

"Fat chance," said the carpenter. In the near darkness, I could see him cross his arms over his barrel chest. "I ain't throwin' in on this."

"You would rather we swim?" Kira asked him.

"Oh, —!" Quint growled, borrowing one of Gut's favorite phrases. "Ye wouldn't!"

"We'll have to," I said. "Unless you can help us make a raft."

He stewed for another minute or two, but then he gave in. We went below, and soon enough, we'd scavenged enough busted pieces of the hull to build a decent raft under his direction. We gathered a few long, narrow boards to serve as oars, then carried everything to the gaping hole on the gun deck that had been cut open to toss the cannon overboard.

"Anybody asks, I didn't help ye," Quint muttered, looking over his shoulder at the hanging forest of hammocks behind us, filled with snoring pirates.

"Don't worry," I said. "And thank you."

I knelt down and hugged him. Kira did the same. He and Guts sort of grunted affectionately at each other.

"Yer all fools," he told us.

"I know," I said. Then we slid the raft through the hole, and I jumped out after it as fast as I could, because I knew if I stopped to think about it, I'd lose my nerve.

WE WERE QUIET ENOUGH hitting the water that nobody poked their head over the deck rail to see what the noise was, and the fog was so thick that the lookout in the crow's nest couldn't see us. We got under way pretty quickly, and soon the only challenge was making sure we were paddling in the direction of the distant voices shouting at each other in Cartager.

The raft was about eight feet long but only a few feet wide. We arranged ourselves in a row, with Kira in front and me in back. She did her rowing on alternating sides so we could keep to a straight line even with Guts and me sticking to the sides we favored—the left for Guts and the right for me, because his hook and my injured wrist made it hard to paddle any other way.

"Good thing I busted the right wrist, or we'd be moving in circles," I said.

"How'd ye bust it?" Guts asked.

I pretended not to hear him.

"How'd ye bust the wrist?" he repeated, turning his head to look back at me.

"Landed on it wrong."

"When?"

"When the first round hit."

I couldn't help lying. *When I fell out of a hammock* was just too embarrassing, and it had been bad enough admitting it to my uncle.

"How did you bust yours?" Kira asked Guts.

Then it was Guts's turn to be silent. Which was a sign of just how special his relationship with Kira was—if anyone else had asked him about his lost hand, they would have gotten a few mouthfuls of curse words.

"Or was it always missing?" she added.

I saw his shoulders twitch. But he still didn't say anything.

"I'm only curious," she said. "It's okay if you don't want to tell me."

He twitched again. Nobody spoke.

"Was a card game," he said finally.

Then he twitched a couple more times and went quiet. I figured that was the end of it. But a minute later, he coughed and started again.

"We was in port. Jonny Adder from the *Frenzy* come over to play poker, 'long with some of his crew. I was playin' guitar for 'em. Jonny liked the sound of it. Kept askin' Ripper to sell me to him. Ripper kept sayin' I weren't fer sale.

"But the cards weren't goin' Ripper's way, and he'd been drinkin' hard. Late in the game, he gets a hot hand, wants to go all in. But he ain't got the coin left for it. Short twenty gold."

Guts coughed some wetness from his lungs.

"Jonny'd offered twenty-five for me. So Ripper takes five gold out o' the pot, says, 'Now's yer chance. Boy's in the pot at twenty-five.' Time comes to show. Both Jonny and Ripper are holdin' jack straight. So they gotta make a split.

"Jonny says he wants me fer his half. Ripper says no. Goes back an' forth. Both of 'em get hot. Then Ripper draws his sword. Says, 'We'll split him like the pot. You get the head, I keep the rest.'

"Jonny says, 'The head ain't worth a copper. I just want his hands.' Ripper says, 'Fine. Split those, then.' And that's what he does. Gives my left one to Jonny, keeps the rest for himself."

Kira and I had both stopped paddling. For the longest time, nobody spoke.

"Guts, I'm so sorry," said Kira, her voice breaking as she said it.

"Ain't yer fault."

"Burn Healy's going to kill him," I said.

"Hope he does," said Guts. Then he twitched. "Keep paddlin', you two."

We quit talking after that, keeping our ears trained on the voices as they slowly got louder. By the time we passed the first scattered rocks of the Fangs, we could make out other sounds besides the yelling—grunts, groans, creaking wood and rope, the splash of heavy objects plunging into the water . . .

Out there in the fog, they were working like their lives depended on it. And from the tone of the voices floating back to us, it was clear it wasn't going well.

Even though we were expecting to come upon them, it was still a surprise when the first Cartager lifeboat appeared through the gloom, carrying a dozen sailors, all straining at an anchor rope that ran upward from the water, vanishing into the fog.

Healy had been right—the man-of-war was too fat to kedge. But it hadn't stopped *Li Homaya*'s men from trying.

We weren't nearly as surprised to see them as they were to see us. Every jaw dropped, although pretty quickly their faces went from shock to fury. If they'd been armed, we would have found ourselves looking down their gun barrels.

Kira spoke to them, and their faces turned again, this time to confusion. Then one of them yelled something into the gloom behind him.

As the yells echoed down the line, spreading the news that we'd arrived, one of the men in the boat suddenly sat up straight, his eyes bugging out at Guts.

"Se Guts! Lamana moy!"

As the rest of the men looked closer at Guts, their expressions changed yet again, this time to something strangely like pleasure—and I remembered I was traveling with the most famous one-handed guitar player Pella Nonna had ever known.

"Ay, Gussie!"

"Sima lamana, Gussie!"

"Booya lamai, Guts!"

"Evenin' to ye," Guts replied, his shoulders twitching up a storm. His back was to me, but I'm pretty sure he was blushing. He'd never been too comfortable taking praise from strangers even under normal circumstances, and this was about as far from normal as it got.

But it helped us. Between him and Kira—who, as one of *Li Homaya*'s former court translators, collected a few greetings of her own as we floated past a series of lifeboats, all deployed in various desperate efforts to get the man-of-war unstuck—I started to feel much less worried that we might get shot before we could deliver our message.

Then the man-of-war appeared, looming over our heads. From the weather deck to the waterline, it was easily twice as tall as the *Grift*, and when I realized there was a cargo net hanging over the side down to the water, and we'd have to climb it if we wanted to speak with *Li Homaya*, I started to feel dizzy.

Once we'd gotten close enough to grab the net, Kira called to the sailors in the nearest boat, and they helped us secure our raft and oars to the bottom of the netting so they wouldn't float away. Then we started the climb.

Rowing had been hard enough, but getting up that net—and

the effort it took to keep the pain in my wrist from overwhelming me—drained whatever energy I had left. Once we reached the top and set foot on the deck, I spent the first couple of minutes doubled over, gasping for breath and praying I wouldn't pass out.

When I finally got it together to straighten up and look around, I realized Kira's reunion with her former employer—*Li Homaya*, the swollen-bellied Viceroy of New Cartage, the man I hoped would bring Roger Pembroke to justice—had not only started already, but was pretty much over.

The Cartager leader, who looked a lot less swollen and a lot more worried than he had when I'd last seen him swigging wine at a formal dinner in his palace, was in the middle of a tense conference with his purple-uniformed lieutenants.

Guts and Kira were standing a respectful distance away from them. I joined my friends.

"Are you all right?" Kira asked.

"Fine," I said. Which wasn't really true, but it was close enough. "What's he going to do?"

"It is hard to tell. They are arguing over whether I am trying to trick them."

One of the lieutenants was making an impassioned speech to the group, complete with sweeping, melodramatic waves of his hands. He was in midwave when *Li Homaya* had had enough of it and grabbed the man's hand, shoving it back into his chest.

Then *Li Homaya* spat out a string of words that Kira later translated as "The girl doesn't lie. I'm taking my city back."

Within seconds, orders were getting yelled left and right, and the deck of the ship—which had been a frenzy of hauling, kedging, punting, and pulling—grew twice as frenzied and three times as confused. Every man on board quit trying to save the ship and prepared to abandon it, but not before packing up everything that might be useful in a fight and hadn't already been tossed overboard.

We watched in a daze until it occurred to us that the ship we were standing on was going to be smashed to bits at sunrise, and the cargo net that was our only route off of it was now as crowded as Pella Nonna's main street on a market day. So we got in the line that had formed in front of the net, and eventually managed to climb back down to the water, only to find that our raft had been commandeered to float a crate of rifles to shore.

There was a minute of panic, followed by a few minutes of treading water and begging that got us nowhere until we lucked onto a particularly rabid guitar fan who was commanding one of the rowboats. He had his men haul us up out of the water, and we managed to wedge ourselves into the boat alongside more sailors, dried beef, and ammunition crates than should have reasonably fit in the space.

I spent the next twenty minutes sitting on a Cartager's lap, with someone's elbow wedged in my ear. The man whose lap I had to sit on was even less thrilled about it than I was.

Finally, we reached the shore. The chaos of the ship had moved to the beach, and it took us quite a while to find our discarded raft among the haphazard piles of Cartager weapons and equipment.

By the time we found the raft, I'd realized we didn't need it.

"We have to go with them," I said.

"What?"

"We have to go. To help stop Pembroke."

Guts looked at Kira. She winced.

"Egg, we have a plan—"

"This is better—"

"—to find my people"—she spoke over me, her voice rising— "and recover the Fist of Ka."

"None of that matters if Pembroke wins!"

She didn't answer. She just stared at me.

The look in her eyes said it all.

There was one thing more important to Kira than destroying Roger Pembroke: her god, Ka.

And Ka's Fist, which she believed was the only thing that could truly save her people.

Looking into those eyes, I knew it didn't matter how much I argued with her. She had a map, and a plan, to find the Fist. And she was going to stick to it.

I tried anyway. "We can still find the treasure," I pleaded. "We'll just go to Pella first. As soon as *Li Homaya* retakes the city, we'll get on a ship to Edgartown—"

"There *are* no ships from Pella to Edgartown," she said. "Cartage and Rovia are enemies. They do not trade. If we go to Pella, we'll be stuck there."

I looked at the preparations going on around us. *Li Homaya*'s men were almost ready to march. I had to go now, or not at all.

"Then we'll have to split up."

My stomach dropped as I said the words.

"Nuts to that!" growled Guts. He was twitching up a storm. "Gotta be a *pudda* way to do both!"

But there wasn't. And there was no time left to argue.

"You still have the map I drew?" I asked Kira.

She nodded.

"*No!*" Guts yelped, practically in tears. "— *pudda glulo* —! Gotta stick together!"

"We can't, Guts," Kira said softly. "There's no other way."

I could feel tears welling up behind my eyes. I didn't want to split from Guts any more than he wanted to split from me.

But after what I'd seen between him and Kira on the *Grift*, I knew that if there was a choice to be made, he belonged with her.

"You stay with Kira," I said. "I'll be okay—"

"— you, ye —!"

"— *you*, ye — *billi glulo domamora!*" I shot back.

I'd never cursed at Guts before, let alone like that, and the shock of it made him laugh.

It made me laugh, too—which was a relief, because if I hadn't laughed just then, I would've cried.

Li Homaya was just down the beach, in the middle of a little purple swarm of his lieutenants. "Can you speak to *Li Homaya* for me?" I asked Kira.

"You are sure you want to go with him?"

I nodded. "I'm sure."

She walked over to *Li Homaya*. Guts and I followed.

The Viceroy turned at the sound of her voice. She asked him a question in Cartager.

He looked past her to me. His lip curled. Then he asked a question of his own.

Kira translated for me.

"He wants to know what good you are to him."

That was a tough one. "I speak Rovian. And I could . . . scout for him. I've been over the land before. And I'm small, so people won't notice me."

Kira translated it. *Li Homaya* snorted. I didn't need a translation to know he wasn't convinced.

"Tell him Roger Pembroke killed my father," I said, my voice shaky with emotion.

She told him. *Li Homaya*'s mouth split into a sour smirk. He said a couple of sentences, shaking his head. Then he turned his back on us.

The conversation was over.

I felt my face turn hot. "What did he say?"

"It doesn't matter," Kira said in the soothing voice she usually reserved for calming down Guts. "He is not a kind man."

"Just tell me what he said!"

She sighed. "He said all fathers die eventually. And he is leading an army, not a camp for boys."

The anger was boiling up inside me. I wanted to scream. Or hit something. Not something, someone: *Li Homaya*.

"Nuts to him," said Guts.

For a while, we just stood there—me seething, and the other two not knowing what to say.

"C'mon," Guts said finally. "Gotta get back to the *Grift* 'fore the sun rises."

As I followed them back to our little raft, I thought about going to Pella anyway—following the Cartagers as they marched, or striking out on my own and getting there ahead of them.

I can find the way just fine. And I'll eat . . .

I didn't know what I'd eat. I didn't have any supplies, or weapons, or anything except the shirt on my back.

I can steal a rifle from them. And powder, and shot, and . . . and . . .

In the end, I got on the raft. But the anger kept building, until I could feel it burn all the way to the tips of my ears. As we pushed away from the shore, I silently cursed *Li Homaya* and all his men with the foulest words I knew.

And I wondered if my uncle had been right about *Li Homaya* after all.

Even if he wasn't, Healy was dead-on about one thing: there was no point in trying to divide the Blue Sea into good and bad.

As far as I could tell, the only men on it were bad and worse.

CHAPTER 16

LANDFALL

I SULKED FOR MOST of the next hour as we paddled back through the fog.

Li Homaya's refusing to take me along probably shouldn't have upset me as much as it did. Even as I stewed over it, a part of me had to admit he was right. I wasn't a soldier, I didn't have any skills or knowledge that might help him . . . I didn't even speak Cartager.

But I was furious just the same. And I didn't snap out of it until Kira gave me something new to worry about.

"What if we can't find the *Grift* in the fog?"

"Tough to miss once she starts firin'," Guts pointed out. "Bigger problem, tho'—wot if she sinks that ship and sails off 'fore we can get to her?"

I thought about the situation for a moment.

"That might not be the biggest problem," I said.

"Wot is?"

"What'll the pirates do to us when they find out we've crossed them?"

I'd managed to ignore that question when Quint had brought it up, because I knew *Li Homaya* and the Cartagers were the only ones who might be able to knock off Roger Pembroke. But now there was no ignoring it, and the way Kira and Guts fell silent made me realize they were as worried about it as I was.

"We can't turn around," Kira said finally. "The Cartagers will not have us. And we'd be left in Moku territory."

Having been captured by the Moku once before, none of us were exactly eager to repeat the experience.

"Take our chances with the pirates, then," said Guts, his shoulders twitching.

After the last couple of days, I wouldn't have thought I still had it in me to be afraid. But my stomach churned the whole rest of the time we were on that little raft.

Fortunately, we weren't on it for long. Daybreak came quickly, and the fog was just starting to lift when the *Grift*'s guns erupted, lighting up the gray sky with bursts of orange a few hundred yards from us.

By the time we paddled within hailing distance, the guns had stopped and the fog had burned off enough to reveal the distant, burning hulk of the last Cartager man-of-war, listing badly on the Fangs. If she hadn't been so firmly beached, she would've keeled over and sunk before we finished climbing the rope ladder that had been thrown over the side of the *Grift* to let us back on the ship.

Healy met us at the deck rail, along with Quint and a dozen other pirates. There was a tight smile on my uncle's face.

"On behalf of the crew, I'd like to thank you three," he said.

We must have looked as shocked as we felt, because he quickly added an explanation.

"The carpenter told me what happened," he said, nodding at Quint. "It was quite brave of you to volunteer to go over the side and seal the breach with sailcloth so he could get a better handle on the patch. And I'm sure you must have been quite frightened when you drifted off and spent the next few hours lost in the fog. Good to have you back."

Just in case we were tempted to think he believed what he was saying, he let the smile drop at the end of his speech and shot me a look that could have melted steel.

"We won't speak of this again," he said.

And we didn't. Although I did wonder if the rest of the pirates knew what we'd been up to, or if anyone had noticed that the burning of the man-of-war was strangely unaccompanied by the anguished screams of dying men.

But even I wasn't dumb enough to ask about that.

After that, we went below and slept through the whole rest of the day, getting up just long enough to eat practically a whole bucket of rations each before going right back to our hammocks and sacking out again.

I lay awake for a couple of hours that night, working out what I'd do once we reached Edgartown. Kira was going to find her old tutor and get his help in tracking down the Okalu, translating the map, and trying to find the Fist of Ka.

Guts was going with her. And so was I.

But first, I had to find Millicent. She was almost definitely still on Sunrise Island—but if I didn't move fast, her mother would ship her off to some Rovian boarding school on the Continent, and it'd be months or even years before I could find her.

What if she'd met someone else by then? Someone like that Cyril fellow—older and richer than me?

What if she was with that Cyril fellow right now, back on Sunrise?

What if they were *actually* planning to get married?

I had to get to Sunrise. And fast. I wouldn't be welcome there. It was Pembroke's island, and even if he was down in Pella, his men would know me by sight—those "*WANTED*" posters had seen to that—and if they got their hands on me, it wouldn't be good.

My uncle could help. I'd ask him the next chance I got.

No. I couldn't. I'd pushed my luck with him far enough already. I couldn't just go begging him for more help.

Unless I could find the right way to ask.

I'd figure it out. I'd make it work. I'd find Millicent somehow.

I had to. I was in love with her.

BY THE TIME we got up with the sun the next morning, the *Grift* was sailing into a wide bay on the southern tip of a lush, hilly green island so big that at first I thought it was the mainland.

Then Edgartown came into view. It was the second-largest city I'd ever seen behind Pella Nonna—a mile-wide spread of pointy-roofed Continental buildings, nestled under a hillside topped by a giant stone fortress.

Quint thought we were insane to be sailing within range of the fortress's cannon.

"An' us flyin' the red and black? Be smashed to bits any

second!" he yelped at Ismail, who was standing with us at the forward rail.

Ismail smiled. "Look up, friend. We fly Rovian flag today."

We turned and craned our necks to peer up at the mainmast. Sure enough, Healy's pirate flag had been struck, replaced by the blue cross of Rovia.

"Flag ain't gonna throw nobody off! The whole world knows wot Burn Healy's ship looks like."

"Nah," said Ismail. "Is good, man. We go to Edgartown long time. Years now."

"Tell another!" snorted Quint.

"Is true. Not all together. Usually, we dock in cove to north. Take launches down to city. Ten men each. Captain make us change clothes, look fancy. This time little bit different. Never dock in port before. But is okay. We need shipyard for repair. And these Rovians owe us big now. For Pella."

"What *did* happen in Pella?" I asked. "What did you do for Pembroke and his men?"

"Practically whole thing. Rovians want invade, but only got four warships. Not many guns. They ask captain for help. Healy make plan—middle of night, we sail into lagoon north of citadel. Then we shoot from behind. Cartager cannon all pointed forward, into bay and ocean. Never expect someone shoot from behind. So, boom—we take out citadel. Sink man-of-war in harbor same way. She never even raise sails. After that, Rovians land troops, no problem. Then we help with street fight, too."

Ismail nodded in the direction of Edgartown. "These Rovian guys owe us big. Think now, we walk in front door, they don't complain."

Quint wasn't buying it. "Believe it when I see it," he muttered.

But it seemed true enough—we sailed into the crowded port without so much as a warning shot coming from the shore.

And the flag wasn't the only thing that had changed. The crew's usual deadly seriousness had melted away. They were laughing and joking—especially the gun crews, who had started some kind of contest that, as far as I could tell, involved setting each other's toes on fire.

I would've expected my uncle to come down on them with a heavy hand. But he'd gone as strangely jolly as the rest of them. As we started our final approach to one of the easternmost piers, he showed up on deck, his head and eye freshly bandaged, and called the crew together for a speech that was so different from his usual ones that for a moment I wondered if his head injury was more serious than I'd realized.

"Morning, brothers. Hope you're looking forward to your stay in the Fish Islands. The crab cakes are particularly good this time of year. But for everyone's sake, please don't dine in public until you've had a bath—preferably with soap, because every last one of you smells like a dog's rear end."

A few of the pirates sniffed themselves. No one seemed to disagree. Healy continued.

"A few things to keep in mind: as long as we're in Edgartown, I am *not* Burn Healy. I'm Mr. Longtrousers. Actually, Commodore Longtrousers. I was promoted recently, not that any of you ingrates bothered to send flowers. As for yourselves, congratulations: you've also been promoted, from murderous outlaws to the brave marines of the Forty-Third Rovian Irregulars. Once we've docked, I'll have to ask you to stay near the ship for at least a few hours. You're welcome to disembark, but don't stray past the boardwalks. And mind the ground rules: no robbery, assault, extortion, pillaging, or practical jokes.

"And I can't stress that last bit enough—please, please, *do not set fire* to the toes of any non–crew members. And for Savior's sake, don't start drinking until I say it's okay. Any questions?"

A pirate raised his hand. "When's it okay to start drinking?"

"When I say so."

Another hand. "When will you say so?"

Healy sighed. "Soon as you get paid."

"When do we get paid?"

Healy frowned at the pirate who'd just bellowed out the question. "I didn't see your hand up, Frank."

Frank raised his hand. "When do we get paid?"

"Soon as I fetch the ten million. Any other questions? No? Nobody wants a restaurant recommendation? All right, then. Meeting adjourned."

Quint was standing on the capstan, his mouth open wide enough for a seagull to nest in it.

"Wot the blaze got into *him*?"

"I have no idea," I said. Kira and Guts looked equally stunned.

Ismail was still with us. He grinned.

"Is something, yeah? Captain on shore not like captain at sea. Big relaxed."

"That's *Commodore* to you," came a voice from behind us.

It was my uncle. He gave Ismail a smirk. "And don't you forget it, you dirty Gualo." Then he turned to Quint.

"When we dock, would you mind seeking out the master of the shipyard and giving him a look at the damage? We'll want to get the repairs started as fast as possible."

"No problem, Cap."

"Thanks much. Ismail can join you if he's not too lazy."

"Only just," Ismail said with a wink.

Then Healy turned to me. "Do you have plans for this morning?"

"Not that I know of."

"Good. Come run an errand with me." He reached into his pocket, pulled out a fistful of gold coins, and handed them to Guts and Kira.

"I'll bring him back shortly," he told them. "In the meantime, there's a bakery along the boardwalk you'll want to try. The jelly bread's outstanding. Tell them Commodore Longtrousers sent you, and you'll get a discount. Along with a look of terror, I suspect."

Just the mention of jelly bread made my stomach growl. "Save some for me?" I asked Kira as I followed my uncle away.

SPIGGS, PIKE, MACKIE THE GUNNER, Roy Okemu, and several other pirates were all in the captain's cabin when we entered, arming themselves to the teeth with pistols and knives from a crate of weapons.

"Help yourself," my uncle told me. "No need to load the pistols. It's for appearance's sake more than anything."

I took a pistol and tried to jam it into my waistband. I must have looked pretty ridiculous, because the men all traded amused grins.

"The boy know where we go?" Okemu asked.

"Let's ask him," said Healy. "Do you know where we're going, Egg?"

"To get the ten million gold?" I guessed.

"Smart boy," said Okemu.

"And where might that be?" my uncle asked. "Where's a pirate keep his treasure?"

I thought about that for a moment. "Buried?"

The pirates all laughed.

"Son, if I buried ten million gold, how could I earn six percent on it?"

"What's six percent?" I asked.

More laughter.

"The interest," said Spiggs.

"The what?"

They were laughing even harder now. "Better make him a pirate, Cap," chortled Mackie. "He ain't no businessman."

"Let's try again, son," Healy said. "Where's a pirate keep his treasure?"

"A bank?"

The pirates cheered. Healy gave my hair a gentle ruff.

"You see, brothers? He's teachable."

CHAPTER 17

THE ROVIAN GENTLEMEN'S MERCANTILE EXCHANGE

THERE'S NOTHING QUITE LIKE walking up a busy street in the company of eight terrifying pirates, even if the most infamous of them insists on calling himself "Commodore Longtrousers."

The street didn't stay busy for long. When we turned up the main road from the docks, it was elbow-to-elbow with townspeople, but by the time we reached our destination—a white-columned brick building with ROVIAN GENTLEMEN'S MERCANTILE EXCHANGE chiseled in stone above the doors—most of them had mysteriously disappeared. The few who were left kept their distance. It was like there was an invisible wall surrounding us that repelled anyone who got within fifteen feet.

It's possible it was the smell. Healy hadn't been kidding about that—none of the pirates had seen a bath in who knows how long, and the stink was so ripe you could almost see it rising off their backs. I wasn't much cleaner myself, although at least I'd had a dunk in the ocean two nights earlier.

Crowded or empty, it was a very nice street. The Continental-style buildings were pretty and well kept, and there were quite a few shops that looked interesting, along with a street-meat shack that made my mouth water. But as we passed each one, its door would slam shut, and someone with badly shaking hands would shove a CLOSED sign in the window.

"That's curious. Do you reckon it's a holiday?" asked Healy—or, at the moment, Longtrousers.

"Funny holiday," said Pike, looking up at the clock on the bell tower at the end of the street. "Where the shops all close at nine-seventeen exactly."

"Hope the bank's open," said Spiggs.

"Oh, it will be," said my uncle. "One way or another."

He led us up a short flight of steps to the bank's thick doors. To my surprise, they weren't locked. As my uncle began to push them open, I could hear frantic shouts from inside—but by the time he'd taken his first step inside, the shouting had given way to an extremely nervous silence.

I'd never been inside a bank before, so I can't say whether it was more or less impressive than other banks. But I was pretty amazed—there were big chandeliers, thick rugs on the floors, and lots of gold fixtures that gleamed like they'd been polished to a high shine. Massive, serious-looking desks filled the space here and there, and running the length of the room about a dozen paces from one of the walls was a stone counter with some kind of wooden barricade atop it. Every ten feet or so, there were little gold-barred openings in the barricade, just high and wide enough for a man's head to peer through.

The dozen or so people in the room were all frozen like statues when we first entered. As we approached the counter, some of them made an effort to move around, like they were just going about their business without a care in the world. But they did a lousy job of it.

Healy led the way. Halfway across the room, he passed a ruddy-faced man in a suit who I think tried to say, "Good morning, Mr. Longtrousers!" But all that came out was a series of broken squeaks that sounded more like, "Gya-mana-Mista-Laaghtraii . . ."

"Good day to you, sir," my uncle replied pleasantly. He stopped when he reached the counter. Behind one of the gold-barred openings was a skinny, quivering bald man.

"Hello," said Healy.

"M-m-ma—"

The bald man was having a hard time getting the words out.

"'May you help us?'" Healy suggested.

"Y-ye—"

"Yes, you may," my uncle answered his own question. "The name's Harold Longtrousers. I'm an account holder. And you are . . . ?"

"A-a-al—"

"Why don't we just go with 'Al'? Keep things moving along. Al, my friend, I'd like to make a withdrawal from this account." Healy passed a sheet of paper through the opening, then clasped his hands together and rested them on the counter, smiling politely at Al's face just a couple of feet from his own. The rest of us stood behind Healy in a semicircle.

Viewed up close, Al was not only quivering, but remarkably sweaty. So many rivulets were running down his bald head that I looked up to make sure there wasn't a leak in the ceiling.

"S-s-sure. H-h-how—"

"'How much?'"

Al nodded.

"Ten million gold," said Healy. "Or its equivalent in silver. Is there an exchange rate posted—?"

Healy turned his head to look around the room. So did I, which was why I didn't actually see Al faint. I just heard the *thump* of something long and skinny hitting the floor, and when I turned around, he'd vanished from his little hole.

"Oh, dear. Al's fallen ill." Healy leaned forward, peering through the gold bars. In a much louder but no less friendly voice, he called out, "Could someone else help us, please? And possibly get Al some medical attention?"

One by one, the bank employees all turned to stare at a grayhaired man in a black suit. He was standing near an interior door, his hand on the knob.

The gray-haired man looked for a moment like he was trying to decide whether to flee. Finally, he took his hand off the doorknob and approached my uncle, gulping through a pained smile.

"Yes! Of course. I . . ."

Healy smiled back. "Ah! Mr. Smith-Jones, isn't it? The bank president?"

Mr. Smith-Jones nodded, looking like he'd rather be anything on earth besides the bank president at the moment.

"D-did I hear you correctly? That you n-need to withdraw . . ."

"Ten million gold. Yes."

Mr. Smith-Jones took a deep breath. "Why d-don't we speak in my office?"

The private office of Mr. Smith-Jones was even more fancy than the main room. It was filled with what looked like very expensive but rather fragile furniture—the chairs and settees all creaked loudly as the big pirates settled into them, and Mr. Smith-Jones winced at every creak.

There weren't quite enough seats to go around. I wound up standing against a wall, while Mackie and Roy Okemu perched on either side of the desktop. Roy was so big that Mr. Smith-Jones had to crane his neck to peer around Roy's butt at my uncle, relaxing in a plush leather chair on the other side of the desk.

"Do we . . . ah . . . need . . . everyone . . . ?" Mr. Smith-Jones's eyebrows wiggled in the direction of Roy Okemu's butt.

"Unfortunately, we do. These are, let's see, my"—Healy pointed at each pirate in turn—"accountant, attorney, personal physician, secretary, factotum, stenographer, assistant stenographer, and . . ." He finished up with me. "Bodyguard. So! How's business?"

Mr. Smith-Jones looked like he might throw up. Which made sense for a lot of reasons, including the smell. There wasn't much ventilation in the room, and the weeks-old pirate fumes made even me want to gag.

"Ahhhh . . . not bad?"

"Glad to hear it. I'm assuming this is just a friendly chat while your employees get the ten million together?"

"Well . . . about that . . . um . . . ahhhh . . ."

"Please, Mr. Smith-Jones. Speak freely. I'm not here to make trouble. I'm merely a loyal account holder who wishes to withdraw some money."

"Of course! But . . . well . . . you see, it's *quite a lot* of money."

"Although not nearly as much as I have in my account."

"Yes! Obviously! I realize that."

I was glad to hear my uncle's account had more than ten million in it, because it meant that saving me from hanging hadn't bankrupted him.

"You do have my money, do you not?"

"We do! Of course! But. Ahhhh . . ."

Mr. Smith-Jones spent some time tugging at his shirt collar.

"Could you finish the sentence, please? The part that comes after *but*?"

"Mr. Longtrousers . . . the way a bank works, you see, is, we take in deposits, and then we lend that money out, and it's those loans that allow us to pay interest to depositors like yourself, and . . ."

"Let's skip to the end, shall we?"

Mr. Smith-Jones sighed heavily. He wasn't happy about skipping to the end.

"Well, most of our money, you see . . . it's lent out. So what we have on hand is just a small fraction—"

"How small a fraction?"

"At the moment . . ." Mr. Smith-Jones took a big gulp of air. "About two million."

"Two million gold?"

"Mmmph."

"Let me get this straight. I have, what? Thirteen million on deposit?"

"I'd have to look at the exact—"

"Trust me. It's well north of that. Closer to fourteen, last I checked. And yet, when I ask for just ten of it back . . . you tell me all you've got is two?"

It was a good thing Mr. Smith-Jones was sitting down, because judging by the color of his face, there wasn't any blood left in his head.

"The w-way a b-bank w-works . . ."

Healy held up a finger. The bank president clamped his mouth shut.

"We've had that lesson. Here's one for you. The way a pirate works . . . is I get what I ask for."

It was a good thing the door flew open just then, or I think Mr. Smith-Jones might have died of fright.

Standing in the doorway—or as much of it as he could shove open, given the tight quarters on the other side of the door—was a barrel-chested man with a handlebar mustache. His Rovian military uniform was pinned so full of medals that he rattled when he moved.

Like every other man we'd seen in Edgartown so far, he was flushed and sweaty.

"Mr. Longtrousers!"

"Oh, hello, Governor," Healy said mildly. "It's actually 'Commodore' Longtrousers now. Or have you forgotten that you promoted me?"

"Commodore! Yes! Of course. What, um, uh . . . What is happening?"

"Doing a spot of banking. What's happening with you?"

The Governor-General—at least, I assumed that was him, and if so, he was the supreme Rovian leader in the New Lands and surrounding islands, his authority second only to King Frederick—looked flustered. "I'm . . . well, wondering . . . why you, ah, chose to dock in the main harbor."

"Simple thing, really. My ship sustained quite a bit of damage during the conquest of Pella Nonna that you ordered. Needs to be dry-docked for repairs. During which I decided it was appropriate to give the brave marines of the Forty-Third Rovian Irregulars some shore leave."

"I'm not at all sure that's appropr—"

"But we seem to have run into a bit of a snag, banking-wise," Healy said, in a tone of voice that, while arguably still friendly, made the Governor-General's head and neck draw back inside his stiff-collared uniform like a frightened turtle. "You see, I need to withdraw ten million gold. And your man Smith-Jones here says he's only got two on hand."

The bank president and the Governor-General exchanged looks of pure panic.

"The thing is, Commodore . . . ," the Governor-General began, "that the way a bank works—"

"I've heard enough." My uncle's voice, while calm and level, was no longer friendly. He'd switched to the tone that only he knew how to use—the one that could make a man's insides turn to water.

"Here's what's going to happen." Healy turned to the bank president. "You're going to give me every coin in this bank, down to your last copper. And you"—he shifted his gaze to the Governor-General—"will see to it that every establishment in Edgartown opens its doors to my men, offering lines of credit for them to borrow against. We'll take our rooms at the Four Winds Hotel. Please be so kind as to run ahead and have them prepare hot baths for a hundred and eighty-seven. And tell them to expect a bit of a crowd for lunch."

The Governor-General looked aghast. Healy turned back to the bank president.

"I'll drop by tomorrow for the other eight million. See you then."

He gave the banker a wink with his unbandaged eye, then stood up. As he passed the Governor-General, he gave the man's limp hand a friendly shake.

"If you're not busy for lunch, drop by the Four Winds. We'll catch up. My treat. Cheerio!"

MOST OF THE BANK'S two million gold wasn't actually in gold, but silver—which was about ten times as heavy to carry. In the end, we needed three pack mules just to get it all back to the ship. As Spiggs and three other pirates began to divvy it up, Healy gathered everyone together for another short speech.

"The bad news, brothers, is that at the moment, your coin in hand is just a fifth of what you're owed. The good news is you've got lines of credit all over town. If you'd rather not pay cash for something, just have them put it on Commodore Longtrousers's bill. Please try to pace yourselves—given the amount of repairs the *Grift* needs, we'll likely be here . . . what do you say, Quint? Four, five days?"

Quint shook his head. "Could be longer, Cap."

"So there's that. Rooms and hot baths will be ready in short order at the Four Winds. Please treat the townspeople with respect. And for Savior's sake, try not to get *really* drunk until after sunset."

Half an hour later, the money had been doled out to the crew. Kira, Guts, and I sat on a railing at the end of the dock, eating the leftover jelly bread they'd gotten from the baker's—it was pretty good, although it would have been better hot—and watching a steady stream of newly flush pirates head into town, their pants sagging and clinking under the weight of all that silver.

Guts shook his head. "Pirates with money. Gonna get ugly."

I had to agree. I'd seen what had happened with the field pirates when they were let loose in Port Scratch with fifty silver each—and that had been a lot less money, and a much less breakable town. Healy's men were less ragged and desperate than the field pirates. But they were still pirates. And after what they'd been through the past few days, they were primed to blow off quite a lot of steam.

Kira hopped off the railing. "We need to find Mr. Dalrymple before things get out of hand."

Kira's former tutor lived about fifteen minutes' walk from the port, on one of the narrow side streets that snaked through the hills above the town center. As she led us up one street after another, I wondered how she knew where she was going—but then I remembered she'd lived in Edgartown for more than a year, when her father was trying to get the Governor-General's help to stop Pembroke's slave trade.

Finally, she turned us up a red brick sidewalk that led through a small, well-kept garden to a little green house with white trim. As we approached the door, we heard voices through the open front window.

"And the square root of nine is . . . ?" It was a thin, slightly musical voice, and Kira beamed when she heard it.

"Five?" a boy's voice answered.

"Is it?"

"Four?"

"Now, Trevor, don't go guessing willy-nilly—"

Kira knocked on the door.

"Just a moment!"

"Three?"

"Very good. But we don't guess. We memorize. Sit still and look at your squares. Back in a sec."

The front door opened to reveal a man in a crisp shirt and an unbuttoned sweater who looked exactly like his voice—thin, slightly musical, with kind eyes and unkempt silver hair combed over a poorly hidden bald spot.

Mr. Dalrymple and Kira took one look at each other and both started to cry.

"Oh, my dear . . . !"

There was a lot of hugging, and tears, and a whole series of *oh, my dear!*s from the tutor. It went on long enough that Guts and I started to feel a little awkward.

As I watched them, I wondered what the reunion would be like if I ever ran into my own former tutor—cruel, stupid, lazy Percy, who'd betrayed me to Pembroke and wound up getting run off our plantation after Millicent shot him through the arm.

There'd be a lot less hugging, for one thing. And there might be an *oh, my dear!* or two, but they'd be delivered in a very different tone of voice.

Eventually, Kira and Mr. Dalrymple managed to pull themselves together. She introduced us, then tried to explain how we'd wound up on his doorstep. But the story was too confusing, and he quickly lost the thread of it.

"Come in, come in!" he said. "Plenty of time for all of that."

The interior was remarkably tidy and smelled of fresh-brewed tea—and when the nine-year-old boy who'd just had his math lesson interrupted scrunched up his nose at our arrival, I remembered we were still overdue for a bath.

"Come, come," Mr. Dalrymple said. "You can wait in the kitchen and have a pot of tea, and as soon as Trevor's finished his lesson, we'll get caught up. Did you know Makaro is here?"

Kira's eyes widened. "Here in Edgartown?"

"Yes! At the moment, he's up in the hills collecting berries. But he'll back shortly. He's staying with me."

Kira turned to us, her eyes shining. "Makaro is Okalu. An elder. He can translate the map!"

"What map?" asked Mr. Dalrymple.

"We have a map that leads to the Fist of Ka," she told him.

Now it was Mr. Dalrymple's eyes that widened. "You don't say? Mercy! The gods must finally be smiling on your people. Why, just the other day—"

He poked his head in the living room to make sure his young student wasn't listening. Then he continued in a hushed voice. "Just the other day, two teenagers from Sunrise Island showed up demanding an audience with the Governor-General. Said they had evidence of slavery in the silver mine. Course, they got thrown in jail for their trouble, but it was—"

"What teenagers?" I blurted out.

"I'm sorry?"

"Who were they?" My heart was hammering against my chest.

"I don't know. Rumor was, they were children of some mining executives—"

"Did you see them? What'd they look like?"

"I didn't. But I'm told they were quite the handsome pair."

"Handsome? So . . . they were boys?"

My heart skipped a beat, then started to settle down.

"No. A boy and a girl. He was older than her, I think."

Just like that, it was hammering again. "Where are they now?"

"Still in the jail. Waiting for their fathers to—"

"*Where's the jail?*"

"Straight down the hill."

CHAPTER 18

JAIL

"EGG! WAIT!"

I was barreling down the hill toward the middle of town. Kira and Guts were somewhere behind me.

"Stop!"

I wouldn't have stopped, except it had just dawned on me that I had no idea where the jail was. I let them catch up.

"That was very rude to Mr. Dal—"

"Is this the right direction?"

Kira nodded, panting for breath. "Bottom of the hill. First big street to your right. But don't you think we should talk about how we're going to—"

I took off again.

"Egg!"

I couldn't wait.

Millicent's here.

With Cyril.

Best not to think about that part.

The jail was a wide, low stone building in the middle of town. There wasn't any kind of sign on it that said JAIL, but it was the only building on the block that had iron bars on its windows, so I figured I was in the right place.

I pushed open the heavy door and found myself inside a small entry room manned by two Rovian soldiers. One of them was seated at a large desk, filling out paperwork. The other was hunched over the far end of the desk, playing cards with himself.

There was an iron door against the back wall.

"Is there a girl from Sunrise Island here?"

They both looked up at me.

"What of it?" asked the one at the desk.

"I need to see her. Please."

"On whose authority?"

"Burn—I mean, Mr. Lo—I mean, Commodore Longtrousers."

The soldiers looked at each other with concern. The card-playing one shrugged.

The one at the desk got up, pulled open the iron door, and gestured for me to go inside. As I started to pass, he stopped me and took the pistol from my hand.

"Forgot I had that. Sorry." I'd been holding it so it wouldn't fall out of my pants as I ran.

"Mmm."

As I walked through the inner door, I heard Kira and Guts burst into the room behind me, but I didn't stop to wait.

The jail was split into three iron-barred cells, side by side with a corridor running the length of the room in front of them. There was a single, wide bench in each cell, along with a wooden bucket.

A heavyset, grimy-looking man was asleep on the bench in the first cell.

The second cell was empty.

I walked on to the third cell.

As I approached, I saw a young man sitting up on the end of the bench nearest me. He was tall and lean, with wavy brown hair that fell to his shoulders in a way that was almost pretty. Something was in his lap, and he was stroking it gently, like you would a cat.

There was a much larger something lying across the length of the bench next to him.

He turned his head to look at me. But I wasn't looking at him. I was looking at the something that was lying beside him.

It was another person, curled up asleep. The thing in his lap was her head.

"Who are you?" the young man asked in a deep, husky voice. He sat up a little straighter, and the girl stirred. A lock of her golden-brown hair came loose and tumbled down over his legs.

"I'm . . ."

I forgot to finish the sentence, because she lifted her head just then, and I knew—even before she tucked her hair behind her ear in that certain way she had—that it was Millicent.

Her head was in his lap.

And my stomach was somewhere near my ankles.

"EGG!" She got up and ran to me. "You're alive!"

She grabbed the bars with her hands like she might try to yank them apart. Her face was running through a whole series of emotions all at once—shocked, happy, overcome. Tears were filling her eyes.

Her head was in his lap. Nothing else could penetrate my skull but that one thought.

I heard the inner door open. She looked away from me.

"Kira! Guts!"

"Millicent!" Kira ran to her, and I sort of moved to one side so they could clasp hands through the bars.

"I'm so, so glad to see you!" Still holding one of Kira's hands, Millicent reached through the bars toward me with her free hand.

The look on her face almost set my stomach right again. I reached out for her hand.

It's okay. She loves me. It was only a—

Our hands had met, and she was twining her fingers in mine when I heard the deep, husky voice again.

"Here's a spot of luck . . ." A strong arm draped itself over Millicent's shoulders. Its owner was grinning down at me, all big teeth and sharp cheekbones and bright blue eyes.

He was handsome. Ridiculously handsome.

And tall. It was absurd how tall he was.

His arm's around her. Like she belongs to him.

I looked back at Millicent, at those deep brown eyes that until a moment ago, I wasn't sure I'd ever see again.

There was guilt in them.

She could have stabbed me in the chest right then and it would have hurt less than seeing that guilt.

I pulled my hand away from hers. She winced—*more guilt*—then sort of wriggled out from under the pretty-haired tall boy's arm, and he let her go.

But it was too late. I'd seen what I'd seen.

Now he was holding his own hand out toward me, grinning with those big teeth like a handsome ape.

"You must be the lad from Deadweather. Cyril Whitmore. Pleasure to meet you."

I didn't want to touch his stupid hand. But he kept sticking it out there, and everyone was staring at me, and it seemed like they weren't going to quit staring until I shook it.

So I did—but I didn't come in hard and fast enough, and he wound up gripping my fingers instead of my palm, scrunching them together in a way that stopped just short of being painful.

Then he dropped my hand with what I'd swear was a smirk.

It was a good thing the jailer had taken my pistol away.

"How did you find us?" Millicent asked, wiping the wetness from her eyes.

"Didn't mean to," I said in a sharp voice. Her head drew back, confused—and maybe even a little hurt.

Good.

Kira jumped in. "We heard that teenagers from Sunrise had gone to the Governor-General about the slaves in the silver mine."

Millicent gave a snort of disgust. "It's madness! They're all rotten to the core. Slavery's illegal! King Frederick himself declared it! But we go to the Governor—*ready to prove it*—and he has us hauled off before we've even gotten the words out!"

"No surprise," said the handsome ape, with a surly toss of his pretty hair. "Can't expect a regime like this to reform itself. Whole power structure's got to be overthrown."

"I'm *so* glad you're here!" said Millicent, glancing at me but mostly talking to Kira and Guts now. "We can stop it! I know we can."

"Stop wot?" Guts asked.

"The slavery! In the silver mine!" She looked down the corridor to make sure the soldiers weren't in the room, then lowered her voice. "They're vulnerable now, because most of the soldiers went off to the New Lands with *him*." She spat the last word out, and nobody needed to be told that *him* meant Pembroke. "If we can move quickly—"

Cyril chuckled. "First things first, darling—"

Darling??!!

As my stomach churned, he put his hand on her shoulder again. "We've got to get ourselves sprung from this little mousetrap." He smirked through the bars at us. "Any of you got pull within the regime?"

Guts wrinkled his nose. "Wot's a regime?"

"Powers that be, my friend. The local despot." He stuck his free hand out toward Guts. "Cyril Whitmore. Pleasure to meet you."

Guts shook his hand with a wary look. "Wot's a despot?"

"A dictator. Or in this case—the Governor-General," Cyril said, adding a wink to his stupid smirk. Guts's eyes narrowed, like he wasn't sure if the wink was meant to be friendly or insulting.

Kira turned to me. "Can your uncle get them out?"

Millicent turned back in my direction. The ape's hand was still on her shoulder. "Who's your uncle?"

"It's not impor—"

"Burn Healy," Guts blurted out.

"*What?!*" Millicent stared at me, stunned.

She wasn't even trying to brush Cyril's hand off this time.

If I stayed in that room any longer, I was going to explode.

"But how—" Millicent began.

"I have to go," I said, turning toward the door.

"Egg! Where are you going?" Millicent sounded upset.

Good.

"Are you getting your uncle?" Kira asked.

I stopped and looked back at them.

"No. My uncle's not helping. I'm not, either. They can rot in here."

They were still calling after me when I slammed the iron door shut behind me.

The soldier in the entry room wouldn't give me back my pistol.

In the mood I was in, I guess I couldn't blame him.

I STORMED DOWN THE STREET, my brain running hot with thoughts of violence and revenge as I listened for the sound of Kira and Guts running after me.

But by the time I reached the end of the block, they hadn't even left the jail yet.

That just made me angrier. I thought about disappearing on them, but it wasn't like I had anywhere to go. I could find my uncle, but I didn't want him asking me why I was boiling over with fury.

Her head was on his lap . . .

His arm was around her . . .

He called her "darling" . . .

I paced back and forth at the end of the block for a while. I got a few strange looks from passing townspeople, but there weren't many of them around—most of Edgartown seemed to have gone into hiding from the pirates, even though I suspected the *Grift*'s crew weren't doing anything more dastardly than soaking in warm baths.

After five minutes of angry pacing, Kira and Guts still hadn't shown up. I went back to the jail and paced in front of the door.

By now, I was furious with them, too.

Millicent betrayed me. Now Guts and Kira are, too. Probably sucking up to that Cyril ape like some . . . something . . .

I was so mad I couldn't even come up with words for it.

Finally, Kira and Guts emerged from the jail.

Kira looked furious as she walked toward me.

At least she's angry, too.

"Can you believe her?" I waited for Kira to agree with me.

Instead, she shoved me so hard I almost fell over.

"What is the matter with you?!"

"Me?!"

"Why did you treat her like that?!" She looked like she might slug me. Guts was keeping his distance from both of us.

"Because she—are you seriously—did you *see* them? They were *snuggled up together*!"

"They're in *jail*!"

"What does that have to do with it?"

"Everything! And so what? She thought you were dead!"

"Didn't waste much time!"

Kira shook her head in a kind of amazed disgust. "At a moment like this, are you truly so selfish . . . ? My people are in chains in that mine! And Millicent's trying to help! She is in prison for trying to free them! And you run away, and suck your fingers like

168

a baby, because two people were sitting too close to each other? *In a jail cell?*"

"He was petting her hair!"

It sounded so ridiculous coming out of my mouth that my face went hot with shame.

Kira's eyes narrowed. I hung my head so I didn't have to look at her.

"My father died for this cause," she said. "It is your cause, too. This is Roger Pembroke's silver mine she wants to make free. And you refuse to help because you're jealous of that man in there?"

"He's not a man!" I spat. "Just because he's tall doesn't mean he's a man."

"A boy, then. What are *you* going to be? A boy as well? A little boy? Who pouts? Or a man?"

I wanted to scream and pull my hair out and stomp on things. Because I knew she was right.

"This is *really* complicated—"

"It is not, Egg. It is very simple."

I looked at Guts for support.

"Do you understand? Why I'm so angry?"

He nodded. "Course. Bein' an idiot, tho'."

"What do you mean?"

"Don't want him near Millicent, yeh? So why leave 'em sittin' in jail together?"

If there was any part of me that didn't already want to crawl under a rock and never come out again . . . well, that took care of it.

I wasn't just being a selfish idiot—I was being a self-defeating selfish idiot.

Kira's attitude changed as soon as mine did. She spent the next ten minutes speaking softly to me, trying to make me feel better by telling me what a good person I was, and how much Millicent cared for me, and how this was all a big misunderstanding that was going to work itself out as soon as we'd gotten her out of jail. Kira even hugged me once to get her point across, which made Guts growl in his throat even though he knew it wasn't that kind of hug.

In the end, I was still mad—mad at myself, mad at Millicent, and mad at that stupid, tall, handsome Cyril with the pretty hair.

But I knew if I wanted to be the kind of person who was worth the ten million gold my uncle had paid for my life, I had to figure out how to ignore all of that and do what was right.

I had to get Millicent out of jail. And worse—I had to get Cyril out, too, if I could.

It felt awful. Even so, I eventually got it together to march back into the jail and tell the soldiers that Commodore Longtrousers had ordered the two teenagers from Sunrise to be freed immediately.

Half a minute later, I marched right back out again.

"What happened?" Kira asked.

"They said their orders are to release the prisoners only to their fathers. And if Commodore Longtrousers feels differently, he'll have to come down to the jail himself."

CHAPTER 19

THE MEETING

I WENT TO SEE Burn Healy alone. Kira preferred to go back up the hill, catch up with Mr. Dalrymple, and await the Okalu elder who could translate the Fire King's map. And Guts decided he'd rather spend the rest of the morning with Kira and her kindly old tutor than a couple hundred pirates on their way to getting dangerously drunk.

Which was fine—I was so used to begging my uncle for help that by now, I didn't need any moral support.

I found Healy sitting with half a dozen of his crew at a back table in the crowded dining room of the Four Winds Hotel. If there were any non-pirates left among the hotel guests, they were keeping to their rooms. Healy's men had the run of the place, and—I guess because there wasn't enough hot water for them to all bathe at once—they'd unofficially divided the dining room into clean and smelly sides.

Fortunately, my uncle was on the clean side. His hair was

damp and freshly combed, and he had on a white shirt that was so crisp and new it practically glowed. He'd rolled up the sleeves, and his muscular arms hovered over a large plate of grungy-looking shells, split open to reveal some kind of slimy gray seafood.

Although to be honest, if it hadn't been for the plate, the dining room, and the fact that my uncle was tipping the slippery hunks of muck into his mouth, I never would have guessed it was food.

"Hello, Egg. Just in time for lunch. Have a seat."

The pirate next to him moved over, and I sat down between them.

"Thank you."

"Can't let you stay long without a bath, though. No offense, but you're quite rank. Have you gotten a room yet?"

"Not yet, no."

"Better snap one up before all the good ones are taken. Probably aren't any harbor views left. Are you feeling all right? You look a little flattened out."

I felt more than a little flattened out. But I didn't want to get into why.

"Just a bit, uh . . . tired, I guess."

Healy picked up one of the grungy shells and offered it to me.

"Here. Try an oyster. Perk you right up. They're delicious."

"Are you sure?"

"Oh, quite. I'm on my second dozen. Try it with the horse-radish."

"No offense, but . . . eegh."

Healy leaned back and stared at me with what I hoped was fake disgust. "You are *not* my nephew. There's no nephew of mine doesn't like oysters. Ridiculous."

He sighed and took the oyster back from me.

"What do you want, then? Ham sandwich? Cup of soup?"

"A favor, actually."

"Again? Savior's sake. Is this what parenting's like? Children pestering you all the time, never taking no for an answer?"

"I don't know," I said. "I'm not a parent."

He looked around the table. "Well, who is?"

"I am," piped up one of the pirates.

"Really, Dobbs? Never knew that about you. How many kids you got?"

"Dunno. Never met one."

"Well, how do you know you're a parent?"

Dobbs shrugged. "Just a guess. Been around a while. Odds are. Y'know."

"I don't think that counts. Oyster?"

"Don't mind if I do."

Healy passed the plate to Dobbs, and I was just about to get back to asking for the favor when the Governor-General appeared. He was slightly less red in the face than before, but there were deep worry lines across his forehead.

"Mr. Longtrousers—"

"Commodore."

"I'm sorry. *Commodore* Longtrousers—"

"So thrilled you're joining us for lunch. Make room, brothers. What are you drinking, Governor?"

"Thank you, but I'm . . . not actually hungry. May I speak with you privately?"

"That depends. Can you put a smile on your face?"

The Governor-General tried to smile. He was unsuccessful.

Healy shrugged. "Points for effort." He got up from the table. "Come along, Egg."

THE THREE OF US sat down in a small private dining room. I wasn't sure why I was there. Neither was the Governor-General.

"Does the boy need to be here?"

"Oh, quite. He plays a critical role in my organization."

"How so?"

"He's my gardener. What can I do for you?"

The Governor-General took a deep breath. "While I recognize that you have every right to request as much currency as you have on deposit, you need to know—"

"How a bank works? I'm well aware, thanks. And not terribly sympathetic. If I were Smith-Jones, I'd be spending my day calling in loans."

"Captain Healy—"

"Oh, is this *that* kind of meeting? Well! I'll put my other hat on."

"The hard truth, Captain, is that we could call in every coin on this island, and we'd still be several million short of ten."

"It'd be a start, though. Why don't you do that, and we'll see where we are?"

"Because doing it will create a currency crisis!" The Governor-General's face was turning red. "Our whole economy will go to pieces!"

"Sounds like a real test of your leadership. But I'm sure you'll manage. You're *very* capable."

The Governor-General shut his eyes and squeezed the bridge of his nose with his thumb and forefinger. Healy gave him a supportive smile.

"Buck up, my friend. A pirate in port spends freely. Any coin I put in my crew's hands will eventually wind up back with your merchants. Seems to me that'd be quite *good* for your economy."

"Not if my people are afraid to walk the streets! The presence of your crew has reduced this town to a state of terror!"

"I can't imagine why," said Healy. "We have an agreement, you and I. One of which my men are well aware and have no intention of breaching. Treat us square, and you have nothing to fear."

"Try explaining that to the public. It's not as if our agreement's common knowledge."

"I'm afraid that's your problem."

They were both quiet for a while. I wondered what their agreement was. Healy scratched his cheek thoughtfully.

"If you're truly strapped, why not take the ten million out of Sunrise? Hasn't been a silver ship in five months—that mine must have produced at least ten million by now."

The Governor-General stared at a spot on the table for a long moment.

"No . . . We shipped the silver out before the invasion."

Healy raised his eyebrows.

"Without an escort?"

"It went on the ship that took the *Earthly Pleasure* refugees home. She had a naval escort. We thought it best to . . . empty the pantry, if you will. In the event that the invasion of Pella led to any unanticipated consequences."

"Funny, you didn't consult me about that."

"It was none of your business," the Governor snapped.

"No need to get upset. I'm only trying to be helpful."

"You want to be helpful? Get these pirates out of my town."

"Not without my ten million."

"This is extortion!" The Governor's eyes were burning.

"Funny word to use for a man who only wants his own money back." Healy's smile was gone, and his own eyes had turned dark and cold.

My palms were starting to sweat just listening to them.

"You have no right to do this!" The Governor spoke through gritted teeth. "Our agreement does *not* include your marching into my city with a pack of wolves—"

"Our agreement"—Healy's tone shut the governor up in an instant—"did not include a lot of things that wound up happening."

Silence. The Governor took a couple of deep breaths to compose himself.

"The agreement, Captain Healy . . . is based on mutual interest. If those interests diverge, I will be forced to dissolve it—and seek a military solution to the problem of piracy."

"With the forty men you've got left in that garrison? Best of luck, sport. Or have you forgotten that you lent all your muscle out to Roger Pembroke and he hasn't gotten around to giving it back?"

The Governor's eyes narrowed. His temper was rising again. "You set me up! Didn't you? You planned all along to march in here the moment I—"

"No!" The sudden fury in my uncle's voice made my heart race. The Governor shrank back in his chair as Healy leaned in over the table, looking like he might leap from his seat and attack at any second.

"I keep my promises," Healy spat. "Even to people who don't

deserve it. My men are here by circumstance, not design. And do you know why? Because your golden boy Pembroke was hanging children in the public square down in Pella, and the price of my stopping it was banishment. I've spent the days since then cleaning up the mess you all left with your greed and stupidity."

"What mess?"

Healy shook his head. "I warned you not to invade."

"Nonsense!" blurted the Governor. "You sat in that council and told us you could do it!"

"I said I *could*. I didn't say it was wise. In fact, I told you the opposite: that Pella was easier to take than it was to keep, that the Ripper needed to be dealt with first, and that it was anyone's guess where those Cartager men-of-war might be when the attack came. But you didn't listen. Because Pembroke had whispered a sweet story in your ear about taking Pella before the gold trains came in, and gorging yourselves on riches by year's end. Now it's blown up in your face."

The Governor snorted. He sat up straight in his chair, squaring his shoulders and puffing his chest out. "Nothing's blown up in anyone's face, other than you. Pembroke got the job done. Pella's ours with minimal casualties. And the gold trains will come in soon enough."

Healy stared at the Governor for a moment, searching the man's haughty scowl.

"Oh, my." Healy gave a dry chuckle and shook his head. "You're completely in the dark, aren't you?"

"About what?"

"The reason we couldn't find Ripper Jones before the invasion was because he'd gone to Pella. To cut a deal with *Li Homaya* for my head. When the attack came, they were already out to sea with two Cartager men-of-war."

The Governor's haughty look vanished. "Where are they now?"

"We sank both men-of-war on the Fangs. But *Li Homaya* and the six hundred Short-Ears with him made it to shore. Right now, they're marching down the coast to retake Pella by land. My guess is they'll be there by tomorrow. Pembroke won't know it until the guns start firing—and when they do, he'll find out in a hurry just whose side the people of Pella are on. It won't be yours."

The Governor's shoulders were sagging. His mouth hung open in a look of shock.

"There's more," said Healy. "The Ripper's still out there. I couldn't control him, and I couldn't kill him. He's a wounded animal at the moment, but I'd bet my last coin he'll go all in and launch the raid he's been itching to pull for years. That means either Edgartown or Sunrise. And unlike *my* men, when he shows up, he won't just be looking for a hot bath and a drink."

The Governor was fully deflated by now, like a sail that had gone slack in the wind. "Oh, my Savior . . . ," he whispered to himself, his hand over his mouth. When he raised his eyes to meet Healy's, they were anguished and pleading.

"You've got to do something. Get your men back on the water. You've got to stop him!"

"My ship barely floats. And my men need to get paid. We left Pella before they saw a copper for their troubles. I promised them that ten million to make up for it. If I don't put it in their hands before I ask them to lift another finger, they'll vote me right out. All I can promise you by way of help is that if Ripper Jones comes knocking at Edgartown's door, they'll answer it. But if you haven't treated them square, they might just decide he's a more profitable ally than you are."

The Governor was reduced to helpless stuttering. "I-I-I . . . can't believe this."

"Nor can I. But here we are."

Healy let him sit there for a bit, staring at his hands. Then my uncle nodded in the direction of the door.

"On your way out, please tell the waiter I'd like another drink."

It took the Governor a moment to realize he was supposed to leave. He somehow managed to get to his feet and stagger out.

"Shame about that one," said Healy after he'd left. "Had a nice little thing going until he got too greedy. But then they always do."

I got the sense that a lot of things had just been explained, if only I was clever enough to understand them. But I wasn't. My head was swimming from trying to get a handle on all of it.

"What was your agreement with the Governor?" I asked Healy.

"It's a bit complicated," he said. "But in a nutshell . . . when I started out, years ago, I plundered everything I could get my hands on. Rovian, Cartager, Gualo, Ildian . . . Didn't matter what flag a ship was under. If it was worth taking, I took it.

"The other pirate crews were the same. There were a handful of us, all based out of Deadweather. Mostly working alone. None of us too choosy about who we attacked.

"The trouble with that was, if you plunder the ships of four different countries, eventually you've got four different navies out gunning for you. And when it came down to it, stealing from Rovians never did put the spring in my step that stealing from Cartagers did.

"So I went to the Rovian Governor-General—not this one, but the man who had his job before him—and offered him a deal. Rather than my stealing *all* his silver every chance I got, he could simply pay me a fraction of it, on a regular basis, and I'd let him keep the rest. He was willing, but only if I could hold all the other pirates to the same deal. So I brought them in, and it worked out quite well for everybody.

"Then the Barker War came. Rovia and Cartage went at it, which at first looked like grim news for Rovia, since the Short-Ears had a *much* better navy. But we pirates realized it'd be awfully bad for business if Cartage won—so when the Short-Ears sent their navy to take Edgartown and Sunrise, it was the pirates who turned them back."

"I think I saw that battle," I said. "From the cliffs by my house."

Healy smiled. "That was it," he said. "Right off Deadweather. It was a fine day. And afterward, the Rovian government and I were thick as thieves. Privately, of course—if word ever got out that they were in league with the likes of me, the whole arrangement would have blown up in their faces.

"We had a good thing going—until two very different men came along and botched the whole thing.

"First, Roger Pembroke decided Sunrise Island wasn't big enough to hold his ego and his true destiny was to rule a whole continent. About the same time, Ripper Jones started questioning the arrangement from the pirates' side. He was a Short-Ear himself, and he never could abide the rule against sacking Rovians. It got to the point where I had to personally escort every ship that left Sunrise so he wouldn't pinch it. A couple months back, a ship full of Rovian noblemen coming back from some island holiday turned off course in a fog—and by the time I caught up with them, the Ripper'd had his way with her."

I'd been on that ship, the *Earthly Pleasure,* when the Ripper attacked it. In fact, it was me, not the fog, that was the whole reason it had turned off course—because its wicked cruise director had decided to maroon me on a deserted island as a kind of entertainment for the *Earthly Pleasure*'s rich and cruel passengers.

For a fleeting second, I thought about mentioning this to my uncle. But he was still talking, and it took all my concentration to follow his story.

"I did my best to smooth things over," Healy continued, "but since the Ripper was a Cartager, Pembroke latched on to his attack as a pretext for launching his grand plan and invading Pella Nonna. He persuaded the Governor to go along with it—on the theory that Cartage was weak enough in the New Lands that if we knocked out their big military ships, they'd be finished.

"But when we got to Pella, the men-of-war weren't there. Pembroke thought they'd sailed back to the Continent. But he miscalculated. Now—thanks to you—*Li Homaya*'s about to give him a nasty surprise. And the Rovians are in a right awful mess."

My head was still swimming from trying to understand the situation. There was a knock at the door. It was a waiter, bringing Healy another drink. He tipped the man a gold coin, and we were left alone again.

Healy took a long drink and shrugged. "I think I'll sit the rest of this one out. I've had just about enough of trying to rescue men from their own stupidity. Now—what's that favor you wanted?"

I'd gotten so distracted trying to understand the tangled mess of Rovians, Cartagers, pirates, soldiers, governors, and businessmen smacking each other all over the Blue Sea that I'd nearly forgotten why I'd come to see my uncle in the first place.

"A friend of mine's in jail," I said.

"Already? What did Guts do?"

"It isn't Guts."

His eyebrows jumped. "Not Kira?"

"No."

"Who am I missing?"

I gulped. "Millicent Pembroke."

"Savior's sake!" He got a look on his face like he'd just bitten into a bad piece of meat. "How on earth did *that* happen?"

"She went to the Governor-General and told him she had evidence they were using slaves in the silver mine—"

"Oh, for —'s sake!" It was only the second time I'd ever heard my uncle curse. "You're not opening *that* can of worms, are you?"

"What can of worms?"

"The silver mine."

"I have to," I said. "It's wrong."

"So are a million things in this world. You can't right them all. I thought you just wanted to get rid of Pembroke."

"It's his silver mine—it's him doing the slaving."

Healy slumped back in his seat with an exasperated look. "Haven't you done enough? *Li Homaya*'s marching on Pella as we speak. That was your doing! And if Pembroke loses that city, even if he gets out alive, he'll be bust. The Governor and the rest of them will never listen to him again. They might even manage to take the silver mine out of his hands."

"Would that fix it?" I asked.

"Fix what?"

"If Pembroke loses the silver mine, will they stop using slaves in it?"

My uncle grimaced, like I'd just told a bad joke. "Not remotely, son. Pembroke or not, there's far too many people making far too much money on that mine for anything to change."

I thought about that. The rottenness of it made my stomach turn.

"Don't you think we've got to do something about it?" I asked.

"No. I don't. You've done enough. Let it go. Sit back and eat some chocolate."

I tried to imagine doing just that. I couldn't.

Watching me, my uncle sighed. "Do you even like chocolate?"

"It's okay. But . . . we can't just let it go. We've got to *do* something."

"Why? Pembroke's on a knife edge now. Why do *you* have to do anything else?"

"Because I want to be worth ten million gold," I said.

He winced. But as he kept staring at me, a smile slowly spread across his face.

"Joke's on me, then, isn't it? What can one say?" He raised his hands, palms up, like he was admitting defeat. "I admire your nobility. And best of luck."

"So you'll help me?"

"Oh, heavens, no."

"Please! I just need you to go down to the jail and—"

"Son, the *last* thing I'm going to do is bail Roger Pembroke's fool daughter out of jail. You're on your own with that one."

CHAPTER 20

THE MAP

I WOULD'VE HEADED straight back up the hill to Mr. Dalrymple's house, but my uncle insisted I have a bath and eat lunch first. He set me up in a big room at the hotel with three beds in it, and while I was soaking in what I had to admit was a delightful warm bath, a frazzled-looking man in a hotel employee's uniform dropped off two sets of new cotton shirts and trousers for me and Guts, along with a pretty red dress for Kira.

The hotel man collected my old clothes for washing, encouraged me to call the front desk for fresh bathwater once "the other lord and lady" arrived, and bowed to me when he left. I dried off with a big, fluffy towel and put on the new clothes, which were so comfortable that wearing them made me want to take a nap.

Then I went to the dining room, where I ate a ham sandwich as big as my head.

It was all very pleasant, although I would have enjoyed it more if I hadn't spent the entire time brooding over how Millicent had ripped my guts out, and racking my useless brain for ways to get her and that Cyril ape out of jail.

Bribing the guards was the best I could come up with. Second best was hiring a few of the Healy pirates to storm the jail, although I was pretty sure my uncle wouldn't stand for that. Neither idea seemed like a winner, but they were all I had.

I trudged up the hill toward Mr. Dalrymple's, hoping my friends would have better ideas and trying to cheer myself up with the thought that even if they didn't, they'd like the warm baths, clean clothes, and cannonball-sized ham sandwiches waiting for them back at the hotel.

It took me a while to find the place—the twisty, hilly streets were confusing, and I hadn't taken the time to get decent directions from Kira. By the time I stumbled on the right house, I'd gotten so turned around that I was heading downhill. And I would have walked right past Mr. Dalrymple's house if Guts hadn't called out to me from the porch.

"Oy! Egg!"

He was sitting on the front steps with a glum look on his face. "Where ye comin' from?"

"The hotel. I got lost."

"Got a bath, too, looks like. New clothes."

"My uncle made me. There's plenty for you and Kira, too. Where is she?"

He jerked his head toward the closed door behind him. Then he twitched and scowled.

"What's the matter?"

"Got the map translated."

"Really?" My stomach started to flutter. "What does it say?"

185

"Nothin' good."

I went inside, my head buzzing. Ever since Roger Pembroke had declared it worthless, I'd mostly stopped thinking about the Fire King's map.

But it was the whole reason for everything.

If it weren't for that map, I'd still be living with my family back on Deadweather. My fool sister would be there, too, instead of lounging atop an Okalu temple in the New Lands, preening in a six-foot headdress while a bunch of Moku fed her chocolate and schemed to make her a human sacrifice.

Burn Healy wouldn't be anything more to me than the name of a ruthless pirate I'd heard stories about.

I wouldn't even have heard of Roger Pembroke, or laid eyes on his daughter.

And my father would still be alive.

Now, finally, I was going to find out what all the trouble was for.

KIRA WAS SITTING at the kitchen table, her eyes red and swollen from tears. Mr. Dalrymple was refilling her teacup from a pot with a knitted holder, his lips pressed together in a sad look.

A man I'd never seen before sat next to Kira. He was Okalu, with the same broad nose and full lips that she had. His skin was wrinkled and spotty with age, and his Continental-style clothes hung loose over a bony frame.

All three of them looked up at me when I entered, and I felt like I'd barged in on a funeral.

The old man asked Kira a question in Okalu. She answered him. Then she wiped her nose with a handkerchief and introduced us as he stood up from the table, using a wooden cane to support his weight.

"Egg Masterson, Makaro Uza."

"Hello," I said. He held his free hand out, and I shook it. It wasn't like that Cyril fellow's handshake—Makaro gave me a good grip, and he held it firmly but not too tight.

"Greetings," he said. His accent was so thick it was hard to understand him. "I thank you for your service to my people."

"You're welcome," I said. Although judging by how sad they were, I didn't think I'd done anybody much of a service.

Makaro sat back down next to Kira, leaning his cane against the table. The copy of the map that I'd made for her back on the *Grift* was sitting on the table next to the teapot.

"So you know what it says?" I asked.

Kira began to cry. Makaro put a fatherly hand on her back to comfort her, and she buried her head in his shoulder.

"I'm sorry." I didn't know what else to say.

Guts had come in behind me. Mr. Dalrymple gestured for us to sit down.

"Please, please," he said. "Sit." There were only four seats at the table, but Mr. Dalrymple insisted we take the last two while he fetched a high stool from the other room.

Kira was still crying into Makaro's shoulder. He whispered something in her ear. She nodded, straightening up as Mr. Dalrymple returned with the stool and took a seat just behind Makaro.

"I'm sorry I was so rude earlier," I said to Mr. Dalrymple.

"Oh, quite all right," he said. "Rather extraordinary day, I think. Puts us all at sixes and sevens."

Kira wiped her eyes and blew her nose. "You want to know what it says?" she asked me.

I nodded.

She exchanged a few words in Okalu with Makaro. He pulled the map toward him and lifted a finger, shaky with age, to hover over the first line of hieroglyphs. Then he began to speak Okalu in a low voice, his finger moving across the lines as he spoke.

Kira took a deep breath and started to translate the century-old words—the ones I'd copied down from the tomb wall and carried with me, over weeks and miles and endless trouble, without knowing until now what they meant.

"'I am Cromazol the scribe,'" she began. "'Servant of Hutmatozal Fire King—man-god, instrument of Ka, father of the Dawn Princess. His body here dead, his soul eternal. This is the story of his end.

"'Two days before solstice we Okalu traveled in large number to the Place of the Sunrise, to give to Ka his bride the Dawn Princess, and the gifts of her dowry.

"'The Stink-Men waited there in a trap. They slaughtered us by hundreds. Hutmatozal Fire King raised his Fist, but Ka gave no answer. Our magic failed, our princess was slain, our tribe was shamed.'"

It was just as Millicent had described the legend: the Okalu had gone to their temple on Sunrise Island for the yearly Marriage of the Sun ceremony, bringing a treasure with them as an offering . . . and were ambushed by Cartager soldiers.

Kira continued the translation.

"'Five of us remained, with the body and the dowry of the

Dawn Princess. We followed the Fist across the water to the Sweat-Place, where lived Thunder God Ma, the Death-Lover.'"

That must have been Deadweather. What with the volcano and all, I guess it was as good a place as any for a thunder god to live.

"'Hutmatozal Fire King offered the Dawn Princess and her dowry to Ma the Death-Lover in his sacred place, atop the Red Cliff, above the Valley of the Choke Plants.'"

Makaro used his finger to circle the middle section of the map—the squiggles, shapes, and dotted lines that I'd always figured weren't hieroglyphs but an actual map. Until now, I'd had no idea what place it depicted.

"Makaro says this is a map," Kira said. "Of what, he does not know."

"I know exactly what that is," I said. "There's a valley in Deadweather, below the south slope of the volcano. Full of thick brush. That must be it here"—I pointed to the map—"and above it, between the valley and the volcano, there's a lot of bare rock, in a funny reddish-pink color. The pirates in Port Scratch call it the Devil's Pimple."

I pointed to a large mark on the map. "Looks like they left the dowry halfway across the top of the pimple. If that's where it's buried, we can find it."

I couldn't help smiling. But no one else did.

"That's good, isn't it?" I asked.

Instead of answering, Kira nodded to Makaro. He started reading again, at the spot below the map where the hieroglyphs began again. Kira echoed him in Rovian.

"'Hutmatozal Fire King swore allegiance to Ma in return for his help. We left the Red Cliff and waited for a sign.

"'Thirty days we remained. We ate of the tasteless fruit. Two men died, and we gave their souls as gifts to Ma.

"'When Ma growled from the earth, we returned to the Red Cliff.

"'Ma had ignored our gifts, shaming us further. Hutmatozal Fire King cried out in anger. He demanded of Ka and Ma that they listen—and he pledged the devotion of all Okalu to whichever god would help us.

"'Ka and Ma ignored him again. He cursed them as false. He cast away the Fist of Ka, and buried the dowry in ash. Then he took his own life.'"

Kira paused to take a deep, shaky breath.

"'We carried Hutmatozal Fire King's body to this place, that his soul would observe the sunset for eternity. I die here also, with Zamozol his lieutenant, to serve him in the beyond.

"'This we swear as truth: the man who seeks rescue from gods will die in bitterness. Neither Ka, nor Ma, will save him. The only savior of man is man.'"

Kira was crying again, silently this time.

I could understand why. I'd long since given up hope that the Fist of Ka would help anyone. Finding out, once and for all, that the map didn't hold the secret to some magical power was only the third most depressing thing I'd learned that day.

But until now, Kira had believed, deep in her bones, that finding the Fist of Ka would mean salvation for her people. And the truth was devastating to her.

We sat for a long time, with nobody saying much of anything

except for Mr. Dalrymple, who couldn't stop refilling everyone's tea.

I wondered if I should be doing, or saying, something. I traded looks with Guts for a while. He kept jerking his head, but I couldn't figure out if he was trying to get a point across or his twitch was just acting up.

Finally, I decided to speak. "There's a hot bath and clean clothes waiting at the hotel," I told Kira. "Plenty of food, too. Might make you feel better."

"Sounds like a good idea, dear," said Mr. Dalrymple, patting Kira on the hand.

She nodded but didn't move. Mr. Dalrymple and Makaro exchanged a few words in Okalu. Kira joined their conversation for a moment. Then the two older men got up and shuffled toward the door. Makaro had a bad limp, and his cane made a loud *clack* on the floor with every step.

"Just shut the door behind you, dear," said Mr. Dalrymple. "No need to lock up."

"Come later," Makaro added. "We sit together."

The men walked out, leaving us alone. Kira sighed and pushed her chair back from the table. "I need a bath. And a meal."

"Where the others goin'?" Guts asked.

"Makaro wants to drink something stronger than tea," said Kira. "And Mr. Dalrymple thinks he knows of a pub that won't have pirates in it."

DROWNING SORROWS

WE WERE SITTING at a corner table in a little pub on the edge of town. It was the saddest room I'd ever been in. Even the handful of locals sitting at the other tables looked miserable. I guessed that was because the pirates were in town, and everyone was terrified they might barge in any minute and start pillaging. Or maybe Edgartown was just an unhappy place.

Still, if there'd been a contest for the unhappiest people in an unhappy town, we would've won it going away. For the first couple of hours, after Kira and Guts had gotten baths and food and we'd rejoined the older men, Mr. Dalrymple had made a game effort to buck everybody up.

But he was lousy at it.

"Perhaps there's a bright side," he suggested at one point.

Makaro looked up from his glass of spirits. He'd been staring into it like the secret of his tribe's salvation was floating at the bottom.

"There is no god," he said.

Dalrymple looked horrified. But he soldiered on. "Goodness, I don't think it said *that*. Only that perhaps it's a . . . different *kind* of god than the one you . . . hoped to . . . rely on . . . for . . ."

Kira and Makaro were both staring at him with withering looks. Dalrymple gave up in midsentence, switched from tea to beer, and didn't speak again for another hour.

I was mostly wallowing in thoughts of Millicent. I felt awful for her that she was in jail, awful for me that she was in there with that Cyril, *really* awful for the fact that she'd betrayed me by taking up with him, still more awful because my uncle could get them out but refused to help, and twice as awful on top of it all because I felt like what I *should* be feeling awful for were Kira and the rest of the Okalu, but I was so wrapped up in my own personal awfulness that I just didn't have anything left over.

It was awful.

Around late afternoon, two Rovian soldiers appeared, collected every gold and silver coin the owner had in his till, and gave him a slip of paper in return.

The owner wasn't happy. "This is an outrage!" he bellowed.

"Tell it to the Governor," said one of the soldiers.

"Better yet, tell it to the pirates," said his partner.

That earned him a glare from the first soldier. He corrected himself.

"Did I say pirates? I meant 'Rovian Irregulars.'" But he rolled his eyes when he said it.

The soldiers left. Sunset came, the owner lit a few lamps, and we ordered dinner with our drinks. I told the waiter to put everything on Commodore Longtrousers's line of credit. He looked skeptical when he heard we were with the pirates, but Guts threatened the man with his hook, and that did the trick.

After the dinner plates were cleared, Mr. Dalrymple persuaded Makaro to play a game of cards. They asked if we wanted to join in. Kira just shook her head. I didn't feel up to it, either.

Guts's face twitched hard. "— *pudda* cards!" he snarled.

Mr. Dalrymple blanched. "Sorry! Didn't mean to offend."

Kira elbowed Guts.

"Sorry, too," he mumbled to Mr. Dalrymple. "Don't like cards is all."

We watched Dalrymple deal out two hands, one to himself and one to Makaro.

Kira sighed. I'd never seen her look so sad. In fact, I wasn't sure I'd ever seen anyone look so sad.

"Are you okay?" I asked her. "Is there anything we can do to help you?"

She thought for a moment. "Not me. The Okalu. We have to help them. It is like the map said: the only savior of man is man." Her jaw tightened, and her sad look turned fierce. "We have to free my people from that silver mine."

"Oughta start by findin' the treasure," said Guts. "Fist or not, might still be worth a pile of money."

"We can do it," I added. "If the Dawn Princess's dowry is still buried where the map says it is, I can find it for us."

Kira looked skeptical. "What good would a treasure do us?"

"Buy guns with it," said Guts. "And men."

Kira thought for a moment. Then she shook her head. "We need to get Millicent out of that jail. She will have ideas."

I nodded. As tangled up as my feelings about Millicent were, there was no question she was clever—and as determined as Kira to stop the slavery on Sunrise. "But how do we get her out?"

None of us had a good answer for that. We'd fallen back into another sullen silence when the pub's owner approached. He was a heavyset man with a bushy beard.

"Are you really with them pirates?" he asked us.

"We are," I said.

"What'd your lot come stormin' into town for? What do you all want from us?"

I thought about what the Governor-General had said—that nobody in Edgartown knew of the agreement between the pirates and the government. That made it more than a little hard to explain.

"Do you know how a bank works?" I asked him.

Before he could answer, Guts piped up. "Tell ye wot *I* want." He pointed at the far wall. There was a guitar hanging from it. I'd seen him eyeing it ever since we'd come in. "Play that guitar."

The owner gave him a bewildered look. "You only got one hand!"

"It's all he needs," I said. "He's the best one-handed guitarist in the New Lands."

Kira smiled for the first time all day. "One hand or two—he is the best guitarist anywhere."

The owner snorted. "Have at it."

Guts lit up with a rare smile. He went to the far wall and pulled down the guitar. Then he got a stool from the bar, sat down with his back to the wall, and began to tune up.

Conversations stopped all around the room as everyone turned to stare at the wild-eyed boy with a hook for a hand, bent over a guitar like he actually meant to play it.

Guts finished tuning and looked at Kira.

"Wot you want to hear?"

She smiled again. "'*Samana Bey Na Fila*,'" she said.

It was a Cartager song. I didn't know what the words meant, but I'd been told it was about the end of a love affair, and that's exactly how it had always sounded to me—aching, sad, and full of regret.

Under the circumstances, there were a hundred other songs I'd rather have heard just then. As Guts bent his head over the body of the instrument and began to play, I bit down on my lip and resolved not to cry.

If the weeks away from playing had left him rusty, he didn't show it. His hook flashed up and down the guitar's neck as he filled the room with the sound of heartbreak, pulling note after shimmering note out of the strings.

It was beautiful. And excruciating.

Don't think about Millicent, don't think about Millicent . . .

I couldn't help it. My throat went tight, and it took all I had to hold in the tears as waves of pure emotion poured out from Guts's fingers.

Halfway through the song, I gave up and let the tears go. It was impossible to resist. He was that good.

Kira was crying, too. No surprise there. Makaro looked like he was on the brink as well.

Mr. Dalrymple seemed strangely unaffected. I thought that was odd.

Guts finished the song. Kira, Makaro, and I were clapping so hard my hands hurt. Then I happened to look around, and I realized Dalrymple wasn't alone.

The pub was more than half full, and everyone in it besides the two Okalu was Rovian. A few of them were offering polite, halfhearted claps. The rest just looked bored.

"Not bad," said the bushy-bearded owner. "A little dull. Know anything with a bit more pep?"

Guts's lip curled. "Like wot?"

"'Froggy Went A-Jumpin''?"

"Oh, that's a great one!" chimed in a man at the bar. "Or even better—'Jitterbug's Fancy'!"

"Right on!"

From all around the room, people began to call out requests.

"'Crack, Crack, in the Haystack'!"

"'Boo-Hoo Bettylou'!"

"'Merrily We Skip to Town'!"

I'd forgotten what horrible taste in music most Rovians had.

Guts was turning purple. I braced myself for the explosion.

"Do you know anything by the Piggly Twins?" asked a slightly dim-looking young woman with a ponytail. "They're a-mazing!"

That did it.

"— yer stupid — Pigglies in the —!" yelled Guts. "Rather — a — in the ear than — play that —, ye — *billi glulo porsamoras!* Ye can — yer *pudda hula saca domamora* till the — and the — *blun,* ye —! Ask again, I'll — yer *pudda* —!"

A full five seconds of silence followed. Someone in the back coughed uncomfortably.

"Oh, my stars," breathed Mr. Dalrymple. "He's got quite a vocabulary."

"I think it might be time to leave," I said.

LESS THAN A MINUTE LATER, the five of us were standing in the empty road outside the tavern. It was still early enough in the evening that nobody wanted to turn in for the night, so we walked the side streets of Edgartown for a while, listening to the distant laughter of Healy's men and the occasional tinkle of breaking glass.

Guts and Kira hung back, holding hands and whispering to each other. Mr. Dalrymple and Makaro tried to make conversation with me, and I did my best to keep up my end. But they'd both had quite a lot to drink, and not much of what they said made any sense, except maybe to them.

Eventually, Mr. Dalrymple led us to the door of another pub, but its windows were blacked out, and it didn't seem to be open.

"Strange," he said. "Usually does quite good business on Tuesdays."

He tried the door. To our surprise, it opened. Once we'd pushed past the layers of blankets that had been hung over the door to keep any light or sound from reaching the street, we found a room full of long tables, packed to the gills with townspeople trying to enjoy a night out without drawing the attention of any pirates.

When we entered, conversation dropped off as half the room turned at once to make sure we weren't Healy men ourselves. Then, just as quickly, the chatter started up again.

"Make sure the waiter sees your hook," I warned Guts. "Or we'll have to pay cash."

We squeezed our way into seats in the middle of one of the long tables. The men ordered beers, and the rest of us asked for sugared lemon. As I waited for the drinks to arrive, with Dalrymple and Makaro on one side slurring at each other, and Guts and Kira on the other making moony eyes across the table, I started to think it might be time for me to pack it in and go to sleep.

But I didn't want to be rude, so I figured I'd at least stick it out until the drinks arrived and I made sure we could charge them to Commodore Longtrousers. So I drummed my fingers on the table and tried to amuse myself by eavesdropping on the conversations that were swirling around me. Most of them were about Healy's men and the stir they'd caused.

"Sent the wife and daughter off to Glimmer Bay. Might join them myself if this madness doesn't end soon."

"Don't know why the Governor doesn't call out more troops."

"Outrage is what it is! I pay my tax! Where's our protection?"

Then, underneath the louder voices, I gradually became aware of a much quieter conversation at the table directly behind me, between two men who weren't eager to be heard.

"You have to understand, it's a valuable thing . . ."

"Dunno what I'd do with it is all . . ."

"Where's your imagination? It's his personal seal! Think of the doors that would open."

One of the voices was unpleasantly familiar.

"On Sunrise, maybe."

"Not just on Sunrise—the man rules Pella Nonna now!"

The hairs on the back of my neck were standing up. It wasn't just that they seemed to be talking about Roger Pembroke. It was that I knew one of the men.

"If it's so valuable, why you selling it?"

"Leaving the islands, aren't I? Pembroke name's got no pull on the Continent. But around here . . . possibilities are endless."

"How so?"

"Draw up a letter of credit! Slap the seal on it. Take it to a merchant, walk out with half his store."

I looked over my shoulder. At the bench just behind me, less than a foot away, was the back of a large man's head. His hair was newly cut, and the rolls of fat on his neck were stacked like sausages over his shirt collar.

It was Percy, all right—my lazy, cruel, and stupid former tutor.

"I ain't no writer," said the rat-faced man he was trying to bargain with.

I turned back around and kept listening.

"For a few extra silver, I'll write some out for you," cooed Percy. "Get you started."

"You ain't no writer neither."

"Nonsense! I'll have you know, I once worked as a tutor—in Roger Pembroke's own house!"

My hands were trembling. I had to call him out. I just wasn't sure how.

I heard Rat Face laugh. "*You?* A tutor?"

"Quite a fine one at that."

Guts turned to look at me. "Wot's the matter? Gone all pale."

"Shh!" I said.

". . . where you stole his seal?" Rat Face was asking.

"Course not! It was *entrusted* to me. As a faithful servant—"

I stood up from the bench, turned around, and leaned over Percy's shoulder to address Rat Face.

"He's a liar! And whatever he's selling you, it's a con."

Percy made a funny gasping noise in his throat. Rat Face stared at me, confused.

"Who are you?"

"One of Percy's victims," I said.

"Never seen this boy in my life!" protested Percy.

"Who's Percy?" asked Rat Face.

"He is," I said.

Rat Face glared at Percy. "Said yer name was George."

"It is!"

"You're a bald liar, Percy," I said. Then I looked at Rat Face again. "If you don't want to get cheated, you'd best leave now."

"Where'd *this* crapsack come from?" It was Guts, standing next to me and brandishing his hook over Percy's head.

"Oh, not *you*!" Percy immediately regretted saying that, because it was all Rat Face needed to convince himself that it was time to go. He rose from his seat.

"No-no-no! I can explain—if you—" Percy blubbered.

Too late. Rat Face was on his way out the door.

Percy's shoulders slumped in defeat. He tilted his head and stared up at me with a look of disgust.

"How are you even alive?"

"I managed," I said. "No thanks to you."

"Oughta slit yer *pudda* belly open," growled Guts.

"Back off, you whelp!" Percy was quickly recovering his bluster. "That hook won't stop the gun in my boot."

"Better not use it," I warned him. "My uncle's Burn Healy."

Percy was aghast. "Nonsense! You can't con *me,* boy."

I turned back to the others. "Kira, Mr. Dalrymple—who's my uncle?"

"Burn Healy," they both chimed in.

Percy hesitated. He didn't seem to know whether to believe it. "Look . . . can't we just agree we never saw each other?"

"You betrayed me," I said.

"You shot me!" he yelped, flapping his right arm. "I still can't raise this over my head."

"*I* didn't shoot you."

"Your girlfriend, then. Call it even. I don't want nothin' to do with your lot."

"What were you trying to sell that man?"

"A set of encyclopedias."

"Didn't sound like it. Sounded like it was something of Pembroke's. Like an official seal or something."

"What's it to you?"

"I might have a business proposition for you."

CHAPTER 22

SPRUNG

EVEN THOUGH I HATED Percy's guts—as a tutor, he'd been lazy, cruel, and shockingly incompetent—he was as good a liar as anybody I knew. Even more important, he'd somehow managed to steal a metal stamp of Roger Pembroke's that, when impressed onto a letter or a wax seal, identified a document as having officially come from Pembroke's hand.

And Percy needed money, badly enough that for fifty-seven gold pieces (a number that took us half an hour of haggling to settle on) he agreed to show up at the jail and present an officially sealed letter to the guards ordering Millicent and that Cyril ape to be released into his custody on behalf of Pembroke and the elder Mr. Ape.

Percy even suggested some improvements of his own to the scheme, like wearing a uniform he'd kept from his days as a servant at Cloud Manor, and waiting until that morning's ship from

Sunrise had just docked before showing up at the jail, to make it look like he'd just gotten off the boat.

We agreed to meet him at the hotel the next morning at eleven, when the ship was due in. All we had to do before then was scrape together fifty-seven gold pieces, which we figured wouldn't be too difficult. We had eighteen between us already—and as Guts pointed out, since we'd served on the *Grift*'s crew during the battle, we arguably had a right to some of Healy's ten million, even if it wasn't the full crew share of fifty thousand each.

We approached my uncle the next morning over breakfast in the hotel dining room. Like the handful of other pirates in the room, all of them green and queasy as they stared at their plates of bacon and eggs, he was badly hungover. We were a little bleary-eyed ourselves, but only because the pirates' caterwauling had made it tough to sleep once we'd gotten back to the hotel.

We made our case for the money. Healy nodded, scratching the thick stubble on his cheek.

"Fair enough," he yawned. "I'm a bit short on actual coin at the moment, though. Feel free to run up whatever bills you like at the local merchants, and I'll see what I can do in a few days. Sound fair?"

We looked at one another. This wasn't going to do. We had only eighteen gold, and we needed fifty-seven.

"The thing is," I said, "we've got a, uh . . . pretty urgent need for, um, thirty-nine gold."

"Thirty-nine?"

"Roughly."

"Roughly? So you'd be all right with thirty?"

"Well . . . not roughly."

"Exactly, then?"

"Could be forty," Kira offered. "If a round number's easier."

Healy squeezed his eyes shut for a moment and rubbed his temples. I think that was more because of the hangover than us, but I wasn't sure.

"This about that Pembroke girl? Are you bribing someone?"

We looked at one another. There was no point in lying. We weren't good at it.

"Sort of."

He sighed. "Fine. Just let me finish my battle with these eggs and I'll put the touch on a few of the brothers for the coin. One thing, though."

"What's that?"

"Don't lay out the whole bribe up front. Give them a taste, but hold back as much as you can until the deal's done."

"Good advice, thanks."

"Don't mention it." He forced down a bite of eggs. Then he scrunched up his nose and cocked an eyebrow.

"Fetch a bucket, will you? Not sure these eggs are going to stay put."

They did, but just barely.

It was still two hours before we were due to meet Percy, and I spent them in a rocking chair on the hotel's porch, staring off into space while I tried to decide how I'd act around Millicent if the plan worked and we sprang her from the jail. A night's sleep hadn't left me any less hurt or confused. I loved her—but at the moment, I hated her, too, which was what made it so confusing.

And she'd told me she loved me as well, back in that pit the Moku threw us into at Mata Kalun. Was she lying then? Had she changed her mind? Did it matter that she'd thought I was dead?

She'd had a thing for this Cyril fellow for a long time, I knew that. It went back years, well before she'd ever met me. She'd once said she was going to marry him. Was *that* true? Were they engaged now or something?

If our plan worked, he'd get sprung along with her. I'd have to figure out how to act around him as well. I wasn't looking forward to that.

Maybe I should ignore her. Freeze her out. Shun her, like the townspeople did to Geraldine, the fallen woman in *A Storm Upon the Heath*. But that ended badly for everybody—Geraldine took poison, and the man who loved her, Miles, wound up jumping off a cliff.

I never liked that book.

Should I issue an ultimatum, and demand that Millicent give up Cyril and return to me? That had happened in a few different books—not just *A Storm Upon the Heath* (early on, before everybody started killing themselves), but *Behold a Stranger* and *Silent Came the War* as well.

But the ultimatums hadn't worked in any of those stories. Demands like that just seemed to make everybody unhappy, especially the person doing the demanding.

Then I remembered Lothar the Lone, in *Throne of the Ancients*. His true love, Boresia, had been captured by the Skorgards of Grumm and fed to their nightwolves. After that, Lothar had resolved to walk the earth alone (which was how he got his nickname), a pitiless warrior for justice, vanquishing evildoers like the Skorgards and righting wrongs wherever he found them, all the while refusing any earthly joy, including the civilizing touch of a woman.

He wasn't exactly a barrel of fun to read about—it got so I'd skip the Lothar chapters whenever they cropped up so I could get back to Billicks the Brave, who had a much more positive attitude—but Lothar was definitely noble, and the various maidens he was constantly saving from peril really seemed to appreciate him.

I decided that was the way to go. It'd be tricky, since Millicent wouldn't have been eaten by nightwolves, so I'd still have to talk to her. And I'd have to put up with that Cyril, too.

But I'd treat them both with the kind of stiff, cold formality that Lothar used on people. And when Millicent saw just how noble I was, swearing off all happiness and devoting my every waking moment to heroically good deeds like freeing the silver mine's slaves, she'd realize she had made a terrible mistake.

But it'd be too late for her. Because by then, I'd be Egg the . . .

I couldn't think of a good *E* word to go with Egg. But I didn't need one. I just had to be cold and aloof, and a warrior for justice. If I did it right, sooner or later someone else would give me a good nickname.

My uncle came through with a sack of silver coin, then went back upstairs for a nap. Percy showed up just before eleven, a wax-sealed letter in his hand. He must have seen hard times over the past months, because his old servant's uniform hung so loose I figured he'd lost a good twenty pounds.

He howled when we only gave him a quarter of the money up front, but Guts showed him the rest, and we swore we wouldn't cheat him. Then we had to hang around the dock until almost eleven-thirty before the Sunrise ship came in. Once the passengers started to disembark—it was mildly amusing to see the looks of fear on the wealthy Sunrisers' faces when the harbormaster stopped them to warn that Edgartown had been overrun by pirates—we followed Percy up the hilly streets to the jail.

While he went inside, we waited at the corner.

He was in there just long enough for us to get worried.

Finally, he reappeared, with Cyril and Millicent in tow.

They were both walking with a stiff gait, like it had been a while since they'd stretched their legs. But when Millicent saw us, she broke into a run.

I tried not to stare at her as she approached, but I couldn't help myself.

It was annoying to realize she wasn't looking at me. She had a big smile on her face, but it was aimed at Kira and Guts.

She hugged them both tightly.

"Thank you *so* much!"

I waited for her to try to hug me. But she didn't even look my way.

"It was mostly Egg's doing," Kira said.

"Oh." Finally, Millicent looked at me. Her eyes were cold. "So you decided not to let us rot?"

I tried to say, "I seek only to do what is just," which was Lothar the Lone's standard answer in situations like this. But I was so thrown off by the fact that Millicent had the gall to be angry herself—*her? mad at ME?*—that the words got all tangled up in my mouth.

What came out was "I seek the what just only . . . what to do."

They all gave me funny looks, and I felt my face turn hot.

Just then, Percy and that Cyril ape reached us.

"Thanks for the subterfuge," he said with a wink. "Accommodations were getting a bit tiresome."

"The subter-wot?" asked Guts.

"Gimme the sack, you," Percy interrupted, holding out a stubby-fingered paw.

Guts handed the bag over. Percy shoved his whole arm into it and pulled out a fistful of coins. He looked them over, then let all but one drop back into the bag, raising a racket loud enough that passersby in the street turned to look at us.

He bit down on the coin he was still holding.

"It's real," I assured him. "We're not cheats like you are."

"See about that," said Percy, putting the coin up to his eye so he could examine it closely.

"Excuse me—"

We turned to see a pair of Rovian soldiers approaching. My heart started to beat faster. If Millicent got rearrested, we were all out of ideas for getting her out again.

But the soldiers only had eyes for Percy.

"Are those coins in that sack?"

Percy got a look on his face like a weasel that had just been caught stealing eggs from a falcon's nest. "Just a few," he said in a panicky voice.

"How many?" the soldier asked as his partner whipped out a piece of parchment and a charcoal pencil.

Percy clamped his jaws shut.

"Fifty-seven gold worth," Guts piped up.

"Going to be needing that," said the first soldier as his partner started to write up a receipt. "Governor's orders. You'll be reimbursed when—"

"I've got a wife and kids to feed!" yelped Percy. "The little one's *very* sick! Got no intestine, you see, and—"

"We should be going," I said. I turned to the soldiers. "We'd offer you our silver as well, but he's got it all."

"Move along, then. And mind yourselves—there's pirates about," said the first soldier.

The second soldier gave him a discreet kick in the foot.

"Sorry—not pirates. Rovian Irregulars."

"We shall be *very* careful," said Kira.

"Thank you, Percy!" I said.

Percy was still pleading with the soldiers when we turned the corner. A part of me felt sorry for him. But considering all the rotten things he'd done to me over the years, it wasn't a big part.

WE HEADED BACK to the hotel so Millicent and Cyril could get a bath. Along the way, Kira filled Millicent in on everything that had happened to us since we'd seen her last. I kept waiting for Millicent to turn to me and say something like, "Nice going!" or "Wasn't that brave of you?" or even "I can't *believe* my father tried to hang you in front of a whole city."

But she didn't even glance in my direction.

Meanwhile, Cyril cracked jokes, using words that nobody except him understood. Guts kept asking what they meant, but half the time he didn't know the words Cyril used to define them, either, so the whole conversation sort of went around in circles.

I was determined to sound stiff and formal like Lothar the

Lone, but it wasn't working, because no one was bothering to talk to me. So I was stuck with just walking stiffly, which made me feel like a fool.

By the time we got back to the hotel, I was so angry at everyone that I thought about getting my own room and locking myself inside it. But I couldn't think of what I'd do inside a locked room by myself.

Instead, we got a second room for the girls so they could have some privacy. Kira asked if Millicent and Cyril needed clean clothes, but it turned out they'd brought plenty of their own. Cyril produced some silver coins and pressed them on one of the hotel employees, asking him to "be a good chap and fetch our bags from my sloop."

I'd forgotten Cyril had his own boat. The thought of him and Millicent spending the whole three days' sail from Sunrise alone on it got me even more upset.

And the way Cyril sauntered up to the hotel man and ordered him around like it was the most natural thing in the world reminded me of how rich he was, and made me want to slug him.

Then again, everything about him made me want to slug him.

Especially the way he kept trying to be nice to us.

The girls went to their room, and Guts and I took Cyril to ours. He ordered a hot bath from another one of the hotel men. Then he took off his boots—they were very fine boots, made from some kind of soft leather—and splayed himself out on one of the beds.

"Ah, that's the ticket," he said in a breathy voice. "It's the little comforts you miss when you're incarcerated."

"In-wot-serrated?" asked Guts.

"Imprisoned, old boy," he said.

"I ain't old," growled Guts.

"Figure of speech, my friend." He gave Guts another one of his stupid winks. "But since we're on the subject—how old *are* you?"

"None of yer *pudda* business," said Guts.

"Ah! You speak Cartager. A man of the world. I like it."

"How old are *you*?" I asked him.

"Three months shy of seventeen." He chuckled. "Although if I don't stop letting Millicent drag me off on these deadly crusades, it's possible I won't live to see the party."

He sat up, peering at us through narrow, laughing eyes.

"Tell me—are you fellows as suicidally idealistic as she is?"

"Wot d'ye mean?" asked Guts.

"I mean, are you every bit as determined to wash away the sins of our fathers?"

The way he said it—with that stupid grin still on his face—made the back of my neck prickle.

"*My* father was no slaver," I hissed.

"Don't take offense, old boy." He chuckled again, looking me in the eye as I stared back at him. "But come now—you're from Deadweather? And your uncle's Burn Healy? More than a few sins on *your* family's ledger, I'm su—"

He didn't finish the word, because by then I was nearly on top of him, swinging my fist at his mouth as I went. It was my right one, attached to an injured wrist that was still in a splint—but I was so angry I hadn't stopped to think about that.

If I'd hit my target, I probably would have broken the wrist. And it would have been the first time in my life I'd ever slugged someone without them coming at me first.

But something went badly wrong, and I never made contact.

Instead, I found myself tumbling head over heels as my legs were swept out from under me.

I hit the wooden floor so hard it knocked my wind out. Then there was a scuffle above me, and just as I was starting to lift my head, something big and heavy drove me back into the floor.

It was Guts, with Cyril on top of him. He was trying to thrash his way free, but however Cyril was holding him, it was good and tight, so all the thrashing did was make things that much more unpleasant for me at the bottom of the pile.

After that, there was a lot of grunting and swearing, most of it from me and Guts.

Then I heard a clatter against the wood, and even though my head was being mashed against the floor so hard I couldn't move it, I caught a glimpse of Guts's hook as Cyril kicked it away, underneath one of the beds.

"Hear this, you two—" That was Cyril, somewhere at the top of the pile and sounding more annoyed than angry. "I spent four years studying Ildian martial arts at prep school. Right just now, I can think of about ten different ways to kill you both with my bare hands."

I heard him chuckle. "Mind you, I'd much rather we peacefully coexist. But if you insist on misbehaving, I'll be forced to make things quite painful for you. Do you understand?"

"— yer —, ye — *pudda hula saca!*"

I heard Cyril sigh. I would have sighed, too, if it had been possible. But my lungs were getting crushed.

"Guts," I croaked, "do what he says."

CHAPTER 23

A HOLE IN THE HEART

"TELL ME SOMETHING, old boys . . ."

Cyril was soaking in a warm tub. Guts and I were glowering in the room's two comfy chairs, trying not to stare at him.

He had hair on his chest. A lot of it. I didn't know you could get that kind of chest hair by sixteen. Or "three months short of seventeen," or whatever he was.

"Why do you despise me?" he asked us.

I didn't even know where to start. And it didn't seem like a good idea to answer him. I was still a little shaken up by how easily he'd squashed both me and Guts at the same time.

"Wot's 'despise'?" Guts asked.

"'Hate,' my friend." Cyril tilted his head back, rinsing the soap from his long, pretty-like-a-girl hair. "I mean, it's rather mystifying. We've only just met. And we're all playing for the same team, as it were. So what have I done to get on your wrong side?"

"Moved in on his girlie," said Guts.

"Guts—!" It was the last thing I wanted Cyril to hear.

Too late. The handsome ape's eyebrows sprang up as he gave me the kind of look that made me want to slug him all over again.

"Ahhhh . . . Suddenly, it all makes sense. Did you and Millicent have some kind of fling?"

I stared at the floor, trying to figure out how to convince my face not to turn red.

"Not—I—just, no—nothing." The whole Lothar the Lone, stiff-and-formal thing wasn't working out at all.

"My friend, I am *terribly* sorry. I had no idea she was spoken for."

He didn't look sorry.

Cyril got up from the tub, grabbing a fluffy towel to dry off his ridiculously tall, muscular body. Then he wrapped the towel around his waist and used a second one to dry his hair as he asked, "How old are you?"

"I'm a . . . bit short of fourteen," I said. It was more than a bit. It was nine months at least. I tried to sit up straight so I looked taller.

"Ah! A younger man."

"What do you mean?"

"I mean, Millicent's fourteen and change, isn't she?" He was putting on a pair of trousers from the luggage that had just been delivered to the room. They were, as I could have guessed without even a glance at them, very fine trousers.

"Well, look, my friend—if that's what this is all about, it's out of our hands, isn't it?"

"How's that?" I asked.

"I mean, you can't dictate what's in a woman's heart. Or a man's, for that matter . . . Until I came back from school this last time, I'd never thought of Millicent as anything more than a sort of little sister. It was quite a surprise to discover she'd blossomed into such a fetching young lady . . ."

He paused, three buttons still left unfastened on his silk shirt, and stared off into space with the sort of smirk that made it hard for me not to leap up and take another swing.

But I still hurt in about four different places from the last time I'd tried that.

"And that spunk!" Cyril went on. "Of course, some men might be put off by her outspokenness. Threatened, I suppose. Personally, I find it rather captivating . . ."

He kept smiling at nothing for a few more seconds. Then he shook his head, like he was snapping himself out of it, and gave a little chuckle.

"My point is—if you're the man for Millicent, there's not a thing I can do to change her mind. And vice versa."

"Wot's that mean?" Guts wanted to know.

"'Vice versa'? Means the other way around." Cyril finished buttoning his shirt and walked over to me with that stupid grin still on his face.

"Look, there's no point in *us* getting bent out of shape with each other. It's all up to Millicent. What say we leave it to her, and agree to be friends regardless of how the chips fall?"

He stuck his hand out. I almost didn't shake it, but then I realized this was my chance to make up for the last handshake.

I got him by the middle of his fingers, the same way he'd

grabbed mine back at the jail. Then I squeezed, hard enough that his smirk disappeared for a moment.

At least I could feel good about that.

CYRIL HAD JUST GOTTEN his boots on and was yammering about a "spot of lunch" when there was a knock at the door.

Guts answered it. It was Millicent. When I saw her step into the room, my heart started to thump.

"Hello, darling," Cyril said in a chipper voice.

"Hi."

But she wasn't looking at him. She was looking at me.

"Can I talk to you? Alone?"

I followed her into the hallway. It was empty except for the two of us.

Her hair was freshly washed, and when she turned toward me to speak, she tucked a lock of it behind her ear in that cute way that always made my stomach flutter. There were heavy circles under her big brown eyes, and a few red blemishes mixed in with the freckles that dotted her nose and cheekbones, but they didn't make her look any less beautiful.

"I'm sorry I was cross with you before," she began. "Kira told me how much you've done"—she was staring into my eyes, which made it hard to focus on what she was saying—"and what you've been through. And I know how much you care about me." She took a deep breath. "And I care about you, too."

Then why do you look so sad?

"When I thought you were dead . . . that he'd killed you . . ." Her eyes darted away, and she let out a little shuddering sigh.

"It was awful," she whispered, staring down at nothing. She looked heartbroken.

"I'm not dead," I said. "I'm right here."

"I know." She met my eyes again and tried to smile.

But she couldn't quite manage it.

Something was wrong.

"Millicent . . . Whatever happened between you and—"

"No," she interrupted. "Don't. Please—"

"Don't what?" I couldn't keep the anger out of my voice.

"Do you know how long—?" She stopped herself, then tried to start over. "But it doesn't—it's not just—the thing is . . ."

Her whole face was scrunched up in frustration. She couldn't get a sentence out.

I'd never seen *that* happen before.

"It's complicated," she said finally.

Kira's words from yesterday came out of my mouth almost as fast as they popped into my head.

"No, it isn't," I said. "It's very simple."

She started shaking her head again.

"It's not—"

"It is!" I knew I shouldn't be getting angry. But I couldn't help it.

"Egg, please don't—"

"Just tell me: him or me?"

"It's not—"

"Him or me?"

"Nobody!" In an instant, all my anger got sucked away from me, to burn in the furnace that lit up behind her eyes.

"Savior's sake," she seethed, "can't you see we've got more important things to deal with? It doesn't matter what, or who—"

"I have to know!" I said. "I *have* to!"

"Have to know what?" she demanded. "What's in my heart?" She said *heart* with a little snarl, like she was mocking me.

"Yes!"

She glared at me for a long moment. When she finally spoke, the words came out trembling and tight.

"What's in my heart . . . is a black, rotten hole. Because my whole life . . . everything in it . . . was built on a lie. And an evil one. And nobody—*nobody!*—will lift a finger to fix it! Not the Governor, not the soldiers, not one single stupid person back on Sunrise—even my mother! Who, when she *finally* admits to herself, after all these years, the truth of what he's been doing up there in that mine—all she can think to do is run! To sail off to Rovia, and stick our heads in a box, and pretend that as long as we're not part of it anymore, it isn't our fault!"

Millicent's eyes were welling up with angry tears. But behind the tears, that furnace was still burning. "But it IS. If we walk away, with our fine clothes and our porcelain plates, that we bought with HIS slave money—and we don't do a blasted thing to stop it—we're as bad as he is."

She pressed the heel of her palm into her eye, wiping away the tears. "I don't care if I have to do it myself. I'm going to get those slaves out of that mine. And until I do, *nothing* else matters. Do you understand?"

I nodded.

"Will you help me?" she asked.

"Of course I will."

And I meant it. It wasn't until hours later, when I was lying in bed, unable to sleep for all the thoughts racing in my head about how difficult and dangerous it'd be trying to free those slaves, that a little part of me—a cynical, ugly part I didn't much like— decided it was a neat trick she'd pulled. In less than a minute, she'd managed to quash my anger, shut down any questions about whether she favored me or Cyril, make me feel selfish for even thinking about it, and guarantee there was no chance I'd waver in my determination to help her.

But like I said, that was hours later. At the time, all I could do was agree without a second's hesitation.

She hugged me—not an "I love you" hug, but a "thanks for sticking with me even if it gets us killed" hug—and when she broke the clinch, I had just one question.

"How are we going to do it?"

"That's something we should talk about," she said, which was as close as Millicent ever came to admitting she hadn't the slightest idea.

CHAPTER 24

LAYING PLANS

"THEY'RE PIRATES," Millicent was saying. "Surely if we pay them enough, they'll do the job for us."

"They're not exactly hurting for money just now," I said. "And where would you get that much coin?"

That seemed to stump her. Millicent's only source of funds was her father, who'd not only disowned her, but wasn't likely to open his wallet so she could hire some men to bust the slaves out of his own silver mine.

"Dig that treasure up from Deadweather," suggested Guts.

"There's a treasure on Deadweather?" Cyril raised his head from the pillow it was resting on and cocked an eyebrow. It was the first time he'd opened his mouth since we'd started brainstorming. Until then, he'd been stretched out on one of the beds in our hotel room, gazing up at the ceiling with that annoyingly superior smirk on his face.

"Keep yer *pudda* hands off it, Feathers!" Guts snarled.

"What did you call me?" Cyril asked him.

"Feathers."

"And this is because . . . ?"

"Way your hair looks. Like feathers hangin' down."

Cyril shrugged, then let his head sink back into the pillow. "Suppose I've been called worse."

Millicent was chewing on her fingernail, deep in thought. "Depending on what's in the treasure . . ."

"Forget the treasure," I said. "It doesn't matter how much money we've got to pay them. My uncle will never let his men help us."

"Why not?" Millicent asked.

"For the same reason he wouldn't bail you out of jail. He doesn't want to get involved."

"My people will help," said Kira. "If we go to the New Lands, and find them in the mountains, their warriors will join us."

"How long would it take to get there?" asked Millicent.

Kira shrugged. "Three days' sail? Then a few days overland, into the mountains—"

Cyril chuckled. "And then six months to build a ship that'll hold them all. Or did you think my little sloop could carry enough Okalu warriors to storm a silver mine?"

Millicent shook her head. "Ship or no ship, we haven't got that kind of time. We have to go *now*—while most of the soldiers from Sunrise are still off in Pella Nonna. Once they come back, it'll be too difficult."

"How many soldiers they got now?" Guts asked.

"On Sunrise? I don't know," admitted Millicent. "But not a lot."

"How many is 'not a lot'?" I asked.

"Thirty? Forty?"

"Easy peasy," said Cyril. "That's, what? Seven or eight highly trained riflemen for each of us? What are we waiting for? Let's leave tonight."

"You don't have to be sarcastic." Millicent glowered at him. I couldn't help feeling a little pleased about that.

Cyril sighed and sat up straight. "As much as I admire everyone's idealism, do you have any idea how useless this entire conversation is?"

"We've got to stop it!" said Millicent.

"You *can't*. Not with force. Game it out, darling. Five of us, totally unarmed—"

"We can get arms," I said. "That's easy enough."

"Fine. Say we're armed. And you somehow manage not to shoot your own toes off—"

"I know my way round a gun," snarled Guts.

Cyril sighed. "Whatever. Let's assume you even succeed. Storm the mine, free the slaves, miraculously get them off the island. *Then* what? I'll tell you what: *they'll get more slaves*. It'll be a setback. But in the long run, nothing will change."

"The short run is good enough for me," said Kira. "As long as the Okalu in that mine go free."

It wasn't good enough for Millicent. "What are you saying, Cyril? That the island we grew up on is just evil, and there's nothing to be done about it? We should just get used to it?"

"No," said Cyril. "But the fact is, if you really want to change what men *do*, you've got to change the way they *think*. Who's read *Liberty and Blood*?"

He looked around. None of us knew what he was talking about.

"Who's at least heard of it?"

No takers. "Well, that's rather tragic. What schools do you go to?"

"Never been to no school," said Guts.

"Neither have I," said Kira.

"I had a tutor," I muttered, feeling my face turn red when I thought about how little I'd learned from Percy.

"Are you just trying to make everyone feel bad?" Millicent snapped at Cyril. His smirk vanished, and I nearly smiled myself. Seeing them fight gave me hope.

"No! It's a *very* well-known book. And dangerous. It's the reason I got kicked out of Thistlewick—because my mates and I were secretly printing copies and passing them around."

"How is a book dangerous?" Kira asked him.

"Because of the ideas in it. About rights, and justice, and government—before I read it, I was as loyal a subject of King Frederick as anyone. And if I'd known there was slavery going on in that silver mine . . . well, I can't say I would've been too broken up about it.

"But once I read *Liberty and Blood*, it was like the scales had fallen from my eyes. I realized our whole system of government's rotten to the core, and it's got to be replaced if there's ever going to be any justice in this world."

"What does this have to do with the silver mine?" I asked.

"Everything," said Cyril. "Real, meaningful change starts in here—" He tapped his head. "And change like that doesn't come from a gun. It comes from ideas. What we need to do is get that book in the hands—"

"A book?!" Guts snorted. *"Pudda — blun!* Wot you gonna do? Throw it at people?"

"Let me finish! Get it in the hands of the men who really hold the power. And make them see the folly of their ways."

"No book is going to change my father's mind," Millicent said, in a voice full of disgust.

"And there's no plan the five of us can cook up that's going to liberate that mine," Cyril huffed. "Thirty soldiers are still thirty soldiers."

Then they started to really go at it. I stopped listening to the argument, because I needed to think—if I could just come up with some kind of plan, good enough to not just free the slaves but show Millicent I was worth more than this twittering snob . . .

But the snob was right. We needed men.

"You want change, it's got to come from within!" Cyril was telling Millicent.

Come from within . . .

"They'll do it themselves," I said.

Everyone looked at me.

"The slaves. There's probably hundreds of them. Right? So we just have to arm them, and open the gates or whatever, and they'll do the rest. They'll free themselves."

Everyone's eyes widened . . . except Cyril's, which narrowed.

"You're going to haul two hundred rifles up a mountain? And give them to men who might not even know how to shoot?"

"Not rifles. Slings." I looked at Kira. "Do you know how to make a sling?"

"Of course."

"Could we make a lot of them? Hundreds?"

She began nodding eagerly.

"And there's no shortage of rocks in a mine—"

"Egg, this is brilliant!" Millicent was beaming at me.

Cyril had his mouth slightly open in a look of bewilderment. I couldn't help rubbing it in a little.

"You probably didn't learn this in your school," I said, "but the Okalu fight with slings. If you know how to use one, they're every bit as good as a rifle. And a lot easier to haul up a mountain."

"We'll need money for materials," said Kira.

"I'm sure I can get that from my uncle," I said. "He was free enough with the money we used to bribe Percy. And if we just need rope, cloth, and thread—it can't cost that much."

The mood in the room had turned from gloomy to bright.

"This is really brilliant," Millicent repeated.

"Nice thinkin'," Guts told me.

"Indeed!" said Cyril. The smirk was back on his face. "Congratulations. You've just devised the perfect plan for slaughtering a thousand innocent people."

Everyone turned to stare at him.

"Once again: game it out," he said. "You're going to put deadly weapons in the hands of a couple hundred freed slaves, then set them loose on an island full of the very people who enslaved them? If you think they *won't* take blood revenge on every man, woman, and child—"

"My people would not do that," Kira said through gritted teeth.

"*All* people would do that," he shot back at her. "It's human nature. And what's more—" Cyril turned back to me. "How do you propose to get all those freed slaves off the island? Because without some kind of escape plan, once they've finished slaughtering every Rovian on Sunrise, they'll be stranded there. And sitting ducks for the soldiers who show up to avenge the killing."

The mood quickly turned gloomy again. Now it was Cyril's turn to rub it in.

"Other than that, it's perfect. Just got to tidy up the part where everybody dies."

"Oh, shut up!" snapped Millicent. "It's like you don't even care!"

Cyril looked offended. "Of course I care! There's nothing more important to me than justice—"

"Or at least *talking* about it," scoffed Millicent.

Cyril recoiled like he'd just been slapped. I had to bite my lip not to smile. A few more minutes of this, and there'd be no question who Millicent favored.

"Nonsense! I want to stop that slaving as much as you do! But we've got to come up with a plan that works!"

"Then help us come up with one! Stop shooting everything down with that stupid smirk on your face!"

For a moment, I thought Cyril was going to storm out of the room. I stared at the floor and prayed for it.

Please leave. Please leave. Please leave in a huff.

But in the end, he flopped back onto the bed and started to stare at the ceiling again, only without the smirk this time.

"We need a diversion," he said. "To draw the troops away . . ."

IT WAS ALMOST TIME for lunch when I finally came up with a diversion that made sense to everybody.

"Ripper Jones."

227

"What about him?"

I told them what I'd heard from my uncle about the Ripper—that he'd been itching to attack Edgartown and Sunrise for years, and might even be planning a raid.

"So we'll tell the soldiers guarding the mine that the Ripper's just invaded Blisstown," I said. "And they need to come quick and save us."

From there, it took just a couple of minutes of back-and-forth to settle on the particulars: Millicent and Cyril would run screaming up to the mine, terrified out of their minds because the Ripper's crew had just landed and was going to put all of Sunrise to the knife if every able-bodied Rovian on the mountain didn't rush right down to the port to save the day.

"Then how do we free the Okalu?" asked Kira. "If they are locked up, how do we get the locks open?"

It took hours to puzzle that one out. Eventually, we tracked down a pirate from the *Grift* who'd worked as a locksmith, and learned from him that there were six or eight types of skeleton key, which between them should open just about any lock we might encounter. Then we found a smith in Edgartown who agreed to set us up with a full set of skeleton keys for thirty gold.

After that, it was on to the next question.

"So we're standing outside the mine with a couple hundred Okalu," said Cyril. "How do we get them off the island without starting a war?"

"The same way they came in," said Millicent. "Through the secret port in the cove on the south side of the island. If we do it in the middle of the night, they wouldn't be likely to run into any Rovians on the way."

"What we gonna do for a boat?" asked Guts.

"Birch's slave ship," said Millicent. She looked at Cyril. "When we left, it was docked in the cove. And no one was on it."

"What if we get to Sunrise and it's not there anymore?" Cyril asked.

"Then we'll wait around until it is."

"How do we sail it?"

That stumped everybody. By breakfast the next morning, the best we'd come up with was either to have someone teach us how to sail a ship that big ourselves—which seemed like it could take ages—or hire a crew, which promised to be not only expensive, but difficult.

"If you were a sailor," asked Millicent, "how would you feel about getting approached by five teenagers who wanted to buy your services for a secret mission they wouldn't even describe to you beforehand?"

Nobody said anything. We all knew the answer, and it was depressing.

But then Cyril—who, although he'd stopped sounding scornful when he pointed out problems, hadn't exactly been killing himself to come up with solutions—surprised us all.

"Oars," he said.

We looked at one another. "Is that possible?"

"Long as we have enough. Forty should do the trick. We'll buy them from the shipyard here. Lash them to the deck of my sloop. Then either . . ."

He thought for a moment before continuing. "Either we'll sail straight into the cove, or dock at North Point and carry them overland in the middle of the night. Hide them near the stairs on the cliff top above the cove."

"It'd take forever to get them overland like that," said Millicent. "If we try to get it all done in one night—"

"Better to break it up," said Cyril. "Land on the first night and stow the gear. Spend the next day resting in the woods and scouting the layout of the mine. Then the next night, you and I will create the diversion, and the others will lead the slaves down to the cove."

He grinned. "By George, I think we've got it. All we need are forty oars and half a dozen skeleton keys."

The grin on his face was annoying. I was glad we finally had a workable plan, but until that moment, I'd still been hoping that Cyril would back out of it and wreck his chances with Millicent.

"And two hundred slings," Kira added.

"Are those really necessary?" Cyril asked. "I mean, we've gone to quite some trouble to put something together that'll avoid bloodshed. Do we really need to arm the Natives?"

"Maybe we don't—" Millicent began.

"No," said Kira sharply. "We must have the slings. They will give the men who carry them confidence. And they will help solve any problem that arises."

Cyril smirked. "Of course, by 'solve any problem,' you mean, 'kill anyone who stands in the way'?"

Kira narrowed her eyes. She didn't care for Cyril any more than I did. "Yes," she said. "That is what I mean."

"But it won't come to that," said Millicent. "It's a good plan. It's going to work. And nobody's going to get hurt."

Cyril winked at her. "From your lips to the Savior's ears."

She smiled back at him, and for a moment, I felt like kicking something.

ONCE WE'D WORKED OUT where we were going to buy all our supplies and how much they'd cost, it was my job to hit my uncle up for the money. I found him late that morning in a tavern off the main street, where forty of his men were celebrating Quint's initiation as a full-fledged member of the *Grift*'s crew.

Apparently, the initiation involved quite a lot of drinking. When I got there, Quint was passed out on top of the bar, his skin bright red around the edges of the brand-new flame tattoo that had been inked on the side of his throat. Several crew members were standing over him, swaying boozily as one of them held up a scary-looking tattoo needle.

"Wot say we give 'im another? In a funny place?" the crew member slurred.

They all looked at Healy for his approval.

He shook his head. "One's enough, boys. Needle down. There you go."

They looked disappointed, but quickly perked up again when one of them had the bright idea to shave a Healy mark into the jungle-thick hair on Quint's back.

"This way, Egg. Unless you're looking for a haircut." Healy led me to a far table, where he ordered a beer for himself and a sugared lemon for me. The bandage over his eye had been replaced by a simple black patch.

"You got a patch," I said.

"Mmm. Hoping the eye heals and I'm not stuck with it permanently. Rather annoying to be such a cliché." He shrugged. "So! How are you liking Edgartown?"

"It's all right."

"I see you managed to spring your girlfriend. Kudos on that."

My cheeks flushed. "She's not my girlfriend."

"She is a friend, isn't she? And rather obviously a girl. So, logically . . ."

"How's your problem with the bank coming along?" Anything to change the subject from Millicent.

He lifted his hand, palm down, and waggled it from side to side. "Seem to have hit a wall at six million. They've put the touch on some other towns in the Fish Islands for the last four. But it might be a while. Although"—he looked back at the bar, where the shaving of Quint's back was in full swing—"if the boys keep drinking like this, they'll end up spending four million on credit, and that'll be that."

I nodded, not sure if I was supposed to act like that was a good thing or a bad thing. Or whether this meant I'd have any trouble getting the money we needed from Healy.

"So, um . . . I was wondering . . ."

He smiled. "Is this the part where I'm supposed to get my wallet out? How much do you need this time?"

"Eighty-six gold, three silver?"

"To spend on what?"

I got out the list and read it to him. "Six days' rations for five, forty long oars, one set of skeleton keys, four hundred yards of half-inch rope, ten square yards of sturdy cloth, fifteen spools of size twenty thread, and five darning needles."

He gave me a blank stare. Not one of his terrifying ones. More just confused.

"Darning needles. Of course. I should have guessed."

"Do you, uh, need to know why—"

"No, no! It's *far* more sporting to try to puzzle out just what on earth you're cooking up with those ingredients."

He reached into his pocket and came up with a handful of coins, which he plopped onto the table in front of me. "Should be about twenty there. Get you started. Hunt me down tomorrow after lunch—I'll likely have the rest by then."

"Thanks," I said, getting up from the table.

"But could you do me just one small favor?" he asked.

"Anything," I said.

"Come by sometime when you *don't* need money. Just to have a sit. It's good politics—gets me thinking you actually like me for me."

"I do! Quite a bit! Really!" My stomach went queasy at the idea that he might think I only cared about his money, and that I wasn't thrilled just to have him for an uncle.

"If the money's a problem, you don't have to—" I started to say.

Then he smiled, in a way that I knew meant he understood.

"Go on. Spin your web. I'll still be here when the spinning's done."

I EXITED INTO the sunlit morning and started up the street, gripping the coins tightly in my pocket so they wouldn't jingle and attract the attention of the soldiers who were still prowling the town, confiscating money to give to the pirates.

I was halfway to the corner when Millicent came around it at a run, followed by Guts, Kira, and Cyril.

"*Egg!*" Her face was pale and anguished. As she approached me, she threw a nervous glance back over her shoulder.

"What's the matter?"

"My mother's here."

CHAPTER 25

THE OTHER PEMBROKE

"PLEASE, EGG! YOU'RE the only one who can do it!!"

Millicent had me backed up against a wall. Literally. We were in a narrow alley about a hundred feet up the street from the jail.

She wasn't begging in a flirty way. She was too desperate for that. And I was glad for it—if she'd tried to be flirty, I would have seen right through it and gotten angry.

The desperation was more effective, anyway. I couldn't stand to see her in that kind of distress.

But I wasn't sure I had it in me to do what she was asking.

"Please!"

"Can't we just avoid her?"

"No! If she happens on us, she'll blow up the whole plan! And I can't have her *worrying* so—did you see the way she looked when she left the jail? It was heartbreaking!"

Millicent was right. The brief glimpse I'd gotten, from our hiding spot in the alley, of Edith Pembroke in tears as she walked out

235

of the jail after learning that the daughter she'd come to fetch had vanished . . . It was definitely heartbreaking.

But that was just going to make lying to her face all the more difficult.

"Can't Cyril do it?"

Cyril shook his head. "Sorry, old boy. Afraid she'll never believe Millicent went home without me."

"Then Guts or Kira—"

"She doesn't know them," said Millicent. "They won't have any credibility with her."

"Can I at least tell her the truth? That you're safe, but you can't see her right now, and she should just go—"

"*No!* That'd be disastrous! If she thinks you know where I am, she'll never let you out of her sight. And if she knows I'm in Edgartown, she'll never leave without me. We need her back at home, on Sunrise. That way, if the plan goes wrong, she might be able to help us."

It was the first time I'd heard Millicent admit that our plan might go wrong—and that she'd already been thinking about what would happen to us if it did.

"I thought you hated your mother," I said.

Millicent sighed. "I thought I did, too. But I was just being a brat. After I came back from the New Lands, we talked for hours. Days . . . And I understand now. The way he kept her in the dark, about everything. I can't even be angry at her for being blind to it, because she's so angry with herself. And it's over—she's leaving him. Soon as she can get a boat back to Rovia. Even though it means she'll lose everything she's got."

Millicent's eyes were glistening. "I'm all she has left—and I just keep running away from her. I don't want to hurt her any worse than I already have. Not if I can help it. But we've *got* to get her on the afternoon ship back to Sunrise."

Guts and Kira returned just then, out of breath. They'd followed Mrs. Pembroke after she left the jail.

"Where is she?" Millicent asked them.

"The hotel," said Kira. "She's trying to get a room."

Millicent turned back to me. "You've got to go quickly. If she settles in . . ."

"What am I supposed to say to her?"

"That you paid Percy to bail me out. But then you and I had a fight. And I went back to Sunrise."

"With me," Cyril added.

"With Cyril." Millicent took my hands in hers and squeezed them so tightly it hurt. "Can you do it, Egg? *Please?*"

I would have rather tried to save her from sharks.

"I'm not a good liar," I warned her.

She winced at that, which didn't exactly make me more confident. "You *can* be. You've got it in you. I know you do!"

There was no getting around it. I started toward the mouth of the alley.

"Don't forget to act surprised! Like you're just bumping into her by accident."

That stopped me short. It was one too many instructions. I was staring at my shoes, trying to remember them all, when I felt a hand on my back.

It was Cyril. He murmured advice in my ear.

"Here's the trick to lying, old boy: convince yourself that what you're saying is true."

"How do I do that?"

"Any way that works. If *you* believe Millicent and I are headed back to Sunrise, Edith will, too. Good luck."

He gave me another pat and then sent me into the street.

"We'll wait for you at Mr. Dalrymple's!" Kira called to me as I started for the hotel.

Millicent and Cyril are headed back to Sunrise...

No, they're not. They're right behind me.

This was going to be hard.

SHE WAS STANDING at the hotel reception desk, her back to me, a uniformed servant on either side of her. Her long blond locks were done up in a complicated whorl of braids that fell just below the collar of her emerald silk dress. From a distance, she looked like a queen.

But as I got closer, I could see all the straggles of unkempt hair that had worked their way loose from the braids, and her voice was scratchy and ragged as she argued with the hotel clerk.

"My family has been patronizing this hotel for over a decade—"

"Terribly sorry, madam, but the circumstances are extraordinary—"

"It's *one room*—"

"If I may speak freely"—the poor man's eyes darted about, making sure there weren't any Healy men within earshot—"we're under siege. By a crowd that, frankly, I think it best you avoid at all costs."

A burst of rough laughter went up from the nearby dining room. Judging by the sound of it, a few of the pirates had followed through on their plan to host a cockfighting tournament in there between meals.

Mrs. Pembroke's braids swished as she glanced in the direction of the dining room. But it wasn't nearly enough to scare her off.

"I am perfectly capable of taking care of myself—"

I was nearly on top of them now, and so shaky with nerves that I knew if I didn't blurt it out and get it over with, I'd lose my courage.

"*Mrs. Pembroke?!*" I tried to sound surprised.

Startled, she whipped her head around to face me. In the two months that had passed since I'd last seen her, she looked like she'd aged twenty years. Her face, which had always glowed with health, was gray and hollow.

As she stared at me, eyes wide as saucers, color began to return to her cheeks.

Then she started toward me, moving fast, her stare freezing me in place, and I was just getting my hands up to protect myself from the smacking when she pulled me to her chest in a fierce hug.

My whole body went stiff. It was the last thing I'd expected. I tried to wait it out, but she wouldn't let go. She just kept hugging me.

Then I felt her body start to tremble, and I realized she was crying. So I tried to hug her back as best I could, hoping it'd stop the tears.

"I'm so glad . . ." Her voice was as quivery as her body. "I thought he'd . . ."

She drew back, cupping my face in her hands and staring into my eyes.

"But you're all right! I'm *so* glad . . ." She was smiling through the tears.

I did my best to smile back at her.

"Where's my daughter?"

I shut my eyes and forced myself to remember how Millicent had looked when I first saw her in the cell. Cuddled up next to Cyril.

"She's gone."

That was how I'd decided I could make the lie feel true. Because Millicent really *was* gone. At least to me. For a while, and maybe forever.

Mrs. Pembroke's smile vanished. "What do you mean?"

"She went off. With *that Cyril*." The words came out in a hiss.

"Where did they go?" Mrs. Pembroke's eyes burned as hot as her daughter's ever did. I could feel her fingernails digging into the flesh on my upper arms.

"Back to Sunrise."

She searched my face. "Are you sure?!"

I nodded. "I paid someone. To get them out of jail. Thought she'd stay with me. But she didn't. She went home with him."

The anger in Mrs. Pembroke's eyes was giving way to worry.

"They weren't going to do anything stupid, were they?"

"No." Then I thought better of it, and backtracked. "I don't know."

"Something to do with the silver mine? And the Natives there?"

She knew her daughter well enough. I had to throw her off. But not too far off.

"Nothing, um, dangerous . . . There was a book."

"A book?"

"Yes. That Cyril said he had a book. And if he could get the men who run Sunrise to read it, they'd change their minds."

That seemed to satisfy her.

"When did they leave?"

"Yesterday."

"They left yesterday? For Sunrise? Millicent and Cyril?"

Her eyes were boring holes into mine. She looked like she wasn't quite convinced, and was searching me for something that would settle it one way or the other.

I shut my eyes again and saw Millicent's face, staring at me through the bars of the cell with that awful look of guilt.

I took a deep, shaky breath. "I wanted her to stay with me," I said. "But she wouldn't. She went with him."

Mrs. Pembroke's mouth turned down at the corners—but not from suspicion, or sadness, or even anger.

It was pity.

"I'm so sorry . . ." She hugged me again, and I realized I was a better liar than I'd thought. She believed the whole thing.

I just wished, for my own sake, that she'd only believed most of it.

I STAYED WITH HER for the hour or so it took the Sunrise ship to board its passengers. It seemed like the right thing to do. But it was a hard hour, because the whole time I felt like I was just one wrong word away from wrecking the whole thing.

And the fact that she kept trying to be kind made things even more awkward. Early on, when we were first walking down to the dock, she started to ask me to come back to Sunrise with her.

241

But before she'd even finished the sentence, she remembered that her husband had tried to kill me on three different occasions.

Then her face turned bright red, and she got all flustered and upset.

"I'm sorry—"

"It's okay," I said.

"It's *not* okay."

"Please don't cry. I know it's not your fault."

"But the way he . . . We're leaving, you know," she said. "Millicent and I. We'll never see him again."

I nodded. "Good."

"We're going across the sea. Back to Rovia." She slowed her pace for a moment, thinking. Then she put a hand on my shoulder.

"Perhaps you'd like to come with us?"

"I don't know about that." Which was the truth. Right then, I wasn't sure if going to Rovia with Millicent would be the greatest thing that had ever happened to me, or some kind of excruciating nightmare.

I didn't even know if Millicent would end up going there herself. For all I knew, she was planning to run away again.

Maybe she'd run away with Cyril.

Best not to think about that.

We were nearly to the dock now.

"Who's looking after you here?"

"I have an uncle."

"You do . . . ? I'd like to speak to him."

I didn't see how any good could come of that. "I don't think you should," I said. "He's Burn Healy."

She sucked in her breath in surprise. "Really?"

I nodded.

"I don't believe you."

Stick, the *Grift's* one-legged cook, was hobbling up the dock about thirty feet away. I called out to him.

"Stick! Who's my uncle?"

"Cap'n Healy!" he called back. "Wot of it?"

"Never mind! Thanks!"

"Oh, my," said Mrs. Pembroke. She was quiet for a while after that.

When we reached the pier where the Sunrise ship was docked, her servants set down her luggage trunk for us to sit on. Then she sent them off with money to buy us lunch at the bakery, insisting on paying for it even though I told her I could put it on my uncle's tab, and warned her that flashing coins in public would get them confiscated.

But the servants managed to get us some cheese rolls and jelly bread without getting shaken down by soldiers, and we ate the food in silence, sitting on the trunk.

She kept watching me out of the corner of her eye. It made me uncomfortable, and I wanted to ask her to cut it out. But I didn't want to be rude.

Once we finished eating, the silence got even more awkward. She kept fidgeting with her fingers—there weren't any rings on them, which was odd, because when I lived at Cloud Manor, she'd always worn a lot of them—and I could tell she was gearing up for some kind of speech.

"I want you to know," she finally began, "that Millicent cares for you very, very much."

But.

That was how she said it. With a fat, unspoken *but* at the end.

And after the *but* came *Cyril*.

"When you're at the age you are, feelings between boys and girls can be very—"

"We don't have to talk about this." *Or I will get very angry.*

"I just want you to know—"

"No, really. Please."

Silence.

"What are you planning to do now?"

Bust the slaves out of that mine.

I shrugged.

"Are you going back to Deadweather? Or staying here?"

I had no idea. I hadn't thought about it.

"Or will your uncle send you to school?"

I nodded, because I knew it was what she wanted to hear. "Yes. I'm going to school. Soon as possible."

"Just promise me one thing: that you won't become a pirate."

"I won't," I said.

"Promise?"

"Yes."

"That's good." She put a hand on my back and rubbed it gently.

"If you're ever tempted, just remember—your mother wouldn't want it."

I thought about that.

"Did you know my mother?"

"No . . ." She pulled me to her in a one-armed hug. She meant it to be comforting. But it just made me want to squirm.

"But I've known enough mothers to be sure of it. She'd . . ." Mrs. Pembroke paused. Then took a deep breath and sighed it out.

"She'd want you to be happy. And be able to just be a boy. And not have to grow up before you were ready. All these things that happened . . ."

It sounded like she was starting to cry, but I was barely listening.

I was too distracted by thinking about my mother. How was I supposed to know what she wanted for me? I didn't even know what she looked like.

"They shouldn't have happened to you," she said. "You're just a child. It wasn't right! It wasn't fair . . ."

She was really bawling now, gripping me like a drowning woman. I wriggled my arm loose so I could pat her on the back.

"It's okay," I said. "Lots of things aren't fair. You don't have to get all worked up about it."

SHE WOUND UP CRYING until the ship came and took her away. And she wouldn't stop apologizing to me, even though I kept telling her that she hadn't done anything wrong. I did my best to make her feel better, and tell her what she wanted to hear, but it didn't seem to do much good.

And it was distracting. I just wanted to be left alone so I could think, but by the time she got on the ship, I didn't have any energy left for it.

Once the ship got under way, I walked up the hill to Mr. Dalrymple's to rejoin the others. Millicent was beyond grateful—she tried to hug me, but I'd had more than enough hugging for one day. And I didn't want to talk about what had happened.

I felt twisted and drained, like a rag that had been used to sop up a mess and then wrung out too hard.

Mr. Dalrymple was in the middle of a lesson, which was a

relief, because it meant we could slip out without answering any questions about what we were up to. We went back into town and spent the rest of the afternoon gathering supplies, then making slings in the hotel room.

Guts couldn't sew with just one hand, so instead he went out, hunted down a guitar, and brought it back to the room to play for the rest of us while we worked. Ordinarily, listening to his guitar would have made me happy.

And the way Millicent was being with me—trying to make me laugh, and smiling her perfect smile at me, all while generally ignoring Cyril—should've put me in a good mood, too.

But it didn't. As the day went on, the wrung-out feeling got worse, and my friends' attempts to cheer me up just made me feel even more wrung out, until finally around dinnertime, I had to leave them and go off by myself.

I walked the streets for a while, wondering where this hole inside me had come from and what I needed to do to fill it up. I tried eating a meal, but I didn't have any appetite.

So I walked some more, until finally my feet took me to a table in a tavern where my uncle was holding court.

He smirked when he saw me coming.

"You're here for the rest of your money?"

"No," I said. "I'm just here to sit."

The smirk turned into a smile. He stood up.

"In that case," he said, "come with me. I know somewhere better."

CHAPTER 26

JENNY'S BOY

HEALY LED ME UP a winding series of streets into the hills above the fortress, where the houses were set back from the road and so far apart that it was more forest than town. If it hadn't been for the moonlight, we would've needed torches to light our way.

"So how's the plan coming?" he asked as we walked.

I felt a nervous flutter in my stomach. "What plan?" I said.

"Freeing the slaves on Sunrise," he said. "That's what it's all for, isn't it? The rope, and the darning needles—you're making slings? And the oars are for the getaway?"

"Who told you?"

"I guessed. I'm clever that way." He must have guessed what I was thinking just then, too, because he quickly added, "Don't worry. I'm not going to try to stop you."

I thought about that for a moment. "Why not?"

"Because I'm not your father. And I'm not your savior. It's not my job to protect you from your own foolishness."

"You think it's foolish?"

"Honestly? I think it'll be a bloodbath."

That got me worried enough that I laid out the whole plan for him, in as much detail as we'd worked out. Then I asked him if it still sounded like a bloodbath.

"Hard to say," he said. "You've obviously done quite a bit of thinking about how to avoid it. But one thing I've learned from experience—no plan ever goes off without a hitch. And I do wonder if you've considered whether the people you're saving truly deserve it."

"What do you mean?"

"I mean the Okalu. They're not exactly pure as Mandar linen."

"Nobody deserves to be a slave."

"No. But everybody keeps them."

"Not everybody."

"Yes, unfortunately. Everybody."

I started to tell him that Cartagers didn't. But then I remembered the story he'd told—and the scarred letter *C* that was burned into his back.

"It's illegal in Rovia—"

"And look how well that's working out."

"But that's just . . . Well, the Okalu definitely don't keep slaves."

"Don't they? When you were in the New Lands, did you happen to see any Okalu temples?"

"Yes."

"Really something, aren't they? Mountains, practically. Manmade. Think they built those with volunteers?"

I'd never thought about that before. And it made me angry.

"You don't know they used slaves! You weren't there!"

"No. But the other Natives were. Ever ask a Moku why they hate the Okalu so much? Or a Fingu, or a Flut? Ever wonder why, when the Cartagers first showed up a hundred years ago, the other tribes fell all over themselves to help a bunch of funny-eared, pale-faced foreigners destroy the Okalu Empire? Ever wonder how it became an empire in the first place?"

I wanted to scream. He sounded like Cyril. "So, what, then? The Okalu *deserve* to be slaves?!"

"Settle down. I already said they don't. I'm merely pointing out . . ." He sighed. "Like I seem to do every time we speak, not that it ever seems to sink in with you . . . that the world's a great deal more complicated than good and evil. And it's worth knowing that before you run off and risk your life to save people you've never even met—oh, blast."

We'd reached a crossroads. He stood in the middle of it, his head swiveling from one road to the next.

"You'd think I'd remember . . . Really should get up here more often."

"What are we looking for?"

"You'll see."

Finally, he chose a direction. I followed him.

"I'm not just doing it to save the Okalu," I said. "I'm doing it because it's Pembroke's silver mine."

"Ahhhh . . . Now, *there's* a motivation I can understand."

"I saw his wife today."

"Really? How'd *that* happen?"

"She came to town looking for her daughter. I had to convince her to go home."

"That must have been rather awkward."

"It really was."

We kept walking.

"She says she's leaving him. That she and Millicent will never see him again."

"Can't say I blame them."

"Do you think it'll hurt him? Pembroke?"

He thought about it. "Yes. I do. But probably not as much as most men. He's got his eyes on a bigger prize, Reggie does."

"Why do you call him Reggie?"

Instead of answering, he asked a question of his own. "*Li Homaya's* had plenty of time to retake Pella by now. Do you think he's managed it?"

"I don't know," I said. "What do you think?"

"Depends on the quality of the men he's got with him. Most of the Cartagers we fought in Pella were fat and slack. But if that was because he'd taken all his best men with him to fight me . . . might be he's got a shot."

A thought occurred to me. "If he succeeded—do you think Pembroke could be dead? Even now?"

"I think . . . that a man like Roger Pembroke has a real talent for self-preservation."

A high brick wall had appeared on our right a while back, running parallel to the road. Just ahead, a wide iron gate stood in the middle of the wall.

"Ah! Here we are." My uncle dug in his pocket for a key, which he used to open the gate.

Beyond it, a road led up a tree-lined drive to a red brick house almost big enough to be called a mansion. Healy produced a second key and let us in the front door.

Inside, we couldn't see a thing.

"Hang on . . . Must be a candelabra somewhere . . ."

He bumped and banged around in the dark for a while, until finally I heard the scrape of a match. My uncle's face reappeared in the light of the flame. He was holding a five-pronged candelabra, and once he got all its candles lit, he gave me a brief tour of the place.

It was a magnificent house, full of grand rooms that were all strangely empty. Other than a small table in the entryway where the candelabra had been, and a single overstuffed chair by the fireplace in the sitting room, there wasn't a stick of furniture in the whole place.

"I suppose I should buy some one of these days," Healy said. "Come, see the garden. It's what sold me on the place."

At the back of the house, a set of glass-paneled doors opened onto a back patio that ran the length of the building. Below it stretched a lawn several acres wide, dotted with low hedges and flower beds intersected by walking paths.

We sat down on the top of the steps and looked out over the moonlit gardens.

"It's beautiful," I told him.

"Even nicer when the sun's up and you can actually see it," he told me. "I pay a man to keep the flower beds in shape. For the two afternoons a year when it occurs to me to drop by. Bit of a waste, I guess. Still, after this mess with the bank, it's looking more and more like a wise investment."

"You really should get some furniture," I said.

"I know . . . I think I just hate shopping. Well, that and—I somehow got it in my head that one day I'd meet the right woman and settle down. And when I did, she'd inevitably want to redecorate, so the smart thing was to wait and let *her* buy the furniture.

"Trouble was, I never did find her. It's frightfully hard to meet women in my line of work. They tend to run screaming when I approach. Not sure why. Perhaps it's my breath."

Something popped into my head that made me smile. I debated whether or not to say it out loud.

"No . . ." I told him. "I think it's your face."

He laughed. "You've got a keen eye, son. How are you at shopping for furniture?"

"I don't know. I've never done it."

"You're lucky. It's death."

I decided it was as good a time as any for the question that I'd come to him to ask.

"What was my mother like?"

"I wondered when you might get around to asking that." He leaned back, propping himself up on his elbows as he surveyed his shadowy garden.

"My sister, Jenny . . . was warm as a fire . . . funny as a court jester . . . and tough as nails. What did your father tell you about her?"

"Not much of anything," I said. "He didn't like to talk about her."

"You know why, don't you?"

"I think because it made him sad."

"More than sad. He was heartbroken. He loved your mother to the point of madness. And when she died, he never got over it . . . They were a strange match, in a way. I'm not sure he ever got a single one of her jokes. But he didn't love her any less for that.

And I think for her part . . . his other qualities more than made up for the fact that he wasn't the keenest of wits."

"Like what?"

He thought for a while before he answered. "Trust. That was a big thing with her. She knew your father's heart was good, that he'd stay by her side no matter what. And he did. Even after she was gone, he stuck by her—and that crazy plantation of hers."

"What do you mean, 'hers'?" I'd always thought of it as my dad's plantation.

"That's what it was. The whole thing was her idea." He chuckled. "Trying to grow ugly fruit in the shadow of a volcano . . . At first, I thought it was another one of her jokes. But she was dead serious about it. She actually thought that with enough hard work and strength of will, she could build a legitimate business on an island full of pirates. And I suppose it worked, after a fashion."

"Not sure how well it's working out now," I said, thinking of Adonis and the mess I'd left him in back on Deadweather.

Then I had to change the subject in a hurry, before the guilty feeling could get its hooks in me. "She was funny?"

"Very."

"What kind of funny?"

It took him a while to answer. "The kind . . . that could make a boy who'd been taken from his parents . . . put into chains . . . and worked half to death . . . feel like life was still worth living. And there was hope for better days, if we just didn't quit."

He stopped to wipe his eyes. "Oh, —. Now I've gotten all sentimental."

"What did she look like?" I tried to picture her, but the image wouldn't come.

"Brown hair. Brown eyes. Sort of a . . . crooked mouth. Rather plain, to be honest. Granted, I'm her brother, so maybe there was some physical beauty there I just couldn't see. And she had more than her share of men fall at her feet. But not because of her looks. Strangers would walk past her without a second glance. It was only if they stopped to talk that they were in trouble. That's where the magic of her was.

"There was one boy in particular. A bit older than us, and dashing as all get out. The kind of boy that other boys wanted to be, and girls just wanted to be with. He could've had anyone, and he chose your mother. They were going to be married. But then he got into some ugly business, and she left him over it."

He laughed—a short, surprised sort of laugh.

"That's where you got it from! It was her."

"Got what?"

"That mule-headed sense of good and evil. Your mother was shot through with it. To a fault—she spent the last five years of her life trying to get me to quit piracy, and hating me for it when I wouldn't."

He grimaced. "That's how she was. All or nothing. She was my favorite person in the world—and it got so she wouldn't even speak to me. Then she had to go and die on me without even saying good-bye."

Healy looked up at the sky. "Well, Jenny, you finally got your wish."

It took a moment for me to realize what he meant.

"You're quitting piracy?"

"I have to. I've lost my touch. I mean, look at me—I threw over my crew, I let the Ripper slip free . . . I can't even keep you in line."

He shook his head. "It's time to hang it up. Keep that under your hat, though, will you? I haven't told anyone else yet. Got to get my money out of that infernal bank before I make it official, or they'll go on stiffing me to the end of my days."

"What'll you do? I mean, once you're retired?"

"I don't know." He looked over his shoulder at the big house behind us. "Buy furniture, I suppose. Or not. It's a slightly depressing thought—sitting around here all day, watching the flowers grow."

We were quiet for a while.

"You could always help free some slaves," I suggested, trying to make it sound like I was joking. Even though I wasn't.

He chuckled. "Sorry, boy. Pirate or not, I'm nobody's hero. I don't go around saving people out of some overdeveloped sense of right and wrong."

I thought about that.

"Then why did you save me?"

"I had to," he said. "You were Jenny's boy."

He smiled at me, and for a moment I thought he might change his mind.

"And I owed it to her," he added, "to give you the chance to make the same stupid mistakes she would've made."

I knew then there was no changing it.

He was only going to save me once. The rest was up to me.

SMOKE

WE SPENT THE NEXT two days getting ready—buying supplies, sewing slings, lashing bundles of long oars to the deck of Cyril's sloop—and even considering the dread and uncertainty over what we were about to do, it could have been a very pleasant two days. The work wasn't hard, I was with my friends, we had plenty to eat, the hotel beds were top-notch . . . and the swelling in my injured wrist finally subsided, to the point where it quit hurting and I could take the splint off.

Even so, I was miserable. And all because of the mess between me, Millicent, and Cyril. Whenever I saw her speak to him, I couldn't help pricking my ears up and going into a funk if it seemed like they were enjoying each other's company.

And every time Millicent and I got to talking, Cyril would puff out his chest and crow like a rooster to get her attention back.

Soon enough, she must have decided she was better off avoiding us both, and she started spending all her time with Kira.

They'd whisper to each other in low tones, and then one of them would sort of roll her eyes, and I was sure they were laughing at me. Or possibly Cyril. But probably me.

It was maddening, even more so because not only was it impossible to speak to Millicent alone, but I couldn't get Kira alone, either—and I desperately wanted to, so I could grill her about Millicent's intentions.

Guts thought we were all acting like idiots, and said so a couple of times an hour. Which just made the rest of us defensive and cranky.

Then we set sail for Sunrise, and it got even worse, because now we were all packed together with nowhere to escape, and Cyril started ordering everybody around like he was the captain. Which he kind of had to—if there weren't any cannonball holes that needed plugging, we were all pretty much useless on a ship except for Millicent—but that didn't make it any less annoying.

"I hate him," I whispered to Guts on the first night as we curled up to sleep between two stacks of oars near the bow. "If he lectures me one more time about reefing a sail . . ."

"Want to shoot him? I got a gun."

"You brought a gun?"

"Brought four of 'em," he said. "Dunno how to use no sling."

"You can't use four guns, either. Not at once."

"Got extras. Case anybody else wants one."

"No, thanks," I said. No matter what happened, I couldn't imagine myself shooting anybody.

Not even Cyril.

It rained on the second night, hard enough to chase us all belowdecks to sleep. It was crowded down in the cabin, and when

I woke up a little before dawn with someone's foot in my face and no patter of raindrops overhead, I decided to relocate to the deck.

I was just about to crawl into my usual spot between the stacks of oars when I heard a voice whisper behind me.

"Good morning."

It was Millicent. She was curled up like a cat in the cockpit.

"Hi."

She uncurled her limbs and sat up, leaving enough room for me to sit down next to her.

I didn't wait for an invitation. In fact, I moved so fast I tripped and almost fell into her lap.

"Careful—"

"Sorry—"

"It's all right."

She yawned and stretched her arms, then folded them tightly over her chest, hugging herself for warmth.

"Are you cold?"

She nodded. I put an arm around her, fully expecting that she'd brush me off. But instead, she burrowed in, so close that a few strands of her hair tickled my face.

Just being close to her made me feel peaceful and contented all the way down to my toes, like someone had covered me in a warm blanket.

It was all I ever wanted, really. Just to be close to her.

I hoped the others wouldn't wake up too soon and ruin it.

"It won't be long now," she said. "Should be there by tonight." She tilted her head and looked up at me. "Are you scared?"

"Not really." It was true enough. I'd had so many petrifying experiences over the past couple of months that what lay ahead didn't even feel particularly dangerous.

"Are you?" I asked her.

"I'm terrified," she said. It came as a surprise—I'd seen Millicent less than self-confident before, but I'd never actually heard her admit it.

"It'll be fine. If things go wrong, we'll just ditch the plan." If that happened, I'd need to get off Sunrise Island in a hurry—but I wasn't too worried about that, mostly because of my uncle. He'd hunted me down on the dock the day before we left and pressed a small sack of gold coins into my hand.

"You get in a fix, buy yourself passage back here," he said. "Anybody gives you trouble, let them know it'll end with me slitting their throat."

"Think that'll work?" I asked. "Even on Sunrise?"

He nodded. "Trust me. Your average Pembroke lackey isn't long on courage—especially with his master off mucking around in the New Lands."

But Millicent hadn't gotten any promises like that, and her eyebrows were scrunched together with worry as she considered what I said.

"I don't know. Even if things *don't* go wrong . . . once we free the slaves, it's not going to be very pleasant for me on Sunrise."

I hadn't thought about that. For Guts, Kira, and me, it didn't matter—it wasn't like we had plans to stay on Sunrise any longer than we had to. But it was Millicent's home. Or had been.

"Aren't you going to Rovia with your mother?" I asked her.

She sighed. "I suppose so. What about you? What'll you do when this is over?"

I thought about it. "Guts wants to go find the Fire King's treasure, back on Deadweather. And I promised my brother I'd go back there and help him with the plantation."

"Is that what you want? To go back to the plantation?"

"No."

"Then don't. You should do what you want."

"It doesn't always work like that," I told her.

"Why not?"

"Sometimes, the thing you want to do isn't possible."

"Nonsense," she said. "You just have to—"

"Your mother asked me to come to Rovia," I blurted out.

She turned her head to me in a sudden jerk, then looked away almost as fast.

"Do you want me to?" I asked her.

"Well, aren't *we* early risers?"

It was Cyril. He practically leaped the steps from the cabin to land in front of us.

Millicent quickly slipped out from under my arm.

"*Do* you?" I asked her again.

She stood up. "We should start breakfast—"

"Millicent—"

"I don't know!" Without looking back, she ducked past Cyril and headed down into the cabin.

He gave me an apologetic wince that was as fake as most of his smiles. "I'm sorry. Did I interrupt?"

I WOULD HAVE BROODED over Millicent all day if something much more unsettling hadn't appeared over the horizon that morning. The leftover haze from the previous night's rain had burned off to reveal the blue-gray peak of Mount Majestic up ahead. A few more hours, and we'd reach the coast of Sunrise.

"Look at that strange cloud," Kira said, squinting into the southern sky beyond the mountain.

The cloud was rising in the distance like a wind-bent tree, with a long puffy trunk that spread wide as it rose, expanding across the sky for miles. Its color was as odd as its shape—mostly white, but shot through with streaks of dark gray.

My stomach suddenly dropped as I realized what I was looking at.

"It's not a cloud," I said. "It's the volcano."

Deadweather was erupting.

Or had just erupted.

Or was about to erupt.

I didn't know which. I'd lived on the shoulder of that volcano, watching it belch and hiss and smoke off and on for thirteen years. But I'd never seen anything like that plume. This was a whole other thing.

For the rest of the day, I fretted over my brother and the field pirates, running through all the possible scenarios in my head.

They had time to leave. They didn't have time. They had time, but no boat. They didn't need to leave at all.

It only looks bad. It's as bad as it looks. It's worse than it looks. They all died instantly. They didn't die at all. They'd suffered unimaginable pain. They're not suffering at all. It's only a nuisance.

The house was destroyed. The house is buried. The house melted in a sea of lava. The house is fine.

They're all fine.

They're all dead.

Adonis will never forgive me. Adonis will be thrilled to see me again.

There's a mess, and I'm going to have to help clean it up.

As we got closer, the plume got bigger. Around late afternoon, just as Sunrise's coastal cliffs were coming into view, ominous brown threads began to appear in the gray-and-white column of smoke.

"So much fer findin' that treasure," Guts muttered.

"Shut up, Guts," Millicent said sharply. She and Kira had spent the whole afternoon telling me not to worry, that it was going to be all right, that maybe volcanoes poured oceans of smoke from time to time without erupting, and I shouldn't jump to any conclusions.

I would've told them not to fuss over me. But all the attention from Millicent was driving Cyril nuts, and I couldn't help milking it a little just to make him suffer. Eventually, he was reduced to what he must have thought was a heroic-looking stance, sitting bolt upright at the tiller and staring at the horizon while the rest of us ignored him.

He was doing such a good Lothar the Lone impression that I started to wonder if he'd read *Throne of the Ancients*, too.

I'd gone back to staring at the plume rising from Deadweather when I heard his voice, in what I'm sure he must have thought was a very serious and grave tone.

"There's more smoke," he said. "It's coming from Sunrise."

I rolled my eyes. *Nice try.*

"He's right," said Guts. "Look over there."

I turned from the distant volcano to the island looming ahead of us. The air around Mount Majestic was clear, but a hazy

262

smudge of black hung low in the sky along the eastern edge of Sunrise.

Something was burning in Blisstown.

HALF AN HOUR LATER, we were closing in on the shore off North Point. The volcano on Deadweather was already forgotten, even by me.

The black smoke rising from Sunrise had faded at first, then sprang up again in a different spot, thicker and darker than before. Both times, it was coming from somewhere in Blisstown, but the island's cliffs kept the harbor hidden from us, and it was impossible to tell exactly what was on fire.

As best we could figure, there were only three possible explanations for what we were seeing. Accident. Cartagers. Or Ripper Jones.

The fact that there were at least two different fires, burning in two different places, seemed to rule out an accident.

And we couldn't for the life of us figure out where a Cartager invasion might have come from. Their only military base within easy sail of Sunrise was on Pella Nonna. Even if Pembroke had lost it by now, my uncle had sunk all the Cartagers' warships.

That just left the Ripper. But nobody was discussing what that might mean, I think because we were all hoping it wasn't true. For all the time we'd spent cooking up a story about Ripper Jones invading the island, we'd never once discussed what we might do if it turned out to be true.

We'd just rounded North Point when the explosion came, louder than thunder. Almost instantly, an angry black cloud billowed up from the cliff above the far side of town.

It was the southern fortress—or what was left of it.

"Must've been the magazine," said Guts. "Somebody blew all their powder."

The northern fortress was coming into view atop the cliff on the near side of us. There was smoke rising from that, too, thin and ragged now—but the hole where one of the fortress walls used to be told us its magazine had been blown as well.

"We're getting out of here," said Cyril, heading for the cockpit.

"Gimme yer spyglass!" yelled Guts.

"What does it matter?"

"Give it!"

Cyril threw him the spyglass, then headed to the tiller. Guts took the spyglass's narrow end in his teeth and telescoped it out, then scanned the harbor.

"It's the Ripper," he said. "*Red Throat*'s tied up at that middle pier."

The sloop began to carve out a sharp turn, away from Blisstown. Kira and I were on the port side, and we both had to duck as the boom swept over our heads.

"Cyril, what are you doing?" Millicent called to him.

"Going back to Edgartown!"

"Wait—let's think about this!"

"There's nothing to think about!" he barked. "They're burning the island!"

"My *mother's* on that island!"

"So's my whole family!" Cyril yelled back at her, his voice rising to a yelp. "But what can we do?!"

"Well, let's talk about it!"

Cyril didn't answer. Instead, he straightened the boat's course, and North Point slid past on the port side as we pulled away from Sunrise.

Millicent turned to Guts. "What will Jones do to the townspeople? If they cooperate, will he leave them be?"

Guts shook his head. "Ripper don't leave nobody be. He'll kill 'em all."

"Cyril, *stop*!" Millicent cried.

"You don't know that!" Cyril yelled at Guts.

"Sure I do," said Guts. "I been on raids with the Ripper. He don't leave nobody alive."

"Not even the Okalu in the mine?" Kira asked.

"Not them neither."

"CYRIL!" Millicent was practically on top of him. "We've got to do something!"

Cyril clenched his teeth and sucked in a deep breath through his nose. "We *are* doing something. We're going back to Edgartown to get help."

Guts shook his head. "No time. Take six days, there and back. Raid like this don't last no six days."

Cyril stared at Guts. Then at Millicent.

But he didn't move to change course.

Guts pushed past me and disappeared into the cabin.

"We have to do something," Millicent hissed at Cyril. "My mother—"

"*I know! I know who's on that island!*" His face was bright red. He looked like he might cry. But he wasn't changing course.

"Maybe . . ." I started to say.

Everyone looked at me.

"Deadweather's only three hours," I said.

"Who will help us on Deadweather?" Kira asked.

I thought about it. The answer was nobody. If there were even people left on Deadweather by now, they were all busted-down field pirates. With no weapons.

Or they were real pirates—and more likely to help the Ripper than to fight him.

I shook my head. "Nobody."

"There's nothing we can do," Cyril said. "We've got to save ourselves."

Millicent sat down next to him. "Cyril . . ." she said in a quivery voice. "We can't just run away. Our family, our friends, everyone—"

"Millicent!" he hissed. "This is bigger than you! These men are killers! You're not invincible—"

"Turn the boat around, Cyril," she said, her voice rising.

"We can't help them—"

"*We have to!*" She took a deep breath, trying to steady herself. "This is the moment . . . of a lifetime. And if you don't do what you—"

"This isn't some melodrama!" he barked at her. "*This is real!*"

"TURN THE BOAT AROUND!" she screamed.

"DON'T BE A FOOL!"

"Better a fool than a coward," she spat.

Cyril's eyes blazed with fury. Millicent had crossed the line. There was no walking back from an insult like that.

Cyril looked to Kira and me, but our faces must have told him we were on Millicent's side. So he tried to laugh it off, but the laugh came out hollow and forced.

"Think you can taunt me into doing what you want? That only works on children, darling. Afraid you'll have to try another tack."

"How 'bout this one?"

We all turned toward Guts's voice. He was standing on the top cabin step. In his hand was a cocked pistol, aimed at Cyril's head.

"Turn the boat around, Feathers."

CHAPTER 28

NIGHTFALL

"IT'S TOO DARK to maneuver—we'll break up on the rocks. We should stop."

We were approaching the entrance to the secret cove where Pembroke's men docked his slave ship. It was the first time Cyril had opened his mouth in almost an hour.

"I'll fire up the lantern," said Millicent. "We'll hang it from the bow."

"What if someone sees it?!" His voice wavered on the edge of panic.

"If there was anyone around," she told him, "*they'd* have a lantern, too. And we'd have seen them already."

She put the lantern in her lap and was drawing a match when Cyril reached out a hand to stop her.

"Don't," he said, sounding defeated. "Not yet. We'll make do with the moonlight till we get inside."

Under any other circumstances, I would've enjoyed how

miserable he was. Instead, I was trying to think of ways to lift his spirits. We needed his help.

We needed all the help we could get.

And ever since Guts had pulled a gun on him, all the life had gone out of Cyril. He did as he was told, bringing the boat around to circle the cliffs of Sunrise until we reached the cove. But he rarely spoke, even though the rest of us had done nothing but talk for the past two hours, puzzling out how the pirate raid had happened and what we could do to help save its victims.

And that annoying smirk of his had disappeared for good.

When sunset had come, flooding the sky with eerie shades of burnt orange and blood red that would have been beautiful if they hadn't felt like the end of the world, I'd been glad for it, because it meant I wouldn't have to see the pasty look of fear on Cyril's face anymore.

Now I was wondering if we shouldn't have spent some time trying to buck him up instead of ignoring him. If we weren't careful, that fear could end up getting us all killed.

"Is there anything I can do?" I asked him. "To help you see better? I could move forward, or—"

"No. Just paddle slowly." The sail was down. Kira and I were on either side of the boat, oars in the water, while Cyril steered from the cockpit.

I watched the black mouth of the cove grow larger as we floated toward it, praying Millicent was right and there weren't any pirates lying in wait inside.

Nobody was supposed to know about this cove except Pembroke and his slavers, but we figured the pirates must have come this way before us. It was the only explanation that made sense.

Sunrise Island was sheer cliffs nearly all the way around—outside of Blisstown's harbor, there was no place to land a ship except the cove.

And if Ripper Jones had tried to sail the *Red Throat* straight into the harbor, he would have been pulverized by cannon fire from the two fortresses. The fact that they'd both been stormed and blown up meant that the pirates must have had the advantage of surprise.

Guts guessed that Jones had landed most of his men at the cove in secret and spread out from there in a surprise attack, leaving just a handful of crew on board to sail the *Red Throat* around to the harbor, where they could load their plunder right from the dock. Guts had seen him use a similar tactic before, against a Gualo missionary outpost down south.

And Guts figured the fact that we'd arrived just as the pirates were blowing up the fortress magazines meant it was still early in the raid—which was good, because no one would be dead yet except for any soldiers who'd tried to resist.

"Way he does it," Guts explained, "is smash anybody with fight in 'em. Then get all the folk together in one spot—church, or meetinghouse, or some such. Lock 'em up an' scare the *blun* out of 'em, so if there's plunder hidden, they'll tell him where. Then gather the plunder, load it all in . . . an' burn 'em alive on his way outta town."

"Does it always go that way?" Millicent asked in a whisper.

"Pretty *pudda* much, yeh."

"He doesn't ever show mercy? Let people live if they cooperate?"

"Nah. Tells 'em he will. But he never does." Guts twitched hard. "He likes it when they burn."

It was around then that Cyril had quit talking.

I couldn't blame him. For a while after that, I had a silent argument going in my head over whether I should tell the others that I thought he was right—that we should turn around and go back to Edgartown, because we were out of our minds to think we could do anything but get ourselves killed.

But the others weren't thinking that way.

"Once we figure out where they're keeping everyone," Millicent said, "we might be able to help them escape."

"Better off doin' what you can round the edges," Guts said. "Big enough island, they probably missed a few folk the first time through. Thing to do is make sure they get themselves hid. Far side of the mountain, say."

"That's where the mine is. They'll go there looking for silver."

"Somewhere else, then. Point is to stay hid till Ripper lifts anchor. Won't be more'n a day."

Millicent was still stuck on the idea of saving everybody. "If they put the townspeople in the meeting hall, there's not more than . . . two doors, I think. But if they're locked in the Peacock Inn, in the big dining room—we might have a chance. There's loads of exits."

As Guts and Millicent kept talking past each other, I watched Kira. She was silent, thinking hard, and I was half hoping she was thinking the same thing I was.

But she wasn't, not at all.

"We have to stick to the plan—and free the Okalu," she announced, loud and firm enough that Guts and Millicent instantly shut up and turned to her.

"We *have* to," Kira repeated.

Millicent got a pained look on her face. "Kira, my mother—"

"The Okalu are the only ones who can help your mother! If they are still alive, and we free them, and arm them with slings—they can stop the pirates."

I knew right then there was no point in suggesting we turn around. For their own reasons, neither of the girls would stand for it.

"The question is," Millicent asked Kira, "*would* the Okalu kill the pirates? Or would they help them kill the townspeople instead?"

Kira's eyes flashed, and she opened her mouth to fire back. But the words never came out, because the logic of what Millicent was saying began to sink in.

Guts twitched and gave a little snort. "Ripper won't take help from no Natives. Ain't even people in his book."

"Then the Okalu will fight," Kira said. "One way or another. And I can talk to them. They will listen to me."

She didn't sound too sure of herself.

"What if we free them," I asked, "and it just makes things worse?"

"Nah." Guts shook his head. "Can't get worse than it is."

I heard Cyril let out a heavy sigh. And once again, I couldn't blame him.

THERE WERE A THOUSAND THINGS to worry about, but as the sloop reached the mouth of the cove, they all fell away except one: *what was in the cove?*

The best we could hope for was the slave ship—so the Okalu

would have a way out, if we managed to free them and they somehow took care of the pirates without everyone getting slaughtered—and no people, because Ripper's pirates would kill us without a second thought, and although Pembroke's slavers were only our second-worst enemies at the moment, they were still enemies.

We got lucky. The slave ship was docked in the cove, tied up snug and taking up so much room that we could barely maneuver past it to tie up ourselves.

And there were no people—or at least, no people left alive. We quickly transferred the stacks of oars from Cyril's sloop onto the deck of the slaver. Then we gathered the bulging rucksacks full of slings, took the pistols and ammunition that Guts handed out, and followed Millicent under the low archway to the steps cut into the side of the cliff.

She stopped short for a moment at the base of the steps. The passageway was so narrow that I couldn't see around the others to learn what had stopped her until it was time to step past it myself.

It was the body of a man, curled up like he was asleep.

But he wasn't asleep.

I climbed the narrow, wet steps as fast as I could, trying not to think about what I'd seen. The deadly drop to the water just inches to my right made me dizzy enough as it was.

I'd just reached the top and was bent over, catching my breath, when I felt a tap on my shoulder.

It was Guts. "See his face?" he asked.

"Whose?"

"The body."

I shook my head no. "I didn't look."

"That *porsamora* from the slave boat. One whose head I kicked in."

Birch. The worst of Pembroke's slavers. The man who'd tortured the map out of me in Pella Nonna.

I might've expected to feel glad, or at least relieved, that a man that evil was dead. But I didn't. I just felt hollow.

And I didn't have time to wonder why, because there were voices in the trees, and they were moving toward us.

THE MINE

WE ALL FROZE in place. Almost as soon as we heard them, the voices stopped. There was a rustle of branches, then nothing.

I heard the *click* of a pistol cocking. Guts.

Then there was a muffled whine that didn't sound quite human, followed by a short struggle that ended in the high-pitched yelp of a lapdog.

My shoulders sagged with relief. Ripper's men didn't have lapdogs.

"Who's there?" Millicent said in a loud whisper as she stepped through the gloom toward the sound. "Come out. We won't hurt you."

"Is that Millicent?" It was a woman's voice, stuffy and rich. "Oh, my dear!"

"Mrs. Wallis?"

I knew the Wallises a little from the weeks I'd spent on Sunrise. They lived in the mansion down the hill from Cloud Manor and had three small children, all of them as yippy as Mrs. Wallis's lapdog.

The children were with her now, terror-struck into silence and each holding the hand of three equally terrified housemaids.

"Where you coming from, child?" Mrs. Wallis quailed.

"Edgartown," said Millicent. "We only just landed."

"Is the . . . landing near here?" She said *landing* in a hushed, embarrassed kind of way, like Pembroke's secret cove wasn't the sort of thing you mentioned in polite company. It made me wonder if all his slaving really was a secret to the people on Sunrise, or if it was just something they didn't talk about.

"It's right over there," said Cyril.

"Why, Cyril Whitmore! Look at you! You're just landing now? Together? And these others . . . ?" She looked at Guts, Kira, and me like she didn't know whether to be glad or frightened of us.

"Never mind us," said Guts. "Where's them Ripper men?"

Her eyelids fluttered at the name. "Everywhere! They went house to house—if the children and I hadn't been up the hill on a picnic, they would've rounded us up, too. My other servants couldn't escape, poor things."

"What happened to them?"

"Taken to Blisstown with the others. Once they sacked Timberfield"—for reasons I'd never understood, people on Sunrise liked to give their houses names—"and all the other homes on the hillside, they marched everyone to town. The children and I hid in the woods until dark. Then set out to try to find the . . . other way out."

"Have you seen my mother?" Millicent asked.

"No, dearie. But . . ."

"But what?"

Mrs. Wallis squeezed her lips together and fanned her face with her hand, even though it wasn't warm out.

"What happened?" Millicent said again.

One of the maids spoke up. "Cloud Manor got the sack, too, miss. We saw it."

"Is my mother alive?"

The maid nodded. "Should be. They herded all the Cloud Manor folk into a cart, sent it to town."

Mrs. Wallis put her stubby hand on Millicent's arm. "Don't you worry, dearie. If she cooperates, they'll leave her be."

"That's what the pirates said," a second maid added. "Yelled it out as they went. Said if we hid, they'd hunt us like dogs. But if we went along all nice-like, we'd be fine."

"We thought about coming out of the woods. Going along with them. Do you think we made a mistake?" Mrs. Wallis asked.

"No," said Millicent, shaking her head. "You didn't."

"And we're going to get you off this island," Cyril announced.

We all turned to stare at him. He nodded gravely.

"It's my duty as a gentleman," he said. "Women and children have to be protected. And there's just room enough for all of us on the sloop."

He'd suddenly found his courage. Funny how it involved turning around and leaving.

"Let's go," he said, turning toward the stairs.

"They can find the boat themselves," said Millicent.

He turned back toward her. "What?"

"We're going to the silver mine."

Cyril stared at her in disbelief. "Millicent, we've got to take them back to Edgartown! We've got to protect these people!"

"They'll be safe as long as they stay hidden. It's everyone else who needs protecting."

She and Cyril locked eyes for a long moment.

"I'm going to do my duty," he said.

"So are we," she replied. "Give us those slings."

He handed her his rucksack. Then he turned his back on her, beckoning to Mrs. Wallis and the others.

"This way, please. I'll keep you safe."

Mrs. Wallis stared at Millicent, bewildered. "Aren't you coming, dearie?"

"Don't worry, Mrs. Wallis," Millicent said. "You won't be in danger as long as you're with Cyril."

The way she said it, even dopey Mrs. Wallis must've known it wasn't a reassurance, but an insult.

Millicent started up the hill. Guts, Kira, and I followed her.

"Where are they going?" I heard Mrs. Wallis ask.

"It's no matter," Cyril replied as his voice faded away. "Here, let me carry your dog . . ."

THERE WASN'T ENOUGH MOONLIGHT to see properly in the woods, so we took to the road. We figured if anybody else was on it, they'd be carrying lanterns or torches, so we'd see them long before they'd see us.

After about a quarter mile, the road turned away from the coast, heading sharply uphill in a series of switchbacks. Millicent set the pace, moving fast enough that I quickly broke a sweat even in the cool night air.

Occasionally, we passed an overlook with a view all the way to Blisstown. There were a few lights twinkling there, and a fire still burned in one of the ruined fortresses. A couple of times, we heard what sounded like the distant echoes of gunshots.

Other than that, it was all too quiet.

None of us talked. Not so much because we were afraid to make noise, but because there wasn't anything left to talk about. We'd planned what we were going to do as best we could, but none of us, not even Millicent, had the slightest idea what to expect when we reached the mine.

Underneath the silence, my brain was churning. I was pretty sure that what had just happened between Cyril and Millicent had busted up any chance of them ever being together, or even staying friends. But I didn't dwell on that for long. There were too many other things to worry about: the mine and the town and the pirates and the Natives and the guns and the keys—*Where are the skeleton keys? Still in the pack? Check to be sure*—and the ship and the oars and Birch's body on the steps and Mrs. Wallis with the dog and the children with the maids and Mrs. Pembroke with the pirates and my brother with the volcano and—*What about my sister? Haven't even thought about her since . . . What if the Moku sacrificed her? What if they're about to? Who's going to save her? I'm a terrible brother. Haven't even lifted a finger to try to . . . WHY AM I THINKING ABOUT THIS NOW? Check the keys again. What if they fell out of the pack? No, there they are*—and the explosions in the fortresses and the townspeople all doomed to die if we didn't do something and the pirates and their plunder and the silver . . .

The silver.

"The pirates are going to be angry," I told the others.

"Why?"

"There's almost no silver on the island."

"How do you know?"

"I heard the Governor-General tell Healy. Back in Edgartown. They were worried about Cartagers attacking Sunrise if the invasion of Pella failed, so they shipped all the silver out early. A couple of weeks ago."

"Don't matter," said Guts. "Silver or not, raid's gonna end the same way."

"*Shh*," said Millicent, raising a hand in warning. Something was coming into view up ahead.

It was a guardhouse, standing in front of a tall, open gate. Nailed to the guardhouse wall was a large sign:

SUNRISE MINING COMPANY
AUTHORIZED PERSONNEL ONLY
TRESPASSERS WILL BE JAILED

There were no guards to stop us, so we continued up the steep road. We were close to the timberline now—the forest on either side of the road was growing thin, and the wind had picked up.

Then the road flattened out onto a wide plateau, and what looked like a whole town suddenly opened up in front of us. There were buildings of all sizes, from squat little huts to long barracks-type structures, to a few giant sheds so big they could've held Cartager men-of-war, masts and all. Great dark hulks of strange machinery were all over the place, hitched to wagons or hanging from scaffolds or just lying on the ground.

And looming behind everything were massive piles of gravel and broken rock that dwarfed even the biggest buildings.

A quarter mile ahead, the plateau ended in a wall of rock that shot up toward the summit of Mount Majestic. At the base of the rock was a gaping black hole thirty feet high and twice as wide.

The only thing missing was people. Other than the remains of a fire that smoldered beneath an iron vat the size of a house, there was no sign of life anywhere.

We walked the whole length of the place, almost as far as the mine entrance, before any of us got up the courage to call out.

"Hello?" Millicent's voice was tentative at first.

She tried again, loud enough to raise an echo. "Hello?"

"HELLO?"

The echoes faded into the night.

Then Kira tried.

"*Se ka?*"

No answer.

"*SE KA?! MASULA TE SE KA?*"

She yelled it twice more. The echo from the last one was dying when we heard a voice, thin and distant.

"*Ka te?*"

"*MATA TANO!*" Kira yelled her reply as we looked around for the source of the voice.

"*Ka te!*"

It was somewhere behind us, back in the direction we'd come from. Kira began to run toward it, calling out in Okalu.

The voice kept answering her, growing louder as we approached.

Eventually, we found its source—one of the massive, warship-sized sheds near the front of the complex, where the road first emerged from the trees.

By the time we reached it, Kira was in a shouted conversation with the Okalu locked inside.

"They are all in here," she said. "We just have to open the door."

It was easier said than done. The only entrance was through a twenty-foot-tall double door that was barred shut by a crosspiece of wood as big as a tree. It must have taken a dozen men to lift it into place.

The four of us started trying to push it up and out of its runner. It was hopeless. Even with all of us pushing at once, it didn't budge an inch.

There was no skeleton key for this kind of thing.

Millicent ran around the entire length of the building, looking for another way in. She came back, panting, to tell us there wasn't one.

And the only windows were all the way up near the roof.

Kira was still calling back and forth in an ongoing conversation with one of the Okalu. I could hear the faint buzz of dozens of voices inside.

"Do they have any ideas?" I asked.

"They say there are explosives. In one of the buildings near the mine entrance."

"Gonna blow the door?" Guts sounded dubious. I was, too.

"Not the door. The wall. The walls are thinner." To prove her point, Kira knocked on one of the doors, then on the wall beside it. The sound from the knock on the wall was higher pitched and more hollow.

I didn't like the idea of messing with explosives that none of us knew how to use. But we didn't seem to have a choice. Once Kira got more specific directions from the Okalu, we ran back toward the mine entrance and started searching the buildings.

None of them were locked—I was starting to wonder why we'd bothered with the skeleton keys—but that didn't make them easy to search, because most didn't have any windows to let in the moonlight. Even in the ones that did, we could barely see anything. Millicent and Kira left Guts and me to do our best while they tried to cobble together torches from the smoldering embers under the giant iron vat.

That seemed particularly dangerous.

"Don't you think," I called to Guts, who'd disappeared into one of the smaller buildings and was clomping around inside it, "that it's a bit stupid to go searching for explosives with a burning torch in your hand?"

"OW!" There was a loud banging noise.

"What are you doing in there?"

He emerged from the building, limping and rubbing his knee. "Nuts. Try another."

I tried two more buildings on my own, blundering around them in the dark and feeling useless. We were looking for barrels of black powder, but I wasn't clear on what size the barrels were, let alone how to identify them by feel. I was walking out of the second building when I heard Guts's yell.

"GOT IT!"

I found him at the door of a small shed, holding an ax in his good hand.

"Get the girls! Tons of these!"

"That's not powder—"

"Ain't gonna use powder! Gonna chop a hole in the wall!"

That made sense. Much more sense than explosives.

"You get the girls," I told him. "I'll start chopping."

I took the ax from him and headed for the shed while Guts ran toward the vat, yelling for Millicent and Kira.

THE WALL WAS THICKER than it looked. By the time Guts and the girls showed up, all them carrying axes, I'd gotten in half a dozen good whacks without much to show for it except a lot of splinters.

"Hit it along the grain!" Millicent told me.

"What do you think I'm doing?"

"Let me try."

I stepped aside to let Millicent take a whack at the splintered gash I'd been working on. Kira was around the corner of the building, looking for a weaker spot that might be easier to chop through, when I heard her call out.

"Guts! Come here!"

"Ugh! Blast!" Millicent had gotten her ax stuck in the wall.

"Here, let me—"

"No, I've—ugh! Fine." She stepped back, giving me room to try to tug her ax out.

"Run down and see!" I heard Kira say to Guts, but I didn't think anything of it. I was too busy trying to yank Millicent's ax out of the wall.

Then a moment later, I heard Guts call out to Kira, but I didn't catch the words. I'd just dislodged Millicent's ax and was handing it back to her when Kira appeared at my elbow, her voice urgent and tight.

"There are torches on the road! Headed up the hill!"

CHAPTER 30

UNSHACKLED

"HOW MANY WERE THERE?" I yelled at Guts as he came around the corner of the shed.

"*Mado laki! Exto padela!*" Kira was yelling through the wall at the Okalu.

"How many what?"

"Torches!"

"Step back! You want your head chopped off?" Millicent had her ax cocked to take another swing at the wall.

"*Kamenaso!*"

"*Casu pata aliza!*" The Okalu were yelling back at Kira.

Shunk! Millicent made contact.

"Twenty?" Guts was twitching hard.

"*Twenty torches?!* How many men?"

"Dunno! Could be more. Lots more."

"*Bataka lamai!*"

My heart was pounding. Twenty torches on the road, heading toward us.

The Ripper's men. It had to be.

Shunk! Millicent struck another blow. The wall was finally starting to split down the grain of the wood.

"Quit gaping and swing your ax!" she yelled at me as she wrestled hers out of the wall.

When Millicent stepped back, I buried my ax head into the top of the crack she'd started—and a four-foot-long fracture opened up with a loud, satisfying *crrrrrk*.

I could hear excited voices on the other side as the Okalu realized we'd breached the wall.

Kira was in a hurried back-and-forth with one of them. I couldn't understand a word of what they were saying.

"Now cut sideways," Millicent told me. "At the top and bottom. So we can—" She flapped her hand back and forth, and I got the idea. If we hacked crosswise into the wall at both ends of the fracture, we might be able to peel open a passage wide enough to let the Okalu out.

I moved a few feet to one side and swung my ax in a sidearm motion at the top of the cut. Splinters flew.

I was yanking my ax out of the wall when Millicent swung her own ax down low, just missing my lower leg.

"Watch it!" I yelled at her.

Kira emptied the slings from a pair of rucksacks. "Get rocks!" she told Guts, handing him the empty sacks. He ran off toward one of the giant mounds of broken rock to collect ammunition.

Shunk!

"Blast!" Millicent's ax was stuck in the wall again.

"Watch your head!" I swung my own ax at the higher spot, a few feet above where Millicent was crouched, trying to tug her ax loose.

"Egg! You trying to kill me?!"

I ignored her. "How close were the torches?" I asked Kira.

"I don't know."

"Well, do we have seconds? Or minutes?" I pulled my ax free and swung it again.

"Not enough of either." She went back to her conversation with the unseen Okalu, her hands busy untangling the pile of slings.

Millicent and I kept swinging the axes as fast as we could, somehow managing not to cut each other in half. The wall shuddered with every swing.

Guts had just returned with two sacks of rocks when one of Millicent's swings produced another loud *crrrrrk,* and for an instant, the fracture opened wide enough that I caught a glimpse of movement on the other side.

"Push it in!" said Millicent. We dropped our axes and shoved against the opening.

A swarm of hands and arms appeared, pulling from within, and I got a whiff of stink like the kind belowdecks on a ship after too many days at sea.

And the arms pulling against the wood were so skinny—*so skinny*—but they were making a fierce effort, and suddenly we lurched forward as the wood splintered away. Millicent and I nearly fell into the shed, and when I straightened up, I saw the first Okalu's face.

He was a ghost—all bone and grime-streaked skin and dark hollows in his cheeks and eyes. His hair was all gone except for a few thin wisps, and the loincloth he wore was as dark with soot as the rest of him.

There was no light in the shed, and I could just barely make out the other men clustered behind him, all as rail-thin as he was. Farther back in the darkness, I could hear the sound of many more—a clanking, impatient mass of men.

Why are they clanking?

"Muto! Muto!" Kira beckoned for the first Okalu to step though the hole that we'd opened up, a couple of feet off the ground and more than wide enough for his skeleton's body.

He hesitated, and the hollow men behind him craned their necks, wondering like we were why he wasn't coming out.

He gritted his teeth and tried to hop over the splintered wood, but he tripped and fell, splaying out onto the ground with a rattling clank—and I realized what all the clanking was coming from, and why he'd had so much trouble stepping over the low section of wall.

His legs were manacled together at the ankles with an iron chain.

"Where are the keys?" Kira asked me.

I looked around for the rucksack I'd left on the ground when I started swinging the ax. After a panicky moment, I spied it a few feet away and quickly fetched the ring of skeleton keys from it.

By the time I did, Kira had helped the first Okalu to his feet, five more were standing beside him, and Guts and Millicent were on either side of the hole in the wall, helping to support the next man so he could get his manacled legs up and over the splintered wood.

I knelt down at the first Okalu's feet and inspected the manacles. Each collar had a small keyhole near the back, just above the tab where the chain attached.

"Hurry, Egg!"

I tried a key. It was too big for the keyhole.

The sound of clanking iron was building on all sides. Helped by Millicent and Guts, the Okalu were filing out of the shed in a steady stream. They crowded around me, blocking out the moonlight.

"Kira, tell them to back away! I can't see what I'm doing."

She did. I could see again, just barely. I went back to the ring and searched the keys until I found a small one.

It was still too big for the lock.

"Hurry!" Kira said again. "The pirates are coming!"

I could hear her handing rocks and slings to the men as they traded urgent words in Okalu over the sound of the clanking chains. But with those chains on their legs, the slings were next to useless, because the men couldn't step forward and put their weight behind the throws.

I fumbled with the ring, looking for the one key—I *hoped* there was one—small enough to fit.

"Hurry!" The fear was rising in Kira' voice.

I dropped the ring.

When I picked it up, my hands found the small key almost immediately. I tried it.

Too big.

290

That's the last one. I could feel panic tightening my throat.

"*Hurry!*"

Try the other one again.

I searched out the other small key, the one I'd tried before.

No. This was different. A squared edge, not a rounded one.

I must have accidentally stuck in the same key twice.

I tried the small square one. It slid into the lock.

But it wouldn't turn.

I jiggled it, back and forth, in and out—

Click.

The first manacle opened on its hinge and fell away.

A few more seconds, and I got the second one off. *Click.*

Clank. The manacle fell off, and the first man was free.

"*Gadda.*" I didn't need to know Okalu to understand he was thanking me. Before I could look up, his bone-thin legs stepped away, and another pair of legs clanked into place in front of me.

"*Hurry,* Egg!" It was Millicent. She didn't need to tell me. I knew.

Click . . .

Click . . .

Clank.

The second set of manacles fell away. Two more skinny legs stepped up, clanking as they came.

So thin . . . Their legs are so thin . . .

Click . . . Click . . . Clank. As I pushed away the discarded manacles, another Okalu stepped up.

Kira was trying to organize the men. Their voices mixed with hers, increasingly loud and urgent.

Click . . . Click . . . Clank.

Click . . . Click . . . Clank.

"We need more stones!" It was Millicent's voice.

The men were running off as soon as I unshackled them. I tried to glance up to see where they were going, but all I could make out were more legs.

Click . . . Click . . . Clank.

Click . . . Click . . . Clank.

They were crowding me again. I didn't have light to see.

"Back away, please!"

They didn't back away.

"KIRA!"

She was gone. I didn't know where.

"Guts! Millicent!"

They were gone, too. *Where did they go?* I felt for the next set of legs. They were turned the wrong way, and I couldn't find the keyhole.

"BACK AWAY! I CAN'T SEE!"

For an agonizing moment, nothing happened.

Then an Okalu voice called out, *"Kotay balu na!"*

Others took up the call. *"Kotay balu na!"*

The circle widened. I could see again, just barely.

Click . . . Click . . . Clank.

Click . . . Click . . . Clank.

"Kira? Guts? MILLICENT?"

Where did they go?

Click . . . Click . . . Clank.

Click . . . Click . . . Clank.

Click . . . Click . . . Clank. The empty manacles were piling up.

I had to scurry backward on all fours to give myself more room to discard them.

The sea of clanking legs moved with me.

Click . . . Click . . . Clank.

Click . . . Click—

A gunshot rang out.

Then a dozen of them, going off like firecrackers.

Voices were yelling—Rovian voices, shouting in anger and surprise—and they were close. *Much* too close.

Now the Okalu were yelling. The clanking around me grew so loud it nearly washed out the gunfire that kept crackling in my ears. The men around me were desperate to get their chains off before the pirates fell on them.

Don't panic. Keep working.

Click . . . Click . . . Clank.

There was no lull between the gunshots now—they just kept popping off, one after the other.

It takes time to reload a gun. There had to be a lot of them for that kind of barrage.

Keep working.

Click . . . Click . . . Clank.

Click . . . Click . . . Clank.

There were screams and grunts and curses and more gunshots and the awful sounds of men fighting to the death with their hands.

They sounded like they were on top of me. I couldn't look up. There were too many chains to unlock.

Click . . . Click . . . Clank.

My hands were shaking.

Click . . . Click . . . Clank.

I couldn't see again.

"BACK OFF!"

"Kotay balu na! Kotay balu na!"

Click . . . Click . . . Clank.

Click . . . Click . . . Clank.

More gunshots. More screams.

"Millicent? Guts? Kira?"

No answer. I risked a quick glance up, in the direction of the road. All I could see were skinny legs and grimy loincloths.

I yelled as I worked. "Speak Rovian? Anyone? Rovian?"

No answer.

Just do your job.

Click . . . Click . . . Clank.

Click . . . Click . . . Clank.

Click . . . Click . . . Clank.

More gunshots. Someone cried out in agony. Men were running, calling to each other in Okalu.

"What's happening?"

No answer.

Click . . . Click . . . Clank.

"Who speaks Rovian?"

Click . . . Click . . . Clank.

"Anybody speak Rovian?"

Click . . . Click . . . Clank.

"I speak."

I looked up. I wasn't sure which of the dozens of men surrounding me spoke Rovian.

"What's *happening*?" I asked.

"Fast! You go fast!"

I lowered my head and kept working.

Click . . . Click . . . Clank.

Click . . . Click . . . Clank.

FINALLY—*HOW LONG had it been? Minutes? Hours?*—I unshackled a man, and when he ran off, no one stepped up to take his place.

I raised my head and looked around. I'd started out maybe five feet from the hole in the shed. Now I was fifty feet from it, with nothing between me and the shed but a dark, ugly field of discarded manacles.

I was staring at that field of manacles, dumbstruck, too numb to wonder why the sounds of battle had died away, when I heard a voice.

"Egg?"

In the predawn gloom, I could see a crowd moving toward me. Skeletons, walking ghosts.

Except for the three in the middle. My friends.

There was no urgency to the way they moved. Just exhaustion.

"What happened?" I asked.

"We won," said Kira.

CHAPTER 31

THE LAST PLAN

"WHERE ARE STAIRS to ship?" The Okalu leader's name was Iko, and he was getting impatient.

"It's not important now," said Millicent, for at least the third time. "The rest of the pirates are—"

"We go to ship first."

"The pirates are in the town!" She was losing her temper.

Iko stopped walking and held up his hand. The few hundred hollow-eyed Okalu on the road behind him—many of them loaded down with jugs of water and sacks of half-spoiled food from the mine's storehouses—came to a stop as well. So did the rest of us.

Iko placed his hands on his hips and stared down at Millicent. Even with his body half wasted from starvation, he was an imposing figure.

"First we load ship," he said. "Food and water. Then we go to town."

"You can leave the supplies by the road and get them later! We have to hurry—"

"*No.* We go to ship first."

Millicent clenched her teeth. "Kira—"

Kira traded words in Okalu with Iko. I tried to read their tone of voice, but neither one was giving much away.

Finally, Kira turned back to Millicent.

"They have to see the ship. To make sure it is there, with the oars, like we said."

"Then they'll help us? Like they promised?"

Kira sighed.

"There are fifty pirates left!" Millicent's voice shook. Dawn was breaking and we hadn't slept or eaten since the day before.

"Maybe not fifty," Guts muttered. Millicent and Kira both looked at him.

"Maybe just forty," he said.

"Kira, they *have* to promise us they'll help!" She turned to Iko. "You *have* to!"

He stared at her, unblinking. "We go to ship," he said. "Or we do not help." He waved his hand toward the side of the road. We were close enough to the cliff that I could see ocean through the trees.

"Is close. You show us."

Kira spoke to Iko again in Okalu.

"I'm not taking them to the ship if they're not going to help us!" Millicent insisted.

Iko replied to Kira. She nodded.

"They will help," she told Millicent.

"I need a promise!"

Iko's mouth split into a grin. "Okay, girl. Promise. Now take us to ship."

BY THE TIME we reached the stairs, sunrise had turned the sky the same eerie reddish orange we'd seen at sunset. The stairs were so well hidden that without Millicent showing the way, I could've walked past the spot a dozen times without seeing it, and I'd been there twice before.

Once she showed them the entrance, Iko gestured to his men. The ones closest to him began to file down the steps—not just the men who were carrying food and water, but all of them.

"Wait—you're just dropping off the food!"

"They see the ship," said Iko.

"They don't *all* need to see it! STOP!"

She pushed in front of them, blocking the way to the stairs.

"Millicent . . . ," Kira began.

"They lied, didn't they?" Millicent's eyes blazed as she glared at Iko. "You *lied* to me!"

His lip curled in a snarl. "What are lies, to the children of slave men?"

"They fought bravely—" Kira began.

"The fight's not over! *We saved them!*" Millicent had one of Guts's pistols in her hand.

She started to raise it.

Everyone moved at once. There was a brief, ugly scuffle, during which both Millicent and a couple of Okalu nearly went over the edge of the cliff. But when it was over, Kira and I were holding Millicent back while the Okalu continued to file down the stairs.

She was in tears, and curses were coming out of her mouth with such a vengeance that even Guts looked a little shocked.

Iko stood between us and the Okalu, staring at Millicent as she raged helplessly at him.

Eventually, she wore herself out and sank to the ground in defeat. I sat down next to her and rubbed her back, because I didn't know what else to do.

The last of the Okalu filed past Iko and disappeared down the steps. Before he turned to follow them, he asked Kira a question.

Her brow furrowed with doubt. She looked down at Millicent and me. Then at Guts.

Guts understood what was going through her head. "Gonna go with 'em?"

Millicent looked up. Her red-rimmed eyes met Kira's.

Kira turned to Iko and shook her head.

"*Ka folay,*" she said.

He nodded. "*Ka folay.*" Then he was gone, leaving the four of us alone on the cliff top.

THE OKALU WEREN'T what you'd call experienced sailors. We sat on a rock at the edge of the cliff, eating leftover biscuits we'd brought from Edgartown and watching the slave ship blunder into every rock outcropping in sight as forty men who'd probably never held an oar in their lives tried to maneuver out of the cove and into the open sea.

I wasn't too worried for them. They'd get the hang of it soon enough. And as long as they could keep the ship pointed west, the New Lands were too big to miss.

The job we'd been left with was a lot harder.

How were the four of us going to stop Ripper's fifty pirates from murdering everyone on the island?

I tried to think, but my brain wasn't good for much. It had been too long since I'd slept.

"It's not supposed to happen this way," Millicent muttered. "You're not supposed to save two hundred people's lives and then just have them run off on you. It's not fair! If this was a book, I'd throw it across the room."

A book.

How *would* they do it in a book?

"*Basingstroke!*"

Millicent looked at me. "What about it?"

"Remember when James was being chased by that squad of cavalry?" I asked her. "And he tricked them into plunging off a cliff? Well, we've got a cliff."

"The pirates aren't a cavalry," she said, sounding irritated. "And there's too many of them. You might be able to trick two people into falling off a cliff. You can't trick fifty."

"Could be just forty," said Guts.

"My point stands," said Millicent, with a roll of her eyes.

"Wot's that mean?"

"Forget the cliff," I said. "What I mean is—we've got to trick them somehow."

"Trick them into what?" Kira asked.

"I don't know. Locking themselves up or something."

"Where?"

"The silver mine," said Millicent.

"None of them buildings gonna hold forty pirates for long."

"What about the mine itself?"

"How would you close it off?" I asked. "It's not like a mine has a front door you can lock."

We were all silent for a moment, thinking.

Suddenly, Guts's whole upper body jerked to life in a massive twitch.

"Blow it up!"

"What?"

"Got black powder! Up at that mine! Sun's up now, we can find it. Get all the — pirates inside the mine and blow the entrance! Bottle 'em up!"

Millicent perked up. "How do we get them up there?"

Guts snorted. "Where all the *pudda* silver is!"

She hurried to her feet. "Let's go. Quickly!"

THE BLACK POWDER was right where the Okalu said it would be, in a storehouse near the mouth of the mine. There were half a dozen short kegs of it, along with several spools of fuses.

But just looking at the mine's entrance, we knew the plan would never work. It was too enormous. No matter how much powder we detonated, we'd never be able to seal the whole thing shut.

Then Millicent came up with another idea.

"The temple ruins," she said.

"What?"

"The Temple of the Sunrise. Where the Okalu used to hold the Marriage of the Sun."

"Mata Kala," said Kira.

Millicent nodded. "Right. What's left of it is just around the mountain."

"But it's a ruin," I said.

"There's a chamber. Underground. With a long tunnel leading in. It's perfect. There's room enough in the chamber for at least fifty people. And the tunnel's narrow—if we set a charge at the entrance, we can collapse it with no problem."

"How do we get the pirates in there?"

"Same way as the mine—we'll tell them that's where the silver is."

"Why would there be a hoard of silver inside the temple?"

Millicent cocked an eyebrow at me. "In a secret underground chamber? Under an abandoned ruin on the side of a mountain? If you knew pirates were invading your island, where *else* would you put your silver?"

HAULING THE BLACK POWDER to the temple ruins was a challenge. It took three hours and the help of the most agreeable mule we could find in the mine's stable—who wasn't very agreeable at all, except compared with the rest of the mules, none of whom would even leave their stalls.

The mule let us load him up without much fuss, but once we started for the temple, he had an annoying habit of stopping in his tracks every few minutes, with a look on his face like he couldn't remember why he was crossing a mountainside with a few hundred pounds of explosives strapped to his back.

When he stopped like that, the only thing that could get him moving again was a smack on the butt, which made everybody nervous on account of the explosives, but which we had to do so many times that Millicent decided we should name him Smack.

It was midday by the time we got Smack across the rocky lower face of Mount Majestic, and Mata Kala—the Temple of the Sunrise—came into view atop a ridge about a quarter mile below us. There wasn't much left of it except a wide foundation, strewn with broken chunks of what used to be massive columns.

Viewed from above, it didn't look like much—but as we came around the side and got a view of it from below the front steps, the way most people would have seen it coming up the ridge, I got a sense of how awesome it must have been in its prime.

Millicent led us around the far end, to a spot about a hundred yards across the rock-studded hillside from the temple. Just past one of the larger rocks was an opening in the ground, flush with the earth so it was impossible to see until you were almost on top of it. Inside it, a set of worn, rubble-strewn steps led down to an underground tunnel just tall enough for a man to walk through.

We followed Millicent down the steps and into the tunnel. It was pitch black, but we'd brought half a dozen torches and a box of matches with us from the mine's storehouses, so we used those to light our way.

After a hundred yards or so—far enough to put us directly under the temple ruins—the tunnel widened into a deep, empty chamber. In the middle of the twenty-foot-high ceiling, an air shaft let in just enough sunlight to see.

Millicent had been right—as long as we could get the pirates inside that chamber and seal off the mouth of the tunnel with the explosive, it was perfect.

Kira peered up at the airshaft, her face lit by the beam of sunlight that streamed down from it.

"What did they use this for?" she asked.

"It must have been to fool people," said Millicent.

"What do you mean?"

"That shaft you're looking at is right behind the temple altar. Which they probably used for the Marriage of the Sun—when Ka took the Dawn Princess and her dowry away with him? Right?"

"Right."

"Well, if you had a princess, and some treasure, and you wanted them to rise up in the sky and disappear . . . but you couldn't *actually* make them do that, because it's impossible—"

"It's not impossible," said Kira, scowling. "Ka exists—"

"I'm not saying he doesn't. But for the sake of argument, suppose he doesn't *actually* take the princess and the treasure away with him. And you still want people to think he does. Wouldn't it be helpful if you had a hole behind the altar you could just drop them into?"

Kira glared at Millicent, and I figured I needed to stop the argument before it got going.

"Come on," I said. "We need to figure out how to blow the tunnel entrance."

POSITIONING THE KEGS was simple—if we stacked them in the recesses just inside the tunnel entrance on either side, no one coming in would notice as long as they weren't looking too closely.

The trouble came when we tried to figure out how to set them off. We needed to be well away from the tunnel, not just so we wouldn't blow ourselves up, but so the pirates wouldn't see us and get suspicious. But the fuses we'd found with the powder burned so slowly that if we tried to light them from any distance that gave us cover, the pirates would've left the chamber and gotten halfway back to Blisstown before the charge ignited.

"Lay a trail of powder," said Guts. "Up the steps and across the slope to them big rocks, where we'll be hidin'."

He pulled a short sword from a scabbard fixed to his belt. He'd taken it from one of the pirates back at the silver mine, and although we'd all gotten on him about robbing the dead, he'd claimed it wasn't robbery at all.

"That there's Lank," he'd snorted. "*Porsamora* stole this off me a year ago. Takin' it back is all."

Now he used his newly recovered sword as a crowbar, sticking it under the lid of one of the kegs to pry it open.

Millicent stopped him. "Wait—powder won't work. You can't get it up the steps."

We quickly realized what she meant. Every step meant a break in the line of powder, so the fire would just fizzle out at the top of the steps.

"We'll have to light it from the bottom," said Kira.

"How are we going to do that? Anybody standing down there will get incinerated."

No one spoke for a moment. My stomach started to churn.

This is never going to work.

"We'll throw a torch," said Millicent. "Into the stairwell."

"You think that'll work?"

"Yes! It'll *have* to." She looked around. About fifty yards from the tunnel entrance were the rocks Guts had mentioned—half a dozen of them, more than big enough to hide behind.

Millicent pointed to the rocks. "We'll wait behind those. Leave plenty of powder on the floor around the tunnel entrance. Once the pirates are inside the chamber, we'll light one of the torches and throw it down the stairwell from a distance."

My stomach was twisting itself into knots.

It's never going to work.

"Right, then," said Guts, putting his sword back in its scabbard. "You two get that powder set to blow. Me an' Egg'll go fetch the pirates."

His voice caught a little on the last sentence. And when I looked at him, there was a worry on his face like I'd never seen before.

In all the time I'd known him, I'd never seen Guts scared of anything. Until now.

It's never going to work.

He was already at the top of the tunnel steps, ready to head down the mountain to Blisstown.

"Comin'?"

I followed him up the steps. My legs felt like lead.

"Wait!" Kira pushed past me, ran to Guts, and wrapped her arms around him.

I turned away—it was a private moment, and I didn't want to ruin it by gawking at them—and when I did, I found myself face-to-face with Millicent, her deep brown eyes staring into mine.

She didn't say a word.

She didn't say she was sorry about Cyril, that she regretted the whole thing, that it was me she really loved and she knew that now, and that if we somehow managed to get through this, she'd never doubt it again.

She didn't have to. The look in her eyes said all of that.

Then I kissed her—or maybe she kissed me, I'm not sure which—and when it was over, she cupped my face in her hands and gave me one last, long look with those eyes that I could have stared into forever.

"Just stay alive," she said.

"You too."

Then I turned and followed Guts down the mountain.

RIPPER'S TOWN

IT'S NEVER GOING TO WORK.

It'll work. It has *to work.*

It won't. We'll never get all the pirates inside that chamber.

Don't think like that. Stay positive.

This is insane.

"Donkey's followin' us."

"What?" I looked over my shoulder. Smack was trotting down the ridge in our direction. It was a little annoying to find out he was capable of moving that fast when he felt like it.

"He's not a donkey," I said. "He's a mule."

"Wot's the difference?"

I thought about it. "I don't know. They're bigger, I think."

"He ain't big."

"Bigger than a donkey."

"— your —! He's a donkey."

"— yours! He's a mule!"

We went back and forth like that for a while. It was stupid, but I didn't mind. As long as we were arguing, I couldn't focus on how insane the whole plan was.

It's never going to—

"That's a *pudda* donkey!"

"He's a mule! Look at his ears!"

"Wot's ears got to do with it?"

"HEE-AW!" Smack had joined the argument.

"See?" Guts twitched. "Donkey noise, that is."

"Why's he following us, anyway?"

"Thinks we got food."

"I *wish* we had food."

"Ever eat donkey?"

"He's a *mule!*"

"— YER *PUDDA* MULE! I ate horse once."

"That's disgusting!"

"It ain't! Same as cow."

"No, it isn't."

"Is!"

Guts must have been as eager for the distraction as I was, because the horse meat/cow meat fight went on even longer than donkey/mule did. And when it was finished, we somehow got into an argument about whether cows had feet or hooves. That led right into one about whether it was okay to eat animals that had feet. On the heels of that came a bitter dispute over the reason why snakes don't have feet.

Then there were a couple of *really* stupid arguments, the subjects of which I'd forgotten almost before they were over.

We were less than a mile above the harbor, spitting curses at each other over whether dolphins were fish or something else, when we saw thick black smoke billowing up over Blisstown.

We're too late. They're burning the hostages.

"Run!"

We sped down the footpath so fast that by the time we reached the outskirts of town, the only things that hurt more than my knees were my lungs. There was a thick haze in the air, and the first half dozen houses we saw were on fire.

Smack had quit following us by then. Donkey or not, he had more sense than we did.

We walked through the dirty haze toward the middle of town, the smoke giving us coughing fits and my cheeks prickling from the heat of the burning buildings, until we came upon two men crouched over something in the middle of the road.

They were Ripper pirates. One of them was using a hand ax to hack at the lock on a small, steel-banded chest. What looked like a crumpled pile of clothes was lying a few feet away by the side of the road, but I didn't peer too closely at it, because I was pretty sure it wasn't just clothes.

We were coughing so loudly the pirates heard us even before we came into view through the haze. One of them rose to his feet as we approached, a pistol in his hand and a drunken snarl on his lips.

"On yer—*Gutsy*?" He lowered the pistol, gaping at Guts.

"Oy!" The second man was looking up from the chest in disbelief. "Where ye come from, dog?"

"Been chained up in that mine by these — *pudda* rich folk," Guts said. "Need to talk to the Ripper."

During the walk from the mine to the temple ruins, we'd

worked out exactly what Guts was going to say to the pirates and when. But he was holding his new short sword in his good hand, just in case.

"Well, ain't you sumpin'?" the one with the pistol said, grinning. "Where's all them boys went up to the mine?"

"Dead," said Guts.

Both men stopped smiling. "Dead how?"

"Come with, ye'll find out when the Ripper does."

"S'posin' ye tell us first?"

Guts twitched. "What fer? Ripper make you cap'n?"

"Watch it, crip—" The one with the pistol started to raise it.

"Lemmy," said the other one, with a note of warning in his voice.

Lemmy looked back at his mate. Then he scowled and lowered his gun.

The one crouched over the chest stuck his hand ax in his belt and stood up, hoisting the chest over his shoulder.

"C'mon."

Only the houses on the outskirts of town had been put to the torch. The rest were still standing, although the streets we passed were a mess, with clothes and furniture strewn all over.

The townspeople who hadn't resisted, which was most of them, looked to be locked up in the big meetinghouse at the end of Heavenly Road. Next door to the meetinghouse was the Peacock Inn, where the pirates had set up their headquarters.

The road in front of the inn was piled with the remains of an island-wide sacking: dozens of busted-open chests, wardrobes, trunks, and cabinet drawers, along with hundreds of once-valuable objects discarded in the dirt—tableware, broken clocks, rolled-up carpets, soiled velvet curtains, and the busted remains of a few hundred wine bottles.

The carriages and wagons that had hauled in the plunder lay abandoned all along Heavenly Road, clogging the street halfway to the pier. Most of the horses still stood in their traces, heads drooping and motionless, like they sensed there'd be trouble if they made a fuss.

A few dozen men were lounging around the Peacock's wide front porch, grazing on piles of food and quaffing wine straight from the bottles. They'd been at it a while—most of them looked ready to burst from one end or another. As we approached, a few caught sight of Guts and began to hoot.

"Looky there!"

"Eees Gussie!"

"Back from the dead, eh, Gutsy? Play us a song!"

"Gimme a spot o' that ham, I might," Guts snarled.

The man he was speaking to lurched to his feet and hurled a giant, meaty shank over the porch railing at Guts—who, with the sword still in his good hand, didn't have a prayer of catching it. Fortunately, I was next to him, unarmed and hungry enough that I managed to lunge sideways in front of Guts, trapping the ham against my chest even as it knocked me into the dirt.

The pirates roared with laughter. But Guts and I hadn't eaten much over the past day, and we tore into that ham without wasting any time worrying about how pitiful it looked. Which just made the pirates laugh harder.

"I seen yew een Pella!" a Cartager pirate called out to Guts. "Why you leave?"

"*Pudda* — richie turned me slave," Guts growled back through a mouthful of ham.

I was choking down my fourth bite when I heard the heavy creak of the Peacock's front door, followed by the sudden roar of a deep, angry voice.

"OY!"

All the laughter and talking stopped in a hurry. It took a terrible kind of power to silence thirty wine-drunk pirates at a snap, and I didn't have to look up to know that the heavy footfalls crossing the porch toward us were coming from Ripper Jones.

He was a beast of a man, everything about him oversized except his tiny Cartager ears. There was a machete in his hand and a sour look in his eyes.

"What's this 'bout my men bein' dead?" His Cartager accent was so thick that the words sounded more like "wa'si 'bou me meb'yeh dea'?"

"Natives done 'em rough," said Guts.

"Wha' Natives?"

"Ones slavin' in the mine."

"'Ow you know?"

"I was with 'em. Richies pinched me an' him"—Guts twitched his head in my direction—"when they knocked off Pella. Took us here, stuck us in the mine with them slaves. They locked us all up when they went down the hill to fight yers. But they was sloppy. Some o' the Natives worked 'emselves loose. Freed the rest. They was fixin' to make fer the cove and sail off when yer men come up the road."

"Buncha savages? Best *my* men? *Pudda blun!*" As he glared at

Guts, the teeth that showed through the Ripper's snarl were filed to sharp points. If he'd stared at me like that, I think I might have passed out.

"Got good news fer you, tho'," said Guts.

"Wha's that?"

"I know where them richies hid their silver."

A ripple of low voices rose up around us.

"Do ye now? Up inna mine?"

"Nah." Guts twitched as he shook his head. "Them richies put it someplace secret."

"*Pudda blun,*" scoffed the Ripper.

"True," insisted Guts. "Take ye there."

"Fer wha'? You tryin' deal me?"

"Don't ask much. Spot on yer crew is all. Fer me an' him." He nodded at me again. "Short numbers, ye can use us."

"Ye had yer spot. Ye done run off."

"Won't run twice."

"Why so?"

Guts lowered his head. "Thought I'd see better days. Wound up in *pudda* chains."

The Ripper scratched his chin through his beard as he stared at Guts.

"Where this silver?"

"Up the mountain. High up. Take ye there."

Ripper looked around at his men. "Mink . . . Barney . . . five more. Get a wagon. Be quick. Wanna leave here by night."

The men he'd called out started toward the porch stairs as the Ripper turned to head back inside the inn. My heart was hammering in my chest.

It's not going to work.

"Wait," said Guts.

The Ripper looked back with a scowl. "Wha'?"

"Wagon can't make it. Tough climb. Just a footpath. And there's lots of silver needs carryin'."

"'Ow much?"

"'Nuff that you oughta see it first." Guts's eyes darted from the Ripper to the men who were scattered across the porch. "Be sure it all gets back to ye."

The Ripper's head drew back in surprise—and the tension on the porch suddenly spiked. A few of the men cursed in anger at Guts as the Ripper stepped toward him, descending the porch stairs with his mouth split in a terrible grin.

"You tell me boys gon' cheat me?"

Guts took a deep breath. His next words came out shaky. "I think . . . long as you come with . . . nobody gonna cheat nobody."

The Ripper was standing in front of Guts now, towering over him. For a moment, it seemed like anything might happen— including Guts getting cut down with a swing of the Ripper's machete.

Then he raised his massive fist and cuffed Guts on the side of the head, just hard enough to remind him who was boss.

"Okay, Gussie. Take me to silver."

THE WORD SPREAD FAST. Within a couple of minutes, the size of the crowd around Guts and the Ripper had doubled, to nearly fifty men, all of them as keyed up with greed as they were with drink.

A few tried to unhitch horses from the wagons to take up the

315

mountain. But they were sailors, not horsemen, and drunk on top of it, so all but one of them gave up in frustration before they even got the horses out of their traces. And the last one quit once he realized he didn't have a saddle, and horses' backs were more slippery than they looked. The others had a good laugh at that.

The Ripper looked over the crowd. Then he singled out a few. "Monkey. Don. Lew. Kurt. Big Jim. Stay here an' watch them lambs." He nodded at the locked doors of the meetinghouse.

The men he'd called out—I remembered Big Jim from the few hours I'd spent with the Ripper's crew, mostly because at four feet tall, he was hard to forget—all winced and scowled, but they didn't talk back.

Guts and I traded a look of worry. Five men left behind was better than fifty, but it was still going to be trouble.

The Ripper saw us look at each other. His eyes narrowed. Then he pointed at me.

"You stay, too," he said. Then he turned to the one they called Monkey. "Lambs give ye trouble . . . burn 'em up."

"Wot 'bout this one?" Monkey jerked his thumb at me.

The Ripper looked my way.

"Yew wan' join me crew?"

I nodded.

"Yew need be tough," he told me.

Then he turned to Monkey. "Make sure he tough."

I was just starting to wonder what he meant by that when a fist I never saw coming slammed into the side of my head.

CHAPTER 33

DESPERATE MEASURES

"NOT BAD. YE CAN take a punch."

I spit some blood into the dirt. It hurt to breathe. The five of them had worked me over pretty good.

"'Ave a pull. Takes the pain away." I raised my head to see Big Jim offering me a wine bottle. He was swaying on his feet from drink. They all were.

I managed to rise to my knees. "Got any water?" I asked.

Talking hurt more than breathing. And for some reason, Big Jim got offended at the request.

"— ye!" He swung the wine bottle, aiming to break it over my head. But I managed to duck out of the way, and he lost his balance and toppled over.

The others laughed. They were lounging on the steps of the inn now, looking worn out from the effort they'd put into beating me up. Two of them were rolling tobacco into cigarettes.

Big Jim popped back up again and gave me a resentful kick in the side as he waddled back over to sit with the others.

"Trouble with this one"—I think it was Don talking—"is 'e can take it. But 'e can't dish it out."

"Wot ye mean?"

"Don't ye remember? 'At's the one we put in the ring to fight Gutsy, back on that richie ship."

They all stared at me. Then a couple of them started nodding.

"Oh, yeh! Couldn't finish 'im!"

Lew chortled at the memory. "Had 'im pinned on 'is belly! Holdin' a cannonball! Just had to brain 'im! One swing! An' he let 'im go!"

Monkey snorted in disgust. "Lost ten silver on you," he growled at me.

"I know where you can get it back," I said.

"That so?"

"That and more. Up the hill." I looked down the road in the direction Guts had led Ripper and the others. They were out of sight now.

Monkey ignored me.

But I had to get these men up the mountain somehow. If I didn't, even if Guts and the girls managed to take out all the others, this bunch would hear the explosion and figure out they'd been tricked.

Then they'd torch the meetinghouse. And after that, they'd kill me.

Unless they killed me first.

Got to get them up the mountain . . .

How?

They'd lost interest in me and turned their attention to ransacking a pile of discarded household items. I watched for a while as Monkey and Lew got into a tug-of-war over a mud-spattered silk shirt. It lasted until they accidentally ripped the shirt in half.

They're drunk. And stupid. And greedy.

An idea started to form in my head.

It was going to be hard to pull off. And if it went wrong, I'd end up taking another beating. Or worse.

But I had to try. My heart began to race as I planned what I'd say.

Do it fast. Or you'll be too nervous to sell it.

"You're all Rovians, yeah?" I asked.

Monkey snorted. "Ain't no Rovian, me. Don't serve no king but meself."

"I mean your blood. Your people come from Rovia? Mine do, too."

"What of it?"

"Shut yer yap, boy," growled Don.

"Just want to know, if I'm joinin' the crew—do they always deal us short?"

"— ye on about?" Don was raising his fist to slug me.

I had to get the words out fast. "'Cause I know how it is with them Cartagers. I crewed with 'em before." I started to slip into a pirate accent. "Stick together, they do. Look out for themselves. And they's crafty! Always spinnin' their webs against honest Rovian folk! Seen it time and again. Put two Short-Ears in a room full o' Rovians, mark my words—them devils'll figure out how to cheat us six ways from Sunday."

Don looked suspicious. But he had lowered his fist.

Lew was slowly nodding. "They *does* talk with each other," he said. "In them slippery voices. I seen it."

"Bet yer lot don't never get a fair share," I said. "Bein' Rovians on a ship run by Short-Ears."

"Now, hang on," said Don. "Ripper treats us square."

"Don't look like it to me," I scoffed.

"How's 'at?"

"Jus' look round," I told him. "How many Short-Ears on yer crew?"

"Ten."

"How many the Ripper leave down here with the lambs?"

"None."

"See? Only ones gettin' cheated are us Rovians."

"How we gettin' cheated?"

"Countin' ye short on the silver," I said.

"—!" cursed Monkey.

Don was skeptical. "How ye know that?"

"How do *you*? Gonna see him count it? Less yer standin' there when they find it, ye ain't never gonna know."

All five of them had their brows furrowed now, trying to puzzle it out. Monkey looked pretty sold. Don, not so much. The others were somewhere in the middle.

I sighed. "Just how it is, I guess. Join this crew, I better get used to the short end of the stick."

I shook my head sadly, climbed the steps, and started to pick at the leftover food like I had all the time in the world to wait for the Ripper to come back.

"Hang on a bit, boyo," Don said. "Talk this out with us."

It took quite a bit more talking—not so much because they

didn't believe they were getting cheated but because they were scared of what the Ripper might do to them if they abandoned their posts. But in the end, greed won out over fear. Ten minutes later, I was leading all five of them on a fast march up the hill toward the temple.

We started out at such a good clip that I was worried we might catch up to the others too soon and the Ripper would order us right back down the hill again. But I was on my third trip up the mountain without much in the way of food or sleep, and by the time we'd gone a mile, my legs were shaking, my lungs were burning, my head was spinning, stabbing pains from the beating I'd just taken were shooting through me with every step I took . . . and I knew I had the opposite problem.

"Hurry up, ye —!" Don was a good twenty yards ahead, and he was getting angry. Lew was right behind him, and Big Jim was somehow managing to keep pace even though his legs were about a third as long as everyone else's.

"—, ye —!" Monkey and Kurt were both lagging behind me, wheezing like a pair of clogged fireplace bellows. I think it was because they smoked too much.

A mile later, they'd all passed me by.

"C'mon, ye —! Show us the way!"

By then, I couldn't even spend the energy to raise my head and see how far ahead they were. I was getting so dizzy it was all I could do to keep my feet under me.

Keep going.

"Move yer —!"

Keep going . . .

I heard Millicent's voice in my head.

Just stay alive.

Somehow, I stayed on the trail.

"THERE IT IS!"

I was almost to the timberline. I could see the barren ridge rising up ahead of me.

Then I was out of the trees, and the grade was so steep I was practically crawling up the slope.

Monkey was lagging, too. I'd caught up to him again. Big Jim was just in front of us.

I raised my head and saw the temple steps in the distance. Off to the right, there was a cluster of men crowding the tunnel entrance. The first batch that had gone up the mountain with Guts.

I couldn't breathe anymore. I was going to pass out.

Just stay alive.

I was on all fours, scuttling up the patchy rock, my arms and legs trembling from exhaustion. The cluster of men was thinning out as the last of the pirates filed into the tunnel. Don and Lew had almost reached them.

I saw Guts. He was coming up out of the stairwell, dodging the men going the other way.

They were trading words, but I couldn't hear what they were saying. He was gesturing to them with his hook, the short sword banging in its scabbard against his leg.

Beyond the tunnel entrance, a thin tendril of smoke was rising from the big rock where the girls were hiding.

They'd lit the torch.

Don and Lew reached the stairs and disappeared down them, past Guts.

Then it was Big Jim's turn.

I was almost there myself, and Guts was looking past me, gesturing with his hook.

"C'mon!"

Where's Monkey?

I'd somehow passed him. He was straggling behind me.

I stepped aside for him.

"Hurry! They'll count it without you!"

Monkey paused at the top of the steps, gulping air.

"GET IN!" Guts screamed. "MISSIN' IT!"

Monkey scowled, and for a moment I thought he was going to stop and scrap with Guts. But then he stumbled down the steps after his crew.

The last pirate was inside.

Kira had been watching from behind the rock. As soon as Monkey's head disappeared from view, she came out at a dead run, torch in hand.

Guts and I began to sprint for her, trying to get as far away from the stairs as we could before the explosion came.

She was twenty yards from us when I heard the roar of a familiar voice, echoing out of the tunnel.

"OY!"

It was the Ripper.

As Kira closed the distance between us, she cocked her arm back and let the torch fly. I ducked, lost my footing, and went tumbling over.

Someone cried out in anguish. I looked up from the ground.

It was Millicent. She'd emerged from the rock and was staring past me in dismay.

I turned to see what she was looking at. Kira and Guts were just in front of me, still on their feet. Guts was pulling the short sword from its scabbard as they stared at the tunnel entrance.

The burning torch was lying atop the stairwell. Ripper Jones was halfway up the steps, his head swiveling from the torch to the bottom of the stairwell.

He must have figured out what we were trying to do, because he mounted the last few steps in one quick stride, grabbed the torch, and swept it up off the ground.

Then he straightened his back and turned in our direction.

He slowly raised the torch over his head, flaunting it like a king with a scepter.

He was laughing at us.

It didn't work.

We'd failed.

I was heaving myself to my feet, ready to run for my life, when Guts took two steps in the Ripper's direction and swung his good arm like he was cracking a whip.

A glint of steel flashed through the air.

Then the torch in the Ripper's hand was falling, straight down, disappearing into the stairwell.

The Ripper jerked his head up, eyes wide and staring at the arm that had raised the torch.

It was still up over his head.

But the hand was gone, severed at the wrist by Guts's sword.

Then the Ripper was gone, too, swallowed up by the column of fire that burst out of the tunnel as the earth shuddered from the explosion.

THE ROAD TO BLISSTOWN

THE FOUR OF US staggered into Blisstown just before sunset. The sky was once again turning its unearthly shades of red and orange, made all the more haunting by the smoke that lingered from the house fires on the edge of town.

It took some work with an ax to bust the chain that barred the meetinghouse door. When we finally got it open, the number of people who spilled out onto the street was a real shock—there were easily a thousand, maybe twice that number. They must have been packed in there cheek by jowl.

Then the crying and the hugging started. I'd never been hugged by a stranger before, let alone by dozens of them. It was touching, I guess, except that my arms and ribs were badly bruised from the working over the pirates had given me, so it actually hurt to get hugged.

And what I really wanted at that point wasn't hugs, but food.

I was trying to make my way over to the piles of it the pirates had left on the porch of the Peacock Inn—which was going fast, because the townspeople hadn't eaten since yesterday, either—when Millicent climbed up on top of the porch railing and began to address the crowd.

"I have something important to say!" she called out.

"THANK YOU!" someone yelled.

"WE LOVE YOU!" called out someone else.

Then they were all crowing, "THANK YOU!" and, "WE LOVE YOU," and people were reaching out from all sides to pat me on the back and shoulders—which, again, was nice and all, except that it *hurt*—and a few feet away, I saw a woman try to plant a kiss on Guts's cheek and nearly get a hook in the neck for her trouble, because he didn't care for it at all. And she was blocking his path to the food.

Millicent had her hand up, waving for silence and saying something I couldn't hear because jowly old Governor Burns, who supposedly ran Sunrise but mostly just did whatever Roger Pembroke told him to, was grabbing me around the neck—*ow*—and yelling, "This boy's a hero!" right next to my ear.

No one was paying Millicent much attention at all.

Then she screamed, "SHUT UP!" at the top of her lungs, and that did the trick.

"We're glad you're all alive," Millicent shouted. "But you need to hear this!"

A thousand people were silent now, their eyes on her.

"We've been to the silver mine," she told them. "The men working there were slaves."

There was a murmur of voices.

"That's illegal!" someone cried.

"Not here!" a woman squeaked.

"Quite an accusation," growled another.

"It's not an accusation!" Millicent yelled back. "It's a *fact*. They were in chains. Every one of them."

I glanced at the Governor. He looked a lot less joyful than he had been a few seconds ago.

"I'm sure," Millicent went on, "that most of you didn't know this. But you know it now. And it's our duty, all of us—to make sure it *never happens again*."

"Never!"

"Course not!"

"It's an outrage!"

A handful of people were yelling things like that. But just a handful.

Millicent's face tightened. "Say *never again!*"

"Never again!" Fifty people shouted it. Maybe not even that many.

Millicent repeated herself, louder this time. *"Never again!"*

"Never again!" Half the crowd now.

"Swear it! NEVER AGAIN!"

"NEVER AGAIN!" This time, she had them all.

Millicent's head turned from side to side, staring out at the crowd. I think she was trying to decide whether or not to believe them.

"We're good people," she said finally. "Let's make sure we act like it."

Then she looked over her shoulder, at the townspeople clustered around the food on the porch behind her.

"And for Savior's sake, leave some food for us! We saved your lives, and we're *hungry*."

The crowd on the road parted for Guts, Kira, and me, clearing a path for us to get up the stairs to the porch. As we reached the top, I found Millicent locked in an embrace with her mother. They were both crying.

When Mrs. Pembroke saw me, she practically knocked over two townspeople in her hurry to get her arms around me. The hug hurt like anything, but this time, I didn't mind.

ONCE WE'D EATEN our fill, it was past dark. Burns sent a crew of able-bodied men up the hill to keep watch on the pirates we'd left at the temple ruin, bottled up and roaring in helpless fury. Eventually, they'd be sent to Edgartown to face justice, and things weren't likely to go well for them at trial.

The rest of the crowd was heading home. A heavy quiet had settled over Blisstown—Millicent's speech might have had something to do with that, but mostly I think it had just dawned on everyone that although the pirates were no longer a threat, they'd left an awful mess. And it was going to take a long time and a lot of trouble to get Sunrise back on its feet.

But none of that was my problem. For the first time in ages, I didn't have any problems—no one to run from or to, no one to fight against or about, no one to stop or save from anything.

And every time my eyes met Millicent's, she smiled at me— with that wonderful, warm smile that was all I'd ever wanted in the world.

I didn't know if what my friends and I had done was worth ten million gold. But I didn't care anymore. Millicent's smile was worth ten million to me. And for the moment, nothing else mattered.

While we were eating, Mrs. Pembroke's small army of servants were hard at work getting her carriage untangled from the crush of wagons and horses along Heavenly Road. When we were finished, all we had to do was climb inside for the trip up the hill to Cloud Manor.

The mansion had been sacked, but not as badly as it could've been. And a wagonload of servants had gotten there ahead of us, so by the time we dragged ourselves up the wide central staircase, there were rooms waiting with soft beds and clean sheets. Someone asked me if I wanted a warm bath, but I was too tired to even answer. I sank my head onto a feather pillow and fell blissfully asleep.

I WOKE UP in a room bathed in red from the morning sunlight that flooded through the curtainless windows.

As I headed downstairs, the house was so silent and peaceful that I winced when the creak of the wooden steps under my feet echoed in the entry hall. At the bottom of the stairs, I got a whiff of fresh-baked jelly bread and quickened my pace.

The light in the kitchen was as red as my room. Mrs. Pembroke was sitting at the corner nook, drinking a cup of tea. The jelly bread was cooling in a pan next to a short stack of plates and forks.

She smiled at me. "Good morning," she said in a near-whisper. I guess she didn't want to break the silence, either.

"Hello," I said.

She picked up a spatula to cut me a slice of jelly bread. "Would you like some tea?"

"Yes, thanks."

She stood up, motioning for me to sit. Then she went to fetch a teacup.

I sat down in front of the jelly bread. It was heavenly. I don't know what they did to it at Cloud Manor that was any different from the bakeries in Edgartown or Blisstown, but the jelly bread at the Pembrokes' beat them all.

Mrs. Pembroke set a hot cup of tea in front of me.

"Are the others still asleep?"

I nodded.

"You should be, too. You must be exhausted."

"Maybe I'll go back to bed. If that's okay."

"I think . . . ," she said with a smile, "that whatever you want to do is okay. For a good long time."

I felt a lump in my throat, and I knew I had to change the subject in a hurry or I might start to cry from how nice she was.

"Why is the light so red?" I asked. "It's awfully strange."

"It is," she said, nodding, and then looked out the window. "Started a few days ago. I think it's got something to do with the volcano."

The volcano. I'd forgotten all about it. I could feel the worry start to creep up through my belly.

"Did it really erupt? Or was it just smoking?"

"I don't know," she said. "Is there a difference?"

"Sometimes it smokes and spits, but that's it," I told her.

"It's never smoked like this," she said. "Not since I've lived on Sunrise."

"My brother's on Deadweather," I said.

"Oh, dear!" She put a hand to her mouth. Then she reached

out and placed her other hand over mine. "I'm so sorry. What can we do?"

"I don't know," I said. I felt like I had to do something. But I couldn't think of what.

"Wait—" She stood up quickly. "Thomas just came up the hill. He said there was a ship—THOMAS!"

Her voice echoed across the house. There were footsteps, and a moment later a servant entered.

"Yes'm?"

"Did you say there was a ship coming into the harbor this morning? From the south?"

"Yes'm. She docked just after sunrise. I saw her from the wagon as I headed up the shore road, and—"

"Any chance it was a Deadweather ship?"

He thought about it. "Might've been. Certainly looked grimy enough." He nodded apologetically at me. "Beggin' pardon, sir."

Mrs. Pembroke turned to me. "Most of our sea traffic comes from the north and east. If it's coming from the south, mightn't it be from Deadweather?"

I nodded. "Could be. That's how we always came here. From around South Point." I started wolfing down the jelly bread as fast as I could.

"I can take you down the hill to check it out," Thomas offered. "Soon as the horses are fed and watered."

"How long would that be?" I asked.

"About an hour."

"That's okay," I said. "I can walk." On foot, I could be there in twenty minutes.

I washed down the last of the jelly bread with the tea. Then I stood up.

"You sure you don't want a ride?" Mrs. Pembroke asked. "Thomas can—"

"No, it's fine," I said.

"Wait—take some money. Just in case you need something."

I TOOK A SHORTCUT through the neighboring properties and into the woods, Mrs. Pembroke's silver jingling in my pocket as I trotted downhill.

If Adonis isn't on the ship . . .

Someone in town might know what happened . . .

I could hire a boat to Port Scratch . . .

I reached the shore road and turned down it, toward the harbor.

What if he IS on the ship?

I'd have to invite him back to Cloud Manor. And he was a terrible houseguest.

In an instant, I went from praying Adonis would turn up safe to hoping he was safe but somewhere far away, where my friends and I wouldn't have to put up with him.

Maybe my uncle could find him a job. Or maybe Deadweather's fine after all, and he didn't need to leave. Or maybe—

Someone's coming up the road.

Maybe it's Adonis!

No, it's just an old man.

HE LIMPED AS HE WALKED, his left arm hanging useless in a dirty sling and his back so bent that the overstuffed satchel hanging from his good shoulder threatened to slip off and fall to the ground. He wore a nobleman's clothes, but they were so filthy it looked like he'd dug them out of a hole in the ground before he put them on.

Or someone had dug him out of a hole in the ground.

Poor fellow. Ripper's pirates must have treated him rough.

As the distance closed between us, I saw his chin jerk up in surprise at the sight of me. He straightened his back, squaring his shoulders, and I realized he was much taller than he'd seemed.

Then his ragged, salt-and-pepper whiskers split apart to reveal a line of white teeth.

I'd just put a smile on his face.

Another grateful Sunriser. I bet he's going to hug me.

He was digging in his satchel.

Savior's sake, he's going to give me a present!

I could get used to this hero business.

I was almost upon him. His head was down, searching his pack. I stopped to wait.

"Good morning," I said brightly.

He finally found what he was looking for.

He raised his head, and I saw his ice-blue eyes for the first time as he drew the pistol and pointed it at my chest.

The grin on his dirty face slowly spread from ear to ear.

"And here I thought my luck had run out," said Roger Pembroke.

THE ROWBOAT

"DOWN THE STEPS."

We were standing on the cliff above the cove where the slave ship had docked. Pembroke was behind me. It was the first time he'd spoken since he'd turned me around, ordered me off the road, and started marching me uphill through the trees with a warning that if I opened my mouth or made any kind of noise, he'd shoot me in the head.

What I couldn't understand was why he hadn't shot me already.

I started down the steps, trying not to look at the dizzying plunge to my left—or at the distant lump at the bottom of the stairs that was Birch's body.

When I reached the bottom, I hurried past the body without a second look.

I could hear Pembroke's footsteps pause behind me.

"Well, that should make you happy," he said. "Keep going."

334

I ducked under the archway that led to the dark inner cove.

"All the way to the back."

The slave ship and Cyril's boat were both long gone, and at first I thought the cove was empty. Then, as my eyes adjusted to the dim light, I realized it extended much farther back than I'd noticed before. I walked along the platform cut into the rock, passing the series of iron cleats where the ships had been tied up. Beyond them, several large storage trunks were lined up against the side of the platform.

Just in front of the back wall, hanging on davits from the ceiling over the water, was a small rowboat.

"Get the boat in the water."

I did as I was told. While I was wrestling with the rowboat, I could hear Pembroke banging around in the storage trunks.

When I heard iron clanking behind me. I risked a glance over my shoulder.

"Did I say turn around? Get it in the water!"

I managed to do as I was told.

"Tie it up."

I wound the bow rope around a cleat at the edge of the platform.

"Now, hold still."

I heard the clanking iron again, coming closer.

Something cold and hard struck me on the ankle.

Then I heard a heavy *click* and felt a weight press on the top of my foot. As I looked down, I felt the cold weight against my other ankle. There was a second *click*.

He'd shackled my legs with the same kind of chain I'd taken off the Okalu slaves.

"Get in the boat. And mind you don't fall in the water. The chains will drown you."

I somehow managed to tumble into the boat.

"Take the rear seat. Turn around. Back to me. That's it."

The boat bobbed, lightly at first, then sharply.

"Turn and face me."

I did. He'd settled into the bow seat, facing forward with the pistol still trained on me. There was a burlap sack at his feet, stuffed with who knows what.

"Start rowing."

I got the oars in their locks and started to row. With all the bruises around my ribs, rowing hurt like a demon, but I managed to maneuver us out of the cove and into the open water. The boat lurched against the rough sea.

The plume from the volcano was smeared across the sky in front of me, thick and angry.

"Did I tell you to stop?"

"No," I said. "But you didn't tell me which way to go, either."

"Deadweather Island. And be quick about it." He glanced over his shoulder. "I'd like to get there while it still exists."

I started to row.

But it didn't make any sense.

"It'll take days to row there."

"Not days. Not if you're quick about it."

"But why?"

"Because you're going to lead me through the Valley of the Choke Plants, to the Red Cliff—do those names ring a bell?"

"Yes. They're from the map."

"And do you know where they are? Can you find them?"

"Yes."

"Excellent. Once we're there, you can dig me a treasure. Perhaps I'll join you, if I'm feeling up to it." He raised his wounded arm a few inches in its sling.

It still didn't make any sense.

"The Fist isn't magic," I told him. "You said so yourself. It's—"

"I don't need magic. I need money. And the dowry of the Dawn Princess ought to be just the thing."

"What if we can't find it?"

"Then it won't be for lack of effort. Come, now—I'm sure you can row harder than that."

I did my best. But the chop in the water was pushing the boat back.

And he was wrong. It'd take days to row to Deadweather.

Smoke was still pouring from the volcano.

This is madness.

"But the volcano—"

"—makes our destination rather hard to miss, doesn't it? So you needn't worry about getting lost."

"It'll kill us."

He shrugged. "Can't say that bothers me. Truth is, I've had quite a run of poor luck lately. Rolled the dice on a rather large gamble and crapped out. So much so that when I loaded this gun, the target I had in mind—"

He raised the pistol to his head. "Was me."

He frowned and gave the pistol a little jerk, pretending to fire it.

"But then you came along." His eyes brightened, and the frown became a smile. "And I realized the Savior Himself had picked up the dice and put them back in my hand for one last throw."

The pistol was pointing at me again.

"Now: is the treasure really there? Is the volcano going to blow? Are we rowing toward certain death? I can see as how these questions might be important to you. But personally, I don't care a fig. As a practical matter, boy—I'm already dead."

He settled back in his seat with a pleasant sigh. "And this is my play for resurrection."

I ROWED FOR A WHILE in silence, trying to make sense of it.

"You need money?" I asked him.

"Rather desperately, yes."

"But you're the richest man I know."

"Was. Mmm. Had a tidy little fortune, I did." He got a wistful look on his face. "A lesser man would have been more than satisfied with that. Not me. I had grander dreams. And they — near came true. If I'd pulled it off, they would have written about me in the history books. This whole part of the world would have been mine."

He sat up, suddenly animated, and leaned in toward me as he gestured with his pistol at the western sky, in the direction of the New Lands. "Do you have *any idea* how much undeveloped potential is in those lands? It's a continent full of riches! With free labor as far as the eye can see! And nobody's got the vision to build it out beyond a couple of petty gold mines. Except me."

He sighed and shook his head. I was about to point out that what he called "free labor," most people called "slaves"—but then he was talking again, too fast for me to interrupt.

"But when you're surrounded by small-minded, fearful little men with no ambition but to hang on to what they've got, and no appetite for risk, no matter how great the rewards—well, you've got to do it all yourself, don't you? Pay for the troops, pay for the ships, pay for the guns, pay for the food—and even then—*even then!*—they all want bribes under the table and ironclad guarantees of a fat cut if you pull it off, and Savior save you if the going gets rough, because they'll all run like rats and leave you to twist in the wind."

His eyes narrowed, simmering with resentment, and I thought he was finished. Then he exploded again.

"And I was *so close*! So — close! If I'd only held Pella a few more weeks, until the gold trains came in . . . it would have been all over. I would have won. If that blustering pig *Li Homaya* hadn't shown up out of nowhere . . . And it was all your fault! Bloody — hell! *It was all your fault!*"

He was spitting rage, waving the gun at my face, and I shrank back from him, wondering how he could've known I'd tipped off *Li Homaya*.

"If your fool of an uncle hadn't run off on me and taken his men with him, I could've beaten back those Short-Ears without breaking a sweat."

The rage ebbed away. He sank back in his seat and gave a heavy sigh as he looked down at his injured arm. "Still can't figure out how on earth *Li Homaya* wound up coming at me from the north."

I was wrong. He didn't know.

I sent them. I sent Li Homaya *to stop you. And it worked.*

"What are you smiling about?"

"Nothing."

He scowled at me for a moment, then went back to his brooding.

"A hundred more men, and I could've held that city. Fifty, if they'd had any fight in them . . . Fifty good men, I'd be there still. That simp Burns and the rest of the king's lackeys would be falling all over themselves to kiss my ring. Instead of scurrying around, trying to cover their rears by hanging the blame on me . . . I mean, the sheer — insanity of it! The way they spoke to me this morning! I'd barely set foot on the dock—"

The rage was boiling up again. "*My* dock! I *built* that dock! I built that whole — town from scratch! Everything they've got came out of *my* hard labor! And the whole lot of them . . .

"It's not just the ingratitude. It's the incompetence! Such a pack of bumbling idiots, I can't even leave town for a month without seeing the whole place sacked! By *a single — ship*! Ripper Jones? He's an oaf! The man can't buckle his belt without an instruction manual! And they let him waltz in and burn down half the town? —! Savior's —!"

It was some curse. Guts would have been proud of it.

"And they've got the gall to suggest it's somehow *my* fault? And that the business arrangement—which had profited them all so handsomely, and for so long—has to be disavowed and discarded just because that little . . . oh, this is where it *really* gets irritating . . ."

He leaned in toward me again, his blue eyes fierce. "Tell me this: what in Savior's name did my daughter say to those people?"

I would've smiled again if the look in his eyes hadn't been so disturbing.

"That there were slaves working the mine. And it was wrong. And it could never happen again."

"Oh, my —! The hypocrisy! How many people heard her say this?"

"Everyone."

"Everyone?"

"Everyone who wasn't dead."

He grimaced. "—! I should have had a son."

He shifted the pistol to his injured hand, grunting a little in pain as he inched the arm halfway out of its sling to keep the pistol pointed at me. Then he rubbed his face with his good hand.

"Well, that's the end of that, isn't it? So much for my grand experiment in respectability . . . I'm done with that game. But I'm not done with them. Not by a long shot. They want to make me a villain? Next time, I'll give them a reason to. When those fools see me again, it won't be pink-fingered Roger Pembroke in a silk shirt. Reggie Pingry's going back to his roots."

Reggie Pingry?

"You're going to find me that treasure . . . and it's going to buy me a fast ship . . . and a hungry crew . . . and every one of those simpering cowards who sold me out is going to know what fear is."

He saw the look on my face, and smirked.

"Didn't your uncle tell you? About his old pal Reggie? Who taught him everything he knows? He used to lie at my feet, begging for scraps. Little Billy Healy. Who wanted nothing more than to be like me."

"That's not true!" His eyes were so wild and demented I didn't want to provoke him by talking back. But I couldn't help myself.

"Oh, it is," he said, nodding. "And then some. But, of course, he wouldn't tell you any of that, would he? 'Cause he wants you to think he's somehow better than I am. And that there's actually such a thing as an honorable pirate."

Pembroke—*or was it Pingry?*—laughed to himself. Then he stared at me for a long time, with a little smile playing on his lips.

"And if he never told you about me and him . . . I suppose it's a given he never told you about me and your mother?"

I dropped the oars. The rowboat was lurching in the waves.

"That's right, boy . . . I could have been your father. I very nearly was."

The smile on his face was almost tender.

And I was going to be sick.

"No . . ."

"Oh, yes. Jenny was going to be my bride. Nothing would have made her happier."

The waves slapped against the boat. My hands were trembling.

"You're a liar."

"I'm far past the need for lies, boy. And I can well understand your sense of shock—I felt the same way when I first made the connection. Standing on those palace steps in Pella, watching you with a noose around your neck. Imagine what Jenny would've thought if I'd hanged her son . . ."

His voice trailed off for a moment. Then he perked up. "Thank heavens for small favors, eh? Get back to rowing."

I didn't move.

"Son, this boat's not going to row itself."

I stared at my feet. And the chains that bound them together.

I heard Pembroke sigh. Then there was a creak and a rustle of burlap. He was digging in his sack for something.

"I'll tell you what," he said. "You row . . . and I won't have to use this."

I looked up. The pistol was still in his injured left hand.

His right hand held a leather whip.

"And if you're a very, very good boy, I'll tell you some stories along the way."

He must have had a lot of practice with a whip. In the end, he only had to crack it once to convince me to start rowing again.

I ROWED THROUGH THE DAY, long past the point of exhaustion. Finally, he let me rest. He had a little jug of foul-smelling water in his sack, and he gave me some of that, along with two strips of rotten meat.

"You've got her face, you know. You're lucky in that. Don't have that horse nose your brother and sister got from your father. I never would've guessed she'd marry such a dog. Must've fallen on hard times after we split up . . ."

He sighed. "All right. Fun's over. Back to work."

IT WAS SUNSET, and the volcano's plume was black and sinister against the red sky. There were blisters on my hands, and my mouth was so parched I couldn't swallow or talk.

I wished *he* couldn't talk. The things he was saying made me sick.

"We had some fun, I'll say that. Your mother certainly knew how to have a good time. And she was so — devoted to me.

Wanted nothing more than to cook my meals, and keep my house, and have my babies . . .

"But it had to end. You know why? Because they were small. Small people. Her and her brother both. Small dreams. Small minds. Small morals. Even Billy, once he'd made a half-decent pirate of himself, couldn't think any bigger than a dirty little corner of a dirty little sea. All the while patting himself on the back for his — Code of honor.

"Do you know what honor is? It's the consolation prize a man awards himself when he hasn't got the guts to do the job."

IT WAS NIGHT, so dark we could barely see each other's faces. There were tiny threads of orange spitting up from the mouth of the volcano to guide my way.

I was breaking down. With every pull of the oars, my whole body shook.

But whenever I tried to rest, he'd hear the blades stop pushing through the water, and the whip would crack.

He'd finally stopped talking about my mother. But he hadn't stopped talking.

"It's money . . . It's always money. Never let them tell you different. Money is power. Money is love. Money is men. Money makes the world go round . . . and round . . . and round . . ."

IT WAS SNOWING.

I'd never seen snow. I'd only read about it. But little dry flakes of it were everywhere now. Sticking to my hands. Sticking to my face.

His voice came through the dark, ragged and weak. "I'm going to win. Do you know why? Because nobody else has the sack to stick their hand in a volcano and pull out a fortune."

THE SKY WAS PURPLE. The water was still. We were close.

I knew now it wasn't snow. It was ashes. Coughed up out of the volcano and sprinkling down over everything.

He hadn't moved or spoken in a while. His eyes were closed. A thin layer of ash crowned his head, and bits of it stuck to his eyelashes. The pistol was tilted to one side, resting against the sling that held his injured arm.

I lunged at him.

But I'd forgotten about the chains. They caught me short, and I fell wrong. He startled awake.

We struggled. The boat rocked wildly, nearly pitching us into the sea.

But in the end, we were back where we started.

Me at the oars.

Him with the gun.

Ashes falling from the sky.

THE SUN MUST have been up, but I couldn't see it anywhere. The sky was dark and raining ash. The volcano loomed ahead, pouring its anger into the heavens.

Still I rowed. I don't know how. I was numb. Floating through a nightmare world.

There was a ship. Pulling toward us. Sails slack. Oars in the water.

I heard voices. Ghosts in the distance.

"Friends of yours?"

I peered through the haze of ash. The ship was off our port side. There were figures moving on the deck. Too far away to make out faces. Too far to hear the words their voices made.

It was too late for words.

HE HAD TO PULL me out of the boat onto the dock, yelling in anger and pain all the while. The pain must have been from his arm. He'd taken off the sling, and he held himself funny as he stood over me. Like a wounded bird protecting its wing.

There was ash everywhere. It choked my throat and burned my eyes.

I shut my eyes. He was yelling at me, but I was beyond caring.

WATER WAS POURING down my throat. I coughed it up, sputtering.

"Here. Drink."

I was in a chair. At a table. In a dark, empty tavern. There was a bucket and a cup in front of me, along with some stale biscuits and half a wheel of cheese. Pembroke was cutting the mold off the cheese.

"Eat up. Hurry."

He left me alone, taking the knife with him. I tried to get up, only to feel the chains bang painfully against my feet.

I slumped back into the chair, and drank and ate.

I WAS ALMOST FINISHED with the cheese when I heard a gurgling noise. I looked up.

Framed in the gray light of the open door was the silhouette of a man. He was missing part of his head.

He gurgled again, and I realized who it was.

"Mung . . ."

Wet ash clung to him like a gray paste. Water dripped from his clothes and hair. His gurgling was loud and urgent. He held out his arms, beckoning toward me.

I stood up, my heart in my throat and the chains clanking in my ears as I shuffled toward him.

I was halfway to the door when a hollow, metallic *thong* rang out, and Mung crumpled to the floor in a heap.

Roger Pembroke stood in the doorway, holding a shovel like a club.

"Where did *he* come from?"

I stared down at the motionless body of my old friend. I hoped he wasn't real. I hoped I'd just imagined him.

I hoped I'd just imagined all of it.

A shovel head struck me on the arm, just hard enough to convince me.

"Time to go."

THE RED CLIFF

"MOVE!"

We were halfway up the ridge, dripping sweat in the shimmering heat as we forced our way through the waist-high choke plants that covered the hillside. It was slow going. My chains kept getting caught in the low branches.

Pembroke was behind me. It was so hot he'd taken his shirt off, and his upper body was caked in the gray ash that blanketed the hillside and dotted the air all around us.

"Move!"

He'd stopped threatening to whip me. It didn't do any good, and he needed me strong enough to dig if we ever reached the top. We were only a few hundred yards from the pink-tinged rock face of the Devil's Pimple, up and across the ridge to the left. But there was a constant, dreadful rumbling under our feet, and from time to time the sky lit up as the volcano spat molten lava into the air.

"Faster!"

I yanked my foot free of a choke plant. "It's the chains," I said. "If you take them off . . ."

He shook his head. "Just move."

"Please . . . I won't run." That was a lie.

"You want them off? Find my treasure."

There was a loud crackling noise up the hillside to our right. We both turned toward it.

Something was breaking a path through the choke plants. At the leading edge of it, the branches shook violently, stirring up puffs of ash before sinking out of view like they were being eaten by some slithering, unseen animal.

"Hurry!" Pembroke shoved me up the hill.

I struggled to push through the vegetation, keeping one eye on the strange commotion to our right. Then I caught a glimpse of bright orange down at ground level, and I realized what was chewing up the plants.

It was lava. A fat stream of it was creeping down the hillside, melting everything in its path.

After that, Pembroke didn't have to yell to get me to move faster. If I was going to drown in lava, it was going to be on open ground, where at least I could see it coming.

Ten minutes later, we were on top of the hill, emerging onto a field of ash-covered shale behind the Devil's Pimple. It was just fifty yards from one end of the Pimple to the other, but fifty yards was a lot of ground to dig up.

And farther up the mountain toward the summit, I could see half a dozen streams of lava slowly oozing toward us.

Pembroke pushed past me, the shovel in his good hand, and

began to stride down the length of the cliff. The shale crunched under his boots.

I found myself staring at a large, red scar on his upper back, just inside the left shoulder blade. His skin was mottled with bits of ash, half covering it, so for a moment I wasn't sure what I was seeing.

It was a four-inch-high *C*, identical to the one on my uncle's back.

Until then, I hadn't really believed anything Pembroke had said about either Healy or my mother. But seeing that scar made me wonder all over again. I gaped at him for a moment, watching as he searched the ground for a sign that would tell him where to dig.

Then I realized his back was to me.

I started to search the ground myself—for a rock big enough to brain him with. But there was a layer of ash over everything, and even as I dragged the chain on my feet across it, turning over the flaky shale, I couldn't find a piece bigger than my thumb.

"GET OVER HERE!"

He was kneeling near the middle of the cliff.

As I started toward him, a booming growl rose from somewhere in the bowels of the earth, and the whole side of the mountain shook so hard it nearly knocked me off my feet.

I heard Pembroke curse in surprise. When I looked up, he was staring toward the summit.

About two hundred yards straight up the slope, the ground had split open, and a fresh geyser of lava was bursting from the open seam and running toward us. The new lava, thinner and more liquid, moved at twice the speed of the older stuff.

"GET OVER HERE!" he yelled again as he stood up and jammed the shovel head into the earth. By the time I reached him, he'd pulled the pistol from his satchel.

He jerked his head at the shovel.

"Dig!"

I looked down. At first, I couldn't tell why he'd chosen the spot. Then, as I looked closer, I saw a rock—larger, smoother, and of a color that was different from either the black shale around it or the reddish pink of the pimple.

There were several rocks like that—rounded stones the size of my fist, worn smooth by the sea. Painted on the biggest one, in colored dye so faint it had nearly vanished, was the image of a firebird.

The rocks were big enough that if I slung one at Pembroke's head, it might kill him.

Which was why he had the gun trained on me again.

"Don't get any ideas. Dig!"

I pulled the shovel out of the ground and started to dig. The loose shale gave way without any trouble.

"Hurry up . . . ! Not there—farther over . . . ! There . . . ! FASTER!"

I looked up from my digging to see why his voice had turned so urgent.

The streams of lava were closing in on us. One thin, fast-moving line was already dripping over the side of the red cliff just a few feet away.

I shoveled faster.

The shovel head struck something solid.

It was wood. Rotten and splintery.

"Give me that!"

He grabbed the shovel, shoved me out of the way, and started digging frantically, grunting from the pain of his injured arm.

I checked the lava flows on either side of us. Back the way we'd come, a three-foot-wide river of the stuff had already reached the cliff.

I couldn't jump three feet with those chains on my legs.

"Help me dig!" he yelled at me.

"Give me the keys!" I yelled back.

"I DON'T HAVE ANY!"

He'd lied before. Or he was lying now. It didn't matter which. I was going to die if I couldn't jump over those lava streams.

I looked over my shoulder at the thin stream right behind me. I could clear that one with the chains on, no problem. But farther past it, I could see an even wider stream, five feet across at least. It was already spilling over the cliff.

I was trapped on both sides.

Pembroke was screaming at me to help him dig, but I ignored him. Nothing he could do to me was any worse than what was going to happen if I couldn't get those chains off.

How . . . ?

Just ahead, the shale was sizzling into vapor at the edges of the thin lava stream. It was slowly sinking below ground level as the lava ate through the rock underneath.

Melt the chains.

I scrabbled forward and sat on my butt near the edge of the stream. Then I raised my legs and lowered the dangling chain into the orange stream.

The iron sizzled as it touched the molten rock and began to dissolve. I felt a sharp tug as the flowing lava sucked my feet down toward it.

The heat on my feet and legs was intense, and getting worse by the second.

Just a few seconds more . . .

Then there was a new and different pain, higher up, around my ankles.

The iron collars were overheating.

I yanked my feet up and away, nearly splattering my lower legs with bits of lava.

The skin on my ankles was burning.

The chain had broken in two, but there were still a few inches of it dangling from either collar, and I knew if I tried to run with those flapping around, I'd break the bones in my feet.

I had to burn the rest of the chains off.

Pembroke was yelling curses at me, demanding help. I didn't even glance back at him.

Instead, I rolled onto my hip to get a better angle, then lowered my left foot toward the lava.

Right away, the collar began to sear my skin again.

Hold it . . . hold it . . .

I ground my teeth against the pain.

Yes!

The left foot was free of its chain. Now the right. I rolled over onto my other hip.

The mountain was rumbling beneath me. Pembroke was screaming. My left ankle was burning with pain.

I lowered my right foot toward the lava.

My leg began to shake. I couldn't make it stop.

I pulled it back, bending the knee and letting it rest on the shale.

Deep breaths. Don't panic.

I tried again.

The iron began to sizzle. The pain of the hot collar rose against my ankle.

I screamed. But I held on.

Then it was done and I was up, limping, hopping, both collars burning hot against my ankles.

It'll cool. It can't get worse.

I heard a roar of fury behind me.

"— *SAVAGES!*"

I turned around. Pembroke was kneeling over the hole he'd dug, halfway between me and the three-foot-wide stream of lava I had to cross to escape. I hopped in his direction, and as I got close, I saw the treasure.

It was piled into a wooden box the size of a small coffin. Pembroke had pried open the lid with his shovel head, and now he was digging frantically through loose mounds of little white seashells, searching in vain for something more.

But there wasn't any more.

The shells were the treasure.

Thousands upon thousands of them. A fortune in Native money.

A century ago, when the Okalu still ruled the New Lands, there was no end to what those shells might have bought. You could have raised an army with them.

Even now, back in the New Lands, there were tribes who traded with them. You could get an awful lot of corn pancakes and blankets for that many shells.

But not a ship. And not an army. Nothing Pembroke wanted.

He plunged his hand into the pile and threw a fistful of shells at me like an angry toddler.

"—!"

Then he turned, reaching back behind him, and I realized too late he was going for his gun. As he brought it back around, I started to run, but I tripped and fell hard on my stomach as the pistol roared.

The shot didn't hit me, but I kicked up so much ash when I fell that I opened my eyes into a cloud of it. I struggled to my knees, eyes burning from the ash, and the first thing I saw when my vision started to clear was Pembroke coming at me with the shovel.

I ducked and rolled, but that kicked up more ash, and I had to squeeze my eyes shut as I spluttered backward. When I opened them again, he was looming up over me, framed in a blossom of orange fire spewing into the sky behind him as he raised the shovel to bring it down on my skull.

Then he was staggering sideways, yelling in pain and surprise, and as he spun away from me, I could've sworn I saw a monkey straddling his head.

I lurched to my feet, woozy and confused, and I heard a screech and a yell and a clank, and then there was a monkey flying past me through the air, off the end of Pembroke's shovel.

"CLEM!"

It was Adonis, running full speed at Pembroke, screaming vengeance for his pet, but there was more fury than brains behind the attack, and Pembroke caught my brother hard in the chest with the shovel and knocked him off his feet.

Adonis landed on his back, coughing blind in his own little cloud of ash. Pembroke started for him.

Lying near my foot was one of the big smooth rocks that had marked the treasure. I picked it up and hurled it at Pembroke's head.

I missed. It sailed right past his nose and struck the shovel near the top of the handle just as he was cocking it back.

The shock of it threw Pembroke off just long enough for Adonis to roll out of the shovel's range and scramble backward toward me in a cloud of ash.

I got to my feet, looking for another big rock, but the only thing within reach was Pembroke's unloaded pistol. So I threw that.

I missed again.

As Pembroke ducked the pistol, I saw a burst of bright orange out of the corner of my eye as a fresh geyser spit up from the hillside not twenty feet above us.

Lava began to pour down the hill toward Pembroke. With all his focus on Adonis and me, he didn't see it coming—but with just three steps along the hillside toward us, he'd be out of its path.

He raised the shovel and took the first step in our direction.

"TELL ME MORE ABOUT MY MOTHER!" I screamed.

He paused.

"What?!"

The lava was rushing toward him.

"I WANT TO KNOW THINGS!"

He snorted in disgust and began moving again. "Too late for—"

"DID YOU LOVE HER?"

The question caught him short for half a second—just enough time for the molten rock to reach his right foot, burning through his boot in an instant and unbalancing him enough that he fell sideways, right into the oncoming stream.

I squeezed my eyes shut at the sound of his scream.

By the time the screaming stopped and I opened my eyes again, there was nothing left of Roger Pembroke but a cloud of vapor.

I turned to look for my brother. He was a few feet away, wailing over the motionless body of his monkey.

"Cleeeeeeem!"

CLEM WASN'T DEAD—or at least, Adonis insisted he wasn't. My brother clutched the monkey to his chest as we ran down the mountain, leaping and dodging the rivulets of lava that seemed to be coming from everywhere at once.

Deadweather was melting under our feet.

Back in Port Scratch, we came across Mung wandering up the main street in a daze, holding a rag to the bloody gash behind what was left of his head.

I would have hugged him, but there wasn't time.

We fetched the oars from Pembroke's boat and piled into the bigger longboat that Adonis and Mung had rowed in from the ship they'd been on—the one Pembroke and I had passed on our way into port.

Then we started to paddle with everything we had.

In my case, "everything" wasn't much. I could barely lift an oar, my eyes were seeing two of everything, and my brain was so addled I didn't really understand what was happening or how I'd wound up in a boat with Adonis and Mung and a comatose monkey.

They tried to explain it to me. The ship they'd jumped from was a patched-together salvage that had taken the field pirates the better part of a week to make seaworthy after they'd hauled it off the beach where it had been wrecked years before. They hadn't had much choice: after the initial, minor eruption that had set the volcano raining smoke and ash over the island, they'd all run down from the plantation to Port Scratch, only to find the town deserted and the *Sea Goblin*—the last functional ship on Deadweather—already a mile out of the harbor.

The field pirates had put to sea as soon as they finished patching the ship together, only to pass Pembroke and me on our way in. Mung had recognized me, and he'd demanded that the field pirates come back and pick me up. They'd voted on it, and saving my life had lost by a margin of thirty-five to two.

But then Mung had persuaded them to let him go alone in one of the longboats they'd piled on the deck in case their salvage sank, and since they had extra, nobody could think of a reason to say no.

It sounded like Adonis had come along mostly out of guilt, which was an emotion I'd never known he was capable of. Clem had initially stayed behind, but once Mung and Adonis got the boat in the water, the field pirates had thrown the monkey in after them.

They'd started for shore, but Adonis couldn't row fast enough for Mung's liking, and about a quarter mile out, there'd been an argument that ended with Mung jumping from the boat and swimming the rest of the way. Which was why he'd showed up dripping wet and much sooner than Adonis, who'd seen Pembroke and me leaving town in the direction of the Devil's Pimple while he was still rowing in.

After Adonis docked, he'd followed us up through the Valley of the Choke Plants, which was pretty easy on account of the trail I'd left by dragging the heavy chain through the brush.

It was a slightly complicated story, and a hard one to explain while rowing for your life from a volcano on the brink of an apocalyptic eruption. Which was why I was still struggling to understand even the basics of it when the volcano finally *did* erupt.

Adonis claims that when the ultimate explosion came, the sky went black, the ocean heaved, and we all screamed in mortal terror until the falling ash grew so thick we couldn't open our mouths anymore. Then we floated, lost and helpless and coughing ash, until Sunrise Island appeared on the horizon, buried under its own layer of gray ash.

And when we pulled into Blisstown, the combination of pirate attack and erupting volcano had turned the rich and colorful place we used to envy into a desolate wreck that was every bit as beaten down and grim as Port Scratch ever had been.

But I don't remember any of that. I read in a book once that bears in cold climates hibernate when winter comes and the land turns harsh, shutting their bodies down until it's spring and life is easier again.

I think something like that must have happened to me. I'd seen more than my share of trouble, and when the eruption blotted out the sun, my body finally decided enough was enough, and that it was time to check out for a while and not come back until somebody else had fixed things, or at least swept up some of that ash.

HAPPY ENDINGS

I WOKE UP. Millicent was sitting at the edge of the bed, looking down at me.

"Oh, hel-lo," she said. "How are you feeling?"

"I love you," I said.

She smiled her perfect smile.

"I love you, too."

She leaned down and kissed me lightly on the lips. Then she straightened up in a hurry.

"Would you do that again?" I asked.

She frowned. "Eventually," she said. "But not until you've cleaned your teeth. And eaten something with a lot of mint. Or perhaps fennel."

She reached her hand out and brushed the hair back from my forehead. "And had a very hot bath. You're quite smelly, you know. I'll fetch a servant to draw the water. I can't wait to tell the others—they'll be *so* glad you're awake."

"How long was I out?"

"A week or more. We were quite worried at first. But then you started to snore, and talk in your sleep, and the doctor said that was a good sign, and you were probably just exhausted."

"Have you been here the whole time? Sitting with me?"

"Every waking minute," she said in a breathy, romantic voice.

"Really?"

She grinned, scrunching up her nose. "No. Not really. I poke my head in a couple of times a day. It was just luck I happened to be here now."

She stood up.

"Do hurry with the bath, won't you? Everyone's dying to see you, but it really would be better if you were less grungy." Her face brightened. "And it's almost lunchtime! Are you hungry?"

"Starving."

"Wonderful! You'll see them all then. We'll have a feast in your honor. Your uncle's here, you know."

"He is?"

"Yes. Arrived the other day. He's staying with us." She lowered her voice conspiratorially. "You'll never believe it . . . but there's a movement afoot to make him governor."

"What?"

She laughed. "I know! It's madness! But the whole island's a complete mess, what with the sacking and the volcano and the mine shutting down, and people seem to think the firm hand of Commodore Longtrousers"—she rolled her eyes at the name— "is just what's needed to set things right.

"Of course, that's provided they can persuade him to take the job," she continued. "He says he's retired. Keeps going on about his gardening. It's rather strange. Anyway . . ."

She started for the door.

"I'll tell Mother to hold lunch until you can join us. And I'll make sure there's jelly bread. But do hurry—I mean, if you're up for it."

"I am. Definitely."

"Smashing! Can't wait to get you on the croquet field. No one else is any competition. Kira's bored to tears by it. Guts keeps breaking the mallets. And your brother's abysmal. Plus he cheats."

"My brother's here, too?"

"Of course. And I have to say, he's been on his absolute best behavior. Although that's not actually saying much, is it?"

"Is Mung okay?"

She smiled. "Mung's *such* a dear. He's been by twice to see you. And it's quite a long walk from the mine, you know."

"The *mine*? What's he doing up there?"

"You don't . . . ? Oh, right—how could you know? It's actually worked out quite nicely. You see, to rebuild Blisstown, we need money. To get money, we need to run the silver mine. To run the silver mine, we need men willing to work it. And at the moment, the only ones who'll do the job are the field pirates from your old plantation. The good news for them is, it pays a lot better than picking ugly fruit."

"Just make sure they don't spend the money on rum," I warned her. "Or weapons."

She nodded thoughtfully. "See, it's issues like this that make me think your uncle might be just the man to run things for a while." She clapped her hands. "Right, then. Any more questions? Or should I see about your bath?"

I thought for a moment. "Just one—did the monkey pull through?"

"You mean Clem?" Millicent sighed. "He did. But I don't know how much longer he's going to last around here. Mother's at her wit's end with him—he's extremely disagreeable, and he poops on absolutely *everything*."

LUNCH WAS WONDERFUL. So was the rest of the day. And the day after that. And the week after that. And the month after that.

For the longest time, life was perfect.

Well, not perfect exactly. There were still ashes from the volcano all over the place. Even weeks later, I was still finding them in my ears whenever I washed up, and in my handkerchief when I blew my nose. Which was often, because the tiny bits of ash in the air caused no end of sneezing.

Even after the worst of the mess had been cleaned up, Blisstown—with its wrecked forts and burned-out buildings— continued to look like a face with half its teeth knocked out. The fancy clothes and fine furniture were slow to return to the shops, and the rich folk who used to strut down Heavenly Road seemed to have lost most of their swagger.

To my surprise, my uncle actually wound up taking the job as governor. He didn't seem thrilled about coming out of retirement, and he swore to quit the minute Sunrise could take care of itself. But in the meantime, he was exactly what the island needed. Now that the workers in the silver mine actually had to be paid, and were a lot fewer in number—not to mention that field pi-rates were nobody's idea of dependable employees—money didn't flow through town as effortlessly as it had when Pembroke was around. And most of it had to be pledged to fixing what was bro-ken, so there wasn't much left over for anyone to get rich.

That made a few of the formerly well-off folks on Sunrise almost irrationally angry, and the squabbles would have been endless if my uncle hadn't been around to occasionally remind everyone in his calm but terrifying voice that if they didn't get along with each other and stop being so greedy, they'd have to answer to him.

It was dull, mostly thankless work, especially compared with captaining a pirate ship. But he seemed to like it, or at least be amused by it. When he came back to Cloud Manor at night, he'd tell Mrs. Pembroke stories about the more ridiculous-acting townspeople that made them both laugh until they were red in the face.

As far as I could tell, they enjoyed each other's company quite a bit.

That was definitely true of the rest of us. Guts, Kira, Millicent, and I spent our days sleeping late, eating well, playing croquet, and exploring the island.

Early on, we took a hike to the summit of Mount Majestic and wound up stumbling on the last unspoiled patch of land within a hundred miles. It was a hillside meadow, just above the tim-berline and nestled in the shadow of an almost vertical outcrop-ping on the eastern face, exactly opposite Deadweather—so it had somehow managed to escape the rain of ash. There were a good five acres of lush green field up there, bursting with wildflowers.

Even better, we were the only ones who knew about it, except for one contented-looking mule we found munching wildflowers. He looked as surprised to see us as we were to see him.

"Smack!" Millicent yelled. "Don't you dare eat all those flowers!"

He couldn't have if he'd wanted to. There were too many of them. We took turns scratching his nose, and at the end of the day, he followed us home and wound up making a place for himself among the livestock at Cloud Manor.

We took him with us every time we went back to the meadow, which was often. We'd bring a picnic, then lounge on the grass and watch the clouds float by while Guts played guitar. I couldn't imagine a happier, more peaceful place on earth than that meadow.

It was even pleasant when Adonis came with us.

He was around a lot at the beginning. We did our best to be nice to him, and he did his best not to act like a bully or an oaf. But it was always a bit of a struggle. And he usually had Clem in tow, who didn't get along with anybody. Eventually, Mrs. Pembroke's patience with the monkey wore out, and she gently but firmly banished Clem to an unused outbuilding. After that, Adonis wound up spending a good bit of his time down there, and the rest of it working for my uncle.

Uncle Billy—which was what Adonis and I took to calling him, because we weren't supposed to utter the name *Burn Healy* for fear of scaring the townspeople, and "Commodore Longtrousers" just sounded silly—had noticed early on that Adonis wasn't quite fitting in. So he started asking Adonis to do little jobs here and there—running messages up to the mine, carting supplies around town, that sort of thing—and Adonis really took to it.

He got paid for the work, which he liked. But I think more than that, he liked the pat on the back my uncle always gave him for a job well done. It certainly seemed to improve his attitude—after a couple of weeks of it, Adonis didn't have to work nearly as hard at not acting like a thug.

Adonis's transformation came as a surprise—but not nearly as big as the one that greeted us when we returned to Cloud Manor late one afternoon. Mr. Dalrymple and Makaro were there, fresh off a ship from Edgartown. They were escorting a slightly overfed teenage girl who was so sullen and quiet that it took me a moment to recognize her as my sister, Venus.

Makaro had returned to the New Lands—he got a little choked up telling us about the reunion he'd witnessed when all two hundred of the freed slaves had finally made their way back to the Okalu remnant in the Cat's Teeth Mountains—and was settling back into tribal life when word arrived of a Moku raid at the edge of Okalu territory.

It turned out to be a rather strange sort of raid. The Moku hadn't fired a shot, but had simply retreated after depositing my sister, bound and gagged, at the base of an Okalu lookout post. The lookout who found her reported that before running off, the Moku had announced that my sister was the Dawn Princess, and the Okalu were to obey her every command.

The Okalu were skeptical of that from the beginning, and grew even more skeptical once they ungagged Venus and she started barking orders in Rovian—which only Makaro understood, and then just barely.

Pretty quickly, the Okalu decided the whole thing was some kind of Moku ruse designed to sap their morale. After some debate, they settled on shipping Venus off to Edgartown, with Makaro as her escort. From there, she made her way back to us.

Venus wasn't happy at all about the situation. It must have been quite a shock to go from being just Venus to the all-powerful Dawn Princess of Mata Kalun and then back to just Venus again.

We all tried to be nice to her, but it was a tall order, because she was every bit as disagreeable as Clem the monkey. She didn't poop on things, though, so Mrs. Pembroke was endlessly patient with her, and worked almost unimaginably hard at making Venus tolerable to be around. In the end, Venus wound up spending most of her time down the road at the Wallises', where the three younger children didn't mind letting her play queen with them as long as they got to pretend to sacrifice her at the end of the day. Which I guess for Venus was a fair trade.

We saw Cyril again just once, and from a distance. He was shopping with his mother on Heavenly Road. We waved to him, but he pretended not to see us, and by the time we entered the shop he'd ducked into, it was mysteriously empty. But Uncle Billy had dealings with Cyril's father, and one day he came home to report that the Whitmores had found a new boarding school in Rovia, and Cyril was on his way there to study political philosophy.

I felt a little sorry for him. There'd been no need to avoid us—we never talked about anything that had happened in the past, even among ourselves. For my part, I only felt the need to bring it up once, when I was alone with my uncle on the back porch of Cloud Manor. It was dusk, and we were watching the brilliant orange-red sunset over Mount Majestic.

"Did my mother . . . ?" I began.

Then I stopped. I wasn't sure how to ask the question.

He gave me a kind smile. "Go on."

"Did she . . . and Reggie Pingry . . . ?"

I didn't have to say anything else. He knew what I was asking.

"They were engaged," he said quietly. "And it might seem hard to believe, but at the time, I would have liked nothing more to see them married. He was like a brother to me."

My uncle watched my face for a reaction. I turned away and stared at the sunset.

"The thing about Reggie . . ." His voice trailed off. Then he started over.

"When you first met Roger Pembroke, what did you think of him?" he asked.

I thought back to that first day at the Peacock Inn—and the charming man who'd rescued my shabby family from a crowd of sneering rich folk and treated us to the most generous lunch I'd ever seen.

"I thought he was handsome, and clever, and kind," I said. "And if he was a general, and I was a soldier, I would have followed him over a cliff without thinking twice."

My uncle nodded. "That's how most people felt when they met him. And some of them never realized the truth until they'd stepped off the cliff."

The door to the house opened, and Mrs. Pembroke appeared. "Dinner's ready, gentlemen," she said with a smile.

My uncle smiled back at her as he stood up. Then he looked down at me.

"We can talk more about this—"

"That's okay," I said, getting up. "Let's just eat."

AFTER A MONTH of nearly perfect, carefree living, Mrs. Pembroke began to gently suggest that we start taking lessons from Millicent's old tutors. When we ignored her, she began to suggest it less gently.

Then she enlisted my uncle on her side, and the game was up. Starting the next morning, lessons began promptly at eight and continued until three. Millicent and I took to it without much fuss. Kira made out all right, too. Her spelling was atrocious, but otherwise she was a keen student.

The others were varying degrees of disastrous. Venus bit the math teacher twice and eventually had to be confined to the dining room with Mrs. Pembroke on an indefinite basis. Guts was even worse. The tutors tried to institute some kind of punishment for him called a "time-out," but since it involved sitting still, it was a complete failure. I did my best to help him study, but even I couldn't convince him that there was any point to learning how to read, let alone add and subtract.

Adonis lasted exactly a week before deciding, after a long conference with my uncle, that it was time to put to sea. The *Thrush*—the ship that used to run ugly fruit for my father, and on which Guts and I had once hitched a ride to Pella Nonna—was in port at Blisstown, on its way back down to the Barkers, and my uncle arranged for Adonis to join the crew as an apprentice seaman.

There was a time when I would have bet he'd be thrown overboard by the crew before they'd lost sight of the port. But my uncle's positive influence on Adonis was pretty solid by that point, and I figured he'd make out all right.

Clem was another story. The monkey was joining Adonis on

the *Thrush,* but I had my doubts that he'd still be on board when they reached the Barkers.

Adonis still wasn't exactly my favorite person on earth, but he'd grown on me. So when I saw him off down at the dock, there was a lump in my throat. Judging by the huskiness in his voice when he said good-bye, there was one in his, too.

He was the first of us to go, but it wasn't long before I realized he wouldn't be the last. Two days later, Guts stormed out of a math lesson, leaving a trail of curses behind him.

I went to try to settle him down. He was outside near the front door, hitting one of Cloud Manor's big front columns with a stick.

"You okay?"

"— done with this *pudda* learnin'," he spat.

"Well, you don't have to hit that column with a stick."

"Want me to hit the — *porsamora* tutor?"

"No . . . Stick with the column."

He gave it a few more whacks, then put the stick down.

His face twitched. It didn't usually do that anymore.

"If you hate the tutoring so much," I said, "I bet my uncle'd let you come work with him instead."

Guts shook his head and twitched again.

"Nah . . . Gotta leave here anyway."

He said it in a quiet voice, but the words landed like a punch in the stomach.

"And go where?"

"Pella first. Play guitar, earn some money. Then down south. Barkers and such."

"What's down there?"

"Family," he said.

"You've got family?" The couple of times I'd tried to ask about one, he'd nearly slugged me.

"Dunno." Guts twitched. "Gotta find out."

"Well, take some time to think it over—"

"Done plenty of thinkin'. Past time I went. See if I can find 'em."

"But . . ."

My throat was getting lumpy. Much worse than it had with Adonis.

"But wot?"

"Aren't we your family now? Me, and Kira, and Millicent?"

"Course! But . . . ain't the same." He cursed under his breath and pressed the back of his good hand to his eye.

"Just gotta know is all," he said. "One way or another."

"You're going to go look for them alone?"

He shook his head. "Kira's gonna come with."

His eyes peeked out from under his shaggy bangs to meet mine. "Come, too, if you want."

I wanted to go with them. But the thought of leaving my uncle—let alone Millicent—was just too much.

Guts and I talked it over for a while, and eventually he agreed not to leave for at least a couple more days, to give me time to figure out what I was going to do.

At first, I didn't say anything to Millicent. But right away, she guessed something was wrong, and when we got to the meadow that afternoon, she asked me about it.

"What's the matter?"

"It's nothing."

"Then why do you look so sad?"

I told her. Guts and Kira were down the hill from us, playing fetch with Smack. He'd gotten pretty good at it for a mule. Back at Cloud Manor, he'd been spending more and more time with the dogs, and I think he'd started to believe he was one, too.

We watched them scamper around, laughing and shouting.

"How can we get them to stay here?" I asked.

"We can't," said Millicent.

"Don't you want them to?"

"Of course I do. But we've all got to leave sooner or later."

"You and I don't," I said.

A shadow crossed her face. My stomach fluttered a little.

"What is it?" I asked her. "Tell me."

"I'm going to Winthrop. At the next term."

The look on my face must have alarmed her, because she quickly put a comforting hand on my chest.

"You should come with me."

I didn't know whether to cry or yell.

"Millicent—it's a *girls' school.* Across an ocean!"

"There's a boys' school nearby. Kirkland or something. You could talk to your uncle. I'm sure he can get you into it."

"I don't *want* to go to a boys' school in Rovia!"

"Well, what *do* you want?" she asked me.

I thought about that.

"I just want everything to be like it is now," I said. "Forever."

She smiled—not her usual smile, but a more wistful one, with sadness creeping in at the corners.

"That's the one thing you can't have," she said. "Nothing stays the same for long. Everything changes eventually."

I looked into her eyes. "Everything?"

The sadness left her smile for a moment.

"Not everything," she said.

Then she kissed me, just to make sure I understood.

For a long time after that, neither of us said anything. Millicent rested her golden head on my chest, and I watched my best friends in the world play in the meadow as I tried to figure out how to keep us all together.

Millicent in Rovia . . . Guts and Kira down south . . . My uncle on Sunrise . . . The future felt like a math problem I couldn't solve.

I never was any good at math.

"What am I going to do?" I said finally.

Millicent shrugged. "Don't think about it," she told me. "We've got today. Let's just enjoy it."

So that's what we did.

Egg began his thrilling adventure in
THE CHRONICLES OF EGG, BOOK ONE:
DEADWEATHER AND SUNRISE

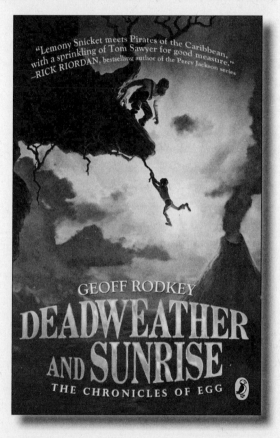

Turn the page to read the first chapter!

CHAPTER 1

DEADWEATHER

Nobody lived on Deadweather but us and the pirates. It wasn't hard to understand why. For one thing, the weather was atrocious. Eleven months out of twelve, it was brutally hot and humid, with no wind at all, so on a bad day the air felt like a hot, soggy blanket smothering you from all sides.

And the other month was September, which meant hurricanes.

Then there was the volcano. It hadn't actually blown in ages, but it belched smoke and shook the earth enough to scare away anybody who might've overlooked the pirates and the weather. The only reason it didn't scare me, even though plenty of things do, was because I'd been born and raised halfway up its slope and didn't know any different.

That's how I felt about the pirates, too. There were two kinds on Deadweather: the normal ones, who hung around down in Port Scratch, drinking and getting into knife fights whenever they weren't off raiding Cartager gold ships; and the busted-down, broken ones, who'd lost too many limbs or eyes or organs to crew a ship, but not enough to kill them outright. A few of those stayed in the Scratch, patching together a living in the taverns and the gun shops, but most of them hobbled up the mountain to work for Dad on the ugly fruit plantation.

I don't know what he paid them—it couldn't have been much, because we didn't have much. But I guess it was enough, since none of them ever staged a mutiny or tried to kill us all in our sleep.

They slept down in the barracks and mostly kept to themselves in the orchards, except for Quint the house pirate, who cooked for us and did some occasional sewing. Dad had his hands full running the plantation, so he left the rest of the housework to the kids—the kids being me, my sister Venus, and my brother Adonis. I was the youngest, which I didn't much like. Adonis whaled on me every chance he got, and even though I fought back as best I could, he had three years on me, so I usually got the short end of it—especially after he turned fifteen and shot up past six feet, with shoulders almost as wide and thick as Dad's.

Fortunately, as Adonis got bigger, he also got more lumbering, so eventually I figured out I could duck the beating by running to the orchards and climbing an ugly fruit tree, way up to where the branches got too thin to bear his weight. He knew Dad would skin him if he hurt one of those trees, so he'd just glower at me from under his heavy, black eyebrows, and shake his fist, and bellow that he could wait for me forever. Then he'd get bored and wander off.

Venus used to knock me around, too, right up until the day I got big enough to take her in a fight. She backed off for good after that, except to constantly tell me how stupid I was, and how Dad

2

had tried to sell me but couldn't find a buyer at any price, and how someday she was going to marry a Rovian prince, and the prince would have me ground up and fed to his horses.

"They'll gobble you up, Egbert, bones and all," she'd say, sneering down her long, sharp nose at me.

At some point, I found out horses don't eat meat, but I never bothered to tell Venus. Just like I never bothered to tell her no prince of Rovia would ever marry a commoner, let alone try to find a wife by leaving the Continent and sailing thousands of miles across the Great Maw to a sweaty little pirate-infested island so unimportant it didn't even show up on the maps of the New Lands in *Geography of the World*.

There was no point in telling her any of that, because Venus ignored any fact she didn't like, and the ones she couldn't ignore, she screamed at. And whenever she screamed, Adonis would come running—not because he cared about Venus one way or another, but just for the excuse—and I'd get slugged, unless I got to a tree fast enough.

And if I did, he'd stand under it and yell the same fist-shaking curse every time: "Treat a lady like that, I'll 'ave the pirates cut yer tongue out!"

Venus was hardly a lady, except in her own mind—she belched when she ate, and picked her nose at the table—and anyway, it was an empty threat. None of the field pirates could stand Adonis, so if he'd ever ordered them to cut my tongue out, the ones who still had legs would have kicked him in the shins.

But Adonis wasn't much for facts, either. Or any kind of learning—I'm not even sure Mr. Sutch managed to teach him how to read properly.

Mr. Sutch was our first tutor, and the only good one, which was probably why he didn't last. This was years back—I was just seven when he showed up, which would have made Venus nine and Adonis ten. I guess Dad had figured out by then that we weren't going to learn to read and write by ourselves—especially since the only book in the house was a chewed-up copy of *Principles of Citrus Cultivation*—so he'd sent out a flyer with the captain of the cargo ship that hauled the ugly fruit harvest up to the Fish Islands.

When the ship came back six months later, Mr. Sutch was on it—all bony and worried-looking, and pulling out a handkerchief every two minutes to wipe the sweat-fog from his glasses. Right from the start, it was obvious he was a bad fit. The volcano and the pirates had him scared out of his pants, and on his first night, I overheard him out on the porch with Dad, complaining in his reedy voice that he'd been lured to Deadweather under false pretenses.

Dad snorted. "Stuff! Don't even 'ave one."

"One what?"

"A wot-ye-say. A faults pretenses."

"What I mean . . . is that your advertisement specifically indicated this position was on Sunrise Island."

"Nah, it didn't."

"Sir, if I may—" I was inside, listening from under the sitting room window, so I couldn't see them, but I heard a crinkling of paper as Mr. Sutch unfolded what must have been Dad's flyer. "Right here, line three—it says 'Sunrise Island.'"

"Nah, look—says '*roundabout* Sunrise Island.'"

"No, it . . . that word there? It's 'roundabout'?"

4

"Wot ye think it was?"

"I honestly didn't know what that word was."

"Now ye do. Says 'roundabout.'"

"That's not even remotely correct spelling!"

"Quint read it fine."

"Who's Quint?"

"House pirate. In the kitchen. Got stumps fer legs. Smart one, he is. Reads AND writes."

"Look, sir . . . spelling issues aside, this island is HARDLY 'roundabout Sunrise'!"

"Wot ye mean? Head down to the Scratch, 'op a boat, east nor'east . . . catch the wind right, be there in three hours. 'At's roundabout, seems to me."

"Well, I'd very much like to do that. And as soon as possible— I think it's the least you can do for me under the circumstances."

"Wot? Put ye on a boat? Can't. 'Aven't got one—I'm a farmer. And the cargo ship's sailed, won't be back till next season . . . Might get one o' the pirates to take ye, fer the right price. 'Ave ye got a gun?"

"What? No! I'm a man of learning."

"Wouldn't chance it, then. Man shows up in the Scratch with money in 'is pocket and no gun, not likely to go well for 'im . . . Looks like yer stuck 'ere, then. So—gonna teach me kids? Or ye gonna pick fruit? 'Cause them's the only jobs need doin' round 'ere."

Once he realized he wasn't going anywhere soon, Mr. Sutch did his best to educate us. But it was a tough job. When he started, none of us could read a word or add higher than our fingers, and when we talked, we all sounded like pirates. That particularly bothered him, because he was a very formal sort, and he couldn't

5

abide the fact that we not only didn't speak what he called "proper Rovian," we couldn't even see the point of it.

"Ye understan' us, yeh?" said Venus. "So wha's the need fer all these *duh*s and *guh*s and *yoooooooo*s?"

"My dear young lady," he said—and kindly, too, not at all sarcastic, because it was still his first day and Venus hadn't bitten him yet—"how can you expect to grow up and marry a Rovian prince if you're not capable of speaking like a princess?"

Looking back, I do wish he hadn't put the idea in Venus's head that all she had to do to marry a prince was start saying "you" instead of "ye," because once it got lodged in between her ears, there was no getting it out, and for years afterward, we had to listen to her natter on about it. But I guess it was effective, because unlike Adonis, she actually did manage to stop talking like a pirate.

The rest of the tutoring she hated almost as much as Adonis did. As for me, I loved it—not so much for its own sake, but because Mr. Sutch was the first person I'd ever met who didn't seem likely to slug me at any second, so spending time with him was a real treat. I did my best to speak properly for him, and to read, and add and subtract and even multiply things, although the multiplying could get pretty tricky.

And when Venus and Adonis complained to Dad, I kept my mouth shut. Fortunately, they didn't get anywhere with their complaints.

"What we 'ave to learn things fer?" Adonis would gripe. "It's stupid!"

"Nah, got it backwards. Need learnin' 'CAUSE yer stupid."

"Wha's the point?"

"Good for ye!"

6

"Why?"

"Just is."

"Why?"

"'Cause yer mum wanted it!"

There was no arguing with that. So my brother and sister just glared daggers at me and went back to their primers, and whenever Dad was off in the orchards—which was most of the time— they made life as miserable as they could for Mr. Sutch. Not that he needed much help to be miserable on Deadweather.

I was almost through the last of his primers and starting to like reading for its own sake when he suddenly disappeared. Venus and Adonis liked to say he was murdered by a field pirate, but the fact that he vanished right around the time a cargo ship lifted anchor for the Fish Islands probably wasn't a coincidence.

Dad would have sent out another flyer, but then the Barker War got going, and for the next year or two, nothing sailed on the Blue Sea unless it had at least twenty guns on it. It was hard times—for the last few months of the war, we had nothing left to eat but ugly fruit, which gave everybody the trots.

The war was named for the Barker Islands, way down south where most of the fighting was. Like all the shooting wars in the New Lands, it was between Cartage and Rovia. They were the only two Continental powers with colonies on this side of the Great Maw, and the only kinds of people around at all except for Natives, who didn't have any guns or ships and who'd been cleared out of the islands so completely that I'd never even seen one up close. There were still tribes of them on the mainland—that's where the gold on the Cartager treasure ships came from—but that was several days' sail from us, and there was no reason to ever go there, since it was all wilderness except for a few Cartager ports like Pella Nonna.

The actual shooting only came near us once. It started as a distant rumble in the darkness, off and on, sort of like thunder but not quite, and at first it hardly seemed threatening. But Dad rousted everybody out of bed, loaded us down with all the food we could carry from the pantry, and started marching us up the hill without telling us why.

He had his pistol belt on, and he carried his rifle, along with a big rucksack stuffed with supplies. Dawn was breaking, but the fog made it hard to see.

"Where are we going?" Venus whined.

"Time fer questions later. Just haul that pack."

"I can't! It's too heavy!"

"Then make Egbert carry it."

After Dad said that, Venus and Adonis both dumped their loads on me, which weighed me down so much that my legs were shaking when I finally caught up with them at Rotting Bluff. Dad kept a single cannon there on a rough stone parapet overlooking the sea to the northwest. We helped him load it—I don't know why, because from the sound of the battle raging out in the fog, there were a lot more ships than one cannon could ever stop. But Dad wanted it loaded anyway. Then we sat and waited, as the battle got steadily louder and more frightening.

"'Oo's fightin'?" For the first time I could remember, Adonis was curious about something.

Dad was hunched over the parapet, his elbows resting on it to hold his beat-up brass spyglass steady as he squinted through the lens into the fog. "Dunno. Cartager Navy, that's certain. Not sure who's takin' 'em on, though. Might be Rovians proper . . . but I think it's the pirates."

"The Cartagers comin' 'ere?"

"'Ere or Sunrise. Could be both."

"Why 'ere? Sunrise got all the silver."

"Yeh. But them rich folks on Sunrise don't steal Cartager gold. Pirates on Deadweather been doin' that longer'n you been alive. Reckon the Short-Ears got a mind to put an end to it. Wipe out the Scratch fer good."

Ordinarily, Dad wasn't much for talking, other than to order us around—and the fact that he was bothering to explain things to us was almost as unsettling as what he was saying. Venus, for one, looked like she might cry. "Wouldn't wipe *us* out, would they?"

"Dunno why not," said Dad.

"I don't want to get eaten!" she cried. I don't know where she got the idea that Cartagers were cannibals.

Dad didn't, either. He took his eye from the spyglass to cock an eyebrow at her. "Nah, won't eat ye. Just slit yer throat."

Around midmorning, the fog lifted, and we finally got a glimpse of the battle on the horizon—two massive Cartager men-of-war and five two-decker galleons were slugging it out against just four single-deck pirate sloops, muzzle flashes blinking through the smoke that hung around their sides.

"Don't much like them numbers," muttered Dad, his face knitting into an even darker scowl than usual.

But as the hours passed, it was clear the pirates were giving better than they got. All but two of the Cartager galleons had gone under before any of the pirate sloops sank, and when the first of the big men-of-war keeled over around midafternoon,

9

Dad—who hadn't lowered the spyglass from his eye for hours—gave a sharp huff of surprise that almost sounded like a laugh.

By sunset, it was over. The men-of-war had burned or sunk, and the last remaining Cartager galleon had been boarded and captured and was creeping back toward Port Scratch behind the two surviving pirate sloops. As he led us back down to the house, Dad's mood was so chipper that I heard him whistling to himself.

We were all headed for bed when we started hearing gunfire from the direction of Port Scratch. Venus got panicky and ran out to the porch, where Dad had settled in with a bottle of rum.

"Is it Cartagers?! Are they coming to eat us after all?"

Dad cocked his head and listened. "Nah. No invasion, that—it's a party."

"A party? For true? Can we go?"

"Nah, girlie. Pirate party's no fun for them's not pirates."

For a week afterward, several times a day Venus would stop whatever she was doing, let out a happy little sigh, and declare, "I'm sooooo glad the Short-Ears didn't come and eat us."

"Wouldn't a' minded feedin' 'em Egbert," Adonis would chime in. Then he'd cackle—no matter how many times he said it, it never stopped being funny to him—and take another swing at me.

BY THE TIME the war ended, we were half starved—and in my case, it wasn't just for food. I'd worked up a taste for reading from Mr. Sutch's primers, but they'd all disappeared with him, and *Principles of Citrus Cultivation* was starting to get pretty tiresome, especially considering that it didn't have much of a story, and I'd read it so many times I could recite big chunks with my eyes closed.

"What ye always readin' that book fer?" Dad asked me once.

"It's the only one we've got," I said.

He just scowled at that, but it must have stuck with him, because when the cargo ships started running again and he sent out a flyer for a new tutor, he wrote "MUST ONE BOOKS" in big block letters at the bottom of it. I secretly fretted over his spelling, but I didn't dare correct it—and I guess it got the point across, because when Percy finally showed up, he brought almost a wagonload of books with him.

I can still remember the first time I saw Percy and his books lurching up toward the house on top of one of the fruit wagons, the horses all lathered from the effort and Percy's massive belly jiggling at every bump. I practically fainted with joy—I'd never seen so many books, and I instantly knew the man who'd brought them to us was going to be the most important person in my life: a teacher, friend, and savior all rolled into one big, fat, sweaty package.

It turned out I was dead wrong about Percy, except for the fat and sweaty part. As horrible people go, he was miles ahead of Venus and could practically outdo Adonis.

When he first arrived, though, we all thought he was some kind of genius. Not just because he had so many books (which we assumed he must have read), but because he acted like a genius would—all scornful and disgusted with how ignorant we were, and capable of tossing around all manner of facts, seemingly off the top of his head.

Percy could tell you everything from where the wind came from (a giant hole in the sky, somewhere west of the New Lands), to why seawater was salty (fish poop), to whether you could multiply fractions together (you couldn't, and if you tried, they'd break). And he spouted his knowledge constantly—that is, during the half hour a day when Dad was within earshot. The rest of the time, he napped. Unless he was eating, which he did so often that Quint took to hiding our pantry food in sacks out behind the woodpile. Sometimes, the rats got into them, but even when they did, they left more for us than Percy.

Percy sussed out pretty quickly how things stood in our house—that Dad wanted us educated but wasn't too clear himself on what that meant—so he struck a deal with Venus and Adonis that they'd pretend to learn while he pretended to teach them, and whatever else they did with their time was fine by him, so long as they left him alone.

At first, he ignored me and could've cared less whether I read his books. So I dug into them, and it didn't take long before I learned enough to realize Percy was a complete fraud, and none of his facts made a lick of sense.

After that, he did his best to keep me away from the books for a while—mostly with a stick, which he could swing pretty fast considering how lazy he was—but the situation was no good for either of us, because it meant I couldn't read and he couldn't nap. So eventually, we struck a deal of our own: he'd let me read the books as long as I kept my mouth shut about what was in them and didn't let on to Dad that Percy was a fake.

It was fine by me, because even though I hated Percy's guts, I figured if he left, he'd take his books with him. And I really loved his books. There were a hundred and thirty-seven of them, and eventually I read them all at least once, even the terrible ones.

The things I learned from them staggered me—and not just the immediately helpful stuff, like the eating habits of horses (no meat, especially human meat, even if it's ground up) or the real reason seawater is salty (I forget, but it's definitely not fish poop). For the first time in my life, I realized there were whole other worlds beyond mine. On the Continent alone, there were cities, and countries, and kings, and castles, all going back a thousand years or more.

And not only did Deadweather turn out to be just a ragged little flyspeck in the Blue Sea a couple hundred miles east of the vast wilderness of the New Lands, but even Sunrise Island—a place that had always seemed, during the twice-yearly trips we took there for holidays and shopping, like the rich and bustling center of the universe—only appeared in *Geography of the World* as an afterthought at the very bottom edge of the Fish Islands map, and wasn't mentioned at all in *A New History of the Rovian Kingdom and Territories*.

Once I started to learn about the larger world, I'd lie awake at night in my little windowless room off the kitchen, and imagine what it would be like to be part of it somehow—to live a life that mattered, to be and to do things worth reading about in books.

But I never thought for a moment it was possible. I wasn't highborn, or rich, or brave, or strong, or even smart—none of those things that made the characters in the novels and the people in the history books so special.

I knew the world was out there. I just didn't see a place for myself in it. And even if there might be, I had no idea how to go about finding it.

It never occurred to me that the world might come find me— and that without my lifting a finger to make it happen, one day my life would change, completely and forever.

But it did. And this is the story of it.

THE CHRONICLES OF EGG

Read the whole
SWASHBUCKLING SERIES!